What readers are saying al

"Hogrefe builds a future world of adventure, chaos, and mystery but ties it back to the true history of the American dream, drawing in the reader to share Portia's quest."

- Joe Bakker, Alpha Omega Academy Principal

The Revisionary is a dystopian with heart. Set in a time when the government uses ignorance to keep its populace under control, Portia is determined to learn the truth—for her brother and her country. Her fierce determination is a timely reminder that some things are worth fighting for, especially love, truth, and freedom.

- Ashley Jones, BigSisterKnows.com.

The Revisionary offers a brilliant exploration of what could be without freedom of speech, expression, ideas, etc., and the role technology could play in the loss of those freedoms. Set in the near future, the world of Portia Abernathy is intriguing, wonderfully easy to lose yourself in, and reminiscent of those found in the popular *Hunger Games* and *Divergent* trilogies. Must read for young and young-at-heart adults alike!

- Jordan, Candidly-Jo.com

Oppression and rebellion are mixed with patriotism and honor in this unique dystopia. As a fan of *The Giver*, *The Hunger Games*, and Bryan Davis' *Reapers*, I felt at home in this new world. The suspense and unexpected twists made me keep turning the pages, desperate to find out what was going to happen to poor Portia. *The Revisionary* has earned its place with other popular young adult dystopian books.

- Cadi Murphy

THE REVISIONARY

by

Kristen Hogrefe

Write Integrity Press

The Revisionary
© 2017 Kristen Hogrefe

ISBN-10: 1-944120-29-7
ISBN-13: 978-1-944120-29-0
E-book ISBN: 978-1-944120-37-5

This book is a work of fiction. The author discovered a good deal of fascinating historical information during her research, and to the best of her knowledge and belief, she represented actual historical facts with integrity. Aside from the historical characters and events, the names, characters, places, and incidents are either products of the author's imagination or used fictitiously. Any similarity to actual people and/or events is purely coincidental.

All quoted Scripture passages are taken from the KING JAMES VERSION (KJV): KING JAMES VERSION, public domain.

Published by Write Integrity Press, 4475 Trinity Mills Road, PO Box 702852, Dallas, TX 75370
Find out more about the author, **Kristen Hogrefe,** at her website, **www.KristenHogrefe.com** or on her author page at **www.WriteIntegrity.com**
Printed in the United States of America.

Library of Congress Control Number: 2017941452

Flag of the ASU

Special thanks to the students of
Alpha Omega Academy
especially our winner,

Brianna Ford,

whose design will become a permanent flag of the
ASU. The designs from our finalists are displayed
at the end of the story.

Congratulations all around.

Dedication

To Devon and Timothy Curtis

"Where there is no vision, the people perish ..."

- Proverbs 29:18

PART ONE THE DRAFT

Chapter 1

Saturday, 9.5.2149
Chrysoprase, Cube 1519

Some people are born with defects like mine. Others are damaged at the hand of another.

Lying flat on a frayed mat, I tug one leg and then the next to my stomach to stretch the tension in my back. Dawn streaks through the cracked pane above me, brightening the dull gray outline of my graduation uniform to navy blue.

I stand and tip-toe across the loft room's cold wood floor. Pulling up the hem of my sack pajamas, I strap on my thigh holster and then try not to trip while climbing down the ladder. Whoever owned the rag dress before me must have been a good foot taller.

Dad is asleep on his mattress, which takes up half the room downstairs. The other half is our kitchen and wooden table.

We've called this converted barn home ever since our ration reduction ten years ago. Ever since the Court convicted Darius and our family shrank to two.

I start the fire and add water to the cast iron tea kettle. Dad says there are rumors of electricity being restored in some of the squares for the first time in decades. For me, a hearth works just as well.

With the kettle set to heat, I slip out back to use the shower stall, pausing only to grab a towel and the wishbone from last night's wild turkey.

I've no sooner shut the door than the growling begins—and I double check the latch. It will hold. I reach for the lye soap and twist open the rusty metal spigot. The cold water drizzles onto my shoulders and dances down my skin. I shiver deliciously. This must be the feeling that makes little sparrows cavort in puddles.

My mind wakes up by spinning lines of verse. I work them out by singing a low alto tune, the best I can manage early in the morning.

Mongrel,
my friend or foe?
If foe, then off you go.
If friend, then don't bite me but a
wishbone.

The growling resumes, louder this time. Either the alley mongrel is extra hungry today, or another mutt has crossed its territory. I shut off the tap, mop the water off my skin with a threadbare towel, and rub dry my pixie-cut hair.

Then, I redress and reach for my Taser. Dad insisted I apply for a permit to carry one when medical pulled me out of a physical education course on account of my back. He figured that if I can't run from danger, I should at least be able to aim at it. The process took a few years and required a security elective class, but the trade-off was worth the hassle.

There are some things in life no one can outrun.

I press my body tightly against the stall frame and peak through a fractured panel. A mutt with matted gray hair and one good eye paws at the door. I relax and re-holster my Taser. I won't need it today. Our alley mongrel is testy but harmless.

I crack open the door and toss the wishbone into the woods. The mongrel bounds after it, and I hurry to the kitchen where my tea kettle puffs steam and whistles like the boy who used to live next door. The simple fragrance of tea and oatmeal wakes Dad, and he joins me at the table. The bench groans under his weight. His mechanical work and years of physical labor have built his naturally thick frame to the size of an ox.

Well, at least compared to me. I'm barely five-feet tall. My mom was small too, or so Dad tells me.

We sip our tea in silence. I won't waste words with another argument.

Dad doesn't want the draft board to call my name. I do. Today, one of us will get our way.

Only the hearth heard those long debates between us. Its crackling tongue, like an old gossip, provokes my memory.

I was a child of nine, unable to sleep in a room bereaved of a brother. "Can't we bring Darius back?"

"Sweetheart, we can't change the ruling. Only the Court could if someone amended the satellite sentencing laws."

"Who could do that?"

His eyes had betrayed the hopelessness of such a reversal, but for my sake, he offered one possibility, one he later regretted. "Why, that would be our Dome Revisionaries. They interpret our Codex, or law book, and decide how to apply or improve it."

Dad never gambled his little girl would pursue training as a

Revisionary candidate, but that's exactly what I did. My scores in school climbed to the top of the charts. I used my accomplishments in language arts, Revisionary theory, debate, and logic as leverage to persuade my professors to enroll me in a Revisionary undergrad program I finished two years early.

But my achievements frightened Dad. "Do you want the draft board to notice you?" He demanded.

"Yes, I do."

"The draft is what Darius defied. I may never see you again if you are drafted."

"We'll never see Darius again if I don't try."

"Darius may already be dead."

"But he might still be alive."

"There's no guarantee you'll succeed."

"There's the chance that I might. You said yourself it's the only way to change the rules and bring Darius back."

"I'll find another way."

"There isn't one."

Dad gave in, but something changed. Many nights and weekends, he never came home. When he did, he looked like soot and smelled like earth. I bandaged everything from cuts to broken fingers, but nothing kept him from leaving again the next night.

Once, I tried to follow him, but he caught me. My gentle father transformed into a ferociously protective papa bear. His warning and whipping sent my feet scrambling home as fast as my sore backside could manage.

After that, I never asked where he went, and he never offered to explain.

When Dad was home in the evening, he invented a game called "Forget and Remember" to help me focus on what we had, not on what we had lost. In the firelight of our small hearth, I also spun my verses. He especially liked the ones that included a riddle for him to solve. Those dusk hours are some of my happiest memories.

To most, the man across the table from me is nothing but an old broken Tooler with knobby fingers and dirty nails. To me, he is everything left that's kind and lovely in the world.

The hearth's chattering fades.

"You'd better hurry up and get dressed." Dad stands and starts for the door. "You don't want to miss the train."

"Where are you going?"

He puts on his leathery hat. "I have something to do first."

My lip trembles in disappointment. I had hoped he would walk with me today. "Promise you'll meet me at the station."

His hand slides off the door latch and reaches for my chin. "Of course, sweetheart." Dad pauses and takes a deep breath. "Even if attendance weren't mandatory, I wouldn't miss the train. My brave girl's quest is a fool's errand, but I'm proud of her spirit."

I search his deep brown eyes, so much like Darius's. "Are we not all fools for those we love?"

He smiles and is gone.

I climb up to my loft and pull the dress off its hanger. The supplied garment is the only new article I've ever owned. Though stiff and starchy, the fabric settles neatly on my waist and stops above my knees.

My regular uniform waits packed in my messenger bag, along with my rationed Taser batteries, my flashlight, and a few toiletries. Unlike some candidates, I won't spend my last evening at home packing if I'm drafted. Small perks of being poor.

My few other belongings line the window shelf by my bed and

include a pocket knife and faded notebook, which holds my collection of verses. I won't be needing those if I leave, so I pull up the edge of my mattress and stuff them underneath.

The walk to the platform takes an hour but feels like less since I do it six days a week to board my train for school. I have no friends to walk with by my own choice. The last people who called themselves my friends were the Danforth brothers. Jotham condemned Darius in court, and Luther never spoke to me afterward. Clearly, who needs friends?

On occasion, the alley mongrel follows me. In return for my scraps, he warns me when more rabid mongrels or looters are around.

Today, I don't walk alone but join the stream of cube dwellers who have started for the platform. Our cube is one among dozens of other population pockets in Chrysoprase, the ninth of thirteen squares that form the ASU or American Socialists United. The other squares refer to us as 'Prase for short, to keep us separate from another square called Chrysolite. We don't mind either way.

Supposedly, the last civilization called squares *states*, but our society places a high value on equality and fairness. As the saying goes, square is fair.

We're required to board the train to the capital cube in Chrysoprase where one ceremony will serve for all graduates in our square. The other twelve squares of the ASU will hold their respective graduations today as well. Collectively, there will be thousands of us graduates.

A gray-whiskered man appears at my arm. "Excuse me, miss, is that seat taken?"

"Yes, I'm waiting for my father. Sorry." He grunts and staggers out of the car to try one farther back. I hadn't realized mine was already full except for the seat beside me.

I fidget with my skirt and press my cheek against the window to look for Dad. This annual pilgrimage reminds us both of what we lost. On a train like this one, the two of us had returned to our cube after the courthouse scene that left a tear in my heart and my spine. Somehow, Dad had carried me through rioting streets to the train.

A blast of steam gushes outside my window as the train prepares to leave, but through it, someone points at me. It's Dad. The lean young man beside him glances at me, and his eyes flicker with recognition. He's another graduate from my class. He nods at my father and disappears to jump on a different car.

Dad grabs onto the pole outside my car and swings himself inside as the train begins to move.

"What took you so long?" I scold.

"Oh, it was nothing."

I arch my eyes. "I saw you talking to that candidate."

He grins and wraps his arm around me. "Maybe I was looking out for a match."

"Oh sure, for the girl who turned down her compatibility testing." I jab him in the ribs. "I'm not going to be another casualty of that system like Candace."

He offers a sad smile in apology but no further explanation.

I cross my arms. "You're a bad liar, you know."

"Then don't ask me what I was doing."

"You have a mean habit of keeping secrets from me."

Dad removes his arm so he can look in my eyes. "Do you doubt I have only your best interests at heart?"

I frown and turn back to the window, wishing Dad would trust me more and shelter me less.

The train pulls to a stop in the capital station an hour before noon. Steam billows from the tracks as I step onto the landing. Maybe tomorrow I'll board the draft train along with a choice number of my peers.

If not, I'll enter the career service system with the rest of my graduating class and most likely, live in my cube till the day I die. A job there would be safer with fewer risks, but I'd never amount to much—or have a chance to change the Codex rulings and bring Darius back.

We step off the platform and follow the stream of bodies toward the open-air auditorium beyond the station.

But first, we have to pass the courthouse. Every year at this spot, my feet grow heavy as if the fetters from Darius's feet have been transferred to my own.

Screams of the phantom rioters make me want to plug my ears, but the echoes are in my memory where I can't block them out. Dad reaches for my hand and tugs me away.

Only when we reach the front stage does he release it. Other graduates form a line behind a check-in station, and one by one, climb the steps to take a seat on the stage.

Dad whispers, "Whatever happens, I am proud of you."

I tip-toe to kiss his cheek. "I love you, Dad. I'll see you back home after the ceremony."

He turns away but not before I see the tear in his eye.

I approach the woman at the booth. She addresses me without taking her eyes off a list. "Name?"

"Abernathy."

She strikes through my name. "Proceed."

I mount the steps and fill the next empty seat. Soon, I'm in the middle of a sea of blue. The girls are in blue dresses, and the boys in blue suits. They look stiff and sweaty, nervous like I am.

To the left of the stage is a row of tables where members of the draft panel have started assembling.

Someone drones for us to rise, and we respond with the precision of soldiers. I feel like a mannequin on display.

Today is not about us. Our diplomas have already been assigned and entered into the national records.

It's about the ASU and our roles to serve it.

The preliminaries bore me. I've long since memorized them. Welcome to the graduation draft ceremony. The ASU is proud of her citizens. All pledge to the ASU and her virtues.

With robotic harmony, we chant our pledge as the panel chairman moves toward the mic.

We pledge allegiance to the Friend
and citizens of the American Socialists United,
and to the virtues for which it stands:
equality, civility, and fidelity.
We pledge to lose ourselves for the public good
and serve our one united nation,
apart from which, we are nothing.

"You may be seated." A voice that sounds like a recording resonates through the square.

It belongs to Bertrand Matteson, president of the Crystal Globe and chairman of the draft panel. His hair is white, though he can be no older than forty-five. Perfectly smooth hands grasp the notebook that holds my fate.

I wonder why he's chosen to attend our ceremony this year when he could have emceed any of the other twelve.

"It is my privilege to introduce the Chrysoprase Class of 2149," he continues with the same velvet voice. "Graduates, you've waited long for this day, so I won't torment you with speeches. When I call your name, please rise. I will announce your career service assignment, and you will respond by saying, 'With honor, I accept.' Then, be seated as I call the remaining names.

"Of the 349 graduating today, only four have been selected for the highest honor: a draft to the Crystal Globe University to prepare for service in the Dome or administrative positions elsewhere.

"I do not need to remind you that all assignments and drafts are final and come with honor. Yours has been chosen with the nation's interests at heart, and I have no doubt you will fulfill your roles and exceed our expectations in a spirit of unity and cooperation.

"In fairness, I will flip this coin to determine your order: heads, alphabetical. Tails, reverse alphabetical."

I bite my lip, rooting for heads. Abernathy would be first, and I could be done with the suspense.

"Tails it is."

I brace myself for the wait.

The names sound like mush coming out of his mouth until he announces someone named Donovan, and I realize he's almost done. And there are still three draft cards left. So far, Matteson has called only one draft, a male on the far side of the stage whose name I can't remember.

Donovan takes his seat, and Matteson resumes. "Danforth, Luther: Court Citizen candidate."

I jolt straight as a young man three rows ahead of me rises to a height and build that rivals my father's.

Luther Danforth.

I hardly recognize the whistling neighbor boy I once called classmate and friend. The last time I saw him, his tangled black hair needed a cut. Now, it is neatly trimmed.

After his brother charged mine as guilty, he had slouched in his family's bench at the trial and ignored my cries. Now, he stands with confidence as if all were right in the world.

I shrink in my seat and grit my teeth to choke back the rising emotion. If Luther's brother betraying mine wasn't enough, we had heard rumors that Jotham later received a draft to the Crystal Globe on account of the bribe he accepted for denouncing my brother. Upon completion of his training there, he secured a seat in the Dome and more comfortable housing in a different Chrysoprase cube for his family. I never saw Luther after that day, and I had never wanted to see him again.

"Draft to the Crystal Globe," Matteson announces with flair.

The audience murmurs in awe, respect, and fear. But all I can think is how nice it must have been to grow up with a brother instead of seeing him only in nightmares.

"With honor, I accept." His voice is a mellow baritone.

The next few dozen graduates pass in a blur. The crowd murmurs as the third draftee, a female, is announced. At last, Matteson calls my name.

"Abernathy, Portia: Revisionary candidate."

I rise, feeling shaky. All eyes fix on me, and Luther turns in his seat. Strong cheek bones define his face, once boyishly round. His eyes are as black as I remember them—only now, they search my face with an expression of disbelief and amazement. I bite my lip and glance away to focus on Matteson.

"Draft to the Crystal Globe."

My head spins. Somehow, I manage to breathe and repeat, "With honor, I accept."

Once seated, I wonder if I imagined the words, but the candidates on either side of me whisper their respects.

"Congratulations, graduates and draftees," Matteson says. "All rise. As is our custom, once I dismiss you, please return to your cubes for your celebration feast before reporting to your career assignments on Monday. As for our four draftees, you will need to report immediately to the panel." He waves his hand toward the solemn-faced assembly on the side of the stage.

"You are dismissed."

Everyone moves at once, and I am engulfed in a sea of blue bodies. When I reach the draft panel, the three other draftees are already there. Luther and the other female are not from my cube. The other male is. He's the same youth Dad spoke to this morning.

I step next to him and farthest away from Luther.

The panel spokeswoman is speaking. "The regular draft train is down. Due to some incidents on the lines, we've assigned an alternate train, but it's coming earlier. Instead of leaving tomorrow, you must be ready to board your trains this evening.

"Abernathy and Foxworth, the train reaches your cube first. Be ready to leave at 2000 hours. Danforth and Collins, plan to board at 2300 hours."

Her eyes narrow and sweep from left to right. "Do not miss your train."

Chapter 2

Saturday, 9.5.2149
Chrysoprase

I step onto the faded platform, the last of the passengers to return to my cube from the ceremony. The late afternoon sun warns that my time at home is short. In a few hours, the draft train will arrive.

Past the platform, cube dwellers assemble along makeshift tables for a simple potluck feast. Families pinch their dolari every year to save for the event since standard food rations never provide anything leftover.

But I'm not hungry.

I'm afraid.

Since I boarded the train after the ceremony, a man with the bearing of a giant and stealth of a ghost has been shadowing me. The green hue of his uniform set against his dark skin now disappears in the crowd of common folk.

He is not an ordinary giant. He is a Gage.

The square fades into the background as I walk home. Alone. Not even the mongrel joins me.

I glance over my shoulder. There is no one—no one I can see but someone I can sense.

I try to run, but my lungs cramp. I slow to a fast walk, cursing my back. Thanks to it, I haven't run for a decade and wouldn't be able to, even if a mongrel pack were chasing me.

But this isn't a mongrel.

Maybe it's not even a Gage.

A new thought terrifies me. Traders haven't darkened our parts for some time, but what if one saw me at the ceremony? What if he saw me board the train alone and followed me?

I shove through our barn-home door and lower the latch behind me.

"Dad?" I turn around to look inside the dim interior. And freeze.

The coals in the hearth are black and cold, much like the man sitting like a stone statue at the table.

I stifle a scream and jump to my loft ladder, scaling it and pulling it up into the loft behind me, as if a missing ladder would keep this giant from getting to me.

But the man does not chase me. I crawl on my stomach to the edge of the loft and peer down. He remains motionless on the seat.

We stare at each other. His features are charcoal-black. Angular, strong bones define his face, offset by silver-colored eyes which study me with intensity. His mammoth build ripples under his dark green uniform, which bears multiple gold stripes.

He is a high-ranking Gage, not a Trader.

"What do you want?" I demand while my left hand feels for the Taser under my skirt.

"You are Portia Abernathy?" He rises and adjusts his belt. My hand quivers. He wears a real handgun, not a Taser like our local Gage.

"Yes."

"I am Gage Gath. I am here to escort you to your draft train."

"Escort me? Why?"

He clears his throat. "Those are my orders."

"But my train doesn't leave for another four hours."

The door groans as someone tries to enter, but the latch holds. *Dad.*

I lower the ladder to the ground, climb down, and rush to the latch. Dad pushes the door open but stops with one foot inside the threshold. Slung on his back is a brown sack bag.

"Dad, this is Gage—Gage Gath," I stammer.

Dad steps in front of me, pushing me behind him. "What is the meaning of this?"

"I am the Gage escort for your daughter."

"I have never heard of such a thing."

Gath flashes a sliver-thick badge with the Gage insignia of a Merlin falcon. "Your family's history raises some concern about fidelity to the ASU. The Dome's Commanding Gage issued orders to escort young Abernathy to the Crystal Globe this evening. I am here to collect her at such a time."

"That time is not yet here." Dad's voice is deep and low. "I would request you leave my home until then."

"Very well. I will wait outside until 1900 hours." The Gage gives Dad a hard look and ducks under the door.

"This is because of Darius, isn't it?" I whisper.

"I'm afraid so." Dad latches the door behind him and moves to the hearth. "Someone wants to make sure his sister doesn't try to run from her draft like he did."

Striking a match, he lights fresh kindling below the old coals and teases a fire to life. I crawl onto the scratchy rug next to him, bring my knees to my chin, and hug them.

"I've worked hard for this chance, and now, do I have to prove myself all over again?" I can't keep the bitterness from my voice. "What if I mess up? What if I fail my training and don't earn a Revisionary seat in the Dome? Even if I do, what if I can't change the satellite sentences and save Darius?" I bite my lip to check the words that give wings to my fear.

Dad pats my cheek. "If there's anyone who has a chance, it's you."

"But can I do this alone? I wish you could come with me." I press my thumbnail deep into my skin to distract myself with the pain.

Dad unslings the bag from his shoulder and places it on the floor before me. "Open it."

"What's inside?"

"We have four hours before you have to leave. I thought we could have our own little feast before then."

I undo the string and pull out a plastic package that's cool and damp. Inside are two fresh fish filets.

"Thanks, Dad." I unwrap each one and set it in the frying pan on the warming hearth.

"There's more inside."

I dig deeper and find wild berries tied inside a cloth handkerchief. They're a little squished but sweet. I lay the napkin between us so we can share them while the filets cook.

"There's one last surprise—a gift for you."

His words are like magic and lift the heaviness from my heart.

I reach into the very bottom of the sack and pull out a small object bound tightly inside a brown rag.

I carefully fold down the sides, embarrassed at how excited the little package makes me feel. Presents are a thing of fairy tales, right next to Christmas trees, which we've never had.

It's a miniature sheath. Inside is a black-bladed karambit with a small grip. It's the shape and size of a razor claw.

I have never seen a knife so beautiful and dangerous.

"You made this? For me?"

He nods. "Turn it over."

On the back side, there's an inscription in the blade. *Fraternitas Veritas.*

"What does it mean?"

"You're the scholar." His bristled face cracks into a grin.

I stare at the phrase, repeating the words which roll off my tongue like music. The words are similar to ones I know: Fraternity, Verity. Fraternity is a group or brotherhood that holds something in common. Verity is truth or fact.

"Brotherhood. Truth." I murmur, then look up at him. "A brotherhood of truth."

"You're too smart for your own good." There's pride and sadness in his voice. "Here, don't forget the sheath. I designed it with straps to make a thigh holster. Try it."

I stretch out my legs and roll up the bottom of my skirt. The leathery straps are thin and surprisingly soft. The blade feels almost weightless, compared to the Taser on my other thigh.

I pull out the blade to stare at it. I'm comfortable using knives to clean food but never as a weapon. And this one can serve no other purpose.

"But what does it *mean*?"

"It means you are never alone," Dad says.

"Who is the brotherhood?"

"I am. You are now. There are others too. We all watch out for each other."

I shake my head. "I don't understand."

"You will when you are ready." He turns the filets over, and the aroma of fresh fish fills the room.

I hold the blade up against the fire to read the lettering again. "And what is verity—the truth?"

"Truth is what will one day set us free from what is wrong and false in our world."

"False." I murmur. "But are we not false ourselves? Think of the game you taught me—to forget the sadness of the past and pretend only good things happened."

Dad pops a berry in his mouth. "It was a poor game for a child. I'm sorry, but sometimes, lies can protect us. However, only the truth can free us."

I slide the blade back into its sheath and curl my arm around his.

He pats my hair. "No one must know that you have this." His touch is gentle, but his words are steel.

"I know. Blades like this aren't legal."

"It's more than the blade. It's the responsibility that comes with it." He hesitates. "Remember that to do the right thing, you sometimes have to break the rules."

"I won't let anyone find this."

"But use it if you have to," he says. "This world is full of wicked men. There are worse kinds of prisons than a satellite."

"I'll be careful."

"Some devils wear handsome faces. Beware those too."

I yank away. "Dad, no. I'm never going for compatibility testing. Not after what happened to Candace."

He breathes a world-weary sigh. "You say that now, but some stranger will want to change your mind. Perhaps he will be a good man, but only time will tell."

I let Dad have his say.

The filets finish cooking, and Dad starts the tea kettle. I bring a remnant candle and napkins to our mat on the hearth. The table sits empty behind us, as it has done many times in my childhood. A picnic on the hearth better fits our mood. We spend the few hours, sipping tea and enjoying a quiet communion.

At 1900 hours, a single knock sounds on the door. I climb the loft for the last time to retrieve my messenger bag as Dad waits for me at the threshold.

I grab him fiercely, not wanting to let go.

"Fraternitas Veritas," he whispers in my ear and then opens the door.

The Gage is a silent guardian on the hour-long walk to the station. Dusk falls, and the howls of mongrels ring in the distance, but none dares approach me with the giant by my side.

When we reach the station, he disappears into the darkness at the edge of the platform. He is a shadow again, waiting and watching.

I stand alone next to the track, nothing more than a shadow myself. On the opposite side of the platform appears another figure, his breath visible in the chilly night air. It must be Foxworth.

He's too far away for me to see his face, but the moonlight silhouettes his wiry, tight form. He is not that big himself, but he is all skin and muscle, a common build for a man from a poor cube.

The blinding lights of our train approach. Minutes later, it brakes within a few feet of me. Swirling steam condenses and frosts the platform.

A car door opens, and the conductor appears. "All aboard."

I step toward him and submit my passport for inspection.

"Abernathy." He checks my name off a list. "You're in sleeper car sixteen." He turns to look behind me. "Next!"

I adjust the small messenger bag on my shoulder and continue down the narrow hallway, scanning for my room number, but I'm distracted by the strange lights coming from the ceiling. There's no visible flame, only a glowing light.

"Hey, if this isn't your room, stop blocking the aisle." A grating voice startles me.

"Oh, I'm sorry," I mumble and hurry farther down until I find number sixteen. I slip inside and let the other candidate pass me.

I leave the door slightly ajar so the strange hallway lighting can shine inside. The small quarters consist of a bunkbed sunken into the wall, a tiny sink, window, and barely enough room to spin around.

I pop the door closed with my shoe and toss my messenger bag onto the top bunk before swinging myself up. No one wants the top, so when my bunkmate arrives from another stop, the poor soul can collapse into her own bed.

I exhale into a lumpy pillow and close my eyes. The train groans to life and falls into a rhythm that makes my eyelids feel heavy.

Sometime later, a scratching noise wakes me, and the compartment door opens, sending a stream of unnatural light into the space. There's a thud. "Ow!" It's soft and low. Baritone low.

I tense and grip the pillow, eyes fixed on my bunkmate.

The man has his back turned to me. His left hand rubs the spot where his head bumped the short door frame.

"Sorry," he mutters and closes the door.

My bunkmate is a man and not just any man. He's Luther Danforth.

He's too annoyed with the cramped quarters to notice me in the dark, but I crouch, poised to jump as soon as he moves away from the door.

"Stuffy in here," he mutters, falls onto the bottom bed, and starts to pull off his shirt.

It's now or never. I leap off the top bunk, landing with all the grace of a frog.

I'm not sure which of us is more startled. His head pops back through his collar as I try to reorganize my limbs on the floor.

"Oh!" He blinks. "I didn't—I'm sorry—Let me give you a hand ..."

But the only hand I need is the one gripping the door handle. I shove it open and with my messenger bag trailing behind, dash into the hallway.

My face warms as I slam the door and ignore the strange stares from passengers lingering in the hallway. I rush past the dining car and lounge, not stopping to make eye contact with the other draftees or acknowledge the glances my way. Most are settling in for the night or getting a drink at the bar, and I am a fit companion for neither.

I push open the door to the observation car at the end of the train. At least it's empty. I collapse onto the U-shaped lounge couch facing the window.

The red cushion is old but clean and comfortable. It will have to do for the night.

Someone shoves open the door behind me, and a gust of air fills the room. I spin in my seat, gripping the back of my velvet couch.

Standing in the doorway is Luther. His shirt hangs askew on his chest, and his face flushes a deep ruddy color.

Is that anger or embarrassment? I don't hesitate to figure out which. I whip out my Taser, aim, and fairly squeeze the trigger when he holds up a desperate hand.

"I didn't mean to scare you." His words come in spurts. "I didn't know it was you—I just saw a cropped patch of blonde hair. Thought it was a puny kid. I mean, not that you're puny. I mean, you are. But that's okay. When you're a girl."

My mouth pops open. I push my jaw on top of the cushion to close it, not knowing what to say.

I hold the Taser ready.

He stammers on. "I don't know why they put you with me—I can see how that's uncomfortable. You can have the bunk, and I'll stay here."

Slowly, I replace my Taser in its hidden holster as I take in his height. Everyone is naturally taller than I am, but my first measure of him was not wrong. He is well over six-feet, like my dad.

"That's okay," I mumble. "Guess neither of us was expecting the other."

He exhales, and his shoulders relax. "Yeah." A half-grin plays at his lips.

"I'll stay here. It's not a big deal." I clear my throat and try to keep a serious face. But the sparkle in his eyes relieves the pressure in my chest. The situation is suddenly funny.

I shake myself. This is Luther Danforth.

"No, I insist." He cocks his head to check the hallway behind him. With the door open, the coarse laughter from the bar echoes into the car. "Some of these candidates are a pretty rough crowd. You're easy prey out here."

I stiffen and pull my Taser back out. "I can take care of myself."

He snorts. "I can see that."

"So leave me alone."

His face grows serious. "Put that away. You won't need it in the bunkroom. You might need it out here. And I don't think you want to fill out a variance report the moment you set foot in Crystal. It might hurt your first impression."

I hate that he's right. Slowly, I stand to my feet and slip past him into the hallway.

He clears his throat from behind me. "You've grown up, Cotton."

My whole body shudders. It's the name he had given me because of my platinum-blonde hair. As a boy, Luther said it resembled the cotton bolls the Harvesters reaped in the work fields. They nicknamed it "white-gold" for its color and value. He had grinned sheepishly and said the description suited me.

No one has called me that since Darius … I stiffen and keep my back to him. "We both have."

"I—I hope we can be friends again."

I clench my fists. "I don't have friends." And hurry down the hall.

Back in the sleeper compartment, I climb to the top bunk and hug the pillow to my chest. For a long time, I listen to the steady rhythm of the train running along the track while my mind replays all the hateful things I've memorized about the Danforth family. I had used a sketch of Jotham for a dart backdrop until it disintegrated. And I may have penned a few verses where a wizard cast a curse on said name.

Yet Luther hasn't changed, except that he's older and perhaps kinder? He seems every bit a naturally likable guy, the kind of person who would make a great … *friend.*

I toss on the narrow bunk.

No.

Never.

Luther stopped being my friend that day in the courthouse, and not even his charming personality is going to change that.

Sometime in the night, the cadence of the train wheels on the track lulls me to sleep.

Chapter 3

Sunday, 9.6.2149
Crystal

"Platform at Crystal Square in thirty minutes!"

The conductor's voice booms from the hallway, jolting me awake. The small window in the compartment is still dark. I guess it's around 0400 hours and that I've slept most of the train ride.

I slide to the floor and kick over something. When I crack open the door, the light reveals a half-spilled bowl of cereal and a paper box of milk. Printed on the milk box are the words, "Morning, Cotton. From a friend."

Luther.

I spin around. The bottom bed is empty. He must have slipped them through the door while I was sleeping.

His simple kindness makes the cereal hard to swallow, but trusting him is out of the question. Jotham had been my brother's so-called friend, and look where that got Darius.

I turn to the small sink and squint into the mirror above it.

Luther's words about a good first impression linger in mind, and I pull the limited supplies from my bag to freshen up.

Not that there's much to do. I wash my face and then remove the clip holding back my bangs before combing through the rest of my pixie cut.

Good as ever.

I slip into the hallway and walk toward the coach car, worried I'll find it crowded. But there are only five candidates, and they're all avoiding eye contact. The rest must still be in their sleeper compartments. I fall into an empty seat and stare out the window.

The lights of Crystal glow in the horizon like a luminescent globe that grows ever closer. It looks unnatural, like the ceiling lights, and makes me wish for the warm radiance of the sunrise.

As the train slows, the car fills with candidates preparing to disembark once we reach the platform.

A pale, slender girl claims one of the few empty seats left—next to me. She smiles with wide brown eyes. "You're the other girl from Chrysoprase, aren't you?"

"Yes." I study her face but can't place it from the fragments of yesterday.

"It's okay. I don't remember your name either. Everything from the ceremony is a blur."

"I'm Portia."

"Lydia Collins—It's nice to meet you, although I feel as if I already know you."

"But you're from a different cube."

"Right, but your face is exactly how I imagined Penelope, the wife of Odysseus, might look."

"Oh." I don't care to strike up a conversation, but this girl makes me curious. Entrance to a Greek mythology elective is as rare as it is difficult. Only Revisionary and Court Citizen candidates receive approval to study ancient texts.

"If I resembled Penelope, Athena would have made me taller too."

Lydia stares at me, unblinking. "I did not notice your height, just your beauty and reserve. And now intelligence. Penelope is a legend, and you are not. If you lack her fair stature, there must be a reason."

I turn to look out the window. "Yes, there's a reason. It's called scoliosis."

"What kind?"

"Idiopathic—At least that's the diagnosis on my records."

"No known cause," Lydia whispers.

"But it's not too hard to guess," I mutter. "A back injury and poor nutrition, plus some fickle genetics, don't encourage strong bone development."

"Well, it would be worse if you had a neuromuscular disorder. Yours is likely treatable."

I look back at her wide brown eyes. Her transparent face is graced with fine, sandy brown hair that falls to her shoulders. "You are remarkable. Are you a dual major? My guess is Healer and Court Citizen."

She smiles again. "Court Citizen. My father is a Healer, and I learned many things from him."

"That explains it."

"What about you?" she asks. "Since you've taken Greek Mythology, I'm guessing you're a Court Citizen candidate too, either that or a Revisionary."

"Revisionary." I yawn and hope she'll take the hint.

But she chatters on. "Mythology was a random elective for

me, but I enjoyed it very much."

Her cheerfulness, though it grates on my tired nerves, is nevertheless hard to dislike. I offer a half smile. "Yes, I liked it too—though Shakespeare was my favorite."

"Shakespeare? What's that?"

I bristle. "*He* was a brilliant writer. His plays are genius."

"Sounds like an elective for an Entertainer."

I sputter. "No, Entertainers are too crass—they would never understand or appreciate Shakespeare. It was an independent study anyway. I had to get a special permit, but the lessons in reasoning and persuasion were more than worth it."

Maybe I've said too much. I blush and try to explain. "You see, I worked hard to get this draft. I want to be a Doctor Revisionary in the Dome."

"I have no doubt you will be."

I exhale at the sincerity of her words. "I wish I had your confidence."

"You do," she says simply, "or you would not dare so great an honor."

The train groans to a stop, and we follow the other candidates onto the harshly lit platform. We all know where to go and nothing about where we're going.

We funnel into five lines for the check-in stations, organized alphabetically by our last names. Lydia and I find the A-E line.

At last, the woman at the desk calls our names. "You're the draftees from Chrysoprase."

"Yes, ma'am."

"Passports."

We hand them to her. She mechanically stamps them. "Abernathy and Collins, you're in Commons 7, Room 604. Here are your keys. Orientation starts at 0700. Next, please." She says the words like something read off a rations box.

Lydia hands me my passport with a grin. "Thank you." If I have to a have a roommate, at least this one has already decided she likes me.

I follow her across a long, blindingly bright courtyard as other draftees scurry around us, dragging their luggage. Lydia pulls a modest suitcase behind her, evidence that her upbringing involved more privileges than mine.

Not that I care. My messenger bag doesn't slow me down.

We reach a smaller courtyard, home to a dormitory with the number seven.

"We made it," Lydia says, her words almost musical with excitement.

She suddenly lowers her voice and blushes. "Don't look now, but you'll never believe who's watching us!"

I see the cluster of male draftees but miss her meaning until we're part way inside the central lounge of our commons. As we reach the stairwell, a tall, blonde candidate stares my way and grins. I trip on the first step and grip the handrail to catch myself.

Though I'm a girl from a poor cube, I immediately recognize him. Everyone in the ASU knows the face of Felix Caesura.

I had once seen a picture of the Friend's only son on a magazine cover. I assumed he was several years older and had looked up to him as the best-looking boy in the nation with every advantage at his disposal.

Now, we share the same playing field and likely the same dormitory. The thought seems both impossible and ironic.

I turn and hurry up the stairwell with Lydia dragging her suitcase behind me.

She gasps for breath when we reach the sixth floor. "Did you see him?"

I nod and scratch the door while trying to insert the key. I give the handle a hard yank and peer inside the dim interior of my new home.

Heavy drapes hang on either side of a large window, allowing the moonlight to filter inside. My eyes quickly adjust. We've entered a small living area and kitchenette, at least triple the size of my home in 'Prase. Just beyond, I make out the shadows of two full-sized beds by the window.

There's even a clock, and the red lettering reads 0450.

I peek outside the window. The courtyard lights shine with perfunctory brilliance below, and in the distance, the crystal peak of the Dome glows like a lone beacon in the nightscape.

Am I witnessing what Dad called electricity? But how can it possibly be available in such large amounts?

The mystery of it all can wait. I throw myself onto the first bed, so plush it seems to swallow me. I'm cocooned in a cloud. I had no idea such a mattress existed.

Lydia collapses onto the second one. "I set the alarm for an hour …"

Beeping wakes me what feels like seconds later, and Lydia slaps the clock with the back of her hand. What an annoying invention. We had roosters back home.

Lydia isn't moving fast, so I help myself to a cold bathroom shower, cold because that's what I'm used to. I'm wide awake when I turn off the water, and quickly dry and redress.

My roommate meets me outside the bathroom, holding a black mug. The contents smell like a witch's magic potion.

"It's coffee!" She slurps.

Coffee.

The word makes my heart race. We always drink tea in Chrysoprase, because it's cheap. Lydia laughs as I inspect the pot—she calls it a percolator—plugged into the wall.

"We have electricity?"

"You saw the courtyard lights last night, didn't you?" she asks. "We even have a phone, lamp, and hair dryer!"

"But how …" I stop and frown. "Lydia, I didn't think electricity had been restored in mass anywhere. My dad said only a few locations had access to the few—oh, what's the word—whatever they had to rebuild after the Rosh League crippled the old order with an EMP."

"The transformers?" Lydia asks. "Well, apparently, they're available here at the Globe. After all, we are one step away from the Dome."

"It's strange so few of us live like this."

"Maybe one day everyone will." She sips her coffee and sighs. "Until that day, I plan to enjoy it while I can."

I don't argue and pour myself a cup. Its contents make me feel as if I can conquer the world.

After Lydia showers, we leave to find the auditorium. I study the courtyard spotlights closer. They are now off and replaced by the soft light of dawn which reveals a small grove of trees and a fountain in the center. Marble slabs beneath my feet seem fitting for a palace.

If this is Crystal, I never want to go back to Chrysoprase.

The auditorium peaks above the other buildings, and we hurry to reach it. Dozens of marble stairs lead up to its entrance, and though an adjacent clock tower shows we're nearly half an hour early, the place already buzzes with other candidates, dressed as we are, in blue uniforms. A few in green and white also appear. I guess they're already enrolled in the Crystal Globe.

Of the massive interior, only the front section is illuminated, drawing us and the other new draftees forward.

"Look, there's Luther!" Lydia says. "And there are two seats beside him. Let's go there."

Luther waves us over, but I balk. "You know him?"

"Of course, silly, he's from my cube. We were classmates together." She eyes me curiously. "How do *you* know him?"

"Never mind," I mutter and reluctantly follow her lead.

"Hey, Lydia, it's good to see you." Luther stands and shakes her hand.

"This is Portia, my roommate," she says, "although I guess you already know each other."

"Yes, we do," he grins. "How was breakfast?"

"Fine, thank you." I take my seat, thankful that Lydia is sitting between us.

"I wonder if the other 'Prase draftee is here." Lydia scans the seats around us. "Isn't he from the same cube as you are, Portia?"

"Yes, I think so."

"What's his name again?" Luther leans forward to look at me.

He asked me a question. I have to answer it—in the name of civility. "The panel spokesman called him Foxworth, but I don't know him. He wasn't in any of my advanced classes."

"That makes sense," Lydia says. "I probably wouldn't know Luther if he and I didn't share the same Court Citizen classes."

The lights flicker a warning, and the auditorium goes silent. Moments later, the walls become screens of light which morph into moving pictures.

The candidates around me respond with gasps of surprise and

delight, but I grip my armrest uneasily and wonder what is real and what is not.

All my life, I have been told digital technology died when a world power called the Rosh League targeted our land with electro-magnetic-pulse warfare. Catastrophic natural disasters had already destroyed half of the country, and this attack crippled the rest. The new order led by our first Friend had more immediate demands than restoring technology, which has lain dormant ever since.

Once, I found an object on the way to school and showed Dad. He had called it a cell phone, but it didn't do anything.

I had thrown it at the mongrel when he got too close.

Now, do my eyes deceive me? Or is this what Dad had called digital technology?

The only images I've ever seen have been faded, crumbling, and in a photo album. These are like living creatures on the screen, changing with every blink of the eye.

"What you are witnessing now is what few have witnessed in our time." A woman's contralto voice narrates. "History, in all its beauty and terror, plays before your eyes."

I search for meaning, but the images flash with such intensity that my head aches trying to give them form. A star-studded flag. A statue. A book. A musket. I think I see them, but I do not know them, and then they vanish. A transparent crystal emblem. A child. A scroll. An olive branch. I know these, for they are the symbols of our ASU pennant.

The voice continues, "You are here because you have the mind to understand and the power to change. Dare to be more than you are in the name of the ASU. Become what it needs to survive the world's next evolution."

The lights go up, and the images vanish. The backs of the chairs in front of us lower to reveal a small, oblong object with a screen that reflects like glass but feels like plastic.

"The trays in front of you contain what we call a tablet," the woman says. "You will see four blanks. Click on each blank and describe an image that you saw on the overhead screen. Your IQs indicate you will have seen three to four."

The voice pauses before one last instruction. "You have two minutes. Make sure you type in no less than three of the fields."

Her words hold an expectation and a warning. *What happens if I don't?*

Chapter 4

Sunday, 9.6.2149
Crystal

A stopwatch blinks on the center display. The two-minute time has begun. Lydia focuses on her screen, pecking letters with painful slowness. Beyond her, Luther stares at his screen, his brows furrowed. He glances my way, a silent question in his black eyes. Perhaps he is wondering the same thing I am: *Which set of images do I type?*

I turn my attention to the keypad and type the second set of images I saw. At least I know what they are. The first four are a mystery.

I finish entering the fourth word when the countdown reaches zero, and the tablet retracts back into the chair. Seconds later, my screen turns gold.

Lydia's and Luther's turn gold as well, but the young man's to my right flashes translucent yellow. The one beyond his turns bronze, and several rows ahead, another displays silver. I blink, and the screens fade to a dull gray.

"What does this mean?" Lydia whispers in my ear.

I have no answer.

A man in a purple suit steps onto the stage. Though his back is to me, his trademark white hair pegs him as Bertrand Matteson.

"Welcome, draftees, to the Crystal Globe." He strides to a small podium in the center of the stage. "I know you're all wondering about that little assessment. Your new life will be full of assessments. You may not immediately understand them, but they are designed to ensure your protection and loyalty to our system. Your advisers will explain them to you and administer correctives if needed."

"Sounds like we're back in grade school," the young man beside me mutters. No sooner do the words leave his mouth than his screen flashes yellow again. His face drains of color.

Matteson continues, "You will soon find that here in Crystal, the highest standards of fairness, civility, and fidelity are enforced. As the core of our nation, Crystal must exemplify the qualities that unite us.

"You, the candidates drafted from our thirteen squares, will receive every privilege and the highest education imaginable. Great privilege brings severe responsibility, one we do not take lightly. I trust you will learn to do the same."

He pauses to smile before continuing. "Perhaps you question our commitment to equality. Already you have noticed advancements that are absent in your home squares. How can we rationalize their employment here?

"We are firm believers in equality but also in the advancement of the ASU. Advances do not happen overnight. They must be manufactured, tested, implemented, and enforced.

"Unfortunately, many people fear change. Our role is to adapt and implement. Your role upon graduation is to accept assignments and enforce our initiatives. One draftee from each field will receive the highest honor attainable, that of a doctor in his field, and earn a representative seat in the Dome. The rest of you will be assigned positions of leadership in other squares.

"Change has to start somewhere, and so it starts here, with you, with me."

The candidates break into applause, and I join in for fear that not clapping may result in my screen flashing yellow too.

Matteson holds up his hand for silence. "We've established that change is necessary, and your class will be the first of many to experience the wheels of progress. Our vision remains the equalization of education. However, until all universities have been retooled with our educators, we believe that proper encoding of our highest achievers will realize our aims in the shortest amount of time."

"That's brainwashing," the young man beside me grumbles.

"Shh!" I warn him, but it's too late. His screen flashes yellow a third time, then turns red.

Report to Sector 16. These words streak across his screen, and he looks at me. "What does that mean?" he asks.

I look into his eyes. They belong to a caged animal. I don't dare speak but shake my head. In my peripheral, I spot the Gage who has moved to the end of our row.

The Gage's mouth moves, and his stern command comes through the chair beside me. *Come with me.*

Somehow, the chair must have built-in speakers, because there's no box-shaped object like the one that amplified our voices on the graduation stage.

The young man has no choice but to stand and step over us to exit. He disappears with the Gage on his heels.

I swallow hard and focus on what Matteson is saying.

"Finally, let me congratulate you on your drafts. I have no doubt you will give your utmost. The Crystal Globe rewards those who do. Equality! Civility! Fidelity!"

We chant the words back to him.

"Next, you will meet with your new advisors. However, remain in your seats until your screen signals that your appointment station is ready. The stations are beyond the auditorium's doors." He points toward the right side of the room. "Your adviser will review your current codes and determine your class allotments. Appointments begin now and run up until lunch. While waiting, review the information on your screens.

"Here's a quick run-down of the rest of your day. Lunch starts promptly at noon. At 1500 hours, return here to receive your individual tablets that contain your reading texts and candidate log-ins. These tablets are personalized to you and your field of study. This technology may be foreign to you, but simply follow the directions on your tablet screen. Respond to the prompts by using the arrow buttons to specify your preferences or selecting the *Enter* key to move on.

"Dinner is at 1800 hours. At 1900 hours, you will congregate in the courtyard for the evening's activity. You are re— ... you will *not* want to miss it."

Clearly, we won't be allowed to skip.

"Remain in your seats until your appointment appears on your screen. Good day, candidates."

Lydia taps me on the shoulder and nods toward my screen where information has started scrolling. Neither of us dares to speak, fully aware that our every word is being monitored.

The familiar story of the ASU's history plays before my eyes in digital clarity. There are no words, nor do there need to be. I've read the story before, and these moving pictures capture every detail of how I imagined it had unfolded.

The year was 2089 when the string of natural disasters, later dubbed the Apocalypse, devastated the population with volcanic eruptions, earthquakes, and tsunamis. Western states were swallowed whole by the sea or separated from the East by a fiercely widened river that cut the country in two. A meteor shower over the Midwest decimated cities, and uncontrolled fires finished what was left.

Survivors fled to the East where the remaining "states" of the then USA were unable to cope with the hordes of refugees. Lack of resources and mounting tensions with foreign enemies resulted in the country's social, economic, and political collapse. The nation's final death knell sounded when a global federation called the Rosh League silenced its communication and technology systems with electro-magnetic-pulse warfare.

The country was crippled. Death and mayhem ran rampant.

And then the first Friend appeared on the scene, calling for a massive restructure of the remaining population. He offered hope and promised to lay the foundation of a new nation. He drew a parallel to a mystical city from an ancient book. Instead of thirteen colonies which began the USA, he mapped out thirteen squares, bearing the names of the twelve foundation stones of "the spiritual New Jerusalem."

Why he called it that, I have no idea. It must be a strange book, because I've never once read it in all my courses.

Added to the twelve would be one cornerstone, Crystal, which would be the purest form of government and leadership.

The squares flash on the screen in consecutive turn from north to south: Amethyst, Jacinth, Chalcedony, Lapis, Topaz, Crystal, Chrysolite, Jasper, Chrysoprase, Sardius, Sardonyx, Emerald, and Beryl.

As the squares morph into one nation and fade into the backdrop, the first Friend's face emerges into focus. He calmed the desperate masses with his optimism and promised to make a reality of a dreamlike fable. Tossed aside were the "failed ideals" of the USA. The Friend replaced them with socialistic standards, captured in the slogan "square is fair." Individual rights were lost so the whole could survive.

Out of the ashes arose a revised nation, the ASU, established in 2090. Though technologically isolated from the world, or whatever was left of it, this nation had slowly recovered from climatic disasters, adapted to global cooling, and crawled into a new era.

My screen flashes my adviser appointment. I smile goodbye to Lydia, squeeze past Luther's legs and walk down the gray aisle. The double doors swing open as if sensing my body. They quickly close behind me, and I stop. Rows of small, portable stations line the long hallway. Above each one is a number, and I start my search for twenty-seven.

At a table inside each station sits a person dressed in purple. Several monitors and a tablet are within their reach. I grimace as a candidate receives an injection. Another begins answering a series of questions on a screen, while another places his fingers on a small, glass-surface device.

I stiffen my back and wonder what my adviser is going to do to me.

Seated at Station 27 is a man in his early thirties with buzzed black hair and a long goatee. Green eyes inspect me through red-rimmed glasses.

"Portia Abernathy," he says. "Take a seat." He enters something on his tablet. Those devices are everywhere.

"I'm Lucius and will be your adviser for your time here." There's a lilt to his voice that tells me he finds his job important.

"A Revisionary candidate," he reads off the screen, "with high marks, no less. You are slated for a full load, four classes each semester. Let's start you with Revisionary Studies 501, Codex Analysis 520, Advanced Literary Interpretation 525, and Simulation."

"What's Simulation?" I fold my hands on my lap to keep from nervously pulling at my skirt.

He smiles patronizingly and glances at his tablet. "Think of Simulation as a hands-on lab elective. The Simulator lets you engage real-time with our Codex and apply it to history—past and present."

"I don't understand."

He sighs. "At the risk of sounding cliché, it feels like time travel, but isn't. The Simulator is a room-sized computer that confronts you with scenarios from history. It's anything but a tourist trip. You must learn from the mistakes of failed codices and correct them by applying your Revisionary training. You must confront their founders and debunk them with our Codex. The technology is stunningly lifelike. Your instructors will initially program your Simulator experiences, but second semester, you will be in control. Think of it as a testing module. Your professors will evaluate your results and implement correctives as needed."

"Okay." I glance away from his face to feign interest in an

oddly shaped trophy on his desk. I don't want him to know how daunting the Simulator sounds to someone who's never used a tablet before today.

"Splendid. I've accepted you into the classes." He taps on his screen. "You're all set to start tomorrow.

"Now, let's talk personal. I'm pulling your file." He swipes the screen. "It looks like you're up-to-date on your immunizations. Your history of scoliosis has been treated?"

"As successfully as possible." I pretend to study the trophy some more. There's something about Lucius that reminds me of spoiled milk. I want to dump my glass and leave.

He punches in a number. "I'm authorizing access to our health spa. Our Healers are highly trained in targeted muscle and massage therapy. If you experience discomfort during your stay, take advantage of their services."

"Thank you."

"Hmm." Lucius's forehead creases into a misshaped W. "What's the story with your compatibility testing? I don't see any notes here."

I clear my throat and shift my weight on the metal chair. "I declined."

"Your age is nineteen."

"Yes, sir, that is correct."

"Oh, drop the *sir*." He waves his hand impatiently. "I could be your brother. Here's what I'll do. I'll write a script for your test. You can take it to medical, and they will evaluate your compatibility and matches."

"No, thank you," I whisper as my heart races. Fragments from my seven-year-old memory surface and remind me of Candace, the beautiful, dark-haired young woman I once called sister. I found her swinging from a rope suspended from her bedroom ceiling the morning of her scheduled union.

She wanted to wed her childhood schoolmate Victor, but the system said they were "incompatible." The superintendent's son Johann, a regular Casanova, may have had something to do with that. Candace's compatibility test confirmed a match with Johann. She was told her results were final, and the union was arranged. I would have hanged myself, too.

No rule requires adolescents to apply for testing. Almost everyone does, but I opted out and skipped my preliminary tests. I will never be a victim like Candace.

The system serves the system—and those who control it. I'll be the one who changes the rules.

"No, thank you," I say, louder this time.

Lucius blinks at my response. "Excuse me?"

"I decline," I say as firmly as civility allows. "I have no interest in being matched. My focus is my education. My goal is to become a Doctor Revisionary in the Dome."

"I understand your disinterest in procreation, but there's no need to deprive yourself of self-fulfillment. An attractive female like you would not be in want of a partner, and I can assure you, Crystal offers only the best candidates."

He pauses to grin. "And here, we're not as old-fashioned as other squares. Your matches don't have to be permanent unions if you don't want them to be."

"I'm not interested. May we continue on another subject?"

"We can revisit this at your nine-week review. I highly suspect, though, you will seek out testing before then, or perhaps you already have someone in mind?"

I lower my voice. "I came to Crystal with one purpose, that of a Doctor Revisionary. Even if I were interested in someone—which I'm not—I wouldn't apply. And if I change my mind, I have no desire for anything less than *till death do us part.*"

That's what Dad had said about Mom, and fourteen years later, he still honors her memory.

The screen next to me blinks yellow.

Lucius's eyes narrow. "I advise you to speak with less conviction and condemnation. Your ideals do not conform to those of the Crystal Globe, or the ASU, for that matter. We believe in the pursuit of indulgence. Abstinence suggests a rebellion against the norm and a defiance of our values."

"I'm sorry you see it that way," I say, nonplused. "Bertrand Matteson challenged us to give our all. That's what I plan to do—and I don't have time for distractions."

Lucius eyes me warily and, with exaggerated motion, swipes to the next screen.

"Place your thumb on the glass in front of you," he says, dryly. He takes prints of all my fingers without another word. I am glad for the silence.

He saves the scans into the system and continues with the next item on his checklist. "Your candidate ID number is 1911. One day, we'll link your thumb prints to your identification, and you won't need this number."

"When will that happen?" I ask.

"It's in the five-year plan." He taps again on his screen. "We have the technology, but implementation takes time. For now, entering this number in any keypad will grant you access into buildings and rooms for which you have authorized access. Memorize it. Tattoo it on your arm. Don't forget it."

"I think I can manage," I say. "I'm good with numbers."

Lucius clears his throat. "Last, let me explain our color system for assessments. Gold is perfect. Your transcripts are gold, and your preliminary orientation screen assessment is gold as well. You are, however, down to silver as a consequence of your callous remark."

I start to object, but he cuts me off. "Civility is one of our core values."

I imagine myself breaking the trophy on his head.

"Bronze is acceptable but low," he continues. "Yellow is a warning. After three warnings, red assigns an automatic corrective."

I flash my teeth. "And what exactly is a corrective?" If only I could keep the sarcasm out of my voice. On cue, my screen flashes yellow.

"Do you really want to know?" Lucius smirks. Before I can answer, he reaches under his desk. I nearly jump out of my seat when he grabs my wrist and stabs me with a two-pronged needle. I flinch and try to pull away as he injects a serum.

He stares me in the eye. "A corrective can come in one of two ways. The first is an injectable dose, designed to retrain the subject's thinking. There are a series of injectable doses, proven 90% successful.

"If unsuccessful, the next phase of correctives is initiated."

He finally releases my wrist, and I yank back, rubbing the spot. I feel dizzy and wonder what dosage he gave me.

Now I want to break his trophy and taser him. I've never been treated like an immunized animal before. I mask my rage with a trembling smile. "And what does this next phase involve?"

He sterilizes the needle for its next victim. "You're going to be a good girl and never have to find out."

Chapter 5

Sunday, 9.6.2149
Crystal

I'm lying on clouds, which makes me care less that my head still feels funny. I roll over and register it's my mattress and not that fabled place called heaven.

"Hey, there." Lydia reclines on her bed and presses an oblong wand. In front of her, a flat screen shows moving pictures with captions below them. "It's about time you woke up. I was getting worried I'd have to leave you and that you'd miss orientation."

"What time is it?" I groan.

"It's almost 1500 hours," she says. "Sorry, you missed lunch. I tried bringing you some food, but there are strict rules here. We're not allowed to take any food out of the lunch hall."

"It's okay." I sit up and rub my head. "What's the matter with me anyway?"

"I was hoping you could tell me that. I found you passed out on your bed when I got here. I left you alone for a couple hours, but I was starting to get concerned since you didn't respond when I called your name."

I rub my head and notice the red spots on my wrist.

My wrist.

The marks, tender to the touch, clear up the fog. Lucius. The injectable corrective. There was a trophy I smashed on his head—or maybe that was in my dream. I vaguely remember getting back to my room and feeling sick.

"I'll be all right," I say slowly. "My adviser wasn't very nice, and I'm tired."

She picks up her bag and glances in the mirror. "Okay, do you want to come with me, or should I meet you there?"

"Go where?" A hazy feeling clings to my head.

"Orientation, genius. We need to leave now, or we'll be late."

I slide off my bed and start for the door, but Lydia just stands there, laughing.

"What's so funny?" I demand.

"You should look in a mirror."

Now I'm laughing too. My hair is a matted mess.

"Be right back." I hurry to the bathroom, comb my hair, and experiment with a small brush Lydia calls *mascara*. Earlier, I watched her insert the brush into a tube, pull it out covered with black goop, and comb it through her eyelashes. She said it made them thicker and brightened her eyes.

I sure could use some bright eyes right now, although mascara is a poor substitute for sleep. It smears. Sleep doesn't.

I still don't look great, but at least the floor feels level again.

We reach the auditorium just in time. The doors close behind us and lock. This late business is serious stuff.

We slide into two seats. The backs of the chairs in front of us fold down to reveal small, black tablets.

The lights in the room dim, but no one steps to the podium. Our screens come to life and prompt us through "activating" the tablets using our candidate ID numbers. Once successful, the program installs something called software customized for our field of study.

I learn terms like home screen and icon and log-in and account settings. I find icons for all my classes and warily eye the black one that reads "Sim," short for Simulation. I watch a dozen tutorials and set up my "preferences." I download my syllabi for tomorrow's classes and start a "document" of notes.

I have barely begun when the lights come back up, and my tablet announces that it is downloading updates and saving my preferences. Good for it.

"Please take your tablets and report to the dining hall in fifteen minutes," a faceless voice echoes through speakers in our chairs.

"What time is it?" I yawn.

"Must be close to 1800 hours," Lydia says. "Wow, we've been in here three hours."

"My head is killing me."

She grins. "Eat something, take drugs, and you'll feel better."

"Drugs?"

"You know, pain killers," she says. "Tell the person at the head of the line you need one, and he'll medicate your drink for you. I saw someone do it at lunch."

Although my system's already in overdrive, I do as Lydia says. An hour later, I'm back in our room, drowsy but pain free. Dinner and drugs do work. I try to concentrate on my tablet and the location finder for my first class, but my eyes keep closing.

And then, my screen blinks a reminder: assemble in the

courtyard at 1900.

I groan. "Lydia."

"What." Her answer is flat, and she is nearly asleep on the bed next to me. She doesn't need a dose of correctives to remind her that we've been up since the train pulled into the platform before dawn this morning.

"My screen says we have to go to the courtyard."

"You go. I'm going to die right here."

I wonder if they accidentally put my drugs in her drink too. "If we skip it, will anyone miss us?"

My tablet flashes a yellow warning. I throw it under my pillow and roll off the bed to kneel beside Lydia.

"Lydia!" I hiss in her ear.

"Whaaaat?"

"They can hear everything we're saying. Someone's listening in through this tablet."

"That's insane. Stop being paranoid."

I lower my voice even further. "My screen flashed at me when I suggested skipping the event."

"It did what?"

"Shh!"

Her brown eyes widen as she takes in my meaning. "Can you turn it off?"

"Try yours first," I say. "Mine might be restricted because of the warning."

She pushes every button she can find, but the tablet will not turn off.

I frown and point to the leather ottoman in the entry way. If we put our tablets there, maybe whoever's listening can't hear us.

Lydia nods to confirm she understands, and we quietly close

the lid on the devices.

"I hope that works," she says, but I hold a finger to my lips. I hear footsteps outside our door.

Someone knocks loudly.

"Who is it?" I stand on my tip toes to peer out the peephole and then shrink back.

A tall Gage stands outside. It's Gath.

"This is a warning that Portia Abernathy must report to the courtyard."

Lydia gasps beside me, but I hold up my hand. "I don't feel well," I say back through the door.

"All candidates must report to the courtyard at 1900 hours. Go to the clinic if you don't feel well. A nurse will prescribe medication."

"I already took something."

There's a pause. "You must either report to the clinic or to the courtyard." His voice sounds recorded. Does everyone here run off scripts?

"Thank you for your message." I force as much warmth into my voice as possible. I know better than to mess with a Gage, especially this one.

There's a muffled response. *Feel better.* Is that what he said? No, I must have heard wrong.

"What do we do now?" Lydia asks.

"We'd better show up for this party." I sigh. "I'm going to pull on some tights and get my jacket."

"Good thinking." The temperature always drops at night, and neither of us knows how long we'll be outside.

When we reach the downstairs lobby, we're almost blinded by the light.

"What's that?" Lydia winces at the brightness.

"Stadium lighting," a voice beside her says. We turn to see a male candidate whose face is painted red.

"But this is the courtyard." I try not to stare at him.

He nods. "Of course, it's Greek night. They put the stadium lights and heaters in the courtyard so everyone has a good time. The lighting will change once we get started. It'll be like a big party."

He glances at our coats and tights and laughs. "You're new, aren't you? You're not going to need those here.

"All you need is to choose the best Greek, and that's Phi Beta Kappa. Go Kappans!"

"What's a Greek?" Lydia whispers as he runs away to join the crowd.

"I've read about them," I say. "It's a fraternity, a group of candidates who have a certain focus."

"Like what?" Lydia shrinks into a corner as two dancers nearly trip over us.

"Dancing?" I suggest. "Some are academic or athletic or service-centered."

"All I see here is self-centered," Lydia says as we find a balcony to overlook the courtyard. It's glowing and hot and sweaty, full of candidates—new draftees, second-year candidates, and alumni—laughing and drinking from luminous lime, pink, and yellow mugs. Tents and platforms form a boundary around the courtyard. Band members tune their guitars, sound technicians check mics, and lighting personnel adjust something called strobes.

For a simple girl from 'Prase, it's sensory overload.

Lydia slips out of her coat. "That guy was right about our

coats. I'm sweating already, and I have to get out of these tights. Do you want to run back to our room?"

"I'll wait here, but would you take my coat? My tights don't bother me."

"Sure." She disappears back inside.

I slide into a porch chair behind the balcony pillars to wait for her.

"Hey there, Frosty."

The voice comes right behind me, but I ignore it, hoping the comment is meant for someone else with whitish-blonde hair.

"I say, Frosty, aren't you going to join the fun?"

Groan.

I turn and nearly jump out of my tights. It's Felix Caesura.

"I—uh—was enjoying the view," I lie.

"You were hiding." He swaggers closer. He's even more intoxicating in person than in his photos. He's blond with chiseled features, a dangerous grin, and sharp gray eyes, almost crystal-blue in the spotlight.

I don't know what to say, so I turn back to the balcony. "It's quite the party."

He steps closer. "So, what are you waiting for?"

"My roommate." I glance at him and then away. Those eyes can see right through me. "She took our coats back to the room. We don't need them here."

"You look dressed for class in that number." He elbows me in the ribs. "Loosen up, Frosty, this is a party."

If he calls me that again, I will blurt out something uncivil. To spare myself another warning, I say, "My name is Portia."

"I'm Felix."

"I know," I say simply, "and this is all I have to wear."

"Where have you been all day? The clothing stations opened after lunch." He slides next to me on the rail, and I edge away from him.

"I missed lunch."

He narrows his eyes. "For being such a pretty girl, you're kind of a prig."

"I'm from 'Prase. I'm not used to boys like you."

He throws back his head and laughs.

I cock my head, and turn my eyes into cadaverous slivers. "I'm not being funny."

"The harder you try to look angry, the prettier you are."

I choke at his breath. "You've been drinking." My youthful ideals about the Friend's son vanish.

I take a deep breath and stick out my chin. "Well, it was nice meeting you."

For a moment, he disappears out of my peripheral vision, but then the hair on the back of my neck starts to itch.

His hot breath pricks my skin. "You can't get rid of me that easily. We're both Revisionary draftees, and I make it my business to know my competition for that Dome seat. I heard some juicy rumors about you and thought I'd see for myself what I'm up against."

He snickers. "I'm not too worried. You're a piece of cake, and I could eat you in one bite. See you around. Frosty."

I keep my back to him. I can't punch someone I'm not facing.

This morning, I thought I would never want to leave this place. Tonight, all I want is to catch a train back to Chrysoprase and return to my boring, underprivileged life.

That life was better than this intoxicating and constricting place where my every word is monitored, my moral fiber is a criminal offense, and no one cares about anyone but himself.

I grit my teeth. No, I won't forget why I'm here. I won't forget Darius.

"Sorry it took me so long." Lydia returns to my side, breathless. "The lights went out for a few minutes. There was a minor glitch with the electricity."

"Everything out here is so bright that I didn't notice," I say. "Glad you're back."

"Did you meet anyone?" she asks. "The people here seem extra friendly."

I snort. "You could put it like that."

She squints at me. "What's wrong? Did something happen?"

I shrug. "Just some guy. He was rude and kept calling me Frosty. It was annoying."

"Excuse me, miss!" A flamboyantly dressed man holding a tray of luminous mugs appears to my left. Can I crawl into a hole now?

"Yes? How may I help you?" I ask, civilly.

"This is for you, courtesy of Mr. Caesura." He hands me a glowing pink mug, frosted with ice. He nods at me and disappears to serve other candidates.

"Caesura?" Lydia gasps. "You met Felix Caesura while I was gone?"

I groan and sniff the mug. A sip confirms it's spiked. "Yes, I wish you'd been here. It was rather awful."

"But he's gorgeous!"

"He's a spoiled brat." I scan around me, expecting a red light to flash. But the blinding amphitheater lighting and music muffle my incivility.

"Something's going on at the center stage," Lydia says.

"Come on. Let's go find out."

I dump the mug's contents and leave it glowing on the railing. The courtyard teems with bodies, a breeding ground for claustrophobia. Lydia seems taken in by the spectacle, and for her sake, I'm glad one of us is enjoying it.

"Welcome, candidates!" A man's voice booms. Lydia edges closer to the platform, and I reluctantly follow.

"Tonight is a big night for you," the voice continues. I don't recognize the man. He's probably scripted, too. "You will choose your Greeks, which will play a major part in your social lives here at the Globe. Around the courtyard are ten stations, each representing one of our campus Greeks. Tonight, you will pick which one you want to join and experience the thrills of initiation.

"You have until midnight to be in your rooms, but the clock doesn't have to stop then. The only limitation is the one you set on yourself—and that of class tomorrow. The night is yours. Enjoy and indulge!"

Lydia frowns. "That's an odd word choice. What kind of Greeks are these?"

My headache returns with vicious force. "Let's just find one and get this over with."

We're surrounded by a cacophony of competing bands and Greek members who scream for our attention. Two men strap a girl into a giant swing on our left, while a guy nervously dives into a pool of goldfish where a sign reads, "We don't catch and release."

"This is bizarre." I keep my shoulder close to Lydia. The girl to my left shrieks as the swing flings her into the sky before jolting her back down.

Lydia shudders. "I hate heights."

I try to lighten the mood. "I'm terrified of goldfish."

She grins. "Let's keep moving."

We're suddenly surrounded by candidates with red-painted faces who chant, "Kappans! Kappans! Kappans!"

I recoil into Lydia and grimace as a tall, red-painted man screams in my face.

"Hello to you too." I cough at his stained breath.

"I'm Arthur, the president of our Greek. Climb the wall, eat the banana bowl, and join us!" He smirks as Lydia's face pales.

Heights.

"And, uh, what's your Greek about?" I shout so he can hear me.

"We're trippers."

"Trippers?" I shake my head. "You mean, like, you trip on things?"

"No, blondie, we day trip around the squares, train hop, sleep on strangers' couches, and explore. We live to experience. Our hobby is to discover the crevices of society."

"Fascinating," I say, intrigued by the idea of exploring the squares. "And all I have to do is climb that wall and eat a basket of bananas?"

"Yeah, girl, it's awesome. You'll totally puke your guts out when you're done."

Bungee jump, swim with goldfish, or climb a wall and eat bananas. I hate bananas, but I can only imagine what tortures the other seven Greeks have invented for their initiates.

"At least there's got to be a harness," I tell Lydia.

She smiles weakly at me. "You first."

The Kappan shakes his head. "No harness. You get up there by yourself, and when you're done, you jump off the back of the wall onto a trampoline net. But our guys won't pull it into place until you're done with the last banana. It's a crazy trust exercise."

The band behind me pounds nails into my head. I can't take much more of this courtyard, so I might as well die stuffed with bananas. "Sure, sign me up." The Kappan hoots and shoves me toward the wall.

The wall has to be two-stories high. I give Lydia one last glance and begin my ascent. My hands ache because I'm squeezing the grips. Maybe I have a fear of heights myself.

Panting hard, I pull myself onto the top, only to find a narrow ledge. I peer over the other side and hear a retching cough below. Must be the last guy. At least he survived the jump down.

The basket brims with at least fifteen bananas.

There's no way. But my choices are to eat the bananas and jump, or painfully climb back down the front and concede failure.

My hands tremble as I peel the first one. I have just squeezed half of it into my mouth when the stadium lights go black.

A wave of darkness spreads across the campus and completes its circuit as the dormitory lights go out, too.

The concert bands and microphones silence, but screams break out. Feet pound on the pavement, and the noise crescendos into a stampede, but I can see nothing. Nothing, that is, but the stars above me.

What's happening? How will I get down if I can't see the grips? And I don't dare jump, because I can't see where the trampoline net is.

Presence of mind, Portia.

I spit out the banana and peer over the ledge into the dark void. "I'm up here! Can someone pull the net?" I yell, but the chaos swallows my words.

I grab the bananas and hurl them like bullets. "Anybody! Can you hear me? Pull out the net."

Only two left.

Clenching the wall with my legs, I lean as far over the edge as I dare and aim for the retreating screams. The last throw nearly topples me.

"I'm stuck up here!" My voice becomes little more than a raspy grunt.

I grab the wall with empty arms. All that remains is the basket, which I punch off the ledge.

"Somebody." But my whisper barely carries to my own ears.

All I can do is wait and hope. Gaze at the stars. And straddle the wall more tightly.

Chapter 6

Sunday, 9.6.2149
Crystal

The evening chill gnaws at my bones. The amphitheater lights have long since cooled, and the courtyard will become my frozen tomb if I don't find a way down this wall.

Several times, I've reached for the closest grips, but my blind attempts have failed. Twice, I nearly fell, scraping my arms. The blood that oozed from the cuts has frozen on my skin.

I lay my chest and head against the wall's narrow top, my arms and legs hanging over either side. A faint clicking sound beats against the pavement, and it grows steadily louder, closer. Listening, I pull back and return to my resting position. My parched throat wants to scream, but my gut wills it silent. There's something sinister about the precision of this machine.

Only, it is no machine.

"Halt!" The boots stomp in unison near the base of the wall.

Gages.

I strain my ears.

"At ease, cadets." A deep and guttural voice gives the command.

I shiver but not from the cold. The voice reminds me of a bad nightmare.

Another man speaks. Though I can't be certain, he sounds like my Gage escort Gath. "Sir, all but eight candidates are checked in to their rooms. Five are confirmed dead. Three are missing."

"Who's missing?" the first demands.

"Abernathy, Ethel, and Merger."

"Abernathy?"

"Yes, sir."

I hold my breath. Why would he care about my name?

"Keep searching." The rasping command comes at last. "These three are either somewhere off limits, or their bodies are shrouded by this darkness."

"Any word on the cause?"

There's a pause. The first clears his throat. "Cadets, continue the drill around the perimeter. Report anything unusual—or any more corpses."

As the mechanical march resumes, he lowers his voice, and I can barely make out his words. "Off the record, we suspect Rogues. They must have insiders here. The three missing are prime suspects, but they may also be victims of the chaos."

"But all three are new candidates."

"What better way to sneak in a Rogue than as a candidate plant? But that's between you and me. The official word will be that a power supply override malfunctioned."

Another pause. "Rogues have enough knowledge of our grid to pull a stunt like this?"

"You leave the Rogue problem to me. I need you to find the missing three. If they're alive, bring them in. Immediately. Especially if you find Abernathy."

The way he says my name makes my skin crawl.

"Yes, sir."

The clicking of their boots fades in the night, and I remain stranded, now branded a Rogue suspect. Whatever that is.

If I don't get down from this wall, I'll be nothing but a corpse myself.

Holding onto the top with my arms, I swing one leg and then the other over the front side, stretching to reach the top grip.

There. I slide my shoe into its narrow indent and search for a second with my other foot. That found, I now face the real problem. I have to let go of the narrow top, but then, I won't have anything to hold.

Biting my lip, I reach down with my right hand to search for a third grip.

And then my left foot slips.

My scream is a hoarse cry. My left arm nearly dislocates as I swing from it alone and claw frantically at the wall with my right.

"Help!" It's a croak, a hopeless sob.

"Portia, hold on!"

Lydia.

Beads of sweat drip from my forehead, freezing before they fall. It has to be almost midnight. The dew is turning into ice.

Beneath me, something scrapes against the wall, and a muffled voice replies to Lydia. Someone is helping her.

"Okay, let go!" A man calls up to me.

Luther.

"We've pulled the net to the base of the wall. Let go, and it will catch you."

I uncurl my fingers and fall. For a few seconds, I'm suspended in air. I squeeze my eyes shut to brace for impact.

I hit the net and rebound. Strong arms reach for me across the mesh and pull me to the ground.

"Hurry! I think someone's coming," Lydia whispers.

Luther lifts me and follows Lydia, running for the dormitory. The lights flicker on when we're halfway up the dark stairwell to our apartment.

Once inside, Lydia closes the door and turns to Luther. "You're a lifesaver, but you need to go. If you're caught breaking curfew, they'll give you correctives. You heard the Gage's orders."

"I'm staying here." He holds me tighter. "I run a bigger risk of getting caught if I try to sneak back into my room. Besides, my roommate is dead. I have no one to tell on me, and as far as the Gage knows, I'm still checked into my room. I'm sure he has other problems than to recheck the entire campus. For all he knows, I'm sound asleep."

My body is a weatherman's nightmare, but I register what these two have risked for me. "Thank you," I say through chattering teeth.

"We've got to get her dry and warm." Luther rubs my shoulders. "Lydia, find something dry for her to wear."

"I'll check her bag."

Luther sets me down and hands me a blanket from my bed. "Take this for now." I stagger to the bathroom to undress and instantly check for my Taser and knife. They're still holstered on my thighs.

At least I didn't lose them.

I loosen the holsters and hide them under a towel in the

bathroom cabinet. I toss my wet clothes in a corner and wrap the blanket around me.

Seconds later, Lydia appears at the doorway with my old uniform and a bathrobe.

"I'll start some hot tea," Luther calls from behind her.

"He's such a good guy." Lydia helps me into the dry clothes. "You're lucky he likes you. Most guys wouldn't give a second thought for someone they met a day ago."

No, a lifetime ago. But she doesn't know that.

I nod dumbly, my mind and heart divided. His brother Jotham gave Darius a death sentence on a satellite, but Luther just saved my life. His brother betrayed his friend to help secure his own promotion, but he risked his safety for mine.

I press pause on my mental sparring match. It will have to wait. Right now, I want to enjoy being alive.

"What happened when I was on the wall?" I ask hoarsely. "I saw all the lights go out."

"Everyone panicked." Lydia wraps the bathrobe around me for added warmth. "I stayed close to the wall to avoid getting trampled as candidates ran to their dorms. Luther found me and helped me to my room."

Lydia guides me to the vanity bench and plugs in a hair dryer to defrost the ice on my hair. "I was so jarred I couldn't speak until we got here. I finally managed to tell him that you were stuck on the wall, and that's when the dorm sirens came on. We were ordered to lock down in our rooms until further notice. Anyone found outside their rooms would receive correctives.

"Luther said he'd come back as soon as he could. Waiting here while knowing you were stuck out there was awful."

The blow dryer strokes fiery fingers through my hair until it's dry and the size of a wet skunk. Lydia has the decency to pat it down before we leave the bathroom.

Luther waits with steaming cups of tea. He helps me onto a couch and hands Lydia and me each a cup.

"You look better already," he says with a smile.

"Thanks to you." I lower my eyes and swallow the tea. It burns my tongue but revives my parched throat.

"What do we do now?" Lydia asks. "We have to report your return, and we all need to have the same story."

I feel cold again. The Gage's words ring in my ears.

"Call your dorm adviser and say you got knocked out, came to, and returned to your dorm," Luther says.

"It's not as simple as that." I relate the conversation I overheard.

"What's a Rogue?" Lydia asks.

"I don't know, but I'm a suspect because of my absence," I say. "I don't want to pull you two into this."

"And Luther, you have to go back to your room," I add. "If you get caught, you'll get pegged as an accomplice."

"What about you?" His face is a solemn mask. "Do you want to face that Gage alone?"

"I don't have a choice." I try to sound braver than I feel. "Knowing you two are on my side is enough."

Lydia sips her tea before speaking. "Then what are you going to do?"

I clutch the tea cup tightly. "Lydia, contact the dorm adviser. Tell her I showed up half an hour ago, nearly frozen. Tell her you called as soon as you knew I was stable. When she asks what happened, say you don't know the story. That makes you impartial and keeps you out of this.

"Luther, you have to sneak out now. Otherwise, you'll be found breaking curfew."

He nods and quickly moves to the sink where he dumps the rest of his tea, then rinses and dries his cup.

I admire his presence of mind: no evidence to prove he was here.

He pauses at the threshold. "I'll see you in class tomorrow, Lydia." He gives me a long, worried look. "Take care of yourself, Cotton."

I swallow a lump in my throat. "Thanks ..." but he is already gone.

While Lydia makes the call, I cocoon myself like an invalid on the couch and ruffle my hair to appear even more distressed.

Seconds later, the dorm adviser and a Gage arrive at our door.

"Come in," Lydia says and backs away. Through squinted eyes, I watch a woman not much taller than myself enter, trailed closely by a goliath Gage whose dark complexion reminds me of a shadow. It's Gath.

The woman introduces herself as Petra, our dorm monitor, and pushes past Lydia towards the couch. "When did she arrive?"

"Half an hour ago."

"What did she say happened?"

"She didn't." Lydia pauses. "She was nearly frozen. I got her into something dry and called you as soon as I could."

Petra circles the couch and whispers into Gath's ear. I close my eyes all the way for fear she'll realize how alert I am. When she speaks again, it's to Lydia. "Thank you for calling us. We'll handle the situation from here."

"If there's anything else I can do—"

"We don't require your assistance any more. We'll take her to the clinic and then for questioning."

Petra's breath comes close to my face. "Can you hear me, Portia?"

I groan and crack open an eye to acknowledge her.

She nods to Gath who slides me into his arms, which feel like rock. There's no use resisting. I keep my eyes closed as they pass through the hall. Someone opens an outside door which blasts frigid air through the robe Lydia wrapped around me. Gath is surprisingly careful with me when he steps into a vehicle.

"She's ice cold."

"She'll be fine," Petra snaps. "She'd better be. The Commanding Gage wants answers."

A nurse at the clinic examines my scrapes and bruises without a word. He dresses them, takes my vitals, and turns to Petra. "She's chilled and running a low fever. She's scraped up a bit, but nothing requires stitches. With plenty of rest, she'll be fine."

"Thank you." Petra nods to Gath who grips me tightly in his arms again.

We emerge back into the night. Headquarters, as Petra calls it, is an illuminated, barbed wire mini fortress on the edge of campus. Gages patrol the perimeter. Petra waves her identification, and we breeze past the guard house.

The bright lights and sudden heat make me dizzy.

"Right this way," a guard tells Petra, and we follow him to an enclosed cell. Two Gages with their backs turned to us are studying a digital map on the wall. The first glances at us, presses some buttons, and the image on the wall vanishes. He mutters something and leaves without acknowledging me.

The other turns to face us, and I shrink further into Gath's arms. The Gage's face is gnarled with age but only fiercer for the wear. He is the Gage from my childhood nightmares.

His black eyes lock on my own with a glint of mockery as Gath sets me down in a hard metal chair in front of a table.

Petra stands somewhere behind us. "Gage Eliab, this is Portia Abernathy."

"Yes, I know."

That rasping voice. It sends shivers down my spine.

Petra continues her report. "The clinic cleared her medical. Do you require anything else from me?"

"Nothing at the present. You are dismissed."

I pull my arms into the bathrobe as the door clicks into place. A black case on the table resembles the one I saw at Lucius's desk.

"Miss Abernathy." Gage Eliab rubs his hands together. "I congratulate you on your draft but had hoped we might meet under different circumstances."

I glance at Gath who stands beside me. He shows no sign of surprise at Eliab's knowing me.

But then, someone had to assign my escort orders.

Eliab drops the niceties and crosses his arms. "What were you doing in the courtyard?"

"I was there for the Greek event." I hug myself more tightly and continue. "One Greek made me climb their rock wall, and that's where I was when everything went black. If you don't believe me, you can ask the president. He said his name is Arthur."

"How long were you on the wall?"

"Hours."

"And how did you finally get down?"

"After several attempts, I climbed part way and fell the rest. I crawled back to my dorm. My roommate found me at our door."

"What time was that?"

"I don't know. I blacked out."

Eliab exchanges a look with Gath, then resumes the questioning. "Did you hear or see anything from the wall?"

I close my eyes. "Everything was black. I couldn't even see my hands."

"And did you hear anything?" He presses the question.

"Nothing." I lie and open my eyes. "May I go back to my room now? I don't understand what this is all about, and I'm tired."

Eliab smiles strangely at me. "You're from 'Prase. You know how dangerous the streets can be at night."

His gaze holds me captive. "There are always the gangs and mongrels to watch out for," I say. "I doubt those are a problem here."

"Miss Abernathy, every square has its night demons. Those who don't belong anywhere make it their business to destroy what they can."

"I didn't hear any mongrels." I shake my head. "After the stampede, the square was deathly quiet. I screamed, and no one heard me."

Eliab's black eyes show no emotion. "Perhaps you should be thankful no one did."

Gath stands stiffer than ever. I feel alone in a room of two machines. "So why am I here?" I ask at last.

I expect him to answer that it's standard procedure, that I'm one of the last candidates to report to her room, that I've broken curfew.

Instead, he steps toward me and leans against the table. It's a deceptively relaxed pose, for he is a cobra poised to strike.

"Miss Abernathy, your draft is impressive, but then, intelligence runs in your family. So does bad blood."

He turns to Gath as I turn to ice. "Do you remember it, Gath? No, you would not have been there."

"I am aware of her family's record," Gath says quietly.

Eliab returns his gaze to me. The smile only masks his fangs. "You *had* a brother."

My throat constricts at his choice of tense. Darius may be gone, but I refuse to believe it's forever. I swallow and lie again. "I don't remember much about him."

"Ah, yes, you were but a child," Eliab murmurs. He fingers the box on the table, exposing the top of his hands—and the scar the shape of a child's bite.

His black eyes turn to blazing coals. "As I recall, there was a young girl at his trial. She broke through the guards to be at her brother's side. One. Last. Time.

"It seems she is still breaking the rules today."

I close my eyes to block out the horror that suddenly feels so fresh, as if Eliab has opened a wound that runs deep in my chest.

I have tried to forget the little girl with tears streaming down her face. Her golden hair was a matted mess, much like it is today. She had pried off her father's arms to dash toward her brother who was being led away.

A stone statue of a guard stepped in front of her, blocking Darius from sight. The Gage grabbed her arm, and she bit his hand.

For a moment, she broke free and ran for Darius—but she did not reach him. A hand yanked her hair and swung her into the air. Her back had crashed into the wall with a painful snap.

Now the stone statue stands before me as flesh and blood.

I uncurl one leg to steady myself, but I cannot steady my voice. "You are *mistaken*. Unlike my brother, I accepted my draft. I am here to make a difference."

"To what purpose?" His black eyes accuse me. "Yes, you're a Revisionary candidate, and your records look impeccable. Yet the fact remains that you are the last candidate to report to her room *alive*—and well past curfew."

He stands, but it is not the position of one preparing to say goodbye.

It is the stance of one preparing to go to work.

He opens the black box. "Naturally, we must call your story into question."

Eliab motions to Gath who steps behind me. I try to stand, but his goliath hand presses hard down on my shoulder, warning me to stay seated.

Struggling would only express the rebellion I feel in my heart.

I jerk my head. Eliab has removed a syringe.

"What's that?"

"Nothing to fear." *That terrifying smile.* "It's a lie detection test. We ask you questions. You give us answers. You go to sleep. You wake up, and don't remember anything—unless, of course, we find you haven't been telling us the truth."

He steps toward me.

In the instant before he injects my arm, I close my eyes and *forget*. I visualize a new memory for the courtyard. I imagine crawling down the wall and back to my room. Alone. In my mind, I see the courtyard, free of Gages, and silent from footsteps.

Silent, that is, from everything but a little girl's cry.

It's the game I've played hundreds of times, the one Dad taught me beside our flickering hearth.

My father is right. Lies can protect us, but I ache for truth.

Chapter 7

Monday, 9.7.2149
Crystal

I am running down a hall, chased by a pack of mongrels. Their black eyes flash red as their breath comes hot on my legs. Before me is a wall I must climb, but the grips are missing. I claw the vertical wall with my hands as one of the beasts pounces.

Someone shakes me.

"Portia, wake up!"

I unclench the pillow and blink. Lydia's pale face stares down at me.

"Are you okay?"

"What happened?" I prop myself up with my arm. My fingers rub a bright red mark that's sore to the touch.

"Tell me what you remember." There's something mechanical about her voice.

I sit up straighter and narrow my eyes. "Did they tell you to ask me that?"

She flushes and bites her lip. Her eyes hold an unspoken apology.

"Never mind," I mutter and fling off the covers. A small pile of clothes is neatly folded on the table. I pick those up and lock myself in the bathroom.

The girl in the mirror is a stranger. Bloodshot eyes stare back at me.

I turn on the shower until the water runs hot. It makes my skin bright pink, but at least I look alive. I lather myself in lotion, redress the cuts on my arms, and comb my wet hair. Bending to open the cabinet doors, I retrieve my holsters, relieved Lydia didn't find them.

I glance at Lydia's cosmetics and cave to the urge to put on makeup—amazing how it feels like armor.

The girl in the mirror is still a stranger. She's hard, but she's human.

The navy suit fits perfectly, and the long sleeves do a nice job concealing my bandages. I pull on a new pair of tights to cover the bruises on my legs and strap on my holsters, wishing I also had something to cover the bleeding wound inside my chest.

I don't remember the lie serum or anything I was asked or answered, but since I'm back in my dorm, I must have passed. However, the faces of Eliab and Gath burn in my memory.

When I emerge from the bathroom, Lydia is gone, and I don't blame her. No doubt someone is scripting her to spy on me. The less she asks, the less she knows, and the less she has to tell.

It's better this way. If I have no friends, I can't hurt anyone. But I can't shake a sense of loss.

I retrieve my tablet from the ottoman and turn it on to review my day's class schedule. I have two classes in the morning, lunch, and then the afternoon free. I plan to sleep from lunch until dinner and then do whatever classwork I have.

I ignore my growling stomach and head to class. I'm the first one there and choose a spot near the front end so I can keep anyone entering class in my peripheral and minimize the number of candidates who sit near me.

While waiting for the professor to arrive, I load my textbook and syllabus. To my relief, no one attempts small talk with me. There is a tense feeling in the room when class finally starts. Whatever happened last night has left everyone on edge. Some whisper, but most say nothing.

After wolfing down lunch, I return to my room and collapse onto my bed. Too soon, the alarm on my tablet goes off.

But there are still three hours until dinner.

I look closer at the alarm. It reads: "Report to gymnasium for physical education."

That notification wasn't there this morning. My physical education requirement was waived due to my medical records.

"Lucius." I want to throw my tablet and break it on the wall, which of course I don't do, because that would mean more correctives.

Still tired but determined not to lose more precious sleep than necessary, I hurry to the adviser cubes and wait impatiently for Lucius to finish with another candidate.

He greets me with his sour-milk stare. "May I help you, Miss Abernathy?"

"Yes, there's something wrong with the scheduling on my tablet. You know my medical history does not allow me to participate in physical education, yet there's a new reminder saying I am to report to the gymnasium for this class."

He frowns. "I remember our conversation." I wait while he types something on his screen. "Unfortunately, I'm not authorized to remove you from this class."

"But who added it to my schedule?"

"I have no way of knowing," he says. "Now, if you'll excuse me, I have work to do."

"But what am I supposed to do?" I protest. "I can't participate in that class."

"I suggest you talk to the coach."

"A coach can't change a roster," I argue. "Where do I need to go to drop the class?"

"You can't drop a class on your own." Lucius rolls his eyes. "You must get permission. If you're enrolled in this class, you must fulfill it unless exempted."

"Then who do I have to see to get my exemption?" I feel my face growing red. "My medical records are in the system. Someone should be able to see them and clear up this mistake."

Lucius glares at me before reviewing another screen. "Your medical files are locked."

"What?"

"As I said, your files are locked. I can't access them—and neither can anyone else without authorization."

"This is an outrage." I stand to my feet. I'm sure a screen flashes yellow somewhere. "I thought Crystal offered the best possible education, and this place can't even read my medical records."

Lucius narrows his eyes and drops his voice. "Someone intentionally froze them, Miss Abernathy. There's nothing you or I or anyone lower than the dean can do to unfreeze them. Now here's my advice. Stop making yourself so unlikable, because someone has noticed you. And it's not in a good way."

I fall back into the seat, unable to keep my shoulders straight. Hot tears of frustration burn my eyes. "Then what am I supposed to do now?"

Lucius straightens and swipes his screen. "Go to class. Good luck, Miss Abernathy."

I am dismissed, but I don't move. I study my small hands and narrow wrists. Any muscle I do have already burns from last night's ordeal. A physical education class might as well be a death sentence to my goal of reaching the Dome.

Someone is setting me up to fail.

I bite my lip. I refuse to cry in front of Lucius. To him, I'm just another number, another candidate, and a mouthy one at that. He has no reason to like me or help me.

My tablet vibrates, and a fifteen-minute warning for class appears. I dismiss the alarm.

"You can pick up your gym clothes and shoes at the clothing station around the corner. If I were you, I'd go to class prepared and hope the coach hears you out. Maybe he will give you a non-physical project to pass the class."

I look up. Lucius stares busily at his screen, but I know he spoke the words.

"Thank you," I mumble. "I'm sorry to bother you."

His green eyes flash at me, but I hurry away before I can read their expression.

Fifteen minutes later, I'm dressed in gym clothes and reach class right before it starts. I peek around my co-ed classmates to where the professor stands in the middle of the gym.

Farther to my right are Luther, Foxworth, and Felix, so I shrink toward the left of the crowd. I don't want to talk to anyone right now. I want to get out of here.

"Gather around, and let's get started," a deep voice calls. "I'm Coach Mariner."

I squeeze between two tall girls to get a visual. Coach is of average height but with an Olympian build. Protruding eyes make his bald head seem even more round than it is. "This class isn't complicated, but it is vital to your curriculum. You may all have the best brains your squares can offer, but if you fail this class, that won't matter.

"Am I clear?"

Murmurs of acknowledgment echo around me, and my legs tremble. This guy doesn't tolerate weaklings.

"Half your grade is from the written portion of this class. The other half is from your performance on the track. The first half of the semester is textbook work. Start training today for the second half if you want to pass."

Mariner paces in front of the line. "You all can read, so download the syllabus on your own time. Before Wednesday, finish chapter one, and be ready for a quiz. We'll start regular discussion then.

"Today is easy or hard. Every last one of you will run a 5K on the outdoor track, just beyond those double doors. As soon as you finish, you're free to go. That means some of you get to leave class early. Others, well, you had better get started if you don't want to miss dinner."

He smirks at us, then flexes, and rolls his shoulders. Next, he reaches into a tote bag at his feet and pulls out a handful of sticker-like sheets.

"I want a straight line. Once you have your marker, start your laps. Your marker will turn from red to green once you're done.

5K means 12.5 laps. Don't dream of leaving until you finish—even if you have to walk. Leaving before completing the laps will result in an automatic corrective."

We form a line, and I try to get toward the back of it. I need to talk to this guy, to convince him that there's been a mistake.

"Next." He slaps a marker on the girl's arm in front of me. She takes off running without a word.

"Excuse me," I say, "but may I have a word with you?"

He slaps a marker on my arm and frowns. "Go to the back and wait."

I nod and step aside for the remaining candidates to pass.

"What is it?" he demands.

"Coach Mariner, there's been a mistake. I have scoliosis, but for some reason, my medical records are locked. When I met with my adviser, he didn't enroll me in this class, but it wrongly appeared on my schedule today.

"When I spoke with my adviser, he told me to report to class and talk to you."

The coach peers at his tablet screen. "I can't access your records either. I see you were enrolled today by priority access administration."

I bite my lip and try again. "But there has to be a mistake. I haven't run a day in ten years or taken a physical education class. My undergrad adviser replaced it with an alternative protection elective."

"The system won't let me remove you from the class." He shrugs. "Clearly someone thinks you need it. Until I see medical records that say otherwise, you're better off starting your 5K."

"Can I apply for a new physical and x-rays to prove I don't belong here?"

"That's a medical issue, not my problem."

"Then, I'll go to medical and get this resolved," I mutter.

"Not until you finish today's class."

"But I can't run!" I protest.

"Walking never killed anyone," he grunts. "Get started. I've got a class to supervise."

I stare after him as he strides toward the double doors.

"Coming?" he barks at me.

I trudge out the doors and observe the track where candidate after candidate start their laps. These candidates have been running for years. For them, fitness is a requirement they have to pass.

It's a death sentence for me.

I can't step on the track with them there. I'll look like a fool and get run over in the process.

"The longer you wait to start, the longer before you finish," Mariner warns. "I'm not waiting here all day."

"I can't run. It isn't my fault that the system made a mistake."

He glares at me. "It's your problem now. You have until the end of the day to run your laps. If your marker isn't green by midnight, you will have to report to medical—for a corrective."

"Thanks for your concern." I can't keep the sarcasm out of my voice. I turn and march back inside the gym, ignoring the stares from my classmates and the scowl from my coach.

I grab my bag and change back into my regular clothes. I can't remove the marker without taking off skin, so I leave it on. Maybe I'll walk the track after dinner to clear my head.

Medical rebuffs me. Only a doctor's script can approve an x-ray, and I have no script on file. They can't break into my medical records either.

"Someone from high priority has intentionally locked them," the nurse tells me.

"What is high priority?" I demand.

Her brows furrow. "Someone from the top, miss. I can't help you."

Eliab. Why would he do this to me? What did I say last night to make him hate me so much? I don't know anyone else *from the top* who would want to ensure my failure—and make it look like my fault.

With no other recourse, I stuff my gym clothes in my bag, along with my Taser, and head to dinner.

I eat in a quiet nook before slipping out for the track.

My tablet came with something called earbuds that allow me to listen to my textbooks. I plug them in, slide my tablet into my bag, and pull it over my shoulder as I step onto the track. Only a few candidates remain, and none are from my class earlier that day.

These crazies run for fun. No doubt they'll ignore me.

I'm tired and hot and completely done with my homework when I finish my 12.5 laps, but my arm marker now reads green.

A remnant of light lingers in the sky, and I'm only too glad to leave the now-deserted track. Deserted, except for a single man seated on the bleachers. How long has he been watching me?

"Hey there, Cotton."

"Luther." My voice sounds limp to my own ears, even though I'm trying my hardest to sound fine.

He jumps off the bleachers. Concern and agitation pinch his face. "You've been out here almost two hours. Why did you leave class earlier? Why didn't you run with the rest of us? Coach wasn't too happy when you walked away. Do you want to make enemies?"

"You sound like my adviser," I mutter. "And for the record, nothing is going the way I want."

"Then learn to run with the flow. That's the only way you're going to survive here."

"I *can't* run." I throw the words in his face. "Someone froze my medical records. No one believes that I have scoliosis and haven't run a mile in my life. Someone wants me to fail. But what do you care?" I fight back tears of frustration—not at Luther, at life.

"I—I had no idea." Luther blinks as if I slapped him.

"Of course, not."

"But you used to be the fastest girl at three-legged races."

"That girl's gone. You don't know anything about me anymore."

The length of a coffin separates us, but the real distance spans a decade estranged by betrayal and bereavement.

Luther takes a step toward me. "I know that your favorite color is the autumn sky, and your favorite insect is the firefly."

I gulp and step back, but he draws nearer. "I know that you're scared of the dark."

A tear, then another, drops past my cheek.

"I know that you dream up verses in your head, and that you're the smartest girl in school. The prettiest girl in school."

He's so close that his breath falls on my face. "I won every three-legged race when you were my partner." Luther chuckles. "Even though you were small, you always kept time with me."

I lower my head and let the tears rain to the ground.

He tips my chin to look me in the eye. "You're still small but no less fierce. Where's the girl I called my best friend? Is she still in there?"

I tremble at his touch. All these years, he has not forgotten me.

"I don't know." I wipe my face with the back of my hand.

He reaches for it and squeezes it. "Then give me a chance to find out."

"I can't run races anymore."

"Then let me teach you. You can learn again."

"But my back."

His eyes cloud. "What happened?"

I look away. "The Healers back home think it was my injury. It never healed right."

He grips my hand tighter and clenches his teeth. "You mean when that Gage threw you."

That's right. He had been there, tucked safely next to his father on a bench in the back.

I swallow and wish I could forget. "Anyway, I don't think it healed right, and after we moved, there was never a lot of food. Good food anyway. Dad did his best ..."

"How bad is your scoliosis?" He lets go of my hands and touches my shoulder. "Lydia isn't the only one with Healer instincts. May I?"

His touch is gentle, kind. Without thinking, I nod and turn my back to him. He runs his palm along my spine which starts straight and then bows outward just above my hips.

"Maybe twenty degrees, maybe less," he says, more to himself than to me.

"Hmm?" I ask.

"It's not severe—as severe as it could be," he says. "Did you get treatment?"

"Dad spent a whole year's health allotment on a cast. I had to sleep in the miserable thing for years."

"It helped." He removes his hand. "I'm sure your Healer knew what he was doing, but at this point, exercise isn't going to hurt you. If anything, it will help strengthen your muscles."

I sit on the bleacher, and he joins me, a new intensity in his eyes. "I could train you. With the right stretches and muscle massages, you could learn to run again."

"Me? A runner? Not likely."

"Lydia's a Healer's daughter," he persists. "She could help with the muscle massages."

I sigh. "I don't think Lydia wants anything to do with me."

He shakes his head. "You're wrong. She told me in class today that she's worried about you."

"Did she also tell you that the Gages asked her to spy on me?"

Luther hesitates. "She told me about last night and that they brought you back unconscious in the early morning hours. She said they wouldn't tell her what happened and to report anything irregular. Lydia's just as scared as you are."

"She'll be fine as long as she doesn't hang around me. You better watch yourself, too. Being my friend might not be the best choice."

His face cracks into a smile. "Too late. I made my choice a long time ago, and I don't plan to change my mind."

I glance around me. The track remains deserted, and we're surrounded by nothing but open air, but even so, I lower my voice. "You say that now, but remember, I'm a Rogue suspect. And even though I passed whatever test the Gages gave me last night, now someone has frozen my medical records and enlisted me in this class. Their only object can be for me to fail and to keep me from reaching my goal."

"And what's that?"

"It's what every Revisionary here wants—a chance to earn a seat in the Dome and work with the Codex itself." I leave off the part about changing the satellite laws and setting Darius free.

Luther grins. "Right. And no one wants a Rogue Revisionary amending the Codex." He laughs at his own joke, but it hits too close to the truth to strike me as funny.

He catches his breath and grins. "Personally, I'd like nothing better than for you to join me as a representative in the Dome. I plan to earn myself the Court Citizen seat slotted for our graduating class. Looks like we both have our work cut out for us."

"But what do I do?"

He grows serious. "You prove you're made of tougher stuff. You prove you're innocent."

The hard bench bites into my thigh, reminding me of the twin holsters under my skirt, and a new thought grips me. *What if I'm not innocent?*

Chapter 8

Tuesday, 9.8.2149
Crystal

The room glows as the earliest traces of daylight filter through cracks in the blinds. This is my first uninterrupted rest in two days—no train ride, no freezing on a rock-climbing wall, no lie serum being stabbed into my arm.

I lie still and enjoy it.

And then the alarm goes off. Lydia presses snooze.

There's no use postponing the inevitable. I trudge to the bathroom to splash my face awake, change, and brush my teeth, feeling human for the first time since I arrived at the Crystal Globe.

The green marker on my arm reminds me I'm still not my own. I hope Coach will remove it on Wednesday but fear it will only be replaced at a later date.

Lydia is still in bed.

"Are you going to breakfast?" I adjust my comforter.

She rolls over to look at me. "Are you?" Her face betrays a

sleepless night.

"Yes, I'm starved. I'll wait for you if you want to join." I turn to unplug my fully-charged tablet and hear Lydia's blanket fall to the floor behind me. She dashes to the bathroom and disappears.

Maybe she wants to talk.

Ten minutes later, she's ready to leave. "Let's take the elevator," Lydia says as we walk down the hallway.

I pause at the entrance to the stairwell. "The what?"

"You know, the closet-sized container that conveys us from floor to floor at the touch of a button." She waits in front of a bronze double-door. "It's electric-powered. Pretty cool."

I stare as the double door pops open, and she steps inside. "You coming?"

I vaguely remember entering this container with Gath and Petra yesterday. The memory makes me hesitate.

"Make up your mind." She places her hand in front of the door to keep it from closing on me. The ride makes my stomach feel strange, but we reach the bottom lounge in one piece.

I readjust my messenger bag as we pass through the courtyard. "How was your first day of class?" I ask.

"It was okay."

"Just okay?"

Lydia sighs. "It was information overload, and I couldn't focus in class." She pauses to look sideways at me. "Yours?"

"Everything was fine, until someone froze access to my medical records and enrolled me in a phys-ed class."

Her jaw drops. "That's awful!"

"You're telling me. I haven't run in ten years, and Coach told me I had to complete a 5K by the end of the day or be punished with correctives."

"There must be some mistake."

"Yeah, I was in the wrong place at the wrong time."

"It's because you got stuck on that wall. You jumped to the top of their watch list. I guess this Rogue threat must be real, because these people are paranoid."

"And we still don't even know what a Rogue is." We reach the dining hall, and I glance at Lydia. "Are you sure you want to hang around me? I don't want to get you into trouble."

She smirks. "Of course. This way, I can keep tabs on your nefarious plot to destroy Crystal."

I snort. "Oh, right. I forgot you're my assigned shadow."

"Yep. I take my job very seriously."

"Now I'm worried."

Lydia raises her eyebrows in a mock serious expression. "You should be. I plan to tell them all about your uneventful eight hours of beauty sleep last night and how you were so enthusiastic to start a new day of classes that you dragged me to breakfast with you."

I squint my eyes and grin. "You wanted to come."

She pauses to tie her sandy brown hair back in a ponytail. "They don't have to know that."

The breakfast food tastes bland, but I feel better. Maybe I've lived most of my life without friends, but having one makes the world a brighter place.

My first morning class goes well, and I'm optimistic that not even Simulation can faze my determination to make today a good day.

That is, until I meet Professor Mortimer who looks as though he's scheduled for the next appointment at the morgue.

Long, spindly arms extend from an already angular body. He combs over what's left of his fine gray hair, and peers at our small class through thick, wire spectacles.

"Boo." Someone blows into my ear.

I jump in my chair and jerk right to see Felix claim the desk next to me.

I frown. "Hello to you too."

"Is this the haunted tour?" he grins and nods toward Professor Mortimer whose back is turned.

Be civil.

"He does look rather awful," I remark. "I hope he's well."

"Oh, he's fine. No doubt he revives himself each night with the blood of a beautiful blonde candidate."

Professor Mortimer begins class and saves me from further harassment. "For those of you who are new to Crystal, our Simulator technology will be like nothing you have ever experienced.

"Technology aside, the concepts here are your real challenge," Mortimer continues. "Here, the playing field is even. How well you know our Codex and how to apply its principles will be your key to scoring high marks, your key to survival."

He pauses to sip a green liquid from a glass tumbler as I shiver at his meaning. He clears his throat. "I am not concerned with survival as a physical reality. Death friends us all."

Felix winks at me and whispers. "Haunted tour."

I shake my head and try to follow the professor's meaning. "Survival is a societal value. I want you to stop thinking of yourselves as individuals. It is an evolutionary flaw of the young. Instead, learn to see yourself as a fiber within a greater social organism. You Revisionary candidates must be loyal to our Codex and embrace your encoding training, or I will personally cut you out like a cancer."

He blinks at us through his spectacles. "Any questions?"

No one moves.

"Good," he says. "We have much to look forward to together. Through Simulator encounters, we will engage with failed codices of the past, learn from their mistakes, and apply our Codex to solve societal problems. We will start together this week. I will then assign group Simulations and eventually individual ones. By next semester, you will be initiating your own Simulations to test and defend your Revisionary thesis.

"Simulation accounts for 60% of your overall grade average. Although I won't dismiss your other classes as unimportant, without 100% from this class, you will never achieve a Doctor Revisionary seat." He flashes a rare smile. "And I'm sure that among this class, many of you are striving for that prize."

I see a hole in his logic. "Question." I blurt out the word before I can stop myself.

All eyes fix on me.

"Yes, candidate?" The professor eyes me with all the warmth of a cadaver.

"We're all fibers in a social organism," I restate his words, "and yet we're pulling separately—as individuals—to attain the highest achievement. Would you—help me understand—how these two components are not in conflict with each other?"

I hold my breath, hoping my innocent tone hides my skepticism.

Mortimer stares hard at me. "What is your name, candidate?"

"Abernathy, sir."

"Candidate Abernathy, would you please come here." It is not a question but a demand.

I slowly rise from my seat, aware that Felix is watching me

closely. I approach the professor and wait, standing poised.

"Hold out your hand, Candidate Abernathy."

I watch uneasily as he picks up a cane. I immediately pull back when he attempts to lash it.

"Do not retract your hand, Candidate Abernathy."

I flush but do not extend my hand again.

His facial muscles twitch. "You hesitate."

I meet his stare. "With all due respect, I do not want a broken hand, sir."

"I am simply trying to answer your question."

My heart is racing. To defy him is to fail the class. I take a deep breath, extend my hand, and brace myself.

The rest of the class gasps for me as the cane cracks against my hand.

Mortimer grabs it and holds it up for the class to see the red mark. He smells like moth balls.

"This is the answer," he says in a voice as thin as ice. "The candidate may strive for what appears to be an individual prize, but to win the prize, she must sacrifice herself. A Doctor Revisionary is a dead individual, but the life blood of the Codex." He turns to stare me in the face. "She will blink at nothing that is asked of her, no matter how contrary it may seem."

He releases my hand, and though I'm trembling, I stare him in the face. "Point made, Professor Mortimer."

I return to my seat, avoiding eye contact with Felix. I keep my wounded hand in my lap, refusing to look at it. I can still move my fingers, so I don't think anything is broken. The pounding of my heart matches the throbbing pain.

Mortimer's cruelty confirms my suspicion. The professors do not want us to learn. They want us to accept without question.

And every fiber of my being rebels. Maybe this is how Darius felt, why he refused to come here, but I can't turn back. I won't turn back.

I focus my attention on my writing hand as the professor resumes his lecture on the immortal merits of our Codex, but my writing is too shaky to read.

"Today, I will introduce you to the Simulator, which for many of you will be a first experience," Mortimer says. "We'll go all the way back to something called the Mayflower Compact. Does anyone know what that is?"

Even if I did know, I wouldn't raise my hand.

He smirks condescendingly at our silence. "Good. This will be your first taste of the civilization we replaced after the Apocalypse."

Mortimer spins to the wall behind him, inserts a small drive into a port, and enters a code. A metallic panel slides down from the ceiling, resembling a man-sized screen, similar to the one on my tablet.

"This is Simulator," he says. "Eventually, you will use your candidate IDs to enter so you can complete group and later individual projects. For now, we will enter as a class."

Mortimer's bony fingers slide nimbly over a screen, entering a series of codes. The classroom lights dim, and the floor illuminates into a translucent blue color, spanning the size of our seating area.

"Let me give you some background on where we're going today." The blue lighting almost makes him look like a skeleton. "A group of non-conformists or rebels from England who called themselves Separatists left their country illegally for a new life in the New World. Their narrow-minded, individualized religious ideals betrayed their country's standards, so their absence was no loss for England.

"When they landed in a place called Cape Cod, Massachusetts, they were miles off course from their planned destination and realized the need for some form of self-government." He pauses for effect. "Amazing, is it not, how even rebels ultimately find the need for some form of order? This attempt at self-organization is what's known as the Mayflower Compact, so-called because of their ship, the *Mayflower*. These Separatists considered this document a social contract for self-order and even claimed loyalty to the king whom they had left, a great hypocrisy if you ask me."

The screen changes color, turning shades of blue that grow more translucent.

"We're going to witness this act on board their ship and then dissect this Compact piece by piece. You see, the purpose of Simulation is to apply our Codex to the failed civilizations of the past. Our Codex offers a powerful contrast to the previous governing failures of the land in which we now live. Through Simulations, you will gain a better understanding of the ASU's aims and vision for a society that upholds the highest standards of civility, equality and fidelity—not individualized rebellion."

The screen is no longer solid, but fluid. The room begins to rock with ocean waves, and I close my eyes to restore a sense of balance. The effect of the Simulator is so life-like that someone behind me retches.

A strong, salty scent and the wail of sea gulls make me forget we're in our classroom.

"One warning before we begin," Mortimer says. "These people may appear to engage you in conversation. Today is observation only. I prefer you not to respond to them, although you can't harm anything by doing so. We're reopening history's pages, not changing it. The only change we hope to accomplish is in ourselves."

The rocking subsides, and I open my eyes. I'm sitting on a narrow, wooden bench in a crowded room. Mortimer disappears into the shadows of the ship, but I sense his eyes on me. My other classmates huddle in the cramped space, which smells of salt and sweat and soiled clothes.

A group of men—I count forty-one in all—hover around a small table, each taking turns signing a document. I can't decide who their leader is, because they all look capable. Their faces, though unsmiling, are not unkind, but honest from hard work. Their shoulders bear an invisible weight of responsibility, but they stand tall—or as straight as possible in the cramped quarters.

The last lays down the quill from signing his name. His eyes hover over the parchment as his voice, a low murmur, restates what he has pledged his life to uphold.

In the name of God, Amen.

We whose names are underwritten, the loyal subjects of our dread sovereign Lord, King James, by the grace of God, of Great Britain, France and Ireland king, defender of the faith, etc., having undertaken, for the glory of God, and advancement of the Christian faith, and honor of our king and country, a voyage to plant the first colony in the Northern parts of Virginia, do by these presents solemnly and mutually in the presence of God, and one of another, covenant and combine ourselves together into a civil body politic, for our better ordering and preservation and furtherance of the ends aforesaid; and by virtue hereof to enact, constitute, and frame such just and equal laws, ordinances, acts, constitutions, and offices, from time to time, as shall be thought most meet and convenient for the general good of the colony, unto which we promise all due submission and obedience.

In witness whereof we have hereunder subscribed our names at Cape-Cod the 11 of November, in the year of the reign of our sovereign lord, King James, of England, France, and Ireland the eighteenth, and of Scotland the fifty-fourth. Anno Domini 1620.[i]

Despite the dank room, the words fan a spark inside me. This kind of daring isn't something I expected to find in a pre-ASU text. What does it mean for my own world?

Lines from our Codex whisper in my mind, yet the words seem empty compared to the ones this man spoke. How can I debunk this document when its words—many of which I do not understand—inspire new courage to live in my heart?

"Lass, what happened to your hand?" The strong, gentle voice startles me. I look up into a weather-worn, kindly face.

"I'm fine." I lower my eyes.

"That's a nasty bruise." His leathery hand reaches to touch my own, but I pull back. I didn't realize Simulation interactions would be this realistic.

"My professor …" I start to say, but the words die in my throat. Mortimer is here somewhere, watching me.

"I'm sure he means only your best." Before I can protest, he's looking at my hand.

"He doesn't want me asking questions," I whisper, "but I have so many." And many now have nothing to do with Mortimer's class.

His brow furrows. "A genuine schoolmaster will not fear

questions, for without questions, how can knowledge be gained?"

The man tears a piece of rough fabric from his sleeve and tries to wrap my hand. But the bandage simply falls to the ground. It's not real. He's not real. Not anymore.

"It's okay," I say hurriedly.

"Well, try not to use it for a few days, and take heart. As you seek to learn, remember that only fools despise wisdom and instruction."[ii]

His words fall like balm on my spirit. "Thank you ... I don't know your name."

"Samuel Fuller," he says. His face grows bleary, and the cramped area turns a foggy green. When next the room focuses, I'm sitting at my desk in the lecture hall.

Gasps and whispering echo off the walls. My fellow candidates are as curious and overwhelmed with the experience as I.

I blink to clear the fog from my mind. What just happened?

Keeping my head down, I glance sideways. Mortimer stands at the front of the lecture hall, eyeing us with half a smile on his face.

"We will follow every Simulation with a Codex criticism review," he begins at last, pacing up and down the aisles. "Today's examination will be oral. In the future, the majority of your reviews will be submitted as reports, which will be graded on the accuracy of your Codex interpretations and applications."

He pauses at the front of class three rows away from me. A male candidate there nervously straightens in his seat.

Mortimer scrutinizes the young man. I want to disappear for the candidate. "Let's start with you."

"Sir?"

"From our Simulation experience, what is one criticism you would bring against the Mayflower Compact?" Mortimer's words sound stilted, as if he's reciting a textbook he wrote.

"I—uh—there was so much to take in," the candidate stammers.

Mortimer taps on the young man's desk. "Look at your tablet, candidate. Today's text will appear there for your reference."

We are all instantly on our tablets, as if doing so will help the young man on the spot.

"I'm waiting." Mortimer stands erect.

"In the name of God, Amen," he mumbles.

"Stop."

"Sir?"

"What is God?" Mortimer asks. "Apply the Codex."

"The Codex does not speak of God," the candidate says.

"Go on."

The young man clears his throat. "It describes and honors the social organism and the unity of thought and purpose we share in the ASU. It affords liberty to those who adopt personal spirituality and practice such things as meditation and mysticism, but with the clear conscience that we ourselves are the highest evolved beings and collectively our final authority. There is no *God*, per se. As a matter of semantics, we ourselves are gods, bound by our pledge to uphold the ideals of equality, civility, and fidelity."

"Bravo." Mortimer mock claps his hands and returns to his podium. "You are right. There is no God. The rebels on The Mayflower held to a naïve notion that there was one true God, the maker of all things. They claimed he had called them to live separate lives to advance their so-called Christian faith—yet maintained that they did so with the utmost respect for their king.

Such a mockery! Citizens are loyal, or they are not. Their history shows us that they rebelled against king and country in a terrible Revolutionary War, won by a stroke of luck, and began a miserable existence here. Hah! Later, they would nearly tear themselves apart in a bloody Civil War."

Mortimer's words unsettle me. From my undergraduate classes, I learned that no country's history, however long or short it may be, can be simply summarized. It is a complex study of factors, of wise and poor decisions, of good and ruthless leaders, of struggle and sacrifice.

I suddenly want to know more about these Separatists and what became of them, what caused this Revolutionary War and the near destruction from within a country they wanted so badly. I also want to know why they would risk everything in the name of a God who doesn't exist.

"These rebels did have a few commendable points in this Compact." Mortimer changes his tone. "Raise your hand when you find them and interpret them with our Codex."

To my right, a confident voice asks permission to speak. It's Felix.

Mortimer recognizes him with a nod, and Felix begins. "In the document, these men talk about covenanting and combining themselves together in a 'civil body politic' in order to better govern themselves. This implies awareness of the need for accountability, something the Codex seeks to provide through its guidance. Our Dome representatives are an excellent example of self-accountability and leadership, submissive to the Friend who upholds the nation's best interests.

"This document also seeks to frame 'just and equal laws,' which are ultimately 'for the general good of the colony' to which these men promise 'all due submission and obedience.' In this respect, it begins to capture the most embryonic forms of our own ideals for equality, civility, and fidelity."

"Well spoken," Mortimer says and lifts his gaze to the rest of the class. "I like to start this class with an evaluation of this document, not because of its historical significance to the previous civilization, but because of its simplicity. In many ways, the Mayflower Compact was an adolescent attempt to provide order. Ironically, that is what makes it such a ripe example for us to criticize and learn from.

"Does anyone else have something to add to Candidate Caesura's comment?"

No one dares add anything to such a well-polished statement. Felix wasted no time positioning himself as the class leader—and ultimately, as the favored candidate for the Dome seat.

Of course, he's had all the prepping in the world.

There's another dramatic pause before Mortimer speaks again. "Your assignment is to examine more documents that I've uploaded to the class portal, which you can find on your tablets. Thursday, I will assign groups of three to review and refute one of those documents. Your group will do a Simulation module on said document and compile a 5,000-word report."

Moaning. I swallow the sound wanting to rise in my own throat to keep any unnecessary attention away from me.

Mortimer smirks. "I advise you to come prepared Thursday with a working knowledge of all documents in your portal. At that time, I will also assign your groups. Any questions?"

Silence.

The fake smile fades from his face.

"One more note," Mortimer says. "If I were not clear, let me make this as simple as possible. You are not equipped to engage with other souls from history. If you speak without first obtaining permission during your next Simulation module, there will be consequences."

I feel my hand and shiver, wishing Fuller's worn cloth could have remained tightly wrapped around it

"Class dismissed."

Chapter 9

Tuesday, 9.8.2149
Crystal

I step outside into the sunlight and feel free—for a moment. My mounting project work will suffocate me if I don't get started soon.

But there's something I want to do first. To avoid talking with any of my classmates, especially Felix, I hurry around the building and take the back route to the library. It stands like a monument at the summit of two dozen marble steps.

The large structure seems ironic in size for a tablet-driven society, but perhaps even Crystal's leaders recognize that history is captured best in the physical documents of time, housed in brick and mortar.

Or not. The elaborate interior is padded with comfortable seating, conference tables, tablet charging stations, and an amusement section which consumes the majority of the main area. A small gallery with portraits of our Friends, present and past, offers an attempt at dignity.

Upstairs are more private study rooms and the reference sections for various degrees—medical, natural sciences, educational psychology, etc. The Revisionary reference section is limited to volumes I practically memorized in my undergraduate classes, and I can't find a trace of a document that speaks to the past civilization, once called the United States of America.

At the end of a long, narrow hallway is another door. Above it, a sign reads, "Basement. Authorized Access Only." Why would the basement access be on the second floor?

To my surprise, the door opens, and I busy myself with the closest book I can find.

A middle-age female emerges. In classic librarian style, she wears black spectacles and pulls her gray-streaked hair back in a bun. "May I help you?"

"Oh, excuse me." I hastily shelve the book. "I'm a Revisionary candidate and am looking for historical books on the past civilization to research a project for my Simulation class. I can't find anything."

"This is the chemistry section." The woman's face holds no humor.

"Of course." I laugh nervously. "I was looking up something for my roommate. Anyway, where would you advise I search?"

She eyes me through narrow spectacles. "What is your ID number?"

"1911."

She turns and enters it in the access panel of the door she just exited. A light flashes red. She shakes her head. "Your professor has not approved your access to the restricted texts section. Until he does, there's nothing I can do to help you."

"Okay, thanks anyway." Flashing a smile, I retreat downstairs, wishing I could find a way to enter the stairway.

Why would texts on the old civilization be kept tightly out of view?

My tablet vibrates with lesson project reminders, and I fumble in my bag to snooze them for now. In doing so, I wince as something rubs roughly against my hand.

My hand. I should wrap it since the bandage Fuller tried to apply didn't stick. Couldn't stick. But its memory is as raw and real as my smarting hand. Professor Mortimer said that in a Simulation, we can't affect history, but somehow, when we intrude into the recesses of time, history has the power to change us.

If only I could harness that power to rewrite the present.

I push through the glass doors back into the light and blink at its brilliance. The light exposes everything for what it is. If history should be feared, I want to know why. If history holds the key to answers my world needs, I want to penetrate the door to its knowledge.

I find Lydia back in our room and tell her about Simulation and the archives as she cleans and wraps my hand. Her face tenses with concern.

"It isn't just you." Lydia puts her gauze spool away. "I think a lot of the candidates are feeling the way we are but are too scared to do or say anything."

I rub my hand which smarts from the antiseptic ointment. "What do you mean?"

"I mean—I'm worried," she says. "Court Scene for me is as scary as Simulation is for you."

"What's Court Scene?"

"It's where we Court Citizen candidates first witness and then participate in live sentencing," Lydia says. "Today, I watched the trial of a candidate who received one too many correctives for not accepting the scientific standing of his department. Portia, he had some excellent points and presented his concerns with respect and intelligence. He's on trial for simply requesting permission to further research his position to see if his hypotheses could hold water."

"What happened?"

"Well, you know how *trial by peers* works." Lydia sighs. "There are only three peers who decide, and two of them are from the candidate's own field of study. The third is the Court Citizen arbitrator. In this case, his two classmates were clearly antagonistic toward him, a bias I thought was to be avoided. The Court Citizen had enough discretion to realize his crime was not worthy of anything more than a type 1 sentence—likely some kind of community service or remediation project—but because the other two condemned him, the candidate is going to a satellite for at least a decade."

"That's awful." I shudder.

"And Portia, it's all because he dared to have a difference of opinion." Lydia shakes her head. "If the Court Citizen hadn't been reasonable, the candidate could have faced death."

I wait for Lydia to work through her thoughts.

"And that's who I'm becoming—the Court Citizen who determines life or death. What if the accused has only committed a marginal offense?" She continues without giving me time to answer. "You know what's even worse? I found out that if a Court Citizen weighs in as the sparing vote on one too many sentences, he is automatically sequestered until a panel reviews his rulings. In other words, I can face prosecution for saving too many people's lives."

"That sounds like incentive to vote guilty regardless if you think the subject is worthy of the sentence."

"How can I live with that kind of burden?" Lydia is near tears. "I can't selfishly condemn a person because I want to save my own skin. I had no idea things worked this way."

"I'm sorry," I say. "I guess we're both in over our heads."

"What's worse is that my first term as Court Citizen arbitrator is scheduled for next Tuesday." She chokes back the rising emotion. "That's the luck of the draw. Only one other classmate goes before I do. Because the number of trials here is unpredictable, the professor starts scheduling us after the first week."

"But you're just beginning your classes here," I protest. "How can you be expected to judge?"

Lydia smiles sadly. "Remember that we've already earned our degrees. Technically, we're both fully approved to administer our professions. We got drafted for special training and service."

I sigh. "I still feel inadequate."

"Tell me about it." She rubs her temples. "At the trials, all our peers will be watching us. Those of us going first are feeling tremendous pressure."

"Pressure to bring down the gavel hard?"

"Exactly." Lydia rises and puts her small first aid kit away, muttering as she does.

"Did you say something?"

She turns back to me. "Luther—he's lucky. His term doesn't come until after our fall break."

"Is there anything I can do to help?"

Her face brightens. "Could you come to the trial? It should be easy to sneak in the back. Knowing you're there would make me feel better."

"I'll come if I can." The promise makes my pulse race. Lydia doesn't know about my childhood dread of the courtroom.

Lydia smiles. "Thanks. How about I make us some tea, and we crank out our homework assignments before dinner?"

"If I can finish one before dinner, I'll be doing well." I laugh and pull out my tablet, which has started vibrating again.

"Well, I don't have a choice," Lydia says. "After dinner, I have to attend a Court Scene module in the library."

"A what?"

"It's an extra-credit seminar or something like that. My professor said there would be a guest lecturer from the Dome."

I'm already so confused between her major and mine that I don't ask any more questions.

The coursework becomes a welcome distraction from our combined fears about Simulation and Court Scene—and the one I will have to face again tomorrow: physical education.

Somehow, the dreading of a thing ensures its prompt arrival.

Wednesday afternoon, I slip into a back seat in gym class and take lengthy notes on Coach Mariner's lecture. At least I won't have any problems with the written portion of this class. I ace the pop quiz he springs on us, and my spirits rise.

But the marker on my arm reminds me that my troubles are far from over.

"Some of you have asked about your arm markers," Mariner says. "The ones you have are semi-permanent and will remain until we switch to the physical section of the course.

"I know that many of you are going to struggle on the anatomical section of this course, so I'm offering extra credit: For every ten miles you spend on the track, you gain half a bonus point on your final grade. I'm capping the limit at 60 miles or three full points.

"Some of you are going to need that extra credit more than others."

I slide lower in my seat. It isn't the subject of human anatomy that has me worried. It's my own anatomy.

"Class dismissed."

Most of the candidates are already dressed in workout clothes and dump their bags at the lockers before running outside. The sun beats down, warming my neck as I trudge toward the stands to watch my classmates run circles around each other.

It's better to let the track thin of candidates before I venture out.

If I walk two miles a day five days a week during the first half of the semester, I can earn those extra points. Maybe with Luther's help, I can pass the physical portion of the class and remain in the running for the Dome seat.

I check the time on my tablet. I have an hour before Luther told me to meet him here for my first track lesson. That's plenty of time to make a good dent in my other coursework.

No sooner have I made myself comfortable on the sun-warmed seat than a runner darts along the edge of the bleachers. I blink in surprise. It's Foxworth. I haven't seen him since the train station.

I pull up my legs to keep from tripping him, and he jerks sideways to miss me. In doing so, something small falls out of his pocket and lands in the dirt.

He doesn't pause to acknowledge me but continues on toward the track.

I lean down, pinch the object, and wipe the dirt off with my thumb. It's a small, silver-colored coin with a man's face on the front. Along the front edge are the words *In God We Trust* and the date, 2007.

I flip it over. The back is so faded and scratched that I can only make out a few words on the edge which read, "E Pluribus Unum" and "Five Cents."

This must be a coin from the past civilization. We don't use coins anymore. But how did Foxworth get it?

I slip my tablet into my messenger bag and stand, scanning the track. Although other runners are chasing laps, Foxworth makes a straight line across the field toward the woods beyond. A second more, and his lean, taut form disappears out of sight.

Clutching the coin in my fist, I run toward the woods and plunge in after him. Although I'm not fast, I'm at home in the woods, and my feet find a deer's trail.

In no time, I'm panting hard and slow to a walking speed. There's no sign of Foxworth, and the deepening woods grow darker.

I am just about to turn back when the woods open into an overgrown clearing. Jagged rocks poke out of thistle patches and undergrowth.

But no, they are not rocks. They are eroded headstones.

This is a graveyard.

In the center is a weatherworn statue shaped like a cross. I stop and stare. Why would a barbaric method of execution be the centerpiece for the dead? I had learned about types of executions in one of my civics classes. We are much more civil today—or at least I think we are. My teacher said executions are rare but instant and painless: one shot to the head. Most criminals go to satellite camps, though. For Darius' sake, I hope they aren't terrible places.

The overhead sky warns me that daylight is fading fast, but there's movement on the far end of the graveyard. I crouch low and strain my eyes.

At the base of a headstone shaped like a winged woman, Foxworth digs with a shovel. The metal hits stone, and the sound echoes like a moan across the open space.

A gravedigger? I cringe as the shovel scrapes the buried casket again. Whatever work Foxworth finds here is better left undiscovered.

I slip the coin into my bag, retrace my steps through the woods, and don't breathe easy again until I've cleared the track without anyone noticing me.

Luther waits for me at the bench. "Where have you been? I was starting to wonder if you changed your mind."

"Sorry, I was taking a walk to—to clear my head. It's been a long day."

His eyes glance at my bandaged wrist. "What's wrong with your hand?"

"That's a gift from my Simulation professor."

He grimaces as I recount the story. "You really do have a problem making friends."

"It's not too late to back out."

Luther cocks his head. "You just want to get out of track training."

I draw in the sand with my shoe. "Guilty."

"Portia, nothing worth having is easy. You need to train if for no other reason than to prove to yourself that you can. You said you want that Dome seat. Prove you're made of the stuff it takes to win even when the odds are against you. If you can't make friends, at least win respect."

His words ring true. I push Foxworth and his secrets from my mind. There are more pressing problems for me to work through right now.

"Yes, I want to run. I want to win."

He grins. "Then let's get started."

The next morning, my alarm buzzes, and I groan.

Everything hurts. Calves. Thighs. Abdomen. Back. Especially back. I waddle like a penguin to the bathroom, and Lydia watches me with a curious face.

"Is that some new dance move?"

I grunt. "Luther is convinced I can pass physical education on my own two feet. I agreed to let him train me, but I haven't run in years. I think I'm going to die."

"Give it a few weeks," she says. "It will get easier."

"Easy for you to say." I start a pot of coffee. At least the aroma makes life smell better. "If my muscles don't stop their spasms, I won't even be able to walk around the track tomorrow."

"Let tomorrow worry about itself," Lydia chuckles. "Focus on surviving today."

I stretch for nearly an hour to get back a limited range of motion, sneak into breakfast at the last possible second, and try to relax during my morning classes. I'm used to mental rigor and breeze through a written exam while the candidate next to me sweats profusely.

My turn will come later. Today's Simulation already has me on edge.

Warily, I slide into my seat in the auditorium, watching Professor Mortimer while pretending to review notes. He doesn't seem to notice any of us as we enter the class.

Felix takes his seat beside me. "Hey, Frosty, how's the hand?"

"Fine." Everything else was so sore this morning that I didn't even pay attention to my hand. I look down at it and see a colorful black and blue peek out from under a clean bandage Lydia applied last night.

"Just some friendly advice—I wouldn't push your luck with Mortimer. Not that I'm worried either way. I can more than handle the competition." He gives me a patronizing smile.

The brat.

I look back at my tablet and bring up my preliminary notes on the eight documents Mortimer added to our class portal.

1. Declaration of Independence (1776)
2. Articles of Confederation (1777)
3. Constitution of the United States (ratified 1788)
4. Federalist Paper No. 1 (1787)
5. Bill of Rights (1791)
6. Monroe Doctrine (1823)
7. Gettysburg Address (1863)
8. Emancipation Proclamation (1863)

I reviewed them for three hours late last night to get a basic idea of each one. Since no external criticisms were available to us, I interpreted them as best as I could on my own, all the while wondering if that library access door could open up answers.

What little I had read of these documents made me hungry for more.

Mortimer begins class with a threat. "I hope you all did your homework. By the end of the period, you will submit a preliminary criticism of the document assigned to your group for a grade."

If a pin drops, it will sound like a gong.

"Without any more delay, here are your group assignments," he continues. "Order and logic are two important tenants of this class, so your group assignments are alphabetical."

I glance nervously at Felix. He presses his lips together and gives me a mock kiss. *You and me*, he mouths and laughs at his joke. All I can do is hope there are enough students with last names starting with A and B to keep us from becoming a team.

"Group one—The Declaration of Independence—will include Abernathy, Bennett, and Caesura," he announces, and I hear no more. How can anyone be as unlucky as I am?

Mortimer concludes the group assignments and shares a summary of them on his screen.

"I'm going to call the first name in each group, and as I do, please stand so your group members can find you," Mortimer says. "Then, all members of a group should move to a respective row, starting on my left.

"Group one—Declaration of Independence—Abernathy."

I stand, but my feet feel as heavy as cinder blocks.

The candidates seated in row one collect their things and step aside for us to fill the row. Felix claims the front seat, and I retreat to the third. A short, thickly built girl with opaque glasses greets me with a timid smile.

"I'm Jael Bennett." She drops her bag next to the second chair.

She reminds me of a mouse. Her round eyes blink uncertainly behind her thick glasses, and she slouches to avoid attention.

"I'm Portia." I smile, less at her and more at the fact that she's unknowingly accepted the position of buffer between Felix and me.

"I'm Felix." He stretches out his hand with an amused smile on his face. *If he picks on Jael, I'll pummel him.* I like her already.

"I work hard and will pull my share, but I don't like people to notice me," she says. "You were so brave yesterday. I would have died."

"Foolish is more like it," Felix says, "but who doesn't love a good fool?"

I clear my throat. "We don't have a lot of time, so let's get started by sharing our preliminary findings on the Declaration. Let's take ten minutes to review our individual documents, noting agreements and points of difference, then twenty minutes to discuss, and a half hour to compile."

"I'm good at compiling," Jael says.

"Perfect. Once we have a consensus, we'll break the writing up into three parts, and Jael will combine and submit."

"Agreed," Felix says. It's the first practical word he's spoken since we met, but then, this group project counts toward both our career grades. We have no choice but to work together.

I wonder how long the ceasefire will last.

Chapter 10

Thursday, 9.10.2149
Crystal

I exhale as Jael presses submit two minutes before the end of class. Other groups scramble to finish as we turn our attention to the new assignment Mortimer downloaded in our class portal.

Jael groans. "One hundred pages of reading."

"Plus, our group outline and thesis by Friday," I remind her.

"Our thesis is easy," Felix says. "The Declaration of Independence rationalizes treason and encourages contempt for established government and order."

I frown. "I don't think it's that simple. The writers' arguments seem worth considering. These were well-educated men who carefully weighed their options. Don't forget they tried to negotiate with England ..."

"Are you sympathizing with the rebel patriots?" Felix mocks, rising to his feet. "I'd be careful if I were you. Don't forget that the only reason we're studying pre-ASU texts is to criticize them in terms of our Codex. Apply the Codex, Portia, and the thesis is simple."

"I'm not saying the colonial patriots were right." I fight to keep the edge out of my voice. "I'm only saying that their document is worthy of *objective* criticism. We can learn from it instead of dismissing it entirely."

"The value placed on equality is something our Codex approves," Jael adds.

"Then what would you suggest?" Felix paces the floor between Jael's and my desks.

"I don't know." I sigh. "I think there's a downstairs research department to the library, but you need special authorization."

Felix pauses in front of me and smirks. "You mean the historical archives? It's not a fun place."

I jolt upright. "You've been there?"

He laughs. "Of course. You forget I did my undergrad work here. You need tenure to access places like the archives."

I stare at him. Maybe Felix won't be worthless after all. "Could you get us inside?"

"What, you want to spend hours breathing musty air and combing through cobwebs?" His eyes grow serious and lock onto mine. "It can be arranged—on the condition you follow my lead and agree to certain conditions."

The idea of Felix setting conditions cools my excitement.

"I don't like spiders, but I'd be willing to brave the cobwebs," Jael says. "I'm free this evening after dinner."

"Then I guess I'm outvoted." Felix's eyes flash with his customary grin. "I'll meet you downstairs in the library's entertainment section at 1900 hours."

Jael swings her backpack over her shoulder. "See you then."

"See you," I say, hoping to cue my own retreat. But my messenger bag is caught on my desk where Felix is now leaning.

And he isn't going anywhere in a hurry. "Have you ever heard the saying *two's company, but three's a crowd*? Jael is definitely crowd material, but you, on the other hand ..."

"Yes, I believe you called me your *competition* at the beginning of class."

"You don't have to be defensive. We're a team now, you know."

"It's one group project."

"Yes, and it counts for a good chunk of our grade for the first two quarters."

I pull harder on my messenger bag. "Okay, so we work together but only until our project ends."

Felix laughs. "Oh, Frosty, I think this is just the beginning of a budding alliance. Something tells me you're going to be useful."

I yank my strap loose. "See you tonight." I hurry away before he can keep me any longer.

I leave the lecture hall and find the courtyard buzzing with activity and noise.

As I hurry closer, I nearly collide with a candidate who's standing motionless and staring blankly at the scene. He's the same young man who sat beside me during orientation. I haven't seen him since the Gage escorted him away.

His face is withdrawn and ashy gray. His faded eyes hold no spark or indication that he remembers me.

"What's going on?" I ask as a group of Gages surround the clock tower.

His voice is a mechanical monotone. "A candidate has been caught tampering with the grid. They cornered the offender. He's hiding in the top of the tower. He can't stay there for long. He will be served justice."

His words are an omen. They no sooner leave his mouth than a dark figure breaks through the glass face of the clock. And there is nowhere to go but down.

I cup my hand to my mouth to stifle the scream rising in my throat as the candidate plummets to certain death. The young man beside me shows no emotional response and disappears into the crowd.

Horror rivets me in place. The twisted body lies motionless, quickly cordoned off by Gages.

One turns and glances my direction.

Gage Eliab scowls at me before assessing the broken body before him. I retreat through the waves of onlookers, wishing I could forget what I saw.

Life, Liberty, and the pursuit of Happiness. This phrase from the Declaration rings in my memory. It paints a stark contrast to the brutal hopelessness of a suicide jumper.

What was that candidate's crime? But it doesn't matter. If he had a chance at the rights esteemed by the Declaration writers, he would not have jumped.

I quicken my step and hope the archives will hold answers.

I arrive at the library before my classmates and dawdle near a bulletin board of announcements. While waiting for Jael and Felix, I scan the flyers and advertisements.

There's a list of elective modules for different fields of study, but Revisionary isn't listed. Beneath the list, though, is a flyer with red lettering that draws my eye. The headline reads, *Explore Cube 1776.*

"Looks like Jael forgot our rendezvous."

I turn to find Felix standing behind me. "I'm sure she'll be here any minute."

She had better be. Two's company. Three is a chaperone.

Just then, Jael appears through the front door, her face beaded with sweat. A knit red scarf hangs lopsided down her sleeve. She sees us and rushes over. "Sorry I'm late!"

Felix arches his brow. "We were about to leave without you."

I hurry to Jael's side and gently rearrange her scarf. "But of course, we waited."

"Thanks," she pants. "I'm excited to explore with you."

"Don't get too excited," Felix says. "You may regret coming once you see the tomb of ancient texts. It's hardly a romantic walk in the park."

But Felix can't dampen Jael's interest. "Right, it's like an archeological expedition."

He rolls his eyes and starts for the stairs. Again, I wonder why the entrance to a below ground archive begins on the second floor.

Felix punches a four-digit code which opens the door and reveals a narrow staircase. At the base of the dimly-lit stairwell, a closed door hides to our right while the expanse of the archives opens before us.

"Where does this door lead?" I ask.

"Not sure," Felix says, quickly. Too quickly.

The stairs end, and we're standing on the far end of a long, narrow room, lined with floor-to-ceiling shelves. Glowing eerily from the ceilings are old can lights, some burned out and some barely doing their job.

The smell is oppressively damp, and I wonder how pre-ASU texts have survived this long in such conditions.

"It's like entering Pharaoh's tomb," Jael whispers.

Felix snorts. "Do you even know who Pharaoh was?"

Jael stiffens. "Yes, he—or I should say, it—was a title given to the rulers of a country once called Egypt. The Egyptians were famous for their architecture, including tombs called pyramids."

Felix pretends to clap. "Bravo. You've clearly done some research—outside the parameters of your regular Revisionary training. I hope it was done under permission and not from misuse of the resources at your disposal."

Before Jael can reply, I step between the two of them. "Where would you recommend we look for pre-ASU texts on the Declaration?"

"Your guess is as good as mine," Felix says. "I think there's a semblance of organization based on continent and time period, but hardly anyone comes down here."

We split up, each taking a row at a time.

Jael's voice punctuates our progress. "What's Germany?" Next, "Does anyone know what *Mein Kampf* means?"

"Just look for anything that says America or The United States," Felix growls. He rounds the corner and shakes his head. "That girl is so distracted."

"I can see why," I say. "What is all this?"

He shrugs. "World history way before our time."

"You mean before the Apocalypse, back when the USA was a technologically advanced nation?"

"Sure, I guess. Probably even hundreds of years farther back than that. Who cares?"

"I'm starting to," I say. "Why aren't we taught all of this?

There's so much we could learn."

He gives me an impatient look. "It's archaic. Why study something that doesn't even affect you?"

"But can't we learn from it?" I turn the corner on a new row. My eyes grow watery as they try to take in the hundreds of faded titles all at once.

I pull a book called *Innovate like Edison* off a shelf and blow dust off the cover. I haven't read half way through page one when Felix snatches it away.

"Focus," he hisses.

"Sorry," I mutter. "I was just curious if I were in the right section. Was Edison an American?"

"Yes, but what does it matter?"

I bite my tongue. *It matters a great deal that privileged people like Felix know more than the rest of us.*

"Anyway, that means we're close." Felix walks away to scan another shelf.

A thick volume at eye level grabs my attention. Printed in large font are the words: *Viktor Rosh.*

"Look at this!" I exclaim.

"Did you find something about the Declaration?" Felix asks.

"No, but it's about someone called Rosh," I say. "Isn't that the name of the league that crippled the USA technologically with some electro-magnetic warfare?"

Felix exhales. "Something like that."

I search his face. He knows more than he's telling me. "Why did the Rosh League do such a thing? What had the USA done to them?"

"How should I know?" He reaches to take away this book as well, but I don't let go.

"I want to know. It has to be important."

He tugs at the book again. "If we needed to know about it, we would."

I hold on tighter. "But why should someone have to decide for us what we do and don't need to know?"

The warning in his eye makes me release my grasp. Disappointed, I watch him place the book on a higher shelf, out of my reach.

"Listen, these archives are off limits to most candidates for a reason." Felix dusts off his hands. "You must receive authorization—it's called a special permit—to study this stuff. If you're going to waste time, we're leaving. I could get in trouble if you or Jael starts spouting off about things you saw here."

"But what's dangerous about these books?"

Felix huffs. "It's about knowing your place. What good will filling one's head with Egypt or Edison or even Viktor Rosh do a medical doctor or a Gage or any of our professions? If people needed to know, they would. Our early leaders had our best interests in mind when they relegated this stuff to the basement, so to speak. They didn't want us getting distracted by what doesn't matter. Saving a human race and survival were on their minds. Thanks to them, our civilization is now thriving—and maybe by not exposing ourselves to what doesn't concern us, we'll escape the fate of these nations and peoples, who are now nothing but mere mentions in decaying books."

His answer sounds nice enough to my ears, but something doesn't make sense.

Before I can stop myself, the question rolls off my lips, "How will we know if we're making their same mistakes if we don't study them?"

Once again, he answers my question with a question. "Do you want to go back, or do you want to look for America?"

"No, let's look for America," I say and turn back to another row of bookcases. I can't waste this chance to learn more about the Declaration.

"Here it is!" I wipe my fingers across a dusty shelf. My eyes scan titles ranging from *The Pilgrim Fathers*, *The Bible*, *Abraham Lincoln*, *The Civil War*, and *Common Sense*. Within me is a burning desire to read them all. I begin to realize this is about more than a good grade on a project. This is about knowledge. This is about answers.

"Here's an American history textbook." Felix hands it to me. I've never seen a history textbook this thick before.

I open to the first few pages. Solemn portraits of men dressed in flouncy outfits make me smile, yet there's a seriousness to their expression that grounds me.

"What's an Indian?" I squint at a photo captioned *Squanto*.

"They were here before the English arrived."

How does he know?

"Flip to the Declaration," he mutters.

"I'm getting there." I wish he wouldn't rush me.

Felix thumbs ahead through pages and pictures. "Ah, here it is." He offers the book back. A picture at the top of the page draws me in. It's of three men gathered around a small round table. Discarded drafts are strewn across the floor. One man with spectacles reviews what looks to be a final draft, while the two others look on. One holds something like a scroll and quill in his hand, indicating authorship. The photo is captioned "Writing the Declaration of Independence, 1776" by Jean Leon Gerome Ferris.

I scan farther down to learn who these three were: Thomas

Jefferson, John Adams, and Benjamin Franklin.

These are men I would like to have known. Surely, they could have taught me something.

"Listen to this." I skim the textbook summary. "When signing the Declaration of Independence, the fifty-six men realized they were guilty of high treason to England and risked their lives, families, and fortunes. Some lost sons in the Revolutionary War. Others had their houses burned or looted. Others lost their estates and faced financial ruin. Some were forced to flee their homes and faced arrest and imprisonment by the British. None of these men could have foreseen the ultimate success of this document—if anything, they saw only the personal dangers involved; yet they hazarded everything they held dear for the cause of a free country."

I look up to see Felix's reaction, but his face remains impassive.

He yawns and gives me a patient smile. "So, they were a bunch of brave rebels who put everything they had on the line."

I feel the need to defend these men. "I think that's rather daring of them."

"Sounds foolhardy to me."

I ignore him and flip to the next page. There, the text of the Declaration unfolds. The words come to life as I whisper them aloud.

When in the Course of human events it becomes necessary for one people to dissolve the political bands which have connected them with another and to assume among the powers of the earth, the separate and equal station to which the Laws of Nature and of Nature's God entitle them, a decent respect to the opinions of mankind requires that they should declare the causes which impel them to the separation ...

I pause and breathlessly turn to Felix. "Could I possibly take this book with me to study?"

He laughs. "I'm starting to think I mistook you for being smarter than you are. Come on, you know the rules about ancient texts. They're contraband. Do you know what would happen if someone discovered this in your room? First, you'd get charged with trespassing and stealing from the archives. Then, I'd get in trouble for giving you access under my permit. We'd both be in for some serious correctives that even I couldn't prevent."

"But why is it such a crime?"

He frowns at me. "Why do you keep asking that? I already told you. Don't forget why we're here. You wanted access for our research project."

He closes the book in my hands. "And now it's your turn to do me a favor."

I grip the cover. "What do you mean?"

"I want access for some research of my own."

"Oh?" I tremble at his closeness and wish Jael would appear.

"You see, the Dome seat is a stepping stone for me. The Friend's term expires next year when the Dome will choose her successor. Just because I'm Juliana's son doesn't guarantee that I'll replace her. I need the CGA to back me."

"CGA?"

"Crystal Gage Administration." He smiles at my confusion. "To earn their loyalty, I need to give them something they want. This week, I discovered a pain point that might be what I need to secure the approval of their Commanding Gage."

"What's that?"

"I need to find the Rogue insider."

Rogue. The word makes my skin crawl. Does Felix know I'm

considered suspect myself?

I try to relax my shoulders. "What's a Rogue?"

"They're troublemakers." Felix mutters and glances away. "You saw their work first hand with that outage on Greek night. Our Gages run a tight ship, monitoring everyone who comes in and everyone who goes out. My sources say there were no security breaches that night, meaning only one thing: someone from the inside sabotaged the electrical grid."

I swallow. "What does any of that have to do with me?"

He picks a stray book off the shelf and blows dust off the cover. "I've done my homework, Frosty. You're the only other Revisionary whose scores rival my own, and I need an ally, not a competitor. Besides, you might stand to gain from this arrangement—in more ways than one."

"What arrangement?"

"You're going to help me find the last insider."

I stall for time to understand his meaning. "The last insider? Do you mean there were several?"

"There were—until today. An anonymous tip led Gages to search a candidate's apartment and found evidence to link one of its occupants to Sunday night's outage. When they confronted him, he fled, and the chase resulted in his death. His roommate proved tightlipped during questioning and is scheduled for trial later this week. He may or may not reveal the third insider."

"How do you know there's a third?"

"Gages hacked the candidate's password: it was *3Musketeers*. If the roommate turns out to be guilty, that means there's one left to find."

"What makes you think I can find him?"

"Because the Commanding Gage thinks he's a new draftee

and from Chrysoprase, no less." Felix pauses for effect. "How convenient that you're from 'Prase? There were only four draftees from that square, including you. A clever girl like yourself can figure out which one demands scrutiny."

I narrow my eyes. "You're asking me to accuse and incriminate a fellow classmate? Why would I agree to that?"

He swaggers closer until his breath warms my face. "There are rumors about you, Portia Abernathy. Rumors say you have bad blood in your family, and maybe you do. What better way to clear your name than to help me find the real source of the problem?"

Felix reaches for my hand. "Besides, if you work with me now, once I'm elected, you can bet your pretty face I'll get you that Dome seat you want."

I flinch as his other hand brushes against my cheek. He laughs. "You might even warm up to me in the process."

A Doctor Revisionary—It's the position I need to revise the satellite laws. But will I be able to change the way things are or simply become a pawn of the system?

He tightens his grip on my hand, and I wince. The bruise from Mortimer's cane still stings. "Do we have an agreement?"

My hand throbs. "I can't make any promises."

"I think you can."

"I'll see what I can do." I yank free, turn, and run.

Two aisle's down, Jael is excavating a massive text on Egypt. "Come on, we're leaving."

She looks up. "Already? Did you guys even find America? Sorry, I got distracted … But hey, are you okay? Your face is all red."

I nod quickly and turn. "Our time's up. We need to go."

Without further explanation, I start for the stairwell, satisfied to hear the Egyptian book thud onto the shelf and Jael's shuffling feet.

I stop abruptly at the base of the stairs. The door. It moved—closed back into place. The access panel beside it flashes green. Someone just passed this way.

Yet Felix is still somewhere in the archives.

I hurry past it and up the stairs to the second level exit with Jael panting not far behind me. The archives hold more demons than answers.

Chapter 11

Thursday, 9.10.2149
Crystal

"I was beginning to think you weren't coming." Luther slowly stands from the metal bleacher. The last colors of the evening sky fade to a dull gray, replaced by the bright spotlights located around the track.

"I'm sorry I'm late again." I drop my bag and start to stretch.

Luther studies me. "Your face is flushed. Where have you been?"

I don't want to tell him about Felix, but I don't want to lie either. "The library archives."

"The what?"

"It's a restricted basement in the library. One of my classmates has access, and I convinced him to take our Simulation group to research our project on the Declaration of Independence."

His eyes widen in surprise. "You're researching the Declaration? You're allowed to do that?"

"It's part of our training. We're supposed to apply our Codex to debunk pre-ASU texts." I hesitate.

"But?"

"But, I'm beginning to wonder …" I don't finish my sentence. Saying it aloud could be considered treason. Thinking it gives me goose bumps.

"You're beginning to wonder if there's some merit to these texts," Luther whispers.

I bite my lip. I won't deny it, but I can't say it. Even though Luther has risked his life for me, his face is a mirror of his brother. Jotham didn't think twice about turning on Darius when he confessed his heart to him. Doing so helped secure him a seat in the Dome.

"What did you find in the archives?"

"Lots of books and no answers."

"Then what upset you?"

I can't tell Luther about Felix. After all, he's now one of Felix's three suspects. "It's nothing. Let's get started."

After another series of painful stretches, we begin our first lap around the track.

Luther jogs next to me. "We're going to run for five minutes, then walk for five minutes."

He continues, "We're starting off slowly, but eventually, we'll build up to longer intervals."

By the end of five minutes, my lungs feel like they're drowning.

"Walk." Luther presses his stopwatch.

I pant for breath and try to walk off the cramp in my side. In no time, we're running again.

We pass the one-mile marker, and I keep going. Luther stays

by my side, breathing effortlessly while I sound like a dying mongrel.

"Walk," he says again. "That was good. You got past the mile. Are you up for two or three tonight?"

"One at a time," I gasp.

"Let's just finish two."

Two down, we head back toward the bleachers to do another series of stretches. Luther hands me his canteen, and I choke down the water.

"The first few weeks are the hardest," he encourages me.

"Great." I sputter.

"This will get easier."

"Easy for you to say." I already feel my back tightening and hope Lydia will give me a massage tonight.

"Look on the bright side." He opens his gym bag to pull out a towel. "At least you've cleared your lungs from all that dusty library air."

It's hard working out with an optimist.

"That reminds me," he continues. "Did you sign up for our Greek's first outing?"

I stare blankly at him. "I didn't even know we had an outing planned."

"We're hopping trains around Crystal and possibly into Lapis this weekend," he says. "We leave after classes let out tomorrow."

"How did you hear about this?"

"Silly, the flyers are all over campus." Luther reaches into his bag and hands me a crumpled flyer. It's the same one I saw at the library earlier this evening.

"What is there to explore in Cube 1776?"

He grins. "There's supposed to be ruins of an ancient library in Crystal. Your archive adventure today made me think of you. Do you want to come?"

I try not to sound as curious as I feel. "What's involved?"

"Well, you have to submit your application by tonight," he says. "There's no cost, but be prepared to couch surf and at least bring a backpack with food and a coat. Another Greek member said the cafeteria will give you some limited food stuffs if you say they're for the trip."

"Are you going?"

"You bet. I never got to explore anything back in 'Prase. I can live out of my backpack for a few days."

I finish off the water. "Thanks for telling me. I'll stop by Arthur's room for an application."

Luther slings his bag over his shoulder but waits for me to grab mine. "Do you want me to go with you? Arthur can be a little too friendly sometimes, especially when he's not sober."

"I'll be fine. Thanks for the work out—I think." I turn to leave, but he follows me.

We walk in silence until we reach my dorm's lobby.

"Remember to drink lots of water tonight. It'll help your muscles recover and prevent lactic acid from building up."

"Whatever you say, coach."

He looks at me seriously. "Are you sure you don't want me to go with you to Arthur's room? Everyone's been a little off since Sunday."

The tragic scene from the courtyard flashes in my memory. Arthur is the least of my worries.

"I'll be fine," I say. "Keep your fingers crossed there's room for one more on the trip."

He turns to leave. "I hope I don't regret inviting you."

I pause. "Why do you say that? You don't think I'm tough enough?"

"No, you're tough. You're just not fast—yet." He clears his throat. "Goodnight, Cotton."

Arthur's room isn't hard to find. The smell in his hallway traces back to his door.

A roommate with dark rings under his eyes answers. "Can I help you?"

I smile, but not too much. "Yes, I want to pick up an application for the Kappan trip this weekend?"

He disappears and returns with a paper. "Slide it under the door sometime tonight." Behind him, Arthur's red hair gives away that he's passed out on the couch.

I force another smile, "Thanks," and hurry toward the elevator.

The form is simple enough. I fill it out and slip it under the door twenty minutes later before I change my mind or Lydia talks me out of it.

I don't tell her until I'm face down on the couch and she's rubbing knots out of my back. "That sounds crazy! There's no way I'm going. Who knows where you'll sleep or what people you're going to meet. Is train hopping even safe?"

"The form said two staff chaperones, who are Kappan alumni, will be coming with us." I wince as her fingers dig deep into my protesting muscles. "We'll be roughing it for two days, but that's nothing new. It's not like I lived a spoiled life in 'Prase."

"You'd better hope you don't get slammed with homework tomorrow." She attacks a knot in my back. "I wouldn't risk getting behind for some crazy trip if I were you."

"I'm working ahead tonight." I dread the long night of project work, but the lure of an ancient library is too much to resist.

I treat myself to coffee the next morning and pain killers during breakfast. Luther is either a genius coach or trying to kill me. I haven't decided which.

He walks over to greet me after gym class and picks up my workout bag before I can stop him. Less than a week ago, I had resolved to keep him at arm's length. Now, a day doesn't pass without him finding new ways to break down my barriers.

I retie my hair to give my nervous energy something to do. "Arthur approved my application."

"That's great." He balances both our bags on his shoulder. "Are you worried at all?"

"What's there to be worried about?"

"Train hopping? Couch surfing? Do you even know what those are?" he laughs.

I give him a hard look. "This was your idea. Besides, you said there are two chaperones."

When we meet up with the tripping group two hours later, I realize the chaperones may be the worst of my problems.

"Please sign in, and Gage Gath will check your backpacks." The soured voice can belong to only one person.

Lucius.

I keep my head down, but it doesn't take a trained bird watcher to pick out my snow-blonde hair.

"If it isn't Miss Abernathy." Lucius checks off my name. "Imagine you choosing my Greek."

Imagine my bad luck.

I clear my throat. "You were a Kappan?"

"Once a Kappan, always a Kappan," he chirps. "Remember that trophy on my desk? That's my president's award for service."

"Right." I still wish I had broken it on his head.

I drop in line behind our current president Arthur whose bright red hair sticks out from under his beanie cap. All the while, I debate whether I should back out while I have the chance.

"Have your backpacks open," Lucius shouts at the line. "I shouldn't need to remind you that this is a non-alcoholic trip."

Arthur spins around, his swollen eyes sullen. "Excuse me." He steps out of line and disappears around the corner. When he returns, his backpack looks deceptively lighter.

Our president.

Lucius being staff alumni shouldn't surprise me.

Gath sticks his baton in my backpack, and I'm glad I holstered my Taser. He avoids eye contact, gives me a terse nod, and moves on to the candidate behind me.

I hurry over to where the "checked in" candidates gather, but my stomach feels queasy.

Luther joins me. "You don't look good."

"I don't feel good." I drop my backpack between my legs.

"What's wrong?"

I cough. "Our chaperones."

"Is that your adviser?" He nods toward Lucius.

"Yes, that's the one. And that Gage? He's the one who ..." but my throat closes up, and I look away. The memory of his mammoth grip on my shoulders as Eliab jabbed me with the serum is too fresh.

Luther places a warm hand on my arm. "Maybe you should stay. This isn't a good idea for you."

I shake my head and pull myself together. "No, I'm going. I won't let bullies get the best of me."

There's a small group of us, fifteen candidates and two

chaperones. At Lucius's signal, we head to the train tracks. A cargo train huffs impatiently, and Gath jumps ahead of the group, yanking open an empty cargo car.

"Everybody in." His voice booms over the hissing sound. The bare car is dark, and I choose a corner where a crack lets in a small beam of light. Luther drops his backpack next to me and slides to the floor.

Though I want to deny it, I'm warmed by his loyalty that borders on possessiveness.

Two of the other three girls on the trip claim floor space to my left, while the other prepares to get cozy with her boyfriend.

Lucius picks a spot by the door. As the train groans to a start, Gath single-handedly closes the door, cloaking the interior in a musty darkness.

"You've got two hours till we reach Cube 1776, our first destination," Lucius says. "There are a couple hostels there, which are expecting us. Stay together when we get off the train. It will be dark.

"Let me tell you a little about this cube," he continues. "No one rebuilt it after the fire, so there are many ruins for us to explore. The cube itself is sparsely populated, and those who do live there are along the Potomac River."

"Why is it called the Potomac River?" I ask. My small voice echoes in the car, but since I can't see anyone's faces, I somehow feel safe in voicing my thoughts.

"It's always been called that," Lucius replies dryly. He clears his throat. "Now where was I? Oh yes, the sparse population. We have a crew that is rebuilding some dams, and some of our own Tooler candidates travel there for internships.

"Otherwise, it's a small river community—fishermen,

trappers. The ruins are off limits to citizens unless you have a permit for exploration like we do."

"But a warning." Gath's voice booms inside our confined space. "You may not take anything from the ruins. If you find something you believe to be valuable, show Lucius or me, and we'll decide whether to leave it alone or bring it back for examination."

"Right," Lucius agrees. "That's all for now. I'd get some shut eye if I were you. There's no guarantee where any of us will sleep tonight." He laughs as if getting no sleep is a funny joke. "But isn't the uncertainty what we Trippers live for?"

The car goes quiet, except for some candidates whispering among themselves.

I prop up my backpack behind me, hoping to keep my back from bruising on the hard floor and walls of the cargo car.

"You had to ask about the Potomac," Luther says. I can hear the smile in his voice.

"There's no crime in asking a question, or at least, there shouldn't be." I think of my hand, still bruised from earlier this week.

"I'm not accusing you," he whispers. "I've just never met someone who has such a desire to *know*. You're going to make a great Doctor Revisionary."

"I have to get to the Dome first."

"You will."

"Do you really think so?"

Luther turns on his side to face me. The light from the crack touches his face, so determined and strong. "We need people like you in the Dome, people who aren't afraid to ask questions and improve the status quo."

"Yes," I agree, "and we also need Court Citizens who judge wisely and pass fair verdicts."

His breath catches in his throat. "About Darius …"

"I didn't mean for that to come up," I say quickly. "I mean we need people—like you—in the Dome, too."

He exhales, and his warm breath brushes my cheek. "Thanks for that." But the sliver of light flitting over his brow reveals anxious creases.

"I'm sorry about what happened," he says. "I have been ever since that day, but Dad made me understand that Jotham did what he thought was right."

"Right for whom? Right for himself?" My voice cracks. "I know all about his Dome assignment."

"That only makes things harder," he moans. "Dad expects nothing less than a Dome seat from me, but I'm trying to do things the honest way. You have no idea how hard it's been to grow up in Jotham's shadow."

"Well, I'm sorry, but at least you had a brother's shadow to grow up in." I can't look at his face any more and pull back into the deeper darkness of my corner.

There's a long pause, followed by a sigh that sounds more like singing.

Autumn
sky, fall. Don't wake
until the rising sun
sets wrong days right and blazes true
again.

I gasp. Those were the verses I wrote the night after Darius' trial. I sang them to the moon through my open window until exhaustion, pain, and heartbreak gave way to sleep.

"I heard you that night," Luther whispers and crawls closer. "I sneaked away when my parents thought I was asleep. I had to see you before you and your dad were transferred. I've never forgotten how broken you sounded. I vowed to do anything I could to make that sun blaze true again.

"And that's what we're going to do one day soon. When we're in the Dome, we'll uphold the laws of our land and condemn bribery and falsehood."

What Luther doesn't understand is that I don't want to uphold our laws. I want to change them.

"I can't undo what happened, but going forward, I can promise to honor and defend the precepts of our land."

Luther certainly isn't the insider Felix wants me to find. He will remain loyal to the system, no matter what it costs him.

There's a rustling noise to my right. "Will you two keep it down? Some of us are trying to sleep here."

The girl says something under her breath and noisily turns over.

Luther shuffles even closer until his hand brushes up against mine. "Cotton, can we please start over? As friends?"

I nod my head in the darkness and squeeze his hand.

This is the second truce I've made in two days, and although this one offers me a friend, neither one leaves me feeling like a winner.

Chapter 12

Friday, 9.11.2149
Crystal

The screeching of the train wheels against the track jolts me
awake. I quickly straighten, embarrassed to find myself leaned up
against Luther's shoulder. The car is a dozen degrees colder than
when we started our trip, and I pull my jacket closer, hoping the
hostels won't be far from the track.

The cargo door groans open, revealing another dimension of
darkness. There are no stadium lights or lamps here to welcome
us.

"Stay close," Gath speaks through the dark, which slowly
takes form as I emerge through the train car's mouth. The cloudless
night reveals a dazzling array of stars and a waxing moon that help
my eyes see shadows in the gray twilight.

The old, splintered platform gives way to a dirt road leading
into the cube. A river rushes on its continuous journey somewhere

beyond us.

The cube is nothing like the manufactured one back home. It consists of three buildings in an L-shape. I wonder how far beyond them are the resident cubes.

Or if there even are resident cubes.

A lone man watches us from the edge of the first building. His stump cigar smolders as he trains his eyes on our group. Gath stiffens and hastens his step toward the two adjacent structures.

The wooden buildings serve as hostels or boarding houses. Lamplight shimmers inside. Lucius takes half the group with him to the first structure, while Luther, some other candidates, and I follow Gath inside the second.

The counter is unmanned. To the left gapes a dark room, quiet except for someone's wheezing snore. Straight ahead twists a darkened stairway. To the right are clusters of empty tables and a bar beyond. Five men play cards around a glimmering lamp.

One stands to his feet. He reminds me of a thick oak, his chest wider than a barrel and his height just under Gath's.

"Evening, Red." Gath extends his hand. Red gives it a hard shake.

"How many this time?" Red's voice sounds like an old river.

"Eight, myself included," Gath says. "This group won't give you any trouble, just looking for a place to bed down for the night, *same as always*."

Red scans the eight of us, and his eyes rest momentarily on me. A flicker of something—of exactly what, I'm not sure—fills them, and then he turns back to Gath.

He nods beyond us to the room we passed on our way in. "You can have the downstairs, *same as always*. It's empty except for old Bart."

Gath pulls out an envelope, probably filled with Greek funds.

Red's face remains stoic, and he is slow to accept it. He starts to say something but simply nods and returns to his card game.

The other players don't bother to acknowledge us. I softly follow the rest of my group and Luther into the darkened room but lag in the hallway. There's nothing but another hard floor waiting for me.

From behind me, someone mutters. "Interlopers."

"Quiet."

Then, slurred droning. "Stupid play money."

I choose the wall closest to the hallway, farthest away from old Bart's loud snoring and the rest of my group who are trying to stay out of the lamp's beam. Somewhere in the dark, someone finds an old couch, and everyone wants a piece of it.

Sliding against the wall, I sluggishly reshape my backpack into a lumpy pillow. I probably won't sleep anyway.

"You coming inside?" Gath's deep voice makes me jump.

I look up, his shadow looming above me. "It seems kind of crowded in there."

"I wouldn't sleep by the door if I were you." His eyes look past me to the hostel's dim hallway, as if seeing beyond. "There's a chair in the corner. You can have that."

"Okay." Before I can move, he reaches under my arms and lifts me off the floor like I'm a paper doll, pushing me toward the back of the room.

I gasp at his touch, nothing like the iron clamp I'd felt before.

In the far corner is an old fabric chair next to a heavily draped window. It feels like a queen's throne compared to the hard ground. Glancing back, I see Gath drop to the floor by the room's entrance, as if guarding a fold of sheep.

I'm not sure what to make of this dual-personality giant. What danger is there in sleeping by the entrance? And why would he give up his chair for me?

I curl up, and gradually, Bart's snoring dims.

Something in the night jars me awake. The sound makes me sink lower into the chair.

The world is still dark, but the hallway comes alive. Boots clomp down the stairs, and voices whisper. The aroma of bacon, burned grease, and black coffee fill the air.

The boarding house buzzes with sounds, although the time can't be much past 0400 hours.

So, this is how some people live. The reality shouldn't surprise me, but I've never imagined living outside the confines of cube life.

I wish I can hear what they are saying, but I'm too far inside the room to make out any words. The voices stop as their owners fill hollow stomachs for the long day. The faint crackling of bacon cues me that the kitchen must be on the other side of our wall.

Holding my breath, I wait for the next sound. The outside door opens, and more boots hit the wooden walkway. The footsteps gradually grow louder as the men round the outside front of the building, walking on the other side of the window by my chair. I resist the temptation to peel back the curtain and look out.

The footsteps stop. They are gone, nothing but ghosts disappearing into the pre-dawn of a new day. Or are they?

I pull back the far corner of the curtain. A lone man stands there, his full-frame silhouetted in the moonlight.

Does he see me? I can't make out his face, only the charred remains of a cigar. There's something in the way he stands that makes my heart beat faster.

I release the curtain and fall back into my chair. Perhaps the men are mere ghosts, and I am but dreaming.

"Wake up and rise. Breakfast is in five minutes." Gath's voice booms into the room. "Outhouses are around back."

The first traces of daylight filter through the crack where the curtains didn't quite close.

Old Bart is gone, and none of the candidates are moving quickly. I slide out of my chair before they notice me and grow jealous of my perch.

Luther is stretching on the floor, limbering up his muscular arms and legs for the day ahead. Black bristles make his jaw look stronger and thicker, more like the man he is and less like the boy I once knew.

That isn't a bad thing, is it?

He gives me a lopsided smile, and I glance away, hoping he didn't catch me studying him.

"How'd you sleep?" He stands and walks with me to the back of the hostel. A hundred yards away at the end of a clearing are two small, wooden outhouses. To the right are some open-air showers.

"Not bad," I say. "Did you hear the commotion earlier this morning?"

"Yeah, that crew sounded like wild horses," he grins. "I asked Gath about them. He says the men are miners and fishermen who travel the river for work."

"Where do they live?"

He shrugs. "Probably in the mountains."

I shake my head. "I thought everyone lived in cubes. I wonder what mountain life is like?"

"Hard."

The stench from the outhouses is sickening, so we split up into the woods beyond.

He's waiting for me in the clearing when I return. "Welcome to the great outdoors." He laughs. "It sure does make you thankful for the accommodations we enjoy."

"It's not all that bad," I say. "We're spoiled in Crystal. I don't have indoor plumbing back home either, but I sure do a better job taking care of our outbuilding."

Luther's grin fades. "I didn't realize how much your dad was demoted."

"It's no big deal." I shrug. "He always took care of me."

"I'm still sorry …"

I cut him off. "I know you are. Let's not talk about it anymore, okay?"

"Yeah." His lopsided smile returns. "Let's go get breakfast, Cotton."

Back indoors, we follow our noses to the dining area where heaps of bacon and grits wait. Some of our classmates are already eating or talking quietly in a corner. Gath stands in the hall, counting heads, and then disappears into the front room to kick awake the stragglers.

Red emerges from the kitchen wearing a faded apron and carrying a large pot of black coffee.

He sees Luther and me come in together, his eyes darting between the two of us.

"Help me in the back?" he asks Luther. "I've got another plate to bring out."

"Sure thing," Luther says. He turns to me. "Go ahead and get started. I'll just be a minute."

I help myself to the country-cooked food and find a cracked spoon to use. I try the coffee as thick as molasses, but my stomach isn't cast iron. I'll pretend I poured it for Luther.

He returns, helps himself to a plate, and sits across from me. I shove the coffee cup toward him.

Luther takes a sip and grimaces. "If I drink the rest of that, I won't sleep for days."

I laugh. "It's too strong for me too, but the food is good."

"That Red is an interesting guy," he says.

"Oh?"

"Yeah, he says the strangest things." He shovels a spoonful of grits in his mouth.

"Like what?" I chew carefully on a gristly piece of bacon.

"He wanted to know if we are, you know, together."

I pause to give my teeth a break. "That's an odd question."

"I told him yes." Luther winks at me. "I don't want anyone thinking you're fair game."

"How chivalrous of you."

"And then he asked what we are studying and where," Luther continues. "So, I told him. And then he asked if we were staying a second night."

"That's strange. Surely Gath worked that out with him in advance."

"Right? I told him I didn't think so, and then he tried to convince me that it takes two days to explore the ruins and that he would keep the room free for us a second night. He said he'd even clear out a room upstairs for you—and 'any other girls.' I told him that he'd have to talk to Gath." Luther pauses. "I got the impression he wants us to stay here again tonight."

I give up on the bacon. "But none of the men seemed pleased to see us last night."

"He was watching you," Luther says. "I saw him look your way. Twice. I think it's a good thing we're moving on today."

I roll my eyes. "Luther, I'm sure it's nothing like *that*."

"Maybe not like *that*," Luther says, "but there's got to be a reason he was watching you. Anyway, it won't matter as long as we leave for Lapis today as planned."

We finish breakfast and meet Lucius's group on the hostel's front porch. The street is deserted except for a stray dog. The men from this morning won't be back until dinner.

Lucius's group looks as haggard as ours. I feel surprisingly rested but try not to let it show.

"The set of ruins is about five miles outside the cube," Lucius says. "Did everyone fill up your water canteens?"

A few candidates shake their heads.

"Well, hurry up!" Lucius barks. "This isn't a walk in the park like back at Crystal. There are no roadside cafes. I hope everyone ate a good breakfast. We'll be back for dinner and then hop our next train to Lapis."

"We head out in five," Gath calls. Candidates split to fill their water canisters or use the outhouse one last time. I don't want to wait around with Gath and Lucius, so I head back inside to see if I can wrap up some greasy bacon to chew on for lunch.

Red has already cleared the tables, and the only sound in the hostel is running water from the kitchen. I step up to the doorway. Red's back is toward me, and he's standing by a panel in the wall. He's making a series of tapping sounds on something I can't see.

"Excuse me."

He flinches but does not immediately acknowledge me. Instead, he hangs up his apron on the panel and then turns to me.

"Yes, miss?" There's that searching look again.

I lower my eyes. "I was wondering if you have any leftover bacon from breakfast. I guess we won't be back until this evening."

"Going to the ruins, are you?" He steps toward the counter where the breakfast scraps are cooling.

"Yes, sir."

"Your first time?" His movements are unhurried as he wraps a few bacon strips in plastic.

"That's right." I glance behind me, hoping he will finish quickly.

"Girls shouldn't come on these trips," he mutters. "Just isn't safe."

"Excuse me?"

Red doesn't offer an apology or explanation. "Besides, you look a little young to be a Tripper." He shakes open a brown bag and stuffs the leftovers inside. I did not expect him to go through the trouble of bagging my food.

"I graduated early."

"You're what, like nineteen?" He reaches for an apple and starts to wash it.

"Yes." I wonder if he will ever hand me the bacon and let me leave.

To my surprise, he adds the apple to my bag. "And you're not from Crystal originally, are you? Your accent—It's maybe Chrysoprase."

I blink in surprise. I've never thought of myself as having an accent. "Why, yes. That's where I'm from."

"Drafted to Crystal because you're the top of your class, no doubt."

"That's right."

"Interesting." He pauses. "I've heard rumors there are some strange happenings in Crystal."

"I should get going," I say and nod toward the door. "My group—they're probably leaving now."

He hands me the brown bag. "Be safe. I hope that will keep you till tonight."

Tonight. It's spoken like a promise.

I stuff the bag in my backpack next to my canteen. "Thanks." I force a smile and make a quick retreat. Outside the hostel, the road is empty, but several hundred yards away, I spot the candidates walking toward the track. I run to catch up. Luther lags behind the rest.

"I see you got in your morning run." He laughs as I gasp to catch my breath. "What took you so long? You should know Gath wouldn't wait for anyone."

I'm relieved to see two other candidates running to join the group as well. At least I'm not the only straggler.

"I went to the kitchen to get some bacon for lunch," I say. "You can thank me later."

"Red must be quite the conversationalist to keep you ten minutes." His tone is accusing.

I squint at him. "He's a strange one—and took his time fixing a whole paper bag lunch for me."

"Not surprised. I'd stall for time too if I were making lunch for a pretty girl."

"Oh, stop it." I swat him on the shoulder. "He's got to be forty or something—old enough to be my dad."

"But he's not your dad."

"It's not like that at all," I say impatiently. "He's—I don't know—curious."

"Curious can get you in a lot of trouble."

Chapter 13

Saturday, 9.12.2149
Crystal, Cube 1776

It's late morning when we reach the ruins of Cube 1776.

Skeletal buildings loom over streets littered with rubble and overgrown with trees and underbrush. This must once have been a place of commerce, a hub of civilization.

"Stay close," Gath says as Lucius counts heads. "There are many buildings we can explore, but only three we're authorized to examine on this trip. More than the rest, they remain structurally sound. Only part of them caught fire. Their main damage is from the decay of the decades."

We form a semi-circle around Gath and Lucius. Although we're tired from the walk, we're no less impatient to start exploring—but not before our chaperones give us one parting lecture.

Once satisfied with the head count, Lucius trains his eyes on us. "The three buildings made up an old library once called 'The Library of Congress.' It belonged to the past civilization, and most of the documents contained inside have long since been scavenged or destroyed. If you happen to find something, bring it to me for identification. It may be worthless, but on the off chance our Revisionaries find it valuable, you could be compensated. Under no circumstances are you to keep anything for yourself."

Gath stands with one hand on his hip, the other resting on a handgun lashed to his belt. It makes my Taser seem like a child's toy in comparison, and I look at his with longing. Only high-ranking Gages are allowed to carry actual firearms any more. It's a fool's hope that a civilian will ever own one.

"Remember, our role is tripping," Gath says. "We trip. We explore. We take nothing but an experience and leave nothing but our footprints."

"Stay in groups of two or more—although that clearly won't be an issue for some of you." Lucius glares at a guy-girl couple at the edge of our group. Neither is paying much attention to him. "We've had our share of accidents on this trip before. Keep an eye for mongrels, although they usually don't bother us this time of day. And watch your footing carefully."

Gath tightens his belt. "If you see someone not part of our group, do not engage with them. Immediately, get out of the way."

"What kind of people would hang out here?" A candidate next to Luther asks.

"Just avoid them if you see them," Lucius says sharply. "I don't expect we'll have any trouble, though."

Gath looks at the sky and then taps his watch. "We'll meet back here in two hours. Be on time or better yet, early." He catches my eye. "You don't want to get left behind."

Gath and Lucius step back, and the group breaks apart.

Luther and I start toward the three crumbling buildings that sit adjacent to each other. Beyond them, other structures entice us to explore.

"I wish I had a map of this place," I say as we pick our way toward the farthest building. "There's so much here, beyond these buildings."

Luther gives me a warning look. "You heard Lucius and Gath. We're not to go past the library."

I wrinkle my nose at him. "Whatever you say, Mr. Rule-keeper."

The massive structure looms before us. The main doors are missing, giving the entrance the appearance of a yawning mouth.

"Did you bring your flashlight?" Luther asks.

"Of course," I say. "Spare batteries too."

"Aren't you prepared."

Still, I'm not ready for how dark the building is. Limited natural light snakes through cracked and missing windows along the perimeter, but the interior walls give the impression of a black hole.

"If we're going to find anything, we're going to have to go deep," Luther says at last.

"Yeah."

"You don't sound like you're in a hurry." The void swallows his words.

"It's creepier than I was expecting. Maybe we should join a larger group—a safety in numbers kind of thing."

Luther shakes his head. "None of our traveling companions strike me as very safe. Five of the guys, Arthur included, sneaked out last night to get drunk. I learned a couple other details I won't bother to share."

"Thanks for keeping them to yourself."

"Gath and Lucius are the only two who know what they're doing." Luther takes a few steps further into the building, flashing his beam through the mist of dust. He waits for me to follow.

"I'm coming." I follow him across what once would have been a beautiful entrance. Now, the tile is cracked and littered with debris where the ceiling has given way.

He offers me a hand to help cross a large hole in the floor. I accept it and watch his face light up. His grasp is gentle and strong.

"Thanks." I jump across. The heat from his hand makes my pulse race. I let go and stuff my right hand in my pocket while gripping the flashlight harder with my left.

Focus, Portia.

"Why do you think Gath and Lucius go through the trouble of sponsoring and chaperoning these trips if most of the candidates come simply to break rules off-campus?"

"Good question. I don't know," Luther says.

Our flashlights sweep the floor around us. Bookcases and broken shelves are a toppled forest of dead wood. Torn pages disintegrate under our boots, crackling like charred leaves.

Every rustling noise conjures images of mongrels and raiders. My body is a time bomb, an adrenaline cocktail of suspense and fear, waiting to be set off.

Luther breaks the silence. "Stairs to your right."

"Do you think they're safe?"

"Nothing about this is safe. I'll go first."

"No, I'll go first," I say. "I'm lighter. I'd rather you carry me out of here than the other way around."

"How noble of you." Though I can't see his face, I hear his

smile.

The stairs groan but lead safely to a second floor, as much of a disaster as the first. I depart from the main hallway down narrower aisles, hoping to find something the previous ravagers may have missed.

Luther disappears down the aisle just beyond.

After minutes of straining my eyes, I find only a torn book cover. I sweep my hand across the layer of dirt to read, *Goodnight, Moon.*

A child's book. The artwork on the cover suggests a bedtime story. An undeniable longing fills me as I remember the few stories Candace once read to me.

"Goodnight, Moon." I ache to know what happens in the story.

Something crashes in the darkness. I drop the book cover and spin my light around.

"Luther?" I whisper into the void.

A trained growl rumbles from somewhere close. My light catches the red eyes of a mongrel lurking at the end of the aisle.

Instinctively, my arm reaches for my Taser.

"Freeze."

The mongrel and I both go rigid. Keeping one eye on the animal, I cock my head sideways to make out a shadow in my peripheral.

"Hand it over, and your friend lives." It's a cold, hollow voice.

Raider. Or worse yet, Trader.

To give up my weapon is to give up my life.

I stall. "What do you want?"

"Your Taser, *wench.*"

Trader.

The click of his double action gives me no time to spare. I light up the shadow and fire my Taser, sending the man howling to the floor. His revolver goes off as the mongrel charges. I can't spin fast enough to focus my light and aim a second time.

Three successive shots beat me to it. I see the fire from the barrel between the broken shelves to my right. My flashlight illuminates the mongrel as it falls lifeless to the floor, inches away.

But my mystery gunman is not the only one ready to open fire.

I drop to my knees as more gunfire cracks open above me. Traders never work alone. Close by, bullets hit their target, and an angry cry goes silent.

I crawl toward the end of the aisle, hoping to find Luther somewhere on the ground nearby.

"Leaving already?" The cavernous voice takes form. The Trader's shadow looks like an ogre, and my Taser only served to light his fuse.

I fall back as he knocks the flashlight out of my hand. The small laser beam on my Taser can't focus fast enough.

The man has bat-like reflexes. But then, men like him are used to the dark.

I trip over the limp mongrel and let out a helpless cry as the man grasps my leg with an iron grip.

Kicking blindly, I hit bone. He snarls but doesn't let go, dragging me toward him.

I scream as he tears off my backpack and jacket, pulling me in for a strangle hold.

There's a whooshing sound, followed by the crack of a cartridge. The Trader curses, grabs his side and suddenly relaxes his grip. I spring free, only to trip again on the dead animal.

Behind me, the man thuds to the ground. He's gagging for air.

Someone has finished him and is heading for me.

I crawl backwards and feel frantically for my Taser as the lethal shadow steps closer on the groaning floor.

"Get up. We need to go."

"Gath!" I gasp in relief. My hand touches my Taser and flashlight, and I gather them up with my torn jacket and pack off the floor.

"There's more where they came from." He pulls me to my feet. "Lucius is rounding up the other candidates."

"Where's Luther?" I ask.

In response, Gath flashes his light around the wrecked shelving. Luther's a heap on the floor, two aisles away.

I fall to his side and put my ear to his chest. He's still breathing.

"Luther!" I shake him.

He only groans.

I reach around him to prop him up. My hand brushes his hair, caked in blood.

"It's his head," I say as Gath bends down.

"They clubbed him badly." His voice is grim. "They weren't after him."

Gath stoops down to slide Luther over his shoulder. Luther is heavy, but Gath only grows stronger under his weight.

He hands me the light. "Keep it down, so we can see our footing."

I lead the way as quickly as I dare, exaggerating my steps so Gath can follow more easily.

Finally, we reach the exit. I fall back, blinking to let my eyes adjust. Gath pauses inside the building's entrance to shift Luther to his other shoulder. I remove my Taser from its holster once more and train it low.

"Where'd you get that?" Gath asks.

"Special permit."

"You know those aren't recognized in Crystal."

I squint at him. "If we get back alive, arrest me then."

He cracks a grin. "I'll look forward to it."

I step outside to scan the perimeter and fall back inside. "All clear."

"Let's move. We don't stop until we're beyond the ruins. Lucius will meet us there with the others."

We silently cross the exposed streets. It takes a small eternity before we're outside the main debris and the ruins begin to fade into the horizon.

Voices ahead make us duck inside a tree cluster. Gath lowers Luther to the ground.

"Wait here."

I nod and pull out my water canteen, forcing some of the liquid between Luther's lips. Again, he groans, fading in and out of consciousness.

He swallows some of the water and gasps, his eyes flickering open.

"Hey." I wipe dirt off his face. "Can you hear me?"

He winces. "Yeah. What happened?"

"We were ambushed. Don't try to talk. Focus on drinking something." I hold the canteen to his lips again.

Luther pulls back when he's had enough. "How'd we get out? There's no way a squirt like you carried me."

At least his humor is returning. "It was Gath."

He nods and closes his eyes.

Minutes later, Gath returns. "Lucius and the others are waiting ahead of us. They saw some Trader tracks heading into the ruins but none coming out. If we move fast, we might beat them back to the cube."

"Luther is awake," I say. "I think he'll be okay with rest and some attention."

Gath slides Luther back onto his shoulder. "Red will fix him up."

"Have you known Red for a long time?"

"We go way back." His voice is quiet, and he offers no further explanation.

When we reach the group, Lucius corrals everyone to start moving. The thirteen candidates with him act like terrified sheep. They're talking loudly and all at once crowding me with questions.

I fall back toward Gath, overwhelmed.

"Silence!" Gath booms. "There will be no talking until we're back in the cube."

Lucius glares at me as if the whole incident were my fault and falls in step on the other side of Gath.

"What happened?" he asks.

"Trader ambush, like Red suspected," Gath says. "I saw the sentry last night but hoped I was wrong."

"No doubt he saw the girls."

"No doubt."

Lucius narrows his eyes at me. "Hard to miss this one."

I gulp. "I had no idea trips were this dangerous."

"They aren't—or they haven't been in the past," Gath keeps his voice low. "But now, something's changing."

Lucius swears. "Rogues."

"Rogues aren't to blame for this," Gath retorts, sounding almost angry. "Raiders and Traders are getting more violent and brazen, because no one's there to stop them."

"Don't all cubes have enforcers?" I ask.

"Enforcers are no match for armed gangs. Gages might have Tasers, but you just found out how well those work against real muscle."

"You have a gun." I look at the handgun lashed to his side. "Arm all the enforcers with them. Give them real weapons."

Lucius glances nervously at Gath. "We did that, once," Gath explains. "And then we had to deal with enforcers abusing power and using it against the people they were meant to protect. That's when we downgraded all basic-level Gages to Tasers. But abuse still happens. Only, no one talks about it."

"Then, let the people arm themselves," I say. "A looter or raider would think twice before attacking an armed citizen."

"Impossible!" Lucius snorts. "That's asking for rebellion."

"No wonder the criminals run rampant," I retort. "There's no one to stop them."

Lucius scowls at me.

But I'm not done making my case. "Who do you see as the real threat here—the code-breakers or the civilians? By not letting the civilians protect themselves, you're encouraging criminal behavior by default."

"Careful, you're starting to sound like a Rogue." Gath's voice is harsh, but he glances at me with respect.

I drop my eyes to the ground and kick at a stone. "What is a Rogue?"

"It's none of your business," Lucius hisses.

"I was ambushed by a Trader," I argue. "How can a Rogue be any more dangerous?"

"Depends on your perspective," Gath mumbles.

Lucius lowers his voice. "You're really getting into this with *her*? Just because we're not at the Crystal Globe doesn't mean her records have changed."

The brief bridge of trust built through the necessity of survival seems to vanish.

"You may be right, Lucius," Gath says at last, "but we're in this together."

"Speak for yourself," Lucius mutters. "I still don't like her."

I look around Gath to catch Lucius's eye. "You know I can hear you."

"You don't like me either, and don't pretend you do." He yanks off his red-rimmed glasses to wipe the sweat beading above his eyes. "This trip will be over soon enough, and as far as I'm concerned, this breakdown into conversational familiarity will never have happened."

"Give me a chance to like you, and let me be the judge," I dare him.

"A chance to like me?" he scoffs. "All right, I felt badly that your medical records were frozen. I actually did, so I looked into who was to blame. It comes straight from the top—suspicion surrounding your ties to a Rogue family member.

"A brother, in fact," he continues without pausing for breath, "a brother who was condemned by the Danforth currently seated in the Dome—who, if I'm not mistaken—is kin to the one Gath's carrying.

"Clearly, you have both bad blood and strange taste in choosing friends. And frankly, I would prefer not to get myself tangled in your problems. Excuse me, but I'm going to check on the group lagging behind us." He retreats to the back of our straggling caravan and begins to harass them to pick up the pace.

"I don't suppose he considered that I can hear everything you guys are saying," Luther mutters.

I feel Gath's eyes on me but can't look at him. My face grows hot, and my vision blurs. I fall back to walk between the lead and middle clusters of candidates. Everyone is too weary to care if I release the tears held in for too long.

My suspicions are correct. Someone wants me to fail—because of Darius.

Darius.

I stop short. Lucius's words take on new meaning. If Darius is a Rogue, then Darius is alive.

Gasping, I run ahead to rejoin Gath and Luther, who is now trying to walk on his own without much success.

"Gath," I pant for air, "What is a Rogue?"

He looks down at me in surprise. "Back so soon?"

"Please, just tell me," I say. "If the Crystal Globe considers me a suspect because of family ties, at least let me know what crimes I'm thought to have committed."

"It's a serious matter," he warns me, "to be considered a Rogue accomplice."

"I haven't done anything," I protest. "You should know. You administered my lie test."

Gath stiffens and gives me a hard glare. "That is confidential."

I forgot Luther. *Luther.*

He collapses onto the ground. It's either a perfectly timed distraction or the sign of a serious head injury.

"We break here." Gath calls to the group behind us, waving us into the shade of a tree canopy. Together, we set Luther against a large oak's trunk.

"I'll be all right," he slurs his words.

"Don't talk." I pull out my canteen and give him the last of my water and the apple. He's too tired to gnaw on the dried jerky, but it helps distract my thoughts as I check the wound on his head. The hair is matted with no fresh blood, which I hope is a good sign.

The stragglers in the group have no sooner reached the resting spot than Gath orders us to move on. We can't risk having the Traders catch up with us.

Half an hour passes. Then an hour. The late afternoon sun sinks fast. Finally, the train tracks appear in the distance.

Gath has been carrying Luther since the clearing. I've fallen into step behind him, not wanting to pester the giant who is showing signs of fatigue from Luther's weight.

"A Rogue," Gath suddenly whispers, his voice hoarse, "is a convict who has escaped his satellite and either formed or joined a band of rebels. The intent is not merely survival. It is to undercut the Dome's government. At first, there were nuisance pranks on our railways and communication lines. Now, they are guilty of cracking into our technology systems and power sources and infiltrating positions and schools of influence. Their numbers are growing, and their message is clear: revolution.

"The bounty on a Rogue is better than a lifetime's worth of rations. If a Rogue is caught and convicted, the sentence is death."

I don't know why Gath decides to tell me this now.

His words extinguish the hope fanning in my heart.

I hope Lucius is wrong, and Darius is still on a satellite. At least then, I have a chance to amend the laws and free him. But I can't shake the whisper of *what if* in my mind.

If Darius is a Rogue, a seat in the Dome won't help either of us. Nothing I do can protect him from the fate assigned to these rebel convicts.

And I simply cannot bear to lose him again.

Chapter 14

Saturday, 9.12.2149
Crystal, Cube 1776

We arrive back at the hostel before the day crews, but the slowing sunlight warns they will be returning soon.

"Everyone, get cleaned up." Lucius waves the candidates toward the open shower out back. "It'll be your only chance before the workers get here, and no one wants to share a stall with them."

The thirteen other candidates hurry away, but I follow Lucius and Gath, still shouldering Luther, inside.

The kitchen steams with baked beans and biscuits, but Red seems to know we're coming. His long, wooden prep table is already cleared, and Gath lowers Luther onto it.

"Head wound, ambushed from behind," Gath says, his voice low. "He's conscious but lost some blood."

"I've seen worse." Red washes his hands and immediately inspects and cleanses the wound. Luther grimaces and clenches his eyes.

Lucius yawns. "We were planning to leave for Lapis tonight."

Red shakes his head. "No good. The train to Lapis is down."

"What?" Lucius straightens and curses under his breath.

Red ignores his outburst. "Besides, this one shouldn't travel until tomorrow at the earliest—and that should be back to the Globe to get a more expert examination. He may have a minor concussion. He's lucky this gouge doesn't go any deeper."

"What happened on the Lapis line?" Gath asks.

Red tightens his lips. "Hard to tell."

"What are the reports saying?" Lucius demands.

"The CGA says Rogues," Red says, "but that's their new favorite line for everything."

"You don't think they're right?" Lucius asks.

Red wraps a bandage around Luther's head. "It's not my concern. You had better hope whoever's behind it don't come south and target the Crystal line, or you're stranded here."

"Then we should leave tonight."

Red frowns. "Not if you've got Traders on your scent. Taking a crew like yours to the tracks to wait for the midnight cargo train is asking for trouble."

"Traders, Rogues, what a mess," Lucius mutters. "Trips never used to be this complicated."

"Welcome to the 22nd Century." Red finishes taping the bandage in place. He looks at Gath. "That's all I can do for now. He needs to drink water, and food won't hurt. Help yourselves to a bowl. I've got to get ready for the men."

He moves to the sink to rinse his hands and stops short. For the first time, he notices me leaning against the wall.

His face softens in concern. "Are you hurt too?"

"No—no, I'm fine," I stammer. "I just want to make sure he's okay."

Red steps toward me. "You're all bloody. Let me have a look."

I glance down and for the first time, realize I'm a mess. My jacket is torn, hanging askew on my shoulders. My shirt is covered with blood—either the Trader's or Luther's or both.

"I'm fine, really," I say. "It was—the other guy."

"The other guy?" Red's face relaxes into a grin, and he turns to Gath.

"Yeah, she tasered the Trader, but it didn't stop him for long. She put up a good cat fight before I finished him off." Gath's voice sounds almost proud.

"You have a license to carry?"

I nod. "Just a Taser. Nothing else is legal, of course."

"Traveling with a Taser isn't legal either," Lucius pounces.

Gath sighs. "I told her."

Lucius snorts. "That's what you need, Abernathy: more correctives back in Crystal."

"I didn't know," I protest but stop short at the sight of Red's face. His eyes widen and then grow warm with approval. It's a look of new recognition, and yet, it's impossible for him to know me.

Despite my protest, he slips off my jacket and inspects my neck, arms, and wrists with a Healer's probing but gentle touch.

"Only scratches," he says at last. "Nothing a good shower won't fix."

"Better hurry, or you'll be sharing the stall with a bunch of hungry, gritty men." Lucius laughs, but neither Gath nor Red smiles.

As if on cue, loud voices and heavy feet sound out front.

"You'd better make sure the others are done out back," Gath

tells Lucius.

My adviser gives me one last smirk and whispers as he leaves. "I'm glad you're not in my group. At least, I don't have to smell you all night."

"The feeling is mutual," I mutter and move toward the table to help Luther. I wrap my arm around him and let him lean on me as he swings down from the table. His weight must be twice my own, but I make a good crutch. With his arm draped across my shoulder, we start for the kitchen door.

"Thanks, Red," I say for both of us.

"Come back and get him a bowl of food and some water," Red invites, and I nod in acknowledgment.

Despite some hard stares, I get Luther into the large lounge room and help him to the chair where I slept.

He lets out a hard breath. "Thanks, Cotton."

"I'm sorry about all of this."

"It's not your fault. I wish I'd heard the guy coming. I would have given him a piece of my mind."

I find a small blanket and roll it into a makeshift pillow, inserting it behind his neck. "Only cowards jump a man from the back."

"Glad the man—the mongrel—got what was coming to them," he mutters. "You're fine, though? You really zapped the guy?"

"Yes, but now, Lucius will nail me for that once we get back."

Luther shakes his head. "I don't think Gath will let him."

"I hope you're right, but I'm not sure. One moment, Gath and I seem to be on the same team, and then the next, I expect him to stab me with another injector. I don't know who to trust."

Luther reaches for my hand. "Trust me, then."

I squeeze it and don't want to let go. With my other hand, I brush his cheek, which is still pale. "Let me get you some food and water. I'll be right back."

Keeping my head down to avoid eye contact with the day crew, I slip into the kitchen where Gath and Red are talking in low tones.

They look up when they see me.

"I came for some water and food for Luther. I don't mean to interrupt."

Red walks past me to look out the door. "The men are here. You shouldn't be seen on the chance one of them is connected to the band of Traders."

"But Luther—"

"I'll take the food and drink back to Luther." Gath places a hand on my shoulder. "You wait here until the men clear out."

Red shoves a bowl of steaming beans into my hands and motions to a stool as Gath leaves with the food for Luther. Without another word, Red moves back to the task at hand, balances two steaming bowls in his hands, and disappears out the door to set out the dinner buffet.

I fall onto the stool as the aroma of beans fans my hunger. Eyes closed, I spoon the savory food to my lips. Its simplicity and warmth remind me of home.

Tomorrow will be a week since I left, but it feels like a lifetime ago. I start to feel homesick, but check my self-pity. I have new friends—or at least people who care enough to keep me from getting killed.

Sitting up straighter, I finish the contents of my bowl and look around the kitchen. Dirty pots and pans clutter the counter. Red's a kitchen crew of one, and he took time away from his own chores to help Luther.

I set my empty bowl in the sink and remove my jacket. After washing my hands, I find the dish soap and fill the sink with hot water. The dishes are the least I can do.

I've just started the first set as Red returns for another steaming bowl. His stare raises the hair on my neck. But I focus on my task, and he leaves again without saying anything.

Half an hour later, the kitchen is clean, and the men's loud voices are muted by the food. Red returns and sets down the last empty bowl, which I begin to rinse.

"You don't have to do that."

"And you don't have to help my friend. But you did, so I want to say thank you."

He watches me for a moment and then disappears inside a closet door as I finish cleaning the bowl and set it on the counter to dry.

When he returns, he's holding a towel, oversized shirt, and wash pail. "There's a room in the back of the kitchen. You can wash up there."

I bite my lip. "Thank you, Red."

"Thank you, Portia."

I accept the gift and hurry to the back door, closing it firmly behind me.

I fill the pail with water from a small nozzle while his words pour over me again. *Thank you, Portia.*

I scrub myself clean. Rub most of the stain out of my jacket. Button up the clean shirt ten sizes too big. Wonder for the hundredth time how he knows my first name.

I wake before dawn to the same stampede of feet and bury my head in my lumpy backpack to drown out the noise.

No use. The combination of a full stomach and exhaustion made me sleep through the night, but now, the hard floor takes its toll. I turn on my side, and my back protests. I grit my teeth to fight the muscle spasm and all its fury.

My body hates me.

But then, I haven't been especially kind to it.

When the spasm subsides, I feel for my shirt, which I left to dry over the arm of Luther's chair. Finding it, I use the dark as a cover to slip out of the extra-large button-up from Red into my own shirt. I fold Red's halfway and leave it on the arm for him to find later.

Then, I feel for Luther.

He's still asleep, but his wrist is warm. He has a low fever. It could be worse, but I don't like the idea of infection.

The clomping boots no sooner retreat outside than Gath bellows from the hallway. "Everybody up and out! We leave in five."

There's no breakfast today. But then, we've already overstayed our visit, and Red hadn't planned on cooking an extra breakfast this morning. I don't even see him to say goodbye.

As we walk in silence toward the tracks, I pull out the last of the bacon from my backpack and slip Luther a piece. We each gnaw on a chewy strand to mollify our stomachs.

He insists on walking without assistance, but I stay close to him. We reach the tracks as the faint headlight from the morning cargo train appears in the distance.

I can't shake a chill as we wait for it to reach us. Red's words of Traders waiting at the tracks ring in my memory.

Luther falls to the ground to rest. I worry that his fever is spiking, but there's no use putting my fear into words.

The river rolls in the distance, but my senses alert me to someone behind me. I whirl, hand instantly on my hip.

"Whoa, nice draw." It's a low whisper.

"Red!" I re-seat my Taser.

"You're all clear. No one's tracking you this morning. My brothers and I saw to that."

My brothers. What does he mean?

He presses a small brown bag into my hand. "That's for the trip."

"Thank you." I'm overwhelmed by his kindness. Yesterday, he was a stranger. Today, he's a friend. No, a brother.

"*Fraternitas Veritas.*"

It means you are never alone, Dad had said.

I gasp in surprise as his words sink in, but Red puts a finger to his lips and slips back into the shadows.

The train howls to a stop as the first hint of dawn flutters through the steam.

The day is here. And Red is gone.

Gath helps me get Luther onto the train but doesn't speak to me. *The lapse into conversational familiarity,* as Lucius called it, seems to be at an end.

Luther passes out on the train, and I doze intermittently. When we pull into Crystal, Gath wastes no time hauling Luther off to medical. I trail behind to make sure he gets checked in okay and then slip out. I don't want anyone to associate Luther too closely with me. For his sake.

Back in my dorm room, Lydia is still asleep. I beeline for the shower to wash away the dank train car smell and then collapse, damp hair and all, onto my bed.

It's early afternoon before I wake to my growling stomach. Lydia is gone, probably to study at the library or participate in another of her modules. I dig inside my backpack for the brown bag from Red. It contains an apple and oatmeal bar.

They satisfy my hunger but only feed my curiosity. My mind replays the words Red whispered at the station—the words my father spoke when we parted. Is Red part of the Brotherhood Dad mentioned?

But who are they, and why are they watching out for a girl like me?

I finish my snack and set out to check on Luther.

"He left an hour ago," the nurse tells me.

"Really?" I ask. "Then he doesn't have a concussion?"

She shakes her head. "No concussion. We gave him a prescription to ward off infection, but his fever is normal at this point. Whoever bandaged him up did a nice job."

"Thanks," I say and start for his dorm.

I knock several times before Luther cracks open the door. Dark circles ring his eyes.

"I'm sorry if I woke you. I forgot you don't have a roommate."

He winces at the light from the hallway and backs into his room where a small lamp gives off a faint glow. "It's okay. I just got out of the shower. Come on in."

He's not wearing a shirt, but then, he often went shirtless when we had played as children. He sprouted tall so fast there was never much meat on his bones. He's anything but scrawny now. No wonder he runs like a machine.

I glance away and close the door. "I stopped by medical, but you were already gone. No concussion is good news."

Luther grunts and pulls on a sweatshirt. "That doesn't mean I don't feel miserable."

"Sorry."

He falls onto a couch and runs his fingers through his damp hair. "The doc said I'll be as good as new in a few days. He gave me a pass to miss class tomorrow, but I don't dare if I want to stay ahead."

"At least you can rest up today."

"Yeah, good thing the Lapis line was down, and we cut our trip short."

I lean against a chair as he closes his eyes. "I can go if you want to sleep."

He cracks open an eye and holds out a hand. "No, stay. That is, if you want."

I hesitate, then reach for his hand and grasp it. "Can I get you anything?"

"Food would be great."

I let go of his fingers. Why does his touch send goosebumps up my arm? Turning away from him, I rummage through his kitchenette. "Oatmeal and tea are your choices." I wish our dorm advisers would let us keep more provisions in our rooms.

"Both."

We share tea and solitude for an hour. When he dozes, I slip out to retrieve my tablet from my room so I can get some studying done.

Lydia is propped up on her bed, doing homework. "How was the trip? I didn't think you were supposed to get back till tonight."

I give her a quick summary of what happened as I dig my tablet out of the ottoman.

"That's awful."

"Yeah, it could have been much worse, though."

Lydia gives me one of those I-told-you-so looks. "You all could have been killed. We should see about changing Greeks."

I grin. "Too late for me. I'm a Tripper now."

Lydia's eyes grow wide. "You would go again?"

"In a heartbeat. Out there, the world is so different from our cubes back home. And it's nothing like Crystal. It's raw and real. Yes, it's dangerous, but there's an honesty about it that's appealing."

Lydia gives me a blank stare. "You're on your own. I've seen my father patch up too many people to invite danger just for thrill."

I frown. "I didn't mean that. There's no thrill in watching your friend's head ooze blood."

"My point exactly."

I want to make her understand but don't want to argue. I adjust my bag on my shoulder and head to the door. "I'm going back to keep Luther company and get some studying done while he sleeps. Want to come?"

"Sure." Her face brightens, and she rolls off her bed. "And then I can make sure the nurse down at medical got his bandage right."

I laugh. "Are you sure that you don't want to switch majors and be a Healer like your dad?"

Her smile fades. "I wish I could, but it's too late for that now. I can't start over again."

"Are you still worried about the trial on Tuesday?" I ask as we head down the hall for the elevator.

"Beyond worried. Let's not talk about it."

Luther is still asleep when we get there, so we make ourselves comfortable on his second couch. I plug in my earbuds to listen to tomorrow's physical education chapter and close my eyes to focus on the concepts.

When I finish an hour later, Lydia is staring at me.

"What?" I pull out my earbuds.

Lydia rubs her eyes. "You can really listen to something and have good comprehension?"

"Sure, why not?"

She shakes her head. "You know that's rare. Most people aren't auditory learners."

"Really? You mean you don't do it?"

"I can't do it. Listening to my textbooks puts me to sleep, and my subconscious retains nothing."

"I never had a chance to listen to my textbooks before coming to Crystal." I bookmark my spot on my tablet. "I thought everyone did to save time."

She rolls her eyes. "Congratulations on being a genius."

"Hardly."

"Will you two stop arguing? You're both ridiculously smart." Luther props himself up on the couch and massages his neck. "Thanks for reminding me how far behind I am on my work."

Lydia laughs. "Welcome to the world of study groups. I'll break down our homework for you if genius here wants to put her earbuds back in."

"Be that way." I exaggerate stuffing in my earbuds. "Let me know when you two masterminds want my humble company again."

Luther tires after about an hour, and Lydia and I leave for

dinner. We take his medical note with us, hoping the cafeteria staff will understand and give us a to-go box for him.

We're fortunate today. The candidate doing head count duty shares a class with both Lydia and Luther and slips in the back to get us a box. We grab a bite to eat and hurry back to Luther's room.

We play a card game as he eats. I brew a pot of tea as Lydia puts a fresh bandage on Luther's head. We talk for another hour. The sun has long since checked out for the day, but we're reluctant to say goodbye.

And then Luther's lamp flickers and dies.

"Must be an old bulb," Luther says as I grope in the dark to find the switch to the main light.

I flip it. I flip it again. "That's odd. The overhead isn't working either."

"I'll try the bathroom," Lydia offers. Seconds later, she calls back. "No good."

I feel for my bag on the couch and fumble for my flashlight. Thank goodness it still works.

Nervous chatter fills the outside hallway. The outage isn't isolated to our room.

"Lydia, we'd better go." I sling my messenger bag back onto my shoulder. "I want to be in our room if there's another dorm check."

"Agreed." She scrapes her tablet and notes off the couch.

Luther stands and walks us to the door. "Be safe."

The hallway teems with candidates, mostly male. A few girls talk in high-pitched voices, and the din gets louder.

"Where'd you get that flashlight?" a man demands. I walk faster and shove open the stair door. Lydia's close on my heels.

Downstairs, the main lounge floods with candidates.

Moonlight streaks through the windows, and I kill my light to avoid attention.

I whisper to Lydia, "Hold my shoulder." Her trembling hand grips my jacket, and I squeeze a path through the crowd.

A microphone screeches on, and a voice drones, "Attention, all candidates, return to your rooms. A mandatory curfew is now in effect until dawn. I repeat. All candidates, return to your rooms. A mandatory curfew is now in effect."

"We've got to hurry," Lydia hisses in my ear.

"I'm trying!" The swarm of bodies reverses the current, and we're swimming against it. At last, I reach a glass door and shove it open.

The courtyard outside surges with candidates, spurred on to a stampede by the announcement that repeats ad nauseam over the loud speakers. Lydia panics and breaks into a run.

"Lydia!" I call after her, but she's gone. A candidate shoves into my side, knocking me into another. I bounce off him and back onto my feet, resisting the urge to run myself.

Instead, I find the building's perimeter and hug it closely to avoid getting swept away.

Somewhere in the dark, a hum hovers above the clamor, followed by a flash of light. A collective gasp responds to the blinding spotlights that shine onto the tallest dorm building, which happens to be my own.

There's a message in the lights. And not just any message.

Fraternitas Veritas.

The blade on my thigh burns like a brand. Who is this Brotherhood? And what is their intent?

A new and terrifying thought strikes me. What if Rogues and this Brotherhood are one and the same?

Boots march nearby and remind me of the present danger. I forgo discretion and run for my dorm as sirens blare the final curfew warning.

I step inside as the downstairs doors lock and join the last trickle of dorm residents fleeing up the stairs.

I swing open my door, collapse inside, and kick it closed.

"Portia!" Lydia rushes over to me. "I'm sorry. I don't know what came over me."

I pant for air and grab my cramping side. "It's okay."

I've barely caught my breath when someone pounds on the door.

"I'll get it," Lydia says, and I step behind her.

Petra and Gath stand there. She glances at Lydia and then me and mutters, "Both present."

As she marks her clipboard, I look at Gath, but his expression is blank.

"What happened?" Lydia asks.

"Stay in your room until dawn," Petra barks and pulls the door shut.

Lydia stares at the door, her face white with fear, but I walk to the bathroom, feeling remarkably calm. At least this time, I'm not stuck on a wall or getting dragged off to an interrogation room.

I prop my flashlight on the counter and take a quick shower. Lydia is watching the courtyard at the window when I emerge.

"They've killed the spotlights. Everything is dark."

The only exception is the Dome's peak, which glows eerily in the distance.

I rub my towel against my wet hair. "We might as well go to bed."

"But what did that message mean?" she asks.

I don't answer her question. "There's no use fretting about it tonight. Let's get some sleep. Maybe there will be answers in the morning."

Lydia shivers. "And hopefully electricity too."

"There are extra blankets in the ottoman if we need them." I flip open the top and pull one out. "I've been using them to bury our tablets at night so no one can listen in on us."

"At least someone else is taking the spotlight off you. I don't think they'll have time to eavesdrop with a real problem on their hands."

"Right?" I laugh for Lydia's sake but inwardly feel even more suspect.

Suspect, because I'm bonded by blood to this mystery Brotherhood who calls me its friend.

An hour, maybe more, passes. Lydia's deep breathing tells me she's asleep, but I can't silence the questions in my mind. Felix's assignment haunts me. The insider can't be someone as loyal as Luther or innocent as Lydia.

That leaves Foxworth. And me.

Maybe if I can find Foxworth, I can find answers.

Chapter 15

Monday, 9.14.2149
Crystal

The night's chill lingers in the dormitory the next morning, and the hallway becomes a funnel of candidates, each hoping for a hot breakfast.

And answers.

The electricity has not returned, and the outage is not isolated to our dorm. As we walk through the courtyard, the usually well-lit buildings hold only vacant, dark windows and cast long shadows.

The cafeteria offers bowls of dry cereal. There will be no hot breakfast today.

No one whispers the unspoken question. We eat in silence and shuffle to our respective classrooms.

Even I have a hard time concentrating in my two morning classes. My tight-lipped professors seem extra testy but don't spring any pop quizzes. Perhaps they know what is happening, but I suspect they don't. Their eyes hold the same anxious fatigue as our own.

Felix waits for me outside my second class. "I missed seeing you around this weekend—heard you went on a trip with your Greek and there was some nasty business involved."

"Hello, Felix. Yes, I'd rather not talk about it." I give him a terse nod and keep walking.

He jumps into step beside me. "Hold up. Here I am, concerned that you're all right, and you're acting as cold as a Trader."

I stop to glare at him. "That's not funny."

"You're right. Traders are no laughing matter."

"And what do you know about them?"

"I'm just glad to see you're safe."

"And you'd like an update."

"That would be nice—if you have something to report."

"I'm working on it. So far, I don't know anything about Danforth or Collins that would lead me to suspect them as Rogues."

Felix studies me. "What can you tell me about them?"

"They're both Court Citizen candidates. Luther seems to be the more ambitious of the two, but his record is flawless. He appears intensely loyal to the ASU."

"Hmm, what about the third candidate from 'Prase?"

"I haven't seen him since our train arrived," I lie, unflinchingly.

"Find out more about him."

I stop and cross my arms. "What if your source is wrong, and the insider isn't from my square? There are twelve other squares, you know. This could be a waste of my time."

"I have no reason to doubt my source." Felix pulls me away from the sidewalk to the building's edge. He lowers his voice. "The CGA's Commanding Gage believes there's a plot being spun inside the borders of 'Prase to aid the Rogues. Can you imagine how much more effective their attacks could become if they've weaseled one of their own inside our ranks?"

I look away, sickened by a new thought. Felix doesn't realize Eliab interrogated me on those very charges. Does Eliab still think I'm the insider—even though I passed the lie test? Or is there someone else he suspects?

Felix inches closer and squeezes my arm. "It would be nice to talk with my future Dome representative in a more relaxed setting. How about my place sometime?"

His touch gives me chills. "I don't mix business and pleasure." I keep my voice civil.

He laughs and runs his thumb along the outline of my jaw. "Aww, Frosty, you need to live a little."

I shove away from the wall and jump back to the sidewalk. "I'll let you know if I learn anything else."

"I'll be looking forward to your next update," he calls after me.

The electricity is still off when I return to my room. Lydia has pulled back the blinds so daylight pours over the library books strewn across her bed.

I toss my messenger bag onto my comforter and pull my gym clothes out of the bureau. "What are you doing?"

She groans and holds her face in her hands. "The trial for my Court Scene class is tomorrow, remember?"

"And what's all this?"

"Records of candidate trials, responses, verdicts, opinions on the verdicts …"

"You're going to do fine." I slip on my gym pants and start stretching on the floor.

"Easy for you to say. You're not the one responsible for someone's life tomorrow."

I stop mid-reach for my ankle. "Is the case that serious?"

"It could be," Lydia says. "Any of the cases could be if the two peers have something to hold against the offender."

"Aren't conflicts of interest identified in peer selection?"

She shakes her head. "Not always. Actually, because the two peers must be from the offender's field and class, I think there's always going to be some kind of bias. I wish we could increase the number of peers and mix up the demographic."

"Have you ever suggested that in class?"

"It's not my place—you know that. The job of revising the Codex belongs to the Revisionary."

I fall back onto the thinly carpeted floor. "Right, people like me."

"I sure hope you get that Doctor Revisionary seat and can start making some changes," Lydia says. "It would help my decision tremendously if you could help me not to be the deciding vote."

"But that's why we need good Court Citizens," I counter. "We need ones like you who will be impartial and actually care about the lives at stake."

"It's still too much pressure." She slams a book shut. "What if I miss something? What if I don't judge correctly? I'd rather cast my judgment after a well-rounded and impartial group of people debated the verdict."

I don't know what to say. I start doing crunches but feel the weight of her silence, expectant of an answer.

I sit up and reach for my toes. "I'll find a way to be there tomorrow."

"Thank you."

She lowers her head back into her books. I stand and slip out early for gym class. Although I don't dare tell Lydia, I'm dreading her trial tomorrow. I haven't stepped foot in a courtroom since Darius's trial.

After the regular lecture, Coach Mortimer dismisses us for the day, and I trudge to the track. It's my new post-class routine.

Plug in the earbuds. Start walking.

My classmates have grown used to the slow girl and breeze past me without as much as a glance.

All except one. A fast, lean male appears on my left and catches my eye. It's Foxworth. He speeds off before I can offer a polite greeting—or ask him about the coin he dropped.

I stop and reach inside my bag to find it, pinching it between my fingers to inspect it more closely.

As I do, the words from the Greek outing surface in my memory. *Play money.* That's what one of the men in Red's hostel had said after Gath gave Red our Greek funds.

Why did he call our currency *play money*? The ASU has been printing our notes indefinitely. I don't even know when they began printing, but the money must have started somewhere. Someone must have agreed on their worth.

Their worth in what?

Too many questions overwhelm my mind. Who decides what a piece of paper is worth? Is it worth anything if not backed by something?

I clench the coin in my fist and watch Foxworth continue running his laps. And what was this coin worth? What was five cents?

What does it matter?

My head hurts, and I don't have the energy to chase down Foxworth for answers. I stuff the coin back into my bag and trudge around the track, feeling trapped in a world that grows more counterfeit with each passing day.

A foreboding grips my chest as I mount the stairs to the judgment court in the Globe. I haven't seen Lydia all day. She left before I woke this morning.

My first two classes drag, and all I can think of are the judgment seat, Lydia seated at it, and the back of a nameless person standing with his head bowed, pleading for her mercy.

I hate my imagination.

When I reach the entrance, a Gage stands like a statue at the door.

"Excuse me, where do I go for the candidate trial?"

He opens his marble-like mouth. "Down the hall to your right."

"Thank you." I slip down the long hall. A few other candidates are milling about, and I mingle with them until they move inside.

I slide into a back seat to watch and open a blank document on my tablet to take notes.

The Court Citizen's seat is empty. Lydia must be somewhere in the back.

A Gage marches the offender into the courtroom. The young man's face is a stoic sheet, and he holds himself stiffly as if bracing for a blow.

The Gage motions for him to be seated as a second Gage accompanies two candidates about my age, a female and male, to the front of the courtroom. The two peers take their seats below the Court Citizen's and wait for Lydia to appear.

She emerges from a back room, dressed in a black robe, her brown hair pulled tightly back. Her face is pale and blank, but her jaw is firm.

As she steps to the bench, the crier calls the court to order. "All rise for the Honorable Court Citizen Collins."

She clears her throat and begins in a low, level voice. "Ladies and Gentlemen of the Court, you are witness to the case of Candidate James Clancy versus the Crystal Gage Administration. Candidate Clancy is accused of aiding and abetting in the tampering of the Crystal Globe's electrical station last week, which left the grid vulnerable to an attack over the weekend.

"His accomplice fled upon Gage attempts at questioning and committed suicide. As the deceased candidate's roommate, Candidate Clancy is suspected of assisting in the unlawful and forced entrance at the electrical outpost. The Court's intent today is to examine the evidence and determine the defendant's role in this act and what, if any, consequences should result.

"Acting as peers are two members of the defendant's electrical engineering class. We will first hear the defense."

Lydia takes her seat as a stout man moves toward the front. Behind him to the left waits the thin young man, his hands clasped on the table. His face, set like a flint, watches his counsel step to the front.

"Ladies and Gentlemen of the Court, I present the defense of James Clancy, second year candidate at the Crystal Globe." The man's voice is loud and crass.

The bellicose voice continues, agonizing over each adjective in his sentences. "Candidate Clancy, in his second term at this university, ranks among the highest in his class for all subjects. He has demonstrated considerable prowess in his field and received nothing but accolades from his professors. He has donated considerable amounts of his time to volunteering in the engineering lab to assist first year candidates. To date, he has received no correctives for any misconduct. His personal records speak to his integrity and ethic. The defendant therefore pleads not guilty to the accusations against him."

I sigh with relief when the counsel returns to his seat. His testimony, short in words, was long in syllables.

"Will the prosecution rise?" Lydia speaks from her seat.

A small man with robust step appears at the front.

"Ladies and Gentlemen of the Court," he begins with efficient charm, "the defendant has made no real defense—other than to paint a reputation that could be said of most candidates enrolled in the Crystal Globe. As you know, this university has built its success on drafting the finest minds in our land. Unfortunately, nature being what it is, I argue the case that wolves have slipped into our midst, their brilliant facades overshadowing their ravenous motives.

"It is true: the defendant presents a healthy record of accomplishments both intellectual and applied. However, let me call into question his choice of companions. The recently deceased Edward Gall was both his roommate and classmate. Gall repeatedly received correctives for uncivil conduct. Some of his actions included disrespect toward authority, tampering with state property, misuse of facilities, and hacking into electrical codes.

"Last Sunday, the evening of Greek night, his fingerprints

matched those found responsible for temporarily shutting down the grid. May I remind you that the ensuing chaos cost several candidates their lives.

"Such a large-scale operation could not have been carried out single-handedly. It is my accusation that his roommate James Clancy sympathized with and assisted in his crimes."

The prosecution turns to Lydia. "Your Honor, I request permission to question the defendant."

"Permission granted. Defendant Clancy, please take the stand."

Clancy rigidly walks forward.

"Candidate Clancy, would you please tell the court your whereabouts on Sunday evening, September sixth?"

"I was in the courtyard along with the rest of the candidate body."

"And what were you doing in the courtyard?"

"Helping man my Greek's initiation booth."

"To which Greek do you belong?" The prosecution's questions fly like darts.

The defendant's answers are just as pointed. "Alphas."

"What is your role in that Greek?"

"Member."

The prosecution frowns and takes a new approach. "Where exactly were you when the outage occurred?"

"At my Greek's initiation booth."

"Can anyone verify this?"

"Ask any one of my Greek's officers."

The prosecution shifts his weight. "Last Thursday, Gages confronted your roommate, because his fingerprints were found in the electrical room. After a scuffle, he escaped them, climbed the clock tower in the courtyard, and then jumped to his death."

Someone moves on my far right, and I tense. It's Felix. He nods at me, a fierce glint in his eyes.

And then I realize why he's here. This must be the case against the Rogue insider he told me about.

"Where were you when all this took place?"

"In class."

"Did you know of your roommate's schemes against the Crystal Globe?"

"I knew he had been in trouble before."

"Specifically, did you know about his role in the electrical breach?"

A pause. "No."

"You knew nothing whatsoever about what he was planning, even though he shared a room with you?"

"My roommate was a very private person."

"Answer the question." The prosecution raises his voice. "Did you, or did you not know anything about your roommate's intentions?"

James Clancy gives the prosecution a cold, hard stare. "If I did, I wouldn't tell you."

The courtroom breathes a collective gasp.

The prosecution waves his hand in a triumphant flourish. "Then by your own mouth you confess your sympathy with this traitor."

The prosecution takes his seat, while the defendant's counsel requests permission to question the defendant.

"Were your fingerprints found in the electrical room?"

"No, they were not."

"Was any evidence found to connect you with the deceased

man's plot against Crystal?"

"No, there was not."

"Is it correct to say that the prosecution does not have any tangible evidence to connect you with the electrical outage incidents?"

"That is correct."

"That is all, Your Honor."

The questions are perfunctory but fill me with new hope for the defendant's case.

But then, the prosecution rises to resume his volley against the defendant. I close my eyes and see another courtroom, much like this one. Much like today, the prosecution in my memory draws out the battle, interrogating the young man on the defense stand. His handsome face is taut with strain but set with grim determination.

The lighting reflects off his hair, highlighting its reddish hues that match the fire in his heart.

Darius was an old twenty-two, two years behind most in his class. Throughout his undergrad, he dragged his feet through his courses. His professors envied his IQ which ranked off the charts, but they wearied of his intentional attempts to fail their classes. The only areas where he allowed himself to excel were the regimental exercises of the Coast Guard and the training of a Tooler. Yes, Darius could design and build anything. His unmatched vigor and mental acumen were the envy of his peers and the admiration of not a few females.

It came as no surprise when, despite his façade of failing grades, the draft board called his name and insisted upon his entrance into the Crystal Globe University—with a dual major, no less—something practically unheard of.

And it came as an even lesser surprise to those who knew him best when Darius refused to comply.

Lydia's voice brings me back to the present.

"The peers will now present their verdicts."

Two sour-faced candidates stand, their twin demeanors suggesting a pre-meditated response.

"Guilty," the first says.

The second echoes the first.

A murmur fills the courtroom. No tangible evidence had been presented—only implied guilt, the art of a seasoned prosecution. Yet the accused now faces an imminent satellite sentence, the duration of which can only be tempered by the Court Citizen.

All eyes turn to Lydia. A man's life weighs in the balance.

"Not guilty." I move my lips but speak the words only in my heart.

Calm passes over Lydia's face. She stands straighter and considers the gavel in her hand. She bangs it on the base to drive home her judgment.

"Not guilty." Her voice is clear and confident. "The defendant will serve a two-year satellite term and return to his home square for remediation and a work assignment. Case dismissed."

The courtroom buzzes with voices, everyone talking at once. The prosecution protests the sentence and studies Lydia through snake eyes.

The defendant's face is a mixture of shock and hope. His counsel stands and follows the Gages and his client through the back door.

I slip out of my seat and hurry outside, suddenly aware of the time. I have less than ten minutes to make my Simulation class.

A commotion on the far side of the courthouse sends me

running to where Gages are breaking up a crowd, cuffing some and cursing at others.

When the scene clears, the bloody face of the defendant emerges.

"What happened?" I demand of a fellow candidate.

"I think it was the Gages," she says. "They suddenly turned and beat the candidate they were escorting from the courthouse. Some candidates saw it and tried to pull them off the handcuffed man, but now, they're a bloody mess too."

Enforcers abusing power and using it against the people they were meant to protect.

Gath's words return to me like a prophecy.

I want to weep. There is no hope of justice anymore.

Chapter 16

Tuesday, 9.15.2149

Crystal

I take my seat in Simulation, finding small comfort in a cupcake that Jael brings me.

"It's red velvet with dark chocolate icing." She licks her lips. "I made a batch this morning. They're good."

"How did you manage that?" I ask, accepting one. "I don't have enough means to make even a pancake in my dorm."

She gives me a secretive grin. "I'm resourceful. Let's leave it at that."

I crack a smile as she innocently offers one to Felix, who refuses with icy politeness.

Jael turns back to me, her face crestfallen.

"If he doesn't want it, I'll take a second back to my roommate." I make a face at Felix. "This is delicious."

"I hope you spent as much time on our rough draft as you did your cupcakes." He walks past her to my desk.

"What's bothering you?" I lick frosting off my fingers.

"I saw you at the courthouse." He lowers his voice. "You saw what happened, too."

"Yes, Lydia asked me to come." I turn to face him. "What do you mean?"

"I thought you said you didn't suspect her."

"I don't."

"She let that candidate off easy—way too easy."

I shake my head. "No, there wasn't enough evidence to convict him. I thought she did the right thing."

"The right thing?" Felix spats. "Whose side are you on?"

I glare at him. "I'm on the side of justice."

Jael's voice intervenes. "Hey, guys, are we all agreed on our final thesis? Do you want to hear it one last time?"

"Sure." I welcome a change of topic.

"I advise you to keep a closer eye on your roommate," Felix mutters and returns to his seat.

"Okay, here's what we've got." Jael scrolls on her tablet and begins reading:

Although the Declaration marks a brave attempt to establish order and civility, it nevertheless fails as a codex, because its contempt for established government ultimately necessitates a return to the imperative it once shunned.

"Sounds good to me," I say.

Felix grunts his consent.

Mortimer calls the class to attention. "Please have your designated group member submit your thesis and outlines at this time."

"That's you, Jael," I whisper. She beams with importance and goes to work on her tablet.

"Please upload your documents to the folder called 'Group Tank.' You should see it in your candidate portal. This location allows you to view each other's submissions. Today, you will be responsible for critiquing each other's work while your groups take turns participating in a five-minute introductory Simulation on your historical document.

"We won't waste any time getting started. Group Abernathy, please step forward. The rest of you, download the critiquing instructions and pace yourselves. Don't forget you have five submissions to critique."

I follow Felix to the front where Mortimer programs our Simulation. His fingers race with familiarity over the control panel. A small light illuminates our feet. The semi-transparent flooring in this room begins to make sense. It is not merely a glossy vinyl but part of the technology interface. It allows Mortimer to control the size of the Simulation, ranging from the breadth of the classroom to a tight square beneath our feet.

He presses a final algorithm into the computer and turns to our group, pointing his bony finger at me. "Remember, your role is observation—not engagement."

The blinding light fades into a translucent blue. The floor beneath our feet transforms into a dusty, dirty lane.

We're standing at the corner of two streets, Seventh and Market, on the threshold of a three-story house.

I hesitate. "Should we knock?"

"No, go on in." Felix motions for me to move forward. "This is Simulation, not a course on courtesy."

My hand grasps the faded brass knob, but someone pulls open the door, sending me staggering inside.

"Oh, pardon me, miss! Can I help you?" A sturdy man with rough hands and an honest face blinks at me in surprise.

"Excuse me," I stammer. "I'm sorry. I'm—my name is Portia—and I'm—I mean, we're—looking for—Mr. Jefferson ..."

His face cracks into a smile. "Pleased to meet you, Miss Portia. I'm Jacob Graff, the bricklayer. Mr. Jefferson and his guests are upstairs, second floor."[iii]

Felix skirts past me, an impatient glower on his face.

"Thanks!" I hurry to chase him up the stairs while Jael pants behind me.

Felix glares at me. "Did you hear what Mortimer said?"

"I can't invite myself into someone else's house," I protest. "Besides, Mr. Graff was right at the door. I had to say something."

"Graff? You bothered with that commoner's name? Bah! Frosty, focus on what matters. We've got five minutes, maybe four, thanks to you."

Felix swings open the second-floor door. Three men huddle around a small writing box and appear too engrossed in their work to notice us.

"It's them!" I whisper in tense excitement. "The writers of the Declaration—Jefferson, Adams and Franklin."

"Shh!" Felix smacks me across the face.

The oldest of the three gentlemen peers over small, round spectacles at Felix. "Chivalry, man! Temper your conduct. That's no way to treat the fairer sex."

Felix's face flushes, and he steps back into the recesses of the parlor, while Jael peeks through the doorway.

Benjamin Franklin motions with his hand. "Come, my dear, are you all right?"

I nod and slowly step forward.

"Jefferson, your writing is sublime!" Adams slams his fist on the table and looks over to the younger man on his left.

Jefferson jumps to his feet and paces the floor, paper in hand. "We're closer, but the words are inadequate. But can you see plainly the common sense of the subject?"

His ink-stained hands grip the rolled draft.

"Yes, plainly," Adams insists. "It's worlds better than anything my obtuse style could have reasoned out. I knew you were the man for the job."

Jefferson's sigh suggests he isn't convinced.

Franklin starts reading again, soon forgetting my presence. I squint over his shoulder. The sunlight from the window warms me with expectancy.

The writing is so slanted and scribbled that I can barely make it out. "We hold these truths to be—*self-evident*; that all men are created *equal*."

"My dear, you read masterfully." Franklin smiles, and I blush, not realizing I had spoken the words.

I hesitate. "Why did you cross out *and independent*?"

"We aren't created independent and free. We must fight for it!" Adams pounds his fist again.

Jefferson's voice moderates Adams' passion. "We must depend on each other and the sovereignty of Providence."

"But go on," Franklin encourages. "The next clause expounds on our equality and substantiates the inherent justness of our cause."

I continue, unable to keep a tremor from my voice, "… that from that equal creation they derive rights, inherent and inalienable …"

"Stop." Jefferson frowns. "Too weak."

"Right," Adams agrees. "Shift the focus to the authority of the Endower to bestow the rights, therefore making unquestionable the authenticity of the creation's claim ..."

Franklin cocks his head. "Adams, your thought is genius, but your words are ponderous."

"I know it." Adams chuckles. "That's why we've got Jefferson here. Jefferson?"

Jefferson's eyes, closed from concentration, suddenly flash open. He slaps his paper onto the table and scribbles furiously, muttering each word with forcefulness. "... that they are *endowed* by their Creator with *certain unalienable rights*; that among these are life, liberty, and the pursuit of happiness."

"That's it!" Adams slaps Jefferson on the shoulder.

Franklin resumes scanning his page of the document, muttering to himself. *Of the people, by the people and for the people.* He sighs and takes off his spectacles. "It's pure poetry. Reasoned eloquence."

Adams nods. "Simple and sublime."

"And common sense." Jefferson taps his quill. "Our argument is reasonable, and our cause is proper."

The candid, authentic relationship of these three endears them to me. Their faces begin to blur, and I close my eyes, not wanting to leave and never wanting to forget the hallowed intimacy of the second-floor parlor.

The blow of a cane against my neck brings my reality into focus with painful clarity. I block a second blow, and when Mortimer strikes at me a third time, I respond with such force that the weapon flies out of his hand.

"Abernathy!" His voice holds nothing but daggers. "I warned you not to engage."

I stand straight and defiant.

"Retrieve my cane."

"No." The brave men in the brick house on Seventh and Market have breathed new courage into me.

"No?" Mortimer's eyes narrow into cadaverous slits.

With all eyes on me, I turn to my class and speak the words branded on my mind.

We hold these truths to be self-evident, that all men are created equal, that they are endowed by their Creator with certain unalienable rights, that among these are life, liberty and the pursuit of happiness.

For a moment, a spell falls on the room, as the words reverberate off the walls and penetrate our hearts.

Then, an alarm sounds, and a red light flashes at the side door. Mortimer grabs my arm with a claw-like grip and marches me toward it.

"Pray your correctives level you out this time, or you'll never survive the next round," he minces the words.

Jael gasps behind me as two Gages appear at the door.

Eliab stands there with Gath at his side. Gath's face is blank. He stares straight ahead as Mortimer shoves me into his grip.

Eliab's face contorts to a scowl. "Somehow, I knew it would be you." I look back to catch Felix's eyes that flash with both suspicion and fear.

"Take her away," Mortimer hisses.

I twist out of Gath's grip to face him. "On what crime?" I demand. Gath reapplies his grasp, firmer this time. He pins my arms behind me and pulls me toward his chest.

Mortimer arches his eyes. "On disrespect of authority."

"Disrespect!" I shoot back at him. "You disrespect us—your

candidates—and do us great disservice by not encouraging our questions and participation."

I rush on. "You fear learning. You fear the truth, and so you conceal it. You bully us with abuses. You want us to accept your word without question. That is not the mark of a real teacher. A real teacher—"

"Silence!" Mortimer screeches. "Be gone with you. Come back only if you learn the error of your ways."

I fight Gath who is trying to lead me away. "And what is my error? Am I not to even know my crime?"

"Your crime is against civility," he condemns.

"Civility?" I bite the words with my teeth. "I call for equality and liberty, and you accuse me of not being civil? A difference of opinion should not be a crime."

Murmurs fill the classroom behind me, and some candidates rise from their seats and stand in their chairs.

Mortimer glares at Eliab. "Can you not silence her?"

"Muzzle the beast," Eliab snarls at Gath.

"State my crime." I spit at him before Gath's hand covers my mouth.

"You sympathize with the reasoning of a failed document, misuse Simulation technology to flatter your own fancy, and wrongly interpret our Codex based on your false assumptions." Mortimer's voice rises to shout above the din breaking out in the classroom.

Candidates pound their arms into the air and call for my release.

Another alarm flashes to the right as Gath drags me through an outdoor exit to a waiting vehicle and pushes me inside.

A third Gage appears, his face anxious. "Sir, the class is in an uproar. If word gets out, we could have a riot on our hands."

Riot. The word stirs up memories from Darius's trial. The resulting riot cost several cube dwellers, and not a few Gages, their lives.

Eliab's face flares. "Lock down the auditorium. No one leaves, and no one enters until I get back. Until then, you're in charge. Call for backup if you need it. I expect to find this situation diffused when I return."

With that, Eliab jumps in the other side of the vehicle, pinning me in the small space between him and Gath. His lifeless black eyes bore through me. "Your brother's riot cost me three good men and stripped me of my rank. It took me five years to regain my command and another four to get where I am today. I'm not about to let another Abernathy do any more damage."

"I have done nothing wrong other than express an opinion," I retort.

He slugs me in the face. Hard.

I try to shake off the pain to my upper cheek. The dim memory of a kindly man peering out from behind round spectacles gives me hope.

Hope that at one point in history, men knew how to be kind.

When the car lurches to a stop, Eliab shoves me out the door behind Gath, and I stumble into him. His face holds no memory of last weekend. I try to shake a sense of loss.

He slaps cuffs onto my wrists, and we march in silence except for the crackling of the gravel beneath our feet.

Armed Gages stand post around the wire fenced compound. The Merlin falcon insignia blazes in the afternoon sunlight above the entrance. Eliab shows his badge at the door, and we pass through.

The inside lobby smells sterile like a Healer's home. Half a dozen candidates sit in the room, staring at their hands or the floor. Their shoulders sag. A screen reads a script. There are no images, only droning words.

Gath checks me in at the counter.

"Portia Abernathy," he tells the woman. Her frizzed, buzz-cut hair and chopped movements are more machine-like than human.

She pulls the file and reads it mechanically. "Abernathy has one minor corrective to date. Take her to 104 for stage one treatment."

"Up it to stage five," Eliab orders. My chest tightens, fearing his meaning.

The woman types on her screen. "Room 515 is ready for stage five treatment."

"Sir?" Gath speaks at last.

"What?" Eliab snaps as the woman slides him an authorization slip.

"Is stage five necessary? A smaller dose may suffice."

"Are you questioning me?"

My breath catches in my throat. Gath is advocating for me.

"Respectfully, I request permission to administer a stage one dose first," he levels his voice. "For many candidates, that is enough. And this one is so small."

"Request denied." Eliab scratches his signature on the paper and pushes it back toward the woman. "If you won't administer the corrective treatment, I'll do it myself."

"No, I'll do it." Gath grips my arm and yanks me after Eliab. We enter and climb five levels up a contorted staircase. The metal floor moans with each step as if mourning the fates of those who have passed before me.

I'm out of breath at the top. The blinding white hallway opens like a throat at the stairway's exit. Windowless, heavy doors line the corridor.

Soundproof doors. How many screams have they swallowed?

I force myself to focus on details.

Eliab enters a four-digit code outside a door, and it automatically opens.

Inside is a small room, fearfully cold. An examination room. There is a long chair, medical prep table and sanitizing station, but all unlike anything I've ever seen in a medical center.

Injectables, syringes, and a control box line the prep table. Out of the box are wires that connect to a dial on the chair.

The chair.

It looks like the creation of a madman.

It's a translucent emerald color. Floating weightlessly inside are corpuscles—something I might read about in a biochemistry textbook. I have never seen anything like it before.

The door locks behind us. Gath opens my cuffs, releases his grip, and moves toward the prep table.

I rub my wrists and narrow my eyes at Eliab. "What is this?"

"Beautiful, isn't it?" He steps toward the chair and slides his fingers over the arm. The floating cells migrate to his touch and disperse as he yanks his finger away.

He repeats the motion. It's like he's arousing barracuda with bait.

"The technology we've developed at Crystal is truly remarkable," he continues, waving a hand over the whole chair as if to arouse it from slumber.

"The chair is heat activated. Our biochemists engineered sensory receptacles that attract and pull toward human flesh through temperature suggestion. The more extreme the temperature, the faster the attachment. Even more amazing is the cell's programmable nature and auto-suggestive power.

"The chair is composed of millions of these cells. The conductive glass chair mold that separates you from this biochemical pool serves as a conductor to bind flesh and science fiction together."

My mind pounds. *To what purpose?*

But fear is Eliab's food. I refuse to feed the beast and remain silent while trying to work my way toward the door.

"We began *testing* the machine's auto-suggestive abilities on criminals. Many of the laboratory tests were too extreme, but there were more than enough subjects to serve the experiments until we reined in the right balance."

He studies me with a smirk. "It's too bad we didn't start developing this technology until seven years ago. Your brother would have made a perfect test subject."

I clench my fists and eye the keypad next to the door.

The chair begins to hum. I jerk my head to look at Gath who stands above the controls with grim determination.

"This machine has reformed many candidates with its corrective abilities. They leave *changed*."

"Changed how?" I stare as the corpuscles begin to vibrate and am unable to mask my terror any longer.

"Changed from rebels into model citizens," he laughs. "Oh, trust me, you'll feel every excruciating tremor as the chair reprograms your thinking with the utmost fidelity to our system.

"You might stay in the top of your class, lacking nothing— nothing, that is, except your *personality*."

I am almost to the door and can practically feel the access

keyboard. Eliab sneers at my desperate attempt. But when I replicate his four-digit code and the door clicks open, his smile fades. He lunges toward me as I fly out the doorway but misses and trips over a wire.

"After her!" he curses.

I run. Never fast enough.

Gath tackles me before I can reach the stairs.

"Gath!" I plead, trying to pry off his iron grip. "Please! Don't do this!"

There's a sharp pain in my thigh as if I've been stabbed. I collapse onto the floor, my leg instantly numb and my world growing fuzzy.

Gath presses his lips against my ear. There's the faintest whisper. *Fraternitas Veritas.*

He drags me like a limp doll back to the room and lowers me onto the steaming chair. Icy cold fingers prick every cell of my body, but I'm soon too anesthetized to care.

"What did you do to her?" Eliab's roar sounds like a distant bell tolling.

"She hit her head on the stairs pretty bad. Don't worry. She'll be reformed once we're done."

"But I want to hear her scream!"

There's a flash of light, and the glowing fog consumes me.

And then, nothingness.

PART TWO TEST OF ALLEGIANCE

Chapter 17

Wednesday, 10.14.2149
Crystal

The morning yawns, stretching its first light through the window onto my face. I flutter my lashes and feel a change, a reset somewhere behind my eyes.

I blink. Scales fall from my imprisoned memory. My vision is clear, but now I actually *see*.

I prop myself up on a pillow and recoil at the sight of my limbs. My skin is a hideous gray. My arms are taut muscle and bone.

To my left, Lydia is asleep. She looks beautiful, peaceful, alive.

I step out of bed, and the floor feels strange. Maybe the feeling has less to do with the floor and more with my legs. They seem strangely strong for looking as ghostly as they do.

I face the bathroom mirror.

A stranger stares back at me, but there's life in her eyes. A faint color creeps into her cheeks.

I wash my face five times, hoping to recognize myself. I shower, and then shower again.

My skin is now bright pink from the scalding water.

Wrapping myself in a towel, I yank open the cabinet drawers, searching for Lydia's makeup. I feel a desperate need to look alive.

As I start to swipe on mascara, the bathroom door opens. I clutch my towel tightly with my left hand.

"What are you doing?" Lydia asks.

My right hand trembles. "What does it look like?" I scratch my eye with the brush and drop the small thing in the sink. I rest my elbows on the counter and stare into the mirror. And uncontrollably burst into tears.

Lydia gasps and puts her hand to her mouth. "You're back!" She hugs me so tightly I can barely breathe.

But her touch sends me into another fit of sobs.

Gently, she slides a bathrobe over my towel so that I can discreetly slip out of it. I tighten the belt and let her lead me to the couch where steaming hot tea waits.

I wipe my face with my sleeve. "You already made tea?"

"I do every morning," she says. "I have every day for the last month, hoping you'll come back."

"Where was I?" I reach for a cup, but my hand shakes.

"Trapped inside yourself." She reaches to steady my hand. "At least, that's how Gath explained it. But he promised it would be temporary. I was beginning to worry he was wrong."

"Gath?" I repeat.

"Yes, he—he brought you back to my room late one night. I'll never forget that day. It was the day I oversaw my first trial as

Court Citizen. You were there. It meant a lot that you came. I wanted to tell you that, but you didn't come back to our room like you usually do after your last class.

"I went to the lecture hall where you have your Simulation class. Or at least, I tried to go there. It was roped off. I was able to gather the pieces of what happened from a few classmates of yours.

"They said one candidate engaged in a Simulation with more involvement than the professor allowed. When she returned, he tried to beat her, but she withstood him. She accused him of abusing his power as a teacher, making an argument against him using a former codex.

"He called Gages to take her away. Something she said stirred the class to her side. No sooner did the Gages haul her away than a whole troop was sent to quell the ensuing class riot."

Lydia pauses. "One girl named Jael—she said she was in your group—identified the candidate as you."

"Jael." The name makes me smile.

"Several candidates were injured and disappeared for the rest of the day. When they returned, and when you returned, you were all *changed*."

My head throbs as I try to remember.

Lydia refills my tea. "Luther and I were worried. When you didn't show up to the track to run with him, he came and found me. I told him what I knew, and we waited. And waited. He refused to go back to his room, not wanting to miss you when you returned.

"It had to be around 0300 hours before Gath showed up at our door. He was carrying what looked like a body bag. We thought you were dead.

"Gath didn't say a word but dropped you on the floor and left, refusing to answer Luther's questions. When we untied the bag, the sight of you made me burst into tears." Lydia bites her lip.

"You were as gray as a corpse, worse than you look now. There are several candidates around campus that look like you do, including several from your Simulation class.

"When you finally woke up, you said you were fine and that you had homework to do. We couldn't reach you—the real you. You talked, walked, and went about your day like nothing had happened, but you were like a breathing ghost."

I drain my second cup of tea. It burns my throat in a good way. "For how long?"

"Today is four weeks, exactly."

"Four weeks?" I gasp. "I don't remember a thing. What have I been doing all this time?"

"Going to class, getting good grades, eating, drinking, sleeping." She stops short. "Everything but living."

"I'm still getting good grades? I don't remember ..."

"Actually living any of it?" Lydia suggests. "That's what Gath said might happen. He said there could be an amnesia when you regained your personality."

"My personality?"

Lydia looks down. "Gath told Luther what happened to you, but neither would tell me. They said it would be—too much for me to take. So, they called it *personality amnesia* and left it at that."

"But you said Gath left me for dead." I struggle with the words as a face forms in my memory.

"He did," Lydia says gently, "but he found Luther a few days later. He explained to him what had happened and told us what signs to look for that you were recovering. He promised you would recover, unlike some of the others."

The dam holding back my memory suddenly breaks open. I

see Franklin, Jefferson, and Adams, then feel Mortimer's cane break down on my neck. There's the class argument, the appearance of Eliab and Gath. A hallway, a hideous chair. I escape, only to be re-captured by Gath. He jabs something in my thigh and carries me to the chair. I am dizzy, deadening the pain. *Fraternitas Veritas.*

I fall face down into a pillow on the couch to catch the uncalled-for tears. They flow fast, like a river that has just been unplugged.

Lydia's hand squeezes my shoulder. "It's okay."

I wheeze and look at her. "Nothing here is okay. It's not okay that I've been acting like a zombie for a month. It's not okay that Crystal thinks they have the right to wipe personalities that disagree with them. And it's not okay that Crystal scientists have designed biochemical torture machines to reprogram individual thinking."

I gasp for breath and suck down the sobs. They won't accomplish anything.

I spring from the couch toward the bathroom to splash away the traces of tears and retrieve the mascara applicator. I am ready to live again. I am ready to fight.

"Wait," Lydia says as I apply my first coating.

"What?"

"I know you want to look human again, but think about what that means." She pries the applicator from my fingers. "If you start to look like yourself, don't you think everyone will notice? You're better off looking like a gray ghost and staying under everyone's radar."

I take the applicator from Lydia and shove it back in its tube. Resisting the urge to comb my hair, I settle for running my fingers through it.

Lydia begins her own makeup, but not even eye shadow and mascara can hide the tired look in her eyes.

"Other than being worried sick about me the last month, how are things going with you?"

She turns to look at me with sadness. "Well, I've learned that the Crystal Globe is all about knowing the right people and how to please them."

She's aching inside and not just for me.

"Are things not going well in Court Scene?"

"Not for me anyway." She sighs. "Do you remember the trial you watched?"

"Um, yes. It's a little fuzzy, but yes. You gave the candidate a two-year term on a satellite."

"I did what I felt was right. There wasn't enough evidence to condemn his life, but later, I learned my professor and peers expected me to judge him guilty. I scored low marks for showing him mercy. And for what purpose? Gages interrogated him to death that evening. Someone thought he knew something more than he was telling."

Felix thought there was a third insider.

"That's awful."

"We're in the same boat. We've both lost our chance to get to the Dome."

"I thought you said my grades were fine?"

"They are, but let's not fool ourselves." She powders her nose. "You and I both know Felix Caesura is in your class, and he's been a rising star over the last month. In light of all the incidents around Crystal and the class revolt you incited, he began championing a program called *See-Say-Save*—a pretty name for a tattling competition. Anyone who sees or suspects disloyal behavior must report anonymously to the CGA."

"Thus, *saving* a life," I mutter.

"I've seen him several times walking with a Gage, and he's fast becoming a campus icon. You may be as smart as he is, but like I said, this place is all about who you know."

Lydia pauses and forces a half smile. "At least Luther still has a shot at the Dome. His turn for a trial isn't for another few weeks, and that's assuming there's a case for him to reside over. Since you stirred the pot, things have been pretty quiet. I think everyone is spooked by all the gray faces on campus."

We grab our bags and head for the door. I pause with my hand on the knob. "Did Gath say if—if my skin color will return to normal?"

"Yes, once your outer skin cells replace themselves, you'll look good as new. You already look better than you did."

I grimace. "That's not very reassuring."

"The key is how you act," Lydia says, giving me a playful shove out the door. "Don't talk unless asked a question. Don't smile. Don't show emotion. Don't say what you want to say."

That won't be easy. "I'll do my best."

"The good news is that fall break starts in two days." Lydia follows me down the stairs. "Get through today and tomorrow, and you'll have a long week at home to avoid public attention."

I nearly trip on the last step. "Home? I'm getting to go home?"

"You're not a threat any more, remember? I went with you to fill out your application to go home for the break. There were a limited number of train seats, but we were both accepted."

"I don't remember any of that." We step outside. The cold, bitter air bites my cheeks, but then, we're into October now.

"I keep forgetting you now have the opposite problem." She falls into step beside me. "I'll try to fill you in on everything that's happened around here since September, but you're on your own to make sure you're ready for class today."

While we wait in the breakfast line, I pull my tablet out and begin scanning the coursework from the last several weeks.

The information is overwhelming. I open the announcements tab to make sure I'm aware of any time-sensitive information from my professors when I see one pop-up reminder from my adviser Lucius.

The announcement reads: *Reminder to schedule nine-week review and compatibility testing.*

I press the cancel button so hard I smudge the screen.

"Put that away, and eat something." Lydia takes my tablet and slips it into my bag. I turn my attention to a heaping plateful of bacon and eggs, the first food I remember eating in weeks. I try to take in everything Lydia tells me and hurry to class early to continue reviewing my assignments.

Sitting like a dumb mute in class turns out to be easy since I feel lost in the lesson. I skim read during class to catch up and squeak out a low A in a pop quiz. At least I haven't lost my edge for picking up on the professor's context clues.

I'm exhausted by noon and sleep until Simulation class, looking ever the part of a zombie when I reach class.

Jael slouches in front of me, not bothering to say hello. I resist the urge to talk to her. In front of her sits Felix who doesn't acknowledge me either.

"Before we get started, please submit the final draft of your group project," Mortimer begins.

I'm relieved that at least in this class, I have a reference point.

We had just started our preliminary outlines on the group project a month ago. I don't remember doing any of the research for it, but apparently, I contributed my share.

"Your group's designated spokesman will present and defend your thesis," Mortimer continues. "A few groups will present today, and the rest will share theirs the week you return from break. Once all projects have been presented, you will then begin your first individual Simulation assignments."

"Have you submitted ours yet, Jael?" Felix asks impatiently.

"Almost done." Her voice belongs to an abused dog.

"Well, hurry up."

I bite my lip and pull up the project file and my individual submission.

I don't recognize my own writing. It sounds like Professor Mortimer more than me.

When Mortimer calls for our group spokesman, Felix rises from his seat and steps to the front of the classroom.

He begins with a superior air. "Our project was to examine the Declaration of Independence and show the lesson from history it demonstrates. Our thesis was as follows:

The Declaration stands as a marked example of a failed codex, because the eventual consequence of a country that begins with contempt for established government and order necessitates an end that requires a return to the same imperative it once shunned.

"I'd like to share with you today how it stands as a magnificent failure in light of our own Codex."

I'm no longer listening, too distracted by the changes to our original thesis. Felix has removed any mention of the Declaration's merits. He's spooning words the professor wants to hear.

My gray ghost cover conceals the fire seething inside.

By the end of class, I feel a new sensation, a pent-up tension inside my tendons and muscles. I hurry back to my room, replace my classwork with my gym bag, and head for the track. A strange muscle memory makes me leave my earbuds and tablet in my bag and start stretching.

For a run.

Yes, I have a desire to run.

Before I can begin to understand it, I'm jogging around the track. I'm by no means fast, but my breathing comes clean and regulated. I brace myself for a side cramp. None comes.

Lap two. Lap three. Lap four. I increase my speed, wondering how long this ability will last.

My legs burn as I reach the one-mile mark. I slow to a stop and find Luther watching me from a bench.

He holds out a water canteen. "Just a sip."

I guzzle it.

"Whoa!" he snatches it away. "That's enough. You've got more running to do."

I gasp. "More?"

"Have you forgotten everything I've taught you about pacing yourself?" He caps the canteen and tosses it into his bag.

"After mile two, you can give everything you have left, but we've got to keep working to increase your stamina if you're going to be ready for the mandatory track exercises after break."

I fall to the ground laughing. "You're telling me that I can run two miles, no sweat?"

"What's wrong with you?" Luther asks. "Of course, you can."

I sit up and feel my legs. No wonder I didn't recognize them this morning. They are taut and muscular, not from starvation, but from training. I reach to stretch and touch my toes just because I can.

Luther lowers himself onto the ground close to me and grabs my hand. He spins me to look him in the eyes. "You're back!"

He throws his arms around me. His warmth makes me feel alive again.

"I can run!" I pull back and smile into his eyes. "You've taught me how to run? I don't remember it."

"All that matters is that you remember who you are," he whispers. "Finally. I was beginning to worry you'd never snap out of it."

"But you believed in me the whole time?" I clutch his hand tighter. "You believed I'd come back, so you kept training me?"

Only a friend would do that.

Luther responds by drawing me to his chest. "Gath said you would. I wanted to believe him, so I did." His lips brush my hair.

I pull back to see tears in his eyes and then hungrily take in the details of his face. His cheeks are ruddy, glowing with color. Then there's his strong nose and full lips—how much I have missed seeing them, or at least remembering them!

I blush and look away, suddenly ashamed of my own ugly skin. "I'm sorry I look awful. Lydia says it's my best cover until I get my bearings."

"You've never looked more beautiful."

"Liar."

He laughs. "Okay, you could use a makeover, but I know the beauty beneath. I see the life in your eyes. And that's enough for me."

"Good answer," I grin. "Want to go for a run?"

He responds by standing and pulling me to my feet. "With

pleasure."

I'm sweaty and exhausted when I return to my room but content. My back is tight, but not unbearable. My new muscles support my spine, and though there is still pain, it's a good pain.

It means I'm alive.

Today's gym class has a new glow to it. I complete my mid-term, the written portion of the class. Even though I had to reread most of the book last night, I ace it.

The last five minutes of class, Coach Mariner answers our questions about the midterm and then finishes with a warning. "You have a week break. Don't get lazy and stop training. Some of you think you have the track portion of this class in the bag, but fitness is a lifestyle, not a pass/fail grade."

He pauses. "I believe in healthy competition, so here are the top standings: Tied for first are Abernathy and Danforth, followed by Caesura and Angler. Foxworth is a close fifth.

"Train hard. Class dismissed."

Tied for first pounds in my head as I walk to my room. If Lydia is right, Felix is a shoe-in and not even genius-quality grades can give me enough edge to win that Dome seat.

Do I still want it?

The thought knocks the wind out of me. Even if I win the seat by some stroke of luck, I doubt what change I can make in the Dome. Our Codex is tightly protected by gatekeepers who refuse to acknowledge the merits of past codices. I've experienced first-hand the punishment for suggesting change.

I hate to admit Dad was right. This goal of mine is a fool's errand.

But what about Darius? I can't give up if there's a chance to help him and others like him who have been wrongly condemned.

I'll find another way.

I quicken my steps and wonder what Dad meant by those words. Maybe tomorrow, I can ask him.

My train is among the first to leave the next morning. There are no sleeper car arrangements. I avoid the passenger seating and retreat to the observation car.

Someone's beaten me to it.

"I thought you might come." Luther stands from the couch by the glass. He strides to my side and wraps his arms around me.

His embrace makes me dizzy, and I let him lead me to the sofa. "We're in a public place. I can't express personality, remember?"

"No one else is here," he whispers. "And I can see anyone coming in the glass."

Which means he can see me in the glass too.

"I know it's my cover, but I look awful." I look away.

He tips my chin to draw my eyes back to him. "Your color is starting to return. If you trim your hair, you'll look more like yourself again."

"I have to do something." My hair is just long enough to pull into a knobby pony tail. I tie it and let my long bangs fall over my face.

Luther grins. "Better."

"I still look like death warmed over."

"That's what you want to look like, remember?"

"What is Dad going to say?"

"Tell him you've been sick."

I shift my position to face him and let my messenger bag slide to the floor. "But how long can I really keep up this ruse? I can't look dead for the rest of my life."

Luther puts his arm around me. "Keep it up until we get into the Dome, until …"

I pull away. "That's almost two years, and assuming I make the Dome is a long shot. I can't act dead to myself for two years. I can barely imagine the next two weeks."

Luther grabs my hands. "Cotton, listen to me. You can't let them know you've recovered. Gath said that you can't survive whatever they did to you again. Maybe you can physically survive it, but you won't be the same.

"The only reason you recovered is that he injected you with an anesthetic and antibiotic, of sorts, before the treatment began."

His words take a moment to sink in. They're hard to believe. "Gath is on our side?"

"*Our side*? That's a funny way to put it. We don't have a side. Our side is the true ASU, and we have to work to restore it. The only way to do that is to make it to the Dome."

I shake my head. "We can't restore a government that thinks torturing and mind sweeping its citizens into submission is any kind of solution."

"Then what do you suggest?" Luther leans back in his seat. "That we set up our own government and form a rebellion? No, that's not sane. I know you've been through a lot, but we have to pursue the right channels. We have a chance at the Dome and making a difference."

"*You* have a chance," I correct him. "I'm convinced that the Doctor Revisionary slot is rigged and not in my favor. Even if I win fair and square, I don't think I will."

"We have to try," Luther insists.

"Are you listening to me?" I plead. "There is no try. We can kill ourselves and still not beat the system. The only way to make things right is to look for answers outside it."

He releases my hands. "No, Portia, I love your passion, but you're wrong. The principles of the ASU will hold out in the end. I believe that."

I set my jaw and speak the treason rising in my heart. "I don't."

"I do, and so I still have to try." He stares beyond the glass, then rises and gently pets my hair. "You've been through a lot. Try to get some rest over the break. Maybe things will look brighter when you return." He disappears out the observation room door.

I want to run after him. I want to make believe he's right.

But I can't. I look back at my reflection in the glass. I will always be Darius's sister, and Luther will always be a Danforth.

The landscape blurs as a mournful dawn breaks on the horizon.

Chapter 18

Friday, 10.16.2149
Chrysoprase, Cube 1519

The walk from the station to my home doesn't take nearly as long. When I run it.

Weeds overrun the front, and not even the alley mongrel greets me. I knock on the front door, which looks older and more worn than I remember. There's no response. I push on it, and it creaks open. An unlatched door means one thing.

Dad's not here.

Sunlight filters through the dusty interior. I check the coals, but they are dark and cold. No one's bothered to light them in days, maybe longer.

Dad's mattress lies empty and hard in the one corner, and I scale my loft. My room remains untouched, just as I left it.

I toss my messenger bag onto my bed and climb back downstairs. I'm tired from the long train ride and haven't eaten since dinner last night.

Our pantry shelf is bare except for four small cans of beans, a half-used pouch of tea leaves, and some spuds.

The pail is empty of kindling, so I snatch it up and go out back to collect some. There's no trace of remnant wild turkey bones. A peek inside the stall reveals a colony of cobwebs, but there's no stench, meaning that even the flies have moved on.

No one has lived here for some time.

I return to the hearth and kindle a reluctant fire. I pop open one of the bean cans and start the tea pot.

Where did Dad go? Why did he leave? Is he okay?

I weigh my options. I can start with my neighbors and see what they know. If I have to, I'll board the work train tomorrow and go to the base where Dad reports.

But right now, I'm too tired. Between the strain from my recent recovery and the absence of my father, all I can do is hold back the tears.

I shovel the beans down my throat and take a few sips of tea before curling up on the scratchy rug and falling into a fitful sleep.

I don't wake until late afternoon. As the sunlight retreats, a chill creeps inside my converted barn home. The only glow comes from the lingering hearth embers.

Shivering, I light them again and climb up to my loft to retrieve my jacket and a blanket. I pull them off my bed and then pause, remembering my collection of verses.

I pull up the mattress and reach in the dark. I retrieve the pocket knife and feel past it.

My fingers come up empty.

It's gone.

I lift my mattress higher, reaching farther underneath for the missing notebook. My hand brushes a crumpled piece of paper and grasps it.

I let the mattress fall back into place and rummage in my bag to find my flashlight. I switch it on and with trembling heart, read the lines.

Daughter,
The night beckons,
And I am old and tired.
Truth hibernates until a new
Day dawns.

Tears roll down my cheeks, as my eyes strain to find hope in the message my father left for me. Is he gone for good? Does night mean death?

"No, you can't leave me," I whisper, but had I not left him?

I can't wait until morning for answers. I wipe my face and yank on my jacket. Our closest neighbor is a block away and may not even remember me, but I have to try.

Scaling the ladder, I shove open the door and ignore the darkness of the alley. It holds no fear greater than the one gripping my heart.

Distant howls punctuate my steps, and I break into a run. There's a small light inside the cabin, and I pound on the door.

A grizzled man with a suspicious face cracks it open.

"Can you help me, please?" I gasp.

"What fer?"

"I'm Abernathy's daughter, home from school, and he isn't here. Do you know where he's gone?"

He strokes his whiskers. "Abram's girl, huh? It's a bad night to be looking for someone you ain't gonna find."

"What do you mean?"

"Abram stopped boarding the service train a month ago. Guess he got his papers."

"What papers?"

"Retirement orders—but them's just a nice way to say they don't need you no more."

"Have you seen him since?"

"Nope. Not since his last day at the train. Never been too neighborly, you Abernathy's."

I gulp. "But where has he gone?"

"To pastures in the sky, I reckon. Now get home, girl. The night is no place to wander."

He starts to close the door, then stops short. His haggard face twitches. "Sorry fer your loss."

I nod dumbly and turn away. It can't be true. He can't be gone. He was tired but strong when I left him.

Hard sobs choke my throat and blur my eyes. The howls grow louder, closer. I focus my eyes on the dark road ahead. Half a block, and I'll be home—or whatever is left of it.

There's a snarl to my left. I spin and pull out my Taser, focusing my beam on the beast. His ragged fur stands in spiky patches on his back, and he crouches to pounce.

I pull the trigger, and he yelps, falling to his side. I flash my light behind him, lighting up half a dozen red eyes lurking in the alley.

I can't fight them all.

I break into a run, and the mongrels charge after me. They may be half-starved, but they can run, better than I can.

One leaps at me from the left, and I discharge another Taser blast into his furry skeleton. But aiming costs precious time I don't have.

I yank out the karambit to slice at another who nips at my leg and cut him across the muzzle.

He retreats with a whimper, but there are too many more to take his place.

A fierce cry pierces the darkness, and the mongrels slow their attack to assess the intruder.

From the back of the pack, shrill yelps break out, but I'm busy trying to evade two mongrels that have ganged up on me. I shoot one and attempt to outrun the other when I see the sickle-swinging shadow that cuts through the fur like a grim reaper.

A fighter's roar echoes from his throat as he takes out one mongrel, then another. When he reaches me, the one hounding my steps flees in terror.

I stare at the approaching man. He stops in front of me and thrusts his tool into the ground. Then, he yanks away the bandana concealing his mouth to take in deep gulps of air.

"Foxworth!"

"Come with me." He doesn't give me time to reply but grabs my hand, pulling me back down the alley and farther away from my home.

"Where are we going?"

"Quiet." His voice is stern. "No one must hear us."

We scale rocks and trek through woods I might recognize by day but confuse me at night. We climb hills, cross two mountain streams, and enter a thick forest. After an hour at Foxworth's breakneck pace, I'm panting like a mongrel myself.

We reach a clearing, and I collapse onto a flat rock as

Foxworth disappears.

He returns moments later to egg me on. "Get up. We're almost there."

Almost where? I want to ask but don't have the breath for it. He saved me from the mongrels. I can only trust he means me no harm.

The woods suddenly open before us. In the dark, all I can see is a steep descent into the earth's gaping mouth.

"Follow me—but careful of loose rocks." Foxworth bounds downward, jumping from one rocky ledge to the next.

I follow as quickly as I dare but soon lose sight of my guide. I grip one rocky boulder and then another as I pick my way downward. I can't see the floor of the quarry and hope I don't disturb a copperhead nest or twist my ankle in a pit.

The ground finally levels out, and the rocks give way to a narrow, grassy trail. Foxworth is gone, but I follow the path.

A shadow darker than the night encroaches. A tall cliff blocks the stars. Ahead is an opening in the side of the rock.

A cave.

I stop to rest, debating my next step. My blood is up, and I'm drenched with sweat, but the night's chill reminds me the harsh winter will visit soon. This den is the place a bear might use to hibernate or another predator might use to …

I jump to my feet. *Hibernate.* The word brings the riddle back to my mind. *Truth hibernates until a new day dawns.*

Ahead, small rocks slide and bounce off larger boulders. Someone or something has disturbed them.

"Portia? Is that you?" The deep voice echoes from inside the cave.

I step forward. "Dad?"

We both run to bridge the gap. He lifts me into his arms in the embrace I thought I'd never feel again. Sweat and soil mingled together form the fragrance I love best.

"I thought you were gone." I manage between sobs. "The neighbor said …"

"I didn't know you were coming." He silences my cry. "If it hadn't been for Foxworth, I might never have known."

"But what are you doing out here? Why aren't you living back home?"

"Shh, not now. Come with me where we can talk." Dad glances behind me at the woods and pulls me further inside the cave.

He holds a small lantern which makes our shadows look like monsters on the rock walls.

"What is this place?" I whisper.

"It's an abandoned rock quarry. It's the perfect hideout."

"Hideout for what?"

He gives me a tired smile. "You'll see soon enough. But first, we need to catch up." Dad moves the lantern in front of my face to look me in the eyes. "And you don't look good."

I had forgotten my gray-like tint. "I'm feeling better."

We bend down to pass through a chiseled doorway. Inside, there's a fire and a pot of steaming stew. Dad motions for me to sit on a blanket, and I wrap it around my shoulders while he scoops me a bowl.

"Eat this, and then tell me your story."

I savor each spoonful and recount what I remember, starting from day one and ending with the day I snapped back to being myself.

Dad listens, his face somber.

I set the empty bowl down with a sigh. "You were right, Dad. I've been a fool for thinking I could change the way things are."

"Maybe not."

"But I can't get a Dome seat, and that means I can't help Darius."

"Perhaps you still can."

I stare at him. We seem to have traded sides of this argument.

Dad stands and checks the door. Then, he returns to his seat on the ground. "Sweetheart, Darius doesn't need your help the way you think he needs it."

I clutch the blanket, waiting for him to explain.

"Darius isn't a satellite prisoner anymore."

His words unhinge my fears. "Do you mean that Lucius is right? That he is a wanted—Rogue?"

"That's what the CGA would call him. To us, he embodies the spirit of our Brotherhood, the spirit of freedom."

"Am I a Rogue, too?" I whisper.

Dad chuckles. "You sound so serious."

"Being a Rogue is serious," I argue. "Do you know that the bounty on a Rogue is more than a lifetime of rations and that a Rogue conviction brings an immediate death sentence?"

Dad grows quiet. "I've heard rumors."

"Well they're true. I witnessed a Rogue suspect on campus commit suicide to escape Gages, and another suspected of connections to him was interrogated to death."

Dad's eyes swell in sadness. "Clancy and Gall—young, brave men with such potential. Their parents were devastated, but they did not die in vain."

I gasp. "You knew them?"

"They were our brothers."

Our brothers. I study Dad carefully. "Will you please start at the beginning? If I am to be part of this dangerous fellowship, I deserve to understand what I'm risking and why."

Dad takes a deep breath. "It all started after Darius's trial. Some other men in our cube and I began talking about what we could do to protect our families—or what was left of them. We decided we needed a place to escape, a place to run.

"We found this deserted quarry and began our digging, tunneling to build an underground network where we could meet and stock food and what little weapons we had."

I lean closer to the fire. "That's why you were gone so much."

"Yes," Dad says. "A few years passed, and our numbers grew. We came to realize that hiding wouldn't solve the real problems, and that's when we heard about the first satellite revolt out west. Rumors spread that a young prisoner staged a daring escape with a couple dozen others. They weren't content to simply escape, though. They took out a whole unit of Gages, stole stockpiled arms, and destroyed the western Gage headquarters."

Dad pauses. "The young man leading the band called himself Abe."

"Was Darius part of his group? Did he escape too?"

The fire crackles in the quiet cave. Dad stares into the flames. "Sweetheart, Darius is Abe."

I narrow my eyes. "Why didn't you tell me? No wonder I've met with so much suspicion in Crystal."

"I didn't tell you to protect you." Dad looks at me across the fire. "Besides, you were set on going to the Dome. You weren't ready to hear the truth."

Lies can protect us.

"What am I supposed to do, now?" I demand. "The CGA has

their hounds sniffing out the last insider, and now, I'm practically one myself."

"You alone choose your path. I won't decide for you. All I ask is that you don't betray the brothers you know."

"Foxworth? Is he a brother?"

Dad studies me with a new fire in his eyes. "He saved your life tonight."

I remember the shadow with the sickle. "I know."

"There's one other, and his concealment is vital to our intel. Even if you guess his name, you must never say it."

A face surfaces in my mind, but the idea is so unsettling I push it away. "Then what am I to do?"

"You do the next right thing, Portia, and then the next right thing after that. You'll find your way."

With Dad, there are never easy answers. "But what is it that the Brotherhood hopes to accomplish?"

"You said yourself that you can't change the system from the inside," Dad says. "It's too corrupt, too far gone for that."

But these men have nothing but raw muscle, hand tools, and a small reserve of firearms. It's hardly the arsenal for a revolution.

"You don't stand a chance against the weapons of the CGA," I mutter.

"We don't plan to fight the conventional way," Dad says.

"I don't see how you can win."

"Would you rather we did nothing? If we don't stand up, then who will?"

His words echo in the cave and remind me of the scene from the simple room at the corner of Seventh and Market. Even farther back than that, the men on board the *Mayflower* hazarded everything for a cause they believed to be right.

Though Dad's shoulders are stooped from hard labor, fire blazes in his eyes. "Portia, there are greater evils in our world than even you have seen. The corruption in government is only the beginning. Abe—Darius—and his band have uncovered an even worse crime being committed against humanity. The ASU is harvesting our land's resources to appease a global dictator and fight his bloody wars. All the while, our population lives in the dark.

"And the satellites? They aren't just prison camps. They are death camps where the blood of our brothers and sisters is spilled to fulfill the endless quota."

My jaw drops. My world becomes suddenly smaller until I'm the size of a pin on a giant pincushion.

"But there, I've said too much. Tomorrow, you must go back to our home. Spend your break alone with your thoughts. You'll find the answer for what you should do."

He stands and adds another log to the fire. "Get some rest. There's a meeting I must attend tonight, but you'll be safe here. In the morning, head due west until you come to the road, and take that back to our place."

"Will I see you again?"

Dad circles over to me and leans down to wrap me in his arms. "I hope so. I have a long journey tonight, and Foxworth and the others will be waiting for me."

"When will I see you again?" I clutch his jacket.

"Hopefully under a freer sky."

Dad kisses my head, then pulls away, and ducks under the door. I jump up to look after him. He does not leave by the front of the cave but disappears into a tunnel deep inside the earth.

A damp and lonely chill seeps toward me, and I retreat into

the small cave room where the fire glows.

Wrapping myself in the blanket, I curl up close to its warmth and dream of my family.

Chapter 19

Saturday, 10.17.2149

Chrysoprase

I leave the cave's shelter at the first hint of dawn, not daring to explore the dark tunnel where Dad disappeared last night.

An urgency pushes me back to our simple barn-home. No one must see me in the woods and guess my night errand. Any curious cube dwellers must think me still asleep in my house—or at least, not wandering far from it.

I stop only to fill my messenger bag with berries to serve both as breakfast and an excuse for any who might question my morning hike.

But I reach home without meeting one person and busy myself with food preparations for the lonely week ahead. The remaining bean cans and spuds will not last more than three days, and I refuse to beg food rations from the cube's ornery officer.

My confused thoughts take refuge in physical activity. I

restring Dad's fishing pole and tramp through the woods to the stream half a mile away. Two hours later, I've snagged a decent bass and two boney pickerel.

I clean them out back beyond the stall and find one of dad's rabbit traps overgrown by brambles. I tear off the vines and search for any bait I can find, returning with a few wild radishes and dandelions.

Most of the small game in our area is overhunted, so the odds aren't great, but I set the trap anyway.

By afternoon, I collapse into my loft bed. Evening comes, and I cook the fish on the hearth. The spattering pan serves as company to my lonely thoughts.

What am I to do?

I ponder that thought long into the night until the hearth grows cold and my mind, weary of itself, shuts off to sleep.

I repeat the same chores day in and out for the whole week, my meals consisting of wild berries, the few fish I can catch, one unlucky rabbit, and wild vegetables.

By week's end, I feel ruddy and strong, the pallor of my skin replaced with a light pink glow. I've spoken no words the whole week but wrestled with my thoughts until I've mastered them.

My last day home, I force myself to leave my solitude and make one trip to the square. My errand seems harmless enough, though it terrifies the very fiber of my being.

No matter. I know who I am, and I know where my allegiance lies.

Later Saturday night, I board the train to Crystal. The other passengers have already bunked for the night, so I slip past the silent lounge to the observation car.

I finger the envelope that protrudes from my messenger bag and tremble at what I am about to do. But I have made up my mind, and I will not falter.

To the perceiving eye, my plan is unchanged. Portia Abernathy is more determined than ever to earn a Dome seat and represent the Revisionary profession.

Only my heart knows otherwise.

When I reach my room in the early morning hours, the first thing I do is retrieve my tablet from the ottoman and schedule my compatibility test with medical for tomorrow. *Won't Lucius be pleased?* I grin smugly and place the envelope on the ottoman before falling into bed for a few hours' sleep.

Though stiff from the long train ride, I rise early and slip outside into the freezing air for the track. The cold bites my lungs, but I press on to complete my laps.

I shower and drink coffee for breakfast. Then, with packet in hand, I stride toward the medical building.

The nurse stares at me from under sagging eye lids. "Can I help you?"

"Yes, I have an appointment for today."

She drones on. "Name?"

"Portia Abernathy."

The nurse types on her screen. "Compatibility test?"

"Yes, ma'am."

She scoots a clipboard toward me. It contains a detailed questionnaire. "Have a seat, and let me know when you're done with that."

I nod and sit in a corner. My hands grow clammy as I fill out my profile, but I grip the pencil with determination. This is the only way I can guarantee an appointment with a medical staff member.

When I finish, I feel cheapened to the level of merchandise. Once my profile hits the system, I'll be nothing more than a listing in a database that is somehow "smart enough" to find me the perfect match.

The way I see it, profiles are like listings for livestock or a new piece of machinery. *What make and model do you prefer? Well, let's see what's available ...*

"Portia Abernathy?"

I look up. Another nurse stands at the hallway door.

"That's me."

"This way, please."

The stiff female accepts my clipboard and leads me to a sterile examination room where she proceeds to take my blood pressure, weight, height, and other physical requirements.

Yep. Those are the same kinds of things one might like to know about cows.

Except who cares what color their eyes are.

I look away as she draws my blood and sit quietly until she's thoroughly satisfied with the rest of her regimen.

"We should have your results in the system within two weeks," she says at last. "Do you have any questions for me?"

"Actually, I do." I hand her the folder I brought with me. "Would you kindly take a look at these?"

"What are they?"

"They're x-rays of my back."

"Surely I can access them from our system."

"That's just it." I heave a mock sigh. "There's been a mix-up in the system, and my medical records are locked. I returned from break with a hard copy to help clear up the system error."

Her face is taut. I hold my breath as she begins typing on a tablet in the wall.

"There's an administrative lock on your records," she says.

"It's a technical glitch," I assure her. "My adviser told me that if I could produce current records, the error could be overridden. Because of the glitch, I've been wrongly enrolled in a physical education course. As you will see from my x-rays, I shouldn't be running."

She finally opens my envelope. Pulling out my x-rays, she pins them up on a light board.

Her shocked expression reveals that my ruse has worked. Her medical professionalism outweighs her administrative concerns.

True to her breeding, she gives me a brief back examination. It doesn't take her long to become convinced that the x-rays match my spine.

"Although I feel good muscle, there's still no reason for you to be running with a back like that," she states. She then pulls up my records on a nearby screen. "You have received and responded successfully to correctives. I see no cause to restrict your medical records. However, I can't unlock them. What I can do is write you a note exempting you from class."

"Thank you." I maintain a demeanor of humble subjection.

"You're welcome." She slips the note and my x-rays back into the envelope and hands them to me.

"Is there anything else you need from me?" I ask.

She shakes her head. "No, you're all set. Best of luck with your class—and your matches."

I smile and leave. I have scored two victories. First, I have pitted the system against the system, using a stupid compatibility test. I've outwitted the odds against me with my own medical records.

Second, I have proved to myself that I'm no longer bound by them. After all, I ran two miles this morning, which according to the nurse, is unreasonable.

I try not to think about Candace and her compatibility test gone wrong. I won't let that happen to me. I've got two weeks before I have to worry about matches anyway, and if someone gets too friendly, I'll simply avoid him.

After all, I know how to run now.

Thanks to Luther.

I hustle to my room and try to concentrate on coursework. But my eyes keep drifting to my running shoes. If I'm honest with myself, the only match I would ever want is with the man who taught me how to use them.

Monday morning, I go through extra trouble to look my best. A week at home with sunshine and exercise brought back the color to my cheeks. Despite her concerns, Lydia trims my hair to a sassy pixie cut. I apply mascara and powder my nose.

I march through my first two classes with ease and arrive early to physical education in a neat black dress and pumps.

Coach Mariner's eyes flicker with annoyance. "Are you planning to run in a get-up like that, Abernathy?"

"No, sir." I hand him the doctor's note.

He reads it and shakes his head. "Well, I never," he mutters. "I'm sorry for the mix-up, Abernathy. You've been a good sport about it, anyway. Tell you what I'll do. I'll give you credit for the whole course based on your performance on the written section."

"Thank you, Coach." I shake his hand and turn to walk out of the room. All eyes are on me, including Luther's.

He jumps up and follows me outside. "What are you doing?"

"Hello to you, too."

He rolls his eyes. "I'm sorry. I'm just worried."

I square my shoulders. "There's no need to be. I'm exempt from the second half of the class. I produced my medical records, and the doctor gave me a pass."

His eyes widen in disbelief. "They unlocked your records?"

"Not exactly, but I got what I wanted."

Luther groans. "Come on, Cotton. Don't you think someone is going to notice?"

"Maybe. I kind of hope they do. Medical and my coach both understand my rights here. I'd love to remind someone farther up that they can't trample on whomever they please."

He shakes his head. "You're the one going to get trampled. I mean, look at you. You look—like a million dolari."

I grin. "No shame in that."

"Don't you get it? That Gage is going to notice. Everyone is going to notice that you're not a mindless zombie anymore."

"Good."

"Not good," he retorts. "You're going to get hurt again, and I can't protect you."

I stiffen my lip. "I'm not asking you to."

My tablet vibrates in my bag, and I pull it out. A new pop-up reads: "Class Schedule Change. Report to Adviser."

I slip the tablet into my bag and look at Luther. He's so at home in his mesh gym shirt and running shorts. Part of me wishes I could stay.

I wiggle my toes in my black pumps, nevertheless determined to move forward with my plan. "Well, you've got a class to attend, and I've got a meeting with my adviser."

"I don't like the sound of that." Luther opens the gym door for me, then pauses. There's a strained longing in his eyes. "Take care of yourself, Cotton."

When I reach the central auditorium building, I take the marble steps by twos. Adviser hours are almost over for the day, and I don't want to give Lucius any more reasons to resent my visit.

He's pecking at his screen, his eyes tightly pinched behind his red-rimmed glasses.

I sit down in an empty seat and watch him for a few minutes before he acknowledges me.

At last, he grunts and looks up. "What do you want?"

I lean forward and pretend to admire his trophy. "My tablet told me to report to you regarding my class schedule change. Besides, I figured it was time for my nine-weeks' review."

He creases his eyebrows. "I didn't issue any schedule change."

I recline in the chair and shrug. "Medical did."

"Medical can't authorize admittance to a class."

"No, but they can exempt me from one if deemed medically necessary." I place my copy of the medical note on the table and slide it toward him.

He scans it and stares at me.

"Since my records were locked, I decided to take your advice and schedule my compatibility test. At which time, I also took the liberty of disclosing my personal x-rays to your knowledgeable medical staff. They quickly recognized a mistake had been made and issued a medical release. Coach Mariner signed off on the physical regimen of his class, and since that is the only section remaining, he changed my class status to complete."

I finish with a yawn. "I assume that meeting with you is a mere formality—or perhaps you want to get our nine-week appointment out of the way?"

Lucius bends forward. "You think you're smart. I warned you that someone at the top intentionally locked your records. Don't think for a second they're not going to notice your little stunt."

"I'd be delighted to discuss my records with them." I slide my chair back. "Is that all for now?"

"Hold on." He swipes across his screen, and his eyes race back and forth. "Hah!" He picks up his phone. "Amanda? This is Lucius. I received a meeting invite from the dean regarding a candidate situation. Is she available now? I have the candidate in question here with me."

I sit poised on the edge of my seat. A meeting with the dean could mean serious trouble or a chance to vindicate myself.

I breathe deeply and wait.

"Very good," Lucius says. "We'll be right down."

He returns his phone to its stand and smirks. "Come with me, Abernathy. The dean has a few questions for you."

I follow him to an elevator and watch in surprise as he pushes a button below 0 labeled a lowercase b. The elevator descends to a floor below ground. The other small letters on the panel indicate that b is not the lowest level beneath the surface.

Maybe this explains the locked door in the archives.

The elevator opens. A pair of Gages stand guard in the hallway, their eyes unblinking. We pass them and walk down a hallway to a reception desk and small lounge.

Lucius approaches the young woman at the counter. "Amanda, I called a few minutes ago about a meeting Candidate

Abernathy and I have with Dean Augusta."

She hesitates. "President Matteson just stepped inside her office. I'm sorry, but I don't know how long their meeting will—."

The intercom at her desk buzzes. "Amanda?" A woman's voice interrupts. "When Adviser Kline and the candidate arrive, please send them in directly."

Lucius Kline. I never imagined a man like him needing a last name.

"Yes, ma'am." Amanda responds. She nods at us and rises from her desk. "This way, please."

We pass through a double conference room door to a spacious office beyond. Sitting at a mahogany desk the size of my bed is Dean Augusta. Standing next to her is President Matteson.

His eyes train on me and spark with curiosity or suspicion. Both, I think.

Dean Augusta presses her lips together into a perfunctory smile. Her hair is a bronze sculpture, and every crease of her purple suit knows its place. "Adviser Kline—and this must be the candidate, Portia Abernathy."

"I'm sorry—We didn't know you had a prior meeting," Lucius stammers.

"No problem," Bertrand Matteson replies for Augusta. I imagine puppet strings pulling above her immaculate hair. "The dean and I were discussing this case. Anything that concerns our candidates concerns me."

The edge in Matteson's voice makes me want to fidget.

Augusta motions to two hard, wooden chairs across from her desk. Lucius and I walk up behind them, but neither of us sits. Matteson remains standing, and somehow, being seated in his presence seems like bad taste.

Matteson makes the decision for us. "Please, be seated."

Augusta clears her throat. "Now, tell us what we can do for you."

Lucius sits on the edge of the chair. "This is the candidate with the medical records in question. Medical recently released her from her physical education requirements due to her producing x-rays of her own."

"And where did the candidate get these x-rays?" Augusta asks.

Her use of the third person annoys me, but I begin with a level tone. "I brought them from home at the end of my fall break since my records here are inaccessible. Your medical professionals were very understanding of my condition, as was my physical education coach."

Matteson moves out from behind Augusta's desk to examine some artwork on the wall while Augusta taps her fingers on her desk. "And what is the candidate's condition?"

I stiffen. "*My* condition is scoliosis."

"Ah, I can understand why that would present difficulties in a physical regimen." Her voice holds no apology.

Matteson readjusts a crooked frame as Augusta continues in a mechanical tone. "The candidate received a series of correctives last quarter?"

I refuse to answer to third person any longer.

Lucius speaks for me. "That is correct."

"What was the reason?"

Lucius kicks my foot.

"It is unclear to me," I say in a flat, robotic tone that rivals the dean's. "I am sure the cause for it was merited. However, I think any inappropriate behavior on my part was provoked by overexertion and strain from my ignored medical condition. Now that appropriate compensations have been made, I see no cause for future conflict."

Augusta opens her mouth to respond, but Matteson holds up a hand. She closes her lips, pressing them firmly together.

Matteson turns his attention back to me. He leans against the edge of Augusta's desk, blocking her from view. "My dear Miss Abernathy, you seem to have been rather underhanded in achieving your objective."

"I appealed to all the proper channels," I say, evenly. "Mr. Kline advised me to take the matter up with medical, which I did today."

Lucius glares at me. "I did *not* instruct her to produce her own records."

"I didn't know what else to do since my records had been *frozen*." I pause for emphasis. "But I had no doubt the Crystal Globe would correct the *oversight*."

Matteson leans forward. A cold smile tugs at his lips. "Miss Abernathy, I don't need to remind you of the black sheep in your family. I'm sure you understand why certain measures had to be taken to ensure your implicit *fidelity* to our educational aims."

My mind reels. I'm stunned the president even knows I exist, let alone is familiar with my family background.

His smile grows strained waiting for my response. I sit straighter and offer my best imitation of his patronizing speech. "I have idolized the aims of this institution throughout my educational career, prizing the Crystal Globe's ideals of *equality* and *fairness*. What more could I ask than an institution that treats all its candidates *impartially* and *individually*?"

His taut features relax into a duplicitous smile. "Perhaps we have misunderstood each other," he says at last. "Dean Augusta will approve Coach Mariner's authorization of your physical education exemption and apply your grade from the first section of his class."

Matteson still blocks Augusta from view, but her fingers tap on a keypad behind him.

"Thank you."

"Dean Augusta tells me your grades are impeccable. I expect your behavior to prove equally flawless for your duration here."

There's a warning in his voice.

"Naturally."

Matteson steps toward the door and gestures for us to rise. The meeting is over. Lucius bolts to his feet, and I follow.

The president extends his hand. I hesitate, then accept it.

His grip is fierce. "I look forward to monitoring your progress with us."

Lucius waves his farewell to Augusta. "Thank you for your time today."

She doesn't look up from her mechanical typing. "It was *our* pleasure." Says the woman who has never used a first-person pronoun in her life.

I follow Lucius down the hall to the elevator. He doesn't speak until the metal doors close.

"You'd better watch yourself," he mutters.

"Neither of them explained how my records became frozen or why someone enrolled me into the physical education class in the first place."

He glares at me. "Dean Augusta and President Matteson do not have to explain anything to you. Clearly, it was a loyalty test."

I snort. "Right, it was simply a test designed to make me fail.

How *uncivil* is that?"

He grabs my arm and brings his lips to my ear. "I don't care what happens to you, Abernathy. But if I were you, I'd start to care." He holds his fingers an inch from my face. "Because you're this close to the scales tipping and not in your favor."

The elevator dings, and the door slides open. Lucius releases his grip and marches out, leaving me behind.

I straighten my dress and walk past the rows of adviser stations and out the exit.

So far, my plan is working. My appearance as a candidate striving for a Dome seat remains intact, and my chances, poor though they are, have improved. My grades are the highest in my class. Now that my physical handicap is gone, nothing but Felix stands in my way of scoring a seat.

Yes, Felix. He tried to use me for intel last quarter. I won't let him use me again.

As I step inside my apartment, something crackles under my feet. It's a green piece of paper someone must have slipped through the crack at the base of the door.

I pick it up and read:

Calling all Trippers! Join the journey to Lapis. Experience the famous Tavern Hall and tour a factory or two. Register by Thursday to guarantee your spot. The train leaves Friday night and returns late Sunday.

I clench the paper and rush back out into the hallway. When I reach Luther's apartment, I'm out of breath.

He opens his door and blinks. "What are you doing here? Did everything go okay with your adviser?"

"Oh yeah, fine, but my meeting isn't what I came to talk about." I hold up the flyer. "Did you get one of these?"

He motions me inside. I drop onto his couch while waiting for his answer.

"Yes, but why are you excited about it?" He rubs his head. "I've barely recovered from the last trip."

"You don't want to go?"

"Not really." He sits across from me. "Besides, there are my classes to consider. My Court Scene trial is coming up in two weeks, and I'm spending every spare moment studying old cases."

I press wrinkles out of my skirt to hide my disappointment. "Lydia wasn't happy with how hers went. She said the professor expected her to be harsher in her sentence, and she received a low grade."

"There's definitely the expectation to come down on the tough side of the law," Luther agrees.

"Would you err on the side of mercy if you weren't sure?" I blurt out the question.

"I don't know," Luther sighs. "Part of me says yes. The other part reminds me that to do the most good, I have to get to the Dome. And to get to the Dome ..."

"But surely nothing is worth sacrificing an innocent life in the process," I insist.

"I'm hoping it won't come to that."

I fold the paper in my hands and stand, forcing a smile. "Well, I'll let you get back to your cases. Sorry to bother you."

He rises and steps between the door and me. "It's no bother. You can stay if you want."

"No, you need to get back to your work, and I should get back to mine."

He rests his hand on the door knob but doesn't turn it. "Are you going on the trip?"

I wait for him to open it, but he doesn't. "I don't know yet."

"I'll go if you want me to."

I adjust my bag on my shoulder and step closer to him and the door. "You should only go if you want to. You can't live your life trying to please people."

"I'm just thinking of one person at the moment." He lets go of the handle to brush my bangs away from my eyes. "And frankly, I can't figure her out." His touch sends goosebumps up my arm.

I laugh nervously and feel for the handle. It's still warm from the heat of his hand.

"Good night, Luther." I give the handle a hard twist. The hallway's cold, stale air is a welcome distraction. I don't look back and quickly head for the stairs.

It's a good thing Luther won't be going on the trip. His head and his heart aren't in the same place. His head wants the Court Citizen slot in the Dome. His heart ... well, I don't know what his heart wants. But if it wants the girl whose loyalty belongs to a Rogue Brotherhood, one of them is going to lose.

And it probably won't be his head.

Chapter 20

Friday, 10.30.2149
Lapis

The train to Lapis lurches to a stop. The dark car erupts into murmuring as its sixteen passengers collide into each other.

I find myself impractically close to someone who smells of brandy and sweat.

Arthur.

How he sneaked his liquor past Gath is beyond me. I slide away from him in the dark until I find an empty spot against the cold, metal wall. Two girls nearby titter about nonsense, but at least they don't reek.

"Quiet," Lucius calls from his corner of the train car.

The door groans open. In the twilight, Gath's dark shadow outlines the door, and dim figures appear outside.

"We have orders from the Friend to seize this train. You will need to get off here."

Gath stands his ground. "We come from Crystal and have permission to take this train to Lapis Square."

"Our orders arrived two hours ago. The train is being redirected farther north to Jacinth. If you choose to stay on it, you do so at your own risk. We can't guarantee your safety or your return to Crystal."

"Where exactly are we?" Lucius demands.

"This is an outpost, ten miles from Lapis Square," the voice returns. "Follow the track, and you'll find your way."

"If you're going north, can't you drop us off there?" Lucius's voice sounds like a shrill whine.

"Negative. The tracks split ahead."

"May I see your papers?" Gath's voice is low and serious. I sit straighter and feel for my bag.

There's a ruffling noise, then a huff. The figures disappear around the side of the train.

"Up and out!" Gath kicks the train car wall. "Unless you want to get left behind."

I grasp my bag and jump to my feet. I'm the first out the door. Arthur barely makes it before the train begins moving.

We watch from the side of the track as our train vanishes around a bend.

We're standing on a splintered wood deck with a dilapidated ticket booth behind us. No civilian has used this outpost recently.

"Stay together," Gath instructs. "Walk two by two. Wander off, and don't blame me for what happens to you."

I fall in step with a groggy female behind Lucius and Gath who lead the way.

"Who were they?" Lucius whispers. "And how did they get authorization to seize the train?"

"Wasps."

Lucius swears under his breath and kicks at a stone. I want to know what Gath means but don't dare interrupt Lucius's smoldering mood.

We've barely walked an hour when dawn breaks, and I hug my jacket tighter as the damp dew falls.

"Hold up!" A candidate from the back calls. A retching sound follows his words.

I gag just listening to it. Someone is puking up his guts.

Lucius steps to the back and returns moments later. "It's Arthur. Maybe we should leave him behind."

"Can't do that," Gath says and disappears. A moment later, he returns with the intoxicated candidate slung over his shoulder.

"Disgraceful."

"You were just like him." There's a hint of a smile on Gath's face.

"I wasn't that bad."

"Yes, you were."

We reach Lapis Square around noon. Undergrowth has swallowed most of the pavement and many structures.

We pause near a short, overgrown wall for a water break. I collapse onto a bench-like concrete slab and stare at the wall. Through the vines, I make out a stone face.

The others seem too tired to notice or care.

"Another few blocks, and we'll reach Tavern Hall," Gath calls. "Line up and head out."

By this time, it's every candidate for himself. The line is a straggling string of exhausted bodies. I fall to the back, pretending to tie my boots, then quickly run up to the wall and yank away the vines. The face takes form.

It's a hard but candid face with hair down to the chin. The rest of the statue has been eroded into a knobby form, but there's wording behind another layer of vines and caked dirt. I climb onto the statue to scrape away enough to read the letters:

EDOM IS A LIGHT

ANY MEN HAVE DIED

I'm trying to make sense of it when pounding feet on the pavement bring me back to the present.

Gath has returned for me. His scowl doesn't mask the concern in his eyes.

"We reached the tavern, and you weren't there. If I didn't lose Arthur, I'm not about to lose you."

I climb down. "I saw a face and wanted to find out what it was."

He grabs my arm. "Hurry up. We've got to go."

His grip. The last time he touched me was … I shudder and yank away.

His face flinches as if I'd slapped him, and he releases me.

"I'm—sorry." We both blurt the words at the same time.

I rub my arm, and he clears his throat. "We should go before the others miss us."

I look into his silver-colored eyes and then back at the wall. "But what does it mean?" The vines fall back over most of the man's face.

He sighs wearily. "Freedom is a light for which many men have died in darkness."

"It sounds like poetry." I whisper. "Who wrote it?"

"It's a statue—one of the few not destroyed from the previous civilization."

I step toward him. "You stopped intentionally. You told us to rest here."

"I did." He turns away, then glances over his shoulder. "Coming?"

I follow him to Tavern Hall, a multi-story structure with a pinnacle tower. It looks as ancient as the overgrown statue.

I gasp. Standing in plain sight in front of the tavern is another statue. It is the same man I saw at the wall. His right arm rests on a thick book, and his left holds onto a cane or a sword—it's too worn to tell.

"Who is he?"

Gath stops and looks at me, a new gentleness in his eyes. "His name was George Washington. But no one here knows that, so keep it to yourself. As far as the tavern is concerned, the man is their mascot and the pardoning saint of weary or happenstance travelers."

We pass the statue of the man and his book. Both seem strangely familiar.

The Tavern Hall door opens to a massive room, filled with roughly hewn tables and chairs. My company sits at a long counter, enjoying steaming bowls of oatmeal.

A grizzled man with a whale's belly appears with more bowls on a tray. His face is a mass of whiskers. His eyes are blue beads of intelligence.

"Thank you, Randolph." Gath slides a bowl toward me and collapses onto a stool to eat his.

"This is the lost sheep?" Randolph stares hard at me. I grip my bowl, not knowing what to say.

Gath speaks for me. "Found her back at the wall, tangled up in the vines. I was telling her about the tavern's patron saint."

Randolph's eyes flicker, but his features relax. He clears his throat, but the strain has left his voice. "Why you bother with these rascals is beyond me."

Gath empties his bowl. "If I didn't, how would I find an excuse to see my old friends?"

"Aye, there's that."

Randolph disappears into the kitchen and returns with yet more bowls. When we're finished, we're so full we could burst.

Randolph watches us with an amused look on his face. "There are two rooms upstairs for you—one for the ladies, one for the gents. *Same as always*."

Gath slides him an envelope. Randolph accepts it without a word, slipping it into his apron pocket.

"Would you show them their rooms, Lucius?" Gath phrases the order as a request. "I'll find out about another train and a factory tour."

Lucius rises and stretches his back. "Follow me."

Gath readjusts his weight on the stool and continues talking with Randolph. I slide off mine and trudge up the stairs behind the other candidates.

The girls' room consists of a bare wooden floor and a few blankets. The other three girls grab for the blankets, so I choose a corner of the floor and lay down my bag.

I know the floor will be merciless to my back, but maybe I won't sleep long.

My eyes close before I adjust all the lumps out of my bag.

I dream hard. There's the statue. George Washington's face looks tired and taut. Then, there's the book. It's big and thick, like the one on which Washington's hand rests.

Next are two symbols that surface from deeper in my memory. A flag, studded with stars. It's stained with blood. Then there's a musket. A hand picks it up. A faceless man charges an unseen enemy.

I bolt awake, the dream fading, but not before I remember where I've seen them all before.

It was orientation at the Crystal Globe auditorium. Images flashed on the screen, and we had to report the ones we saw.

I saw two sets. The second belonged to the ASU. The first set held no meaning to me at the time.

They have meaning now. They are symbols of a lost civilization. It was a civilization where men fought and died for the light of freedom, even if they themselves never saw that light.

It was the civilization of the *Mayflower* passengers and the Compact they established to form order. It was the civilization of men like Jefferson, Franklin, and Adams, of the Declaration of Independence.

But what became of it?

All I know is that the domino effects of the Apocalypse tore it apart physically, and the electro-magnetic warfare crippled it technologically. But what happened to its moral and political fiber? Was there nothing left to re-build again?

I think of my civilization's own story. How the Friend appeared on the stage, promising to restore social order and build a so-called New Jerusalem. How the people, desperate for hope, followed him without question.

But there are so many missing pieces to the puzzle, unanswered questions I never considered before. Why did the people abandon the established order?

What motives actually drive the ASU? The promise for peace and safety secured its hold on the desperate nation. But at what cost?

For almost sixty years, the ASU has governed the land once ruled as the USA. Two generations have no memory of the earlier civilization, and those who would—well, not many people live beyond sixty these days. There is nothing in our society today to remind us of the past or what lies outside our borders.

I roll to my side, but my eyes are no longer tired. There's too much I want to know and so much I'm afraid to ask.

Someone pounds on the door. "Get up!" Gath's voice bellows. "We move out in ten."

My three companions groan beneath their blankets, but I spring to my feet. My muscles immediately protest, and I drop to the floor and grimace through a set of stretches. A few moments later, the spasm subsides, and I rise more cautiously, only too glad to leave the hard floor behind me.

At the base of the stairs, I wait by a frosted window. The worn, stained floor of Tavern Hall creaks as the rest of the candidates trudge down the stairs and gather in small groups, awaiting instruction.

Lucius does a head count. "Has anyone seen Arthur?"

"He's out cold upstairs," a male candidate says.

"Leave him," Gath says and turns to Randolph. "If one of ours stumbles downstairs at some point, tell him to wait here for us to return. He's not to wander outside."

Randolph nods, unsmiling. "I'll put him to work in the kitchen."

Lucius grunts. "That'll teach him."

The thirteen of us follow Lucius and Gath out front. The day is clear, colder than Crystal, but we're many hours and hundreds of miles north of our campus.

We reach a multi-story factory. The cracked wood threshold

opens up into a large shop where clothing wares are folded in drab but neat displays.

Through the threadbare walls, we can hear the spinning and clicking of a hundred machines.

The owners, a sultry woman and her husband, grow indifferent to us once they realize we are not here to buy anything. Only when Gath reveals his permit does the woman agree to give us a tour.

A heavy door in the back opens to a short hallway, which gives way to a massive room. Rows upon rows of tables line both sides of the room, parted by one central aisle.

At crude benches sit women and teenagers whose threadbare fingers work mechanically at sewing machines. Their eyes are glossed over. Their fingers have long since memorized the patterns.

None even look up to acknowledge us.

The distance of a few hundred miles separates the technological marvels of Crystal from the depressed recesses of factory life.

The scene sobers my classmates and me. We leave the factory without saying a word.

When Gath explains that we will be visiting a second factory, we respond with a collective sigh of protest. Lucius silences our complaint with a hard glare, and we trudge along cracked roads. They're a mixture of pavement chunks and hardened mud, like most roads outside Crystal.

After passing a forest of trees and overgrown structures, the road opens to a cleared field. Beyond, we can just see the tops of another tall building. Small stone cottages line the road closer to the factory.

They are bland and uniform, but they are well-kept. Perhaps this factory will not be as hopeless as the first.

Surrounding the factory is a wire gate and guard house. The man standing at his post resembles a Gage, but his uniform is a gray, not green. His expression matches his drab garb.

"Identification, please."

Lucius flashes his badge.

"Is this official business from the Dome?" the man asks.

"No, we're chaperoning candidates on an educational trip."

"Amusement hunters are not welcome."

Lucius's jaw tightens. "I'm official staff at the Crystal Globe. A routine factory tour has never been an issue in the past."

The guard stiffens and steels his eyes as he surveys our group. "This factory requires special clearance from the Dome. If you don't have clearance, you need to leave."

Lucius clears his throat to form a reply, but Gath interrupts him. "Sorry about the misunderstanding. We won't waste your time."

Gath waves us back down the road. The candidates groan again. We're all tired of walking.

"Stop your whining," Lucius barks. "There'll be food and beer back at Tavern Hall."

That seems to appease my classmates, who start chattering. I fall out of their conversation and into step next to Gath. "Has that ever happened before?"

He jerks his head to look at me as if he hadn't noticed my approach. "What?"

"Being turned away," I say. "Has that happened before?"

He shakes his head. "No, but I'm sure there's a good reason."

"What do you think they are making that requires special

clearance?"

"It's none of my business." His tone is flat, final. He clearly doesn't want to discuss it with me, even if he does know.

Typical Gage.

And yet, Gath has been anything but typical. At one moment, he's a cruel enforcer, and at the next, a concerned guardian.

Still, I prefer his silent company to the prattle of my peers. Lucius leads the group, while the two of us bring up the rear.

Tavern Hall finally comes into view. The building, empty as a tomb earlier in the day, now brims over with noise and laughter.

The day laborers have started to arrive for a hot meal and a chance to drown the day's sorrows. Horses, bicycles, and even a wagon fill the courtyard by the statue.

"You'll want to bunker down in your room as soon as we're done with dinner." It's the first time Gath has spoken since we left the last factory.

The bare room and hard wooden floor are hardly my companions of choice for an entire evening.

"Where will you be this evening?"

"Trying to keep the boys from getting into brawls," he mutters. "Tell the other girls to stay with you. I'd rather not have to hunt down Traders in this town."

Traders. The word makes me shudder. "Is Lapis another problem spot for them?"

"There's always the risk they'll wander into a gathering place, looking for potential merchandise," Gath says. "Tavern Hall is a hub around here. Who knows what types of vermin frequent the place."

Inside the hall, hungry customers, mostly men, wait at long bench tables. Including Arthur.

His steaming plate is piled high with beef stroganoff.

Arthur shovels it into his mouth, unaware our group has returned. Lucius walks behind him and knocks over his goblet.

"Hey!" Arthur's face flares, then blushes. "Oh, it's you."

Lucius leans against the table, bending forward. "Glad to see you missed us, Mr. President of the Kappans."

Arthur blushes harder.

Lucius continues, his voice barely louder than a hiss. "You know, when I was president, I not only went on trips, but I also participated in them. You may want to try it sometime."

Gath clears his throat. "All right, group. Clean up, and meet down here for dinner in ten. I'll let Randolph know we're back."

I follow the three girls to the small indoor bathroom. It's a step up from the outhouse at Red's hostel though not much larger than a small closet. But it's clean.

I help myself to a towel and wash the sweat and sun off my face. "Gath told me we should stay in our rooms after dinner."

A tall, thin blonde shoots me a withering look. "What, the big bully wants us to stare at a blank wall for four hours? I don't think so. Not when all the fun's going to be happening downstairs."

I dry my face. "You weren't on the last trip, were you?"

"No. So what?"

"You don't know what getting ambushed by Traders feels like." I hang up the towel on a stubby rack. "I wouldn't recommend it. It's not any version of fun."

"There are Traders here?" The blonde's red-headed friend asks.

"Don't listen to her," the blonde snaps. "She's making up stuff. Since when does the loner care about keeping company with us girls?"

I turn to face the red-head. "There could be Traders. This inn is a traffic hub in these parts. There's no telling what kind of men will visit the place tonight, and that's why Gath wants us in our room."

"Maybe we should listen to her," the third girl says.

The blonde stiffens. "Nonsense. I didn't come on this trip to hole up in a lonely room all night. The loner is bluffing. We wouldn't be allowed on these trips if they were dangerous."

I stare hard at the girl, annoyed that types like her give blondes like me a bad reputation. "Suit yourself. Just don't expect anyone to come rescue you."

I leave the bathroom and jog down the stairs. Gath and Randolph converse in the kitchen doorway.

He frowns as I fall noisily onto a bench. "Something wrong?"

"If those girls get taken tonight, they deserve it," I mutter. "I told them what you said, but they will do what they want."

Randolph's face cracks into an amused smile. "And you won't? Most females will do what they want."

I pull up one leg underneath myself and try to find a comfortable position on the hard bench, which reminds me too much of the hard floor. "I already had a run-in with Traders. Once is enough for me."

Randolph presses his question. "So, you will stay in your room all evening?"

"Sure, why not?" I lie.

"Somehow, I doubt it."

I laugh. There's something refreshing about this man.

Randolph turns to Gath. "If the girls stay inside the inn, my men will keep an eye on them. They might get their feathers ruffled, but they'll be reasonably safe. Once they go outside, though, I can't guarantee their safety."

"You won't have to worry about this one." Gath grins. "She's got brains in her head."

I warm under his compliment. It's the first nice thing he's ever said about me.

"That is the kind I worry about most," Randolph says. "The pretty girl with intelligence—she is the dangerous one."

Gath nods, his smile fading. "Yes, the daring girl is the one most in danger. She knows she's competent, so she takes risks. But she's no match for what lies outside her field of influence. And that field is much smaller than she realizes."

So much for the compliment.

Randolph shuffles to the kitchen door. "The next pot should be ready. Get your crew to circle up at the row of benches right here, closest to the kitchen. And tell the girls they are welcome to stay downstairs, as long as they don't mind becoming—the entertainment."

I bristle at the word. The other girls can do what they want, but I have no intention of cheapening myself like a toy music box.

I eat a sufficient portion of food and leave the table before the others. Randolph intercepts me at the base of the stairs. He's carrying another steaming pot from the kitchen.

"What, leaving so soon? Don't you want seconds?"

"I'm full, thanks."

"But there's no need to hurry upstairs yet. Dinner isn't over, and my apple and dumpling dessert is rather famous in these parts."

"Thanks just the same, but I'd rather be going before the downstairs gets too *crowded*."

Randolph studies me a moment before speaking. I want to

ignore him and continue up the stairs, but his expression keeps me grounded. "You are a proud lass, aren't you? Beautiful and dangerous and proud. But pride is a culture of honor in my family. Pride in dignity, pride in integrity, pride in self-preservation. And I see that in you.

"Here, come with me." He disappears inside the kitchen. I don't want to follow, but he has a commanding way about him. I slowly step inside the kitchen door. The aroma of savory food and sweat overwhelms the small space where Randolph and another man dance around each other, busy at work, in a sequence rehearsed hundreds of times.

Randolph pulls open the oven door, flooding the room with a new sweet and fruity fragrance. He scoops a generous portion of bubbling hot goodness into a bowl and hands the steaming dish to me.

"Take this upstairs," he says. "At the top of the stairs, take an immediate left. It looks like a closet entrance, but it opens up into a small loft. You can see everything down here from up there. It was a favorite spot in my youth when my father owned this inn. There's an old cushion up there, a blanket too. It will be much more suiting to your personality than a bare room."

The dish is almost too hot to hold, but the gesture warms me from the inside out. I smile at this gruff old innkeeper. "Thank you."

"Mind you, don't make a sound, or it will echo in the hall," he warns. "But it is dark up in the loft, so you should be able to see down without anyone seeing you."

I nod and return to the stairs, careful not to spill my bowl. At the top of the stairs, I take a left until the walkway narrows to a dark corner and closet space. Just as Randolph said, it opens up to a small loft, overlooking the hall.

Gath and company are visible below. Randolph reappears with another bowl of stroganoff, then with dessert. Watching my classmates savor theirs while I enjoy mine makes me feel part of the group, even from my perch.

The hall acts as a giant megaphone. Their words and laughter echo up the loft, so I can eavesdrop on several conversations at once.

Except for Randolph's and Gath's. They keep their heads low and whisper near the kitchen door. Randolph nods upward, and Gath peers my direction.

His shoulders relax. He seems almost relieved.

I adjust the cushion and wrap the scratchy blanket around me. The loft is dank and will grow colder as the night wears on. Still, it's a happy substitute to the hard wood floor in the girls' room.

Not that anyone will miss me there. The girls downstairs are already having a busy evening. They'll regret not listening to my warning come tomorrow.

I scrape the bowl clean and set it next to me on the floor. My perch gives me a perfect view of the front door where a steady stream of day laborers flows into the large hall. It quickly fills, and the noise drowns out any chance of further eavesdropping.

I amuse myself with people watching for an hour before I start to get sleepy. I'm shaping half my blanket into a pillow roll when my peripheral picks up a tall man with a barrel-sized chest duck through the doorway, followed by a lean, smaller man.

The first edges around the crowded hallway toward Randolph and Gath. The second man trails silently behind, completely concealed by his hood. The first man's cloak only partially hides his face.

But I'd recognize Red anywhere.

What is he doing here?

The four men withdraw into the kitchen, while general drunken behavior and roughhousing escalate. Arthur lands himself a black eye. Several other boys miss a brawl by seconds and hide in the shadows. The short red-head retreats up the stairs, tousled and generally disheveled in appearance, but she escapes the worst of the night. The other two girls become a popular diversion, but they're too drunk to care.

The last I see of the blonde is a husky fellow carrying her over his shoulder out the door and into the night.

Lucius lounges at a far table, not seeming to mind.

The noise draws Gath from the kitchen, and his face darkens. Within minutes, he rounds up what's left of the haggard crew, including the now unconscious Arthur and remaining girl, and herds them up the stairs.

When he returns downstairs, he barks at Lucius. Though the noise muffles his words, his gestures demand to know where the other girl is. Lucius points at the door and refills his cup.

Minutes later, Gath and two of Randolph's workers leave in search for the girl.

They have no sooner disappeared than another man enters the hall. *An ogre of men.*

His skin is darker than Gath's, and I've seen him once before through the narrow light beam on my Taser.

In the ruins of a library that almost became my tomb.

The Trader. He's alive.

His prowling eyes glint under his hood and scan the room.

Is he hunting Red or Gath for revenge? Surely, he can't know I'm here.

The Trader mingles in the crowd, his head bent low. He limps and leans heavily on a long, narrow cane, evidence of a gunshot wound not fully healed.

I slide lower on my cushion as he speaks a word to one man, than another. Though drunk, the men respond to him with nervous laughs and exaggerated gestures.

My eyes jump between the Trader and the door. Gath has been gone nearly an hour. Red and Randolph haven't reappeared from the kitchen. Lucius slumps in his chair, no longer able to fight exhaustion and the relaxing effects of too many beers.

The Trader edges toward the kitchen and the lonely table where Lucius sits. The man raises his cane above the unconscious Lucius. I clamp my hand over my mouth so I don't scream.

The cane cracks on the table in front of Lucius. He jolts awake and tries to stand, but the cane locks him in place.

His face drains of color. The Trader's back is to me, but the strain in Lucius's eyes reveals his terror.

The Trader pulls something from under his cloak and hands it to Lucius. It looks like a scroll. There's an emblem on it. It looks like the emblem of the ASU.

My mind recoils. What is this monster doing with an official document? Who did he kill to steal it?

Lucius nods stiffly as his eyes scan the document. He rolls it up and hands it to the Trader. Eyes down, he nods to the stairs and mutters something.

The Trader mounts the steps and disappears from my view. Moments later, the landing outside my hidden closet groans under his weight. I hold my breath and tell myself that no one but Randolph and Gath know I'm here.

His steps echo down the hallway, away from me. A door

breaks open. Screams.

I clench my teeth. He's forced his way into our room.

How could Lucius betray the girls?

Betray me? I should have been sleeping there as well.

The screams soften to whimpers. Heavy steps return to the hall and lumber down the stairs. The cloaked man reappears at the base of the steps, alone.

Relief. He has left the girls in their room.

Terror. He didn't find the girl he wanted.

He marches toward the end table, but Lucius has vanished. The Trader's cane scrapes the floor with an angry screech as he heads for the door.

No sooner has he left than Gath reappears at the front door, carrying a body wrapped in a blanket. Matted blonde hair pokes out the end. His two companions follow him wearily, their shirts torn and faces bruised.

Gath looks no worse for wear, except for his grim expression. He mounts the stairs, and the hallway creaks as he reaches it.

There's a deep gasp, then high-pitched voices.

Heavy steps approach my hideout.

Gath squeezes through the door moments later and ducks low to squat next to me.

"The girls say the Trader was here," he whispers.

"Yes, I saw him. He talked to Lucius, then came up the stairs."

Gath's eyes narrow. "Lucius?"

"Yes." I keep my voice low. "The Trader showed him something—It looked like an official document. And then he came up the steps and kicked in the girls' door. Are they all right?"

"Just scared. He didn't harm them. They think he was looking for you."

I grip my blanket tighter. "But why?"

Gath sighs, the day's fatigue catching up to him. "I don't know, but I've had enough trouble for one night. You'd better stay here until morning. Don't come downstairs until I knock twice outside this loft."

I nod as he uncurls his large frame and squeezes back out to the hallway.

An hour, maybe more, passes. The large hall below slowly empties. A boy appears and extinguishes the lanterns hanging from the ceiling, sending the interior into utter blackness.

I close my eyes and hope no cloaked Traders will haunt my dreams.

In the early morning hours, a shuffling noise wakes me. I pull my blanket down from my face to give my ears better space for listening. Perhaps it was a rat.

It comes again, closer this time. This is no rat.

It's the scraping of boots against the narrow floor of my loft.

I am no longer alone.

Chapter 21

Saturday, 10.31.2149
Lapis

The man's breath comes in broken gasps. Perhaps he is injured. Perhaps he doesn't know I am here.

His shadow matches the height and form of the man who followed Red into Tavern Hall earlier tonight.

I lie perfectly still.

"P-Portia?"

Maybe I'm dreaming. I haven't heard this voice for ten years.

I push the blanket away and pull myself up. "Darius?"

His arms answer for him. They are hard and strong, but gentle. I lean into his embrace, feeling his warmth, breathing his scent. It is the fragrance of the woods, the earth, and freedom.

Bristles from his beard tickle my face as he whispers, "I thought I'd lost you."

"Lost me? You've always known where to find me."

He shakes his head. "No, I'd heard you were as good as gone—that you actually wanted to get drafted and become another puppet of the Dome."

I pull back. "I wanted to get drafted to save you."

"Save me? How?"

"Getting drafted to the Globe gave me a chance to become a Doctor Revisionary in the Dome. I'd have access to our Codex and the power to impact change. I thought I could amend the laws and satellite sentencing—and bring you home."

"It would have been a fool's errand."

How much Darius sounds like Dad.

I touch the outline of his face and feel hard lines. Maybe scars. I can't tell which in the blackness. I sigh and lower my head. "I know that now."

"Gath told me what they did to you."

I grow rigid. "What *he* did to me."

Darius grips my hand. "Portia, he saved your life. I know that's not how it looks to you …"

"Yes, I know he injected me with something, but the fact is that he stopped me from getting away."

"There's no place you could have run that Eliab wouldn't have found you."

"You know him?"

He grunts low. "Every brother knows Eliab, the Commanding Gage who has placed targets on our backs."

"He's not especially fond of me either."

"That's because of me, and I'm sorry for that. But as long as you keep up the act of a reformed citizen, you should be out of danger."

I tell him about my meeting with the dean and President

Matteson. The lines in his face deepen. "Why would you do that?"

"It's the only way I could stay at the top of my class, the only way to have a shot at the Dome seat."

"But I thought you said ..."

"I know what I said. I know that even if I do win a Dome seat—and that's a big *if*—I can't bring about the changes I want." I pause and grin into the darkness. "But *they* don't have to know that. As far as the Crystal Globe is concerned, I'm a devoted candidate of the state, eager to pledge herself to its cause."

Darius chuckles. It's good to hear him laugh, even if it sounds like nothing more than a low sneeze. "We're cut from the same cloth, you and I. What's your plan now?"

"My plan is to be ready to serve my brothers any way that I can."

His breath catches in his throat. "You're volunteering to be an insider."

"If that's what you need me to be. Dad says there are only two left inside Crystal."

"We've lost several good men. The risk is great, and I can't promise to protect you."

"I understand that. What I don't understand is what we're fighting against. Oh yes, there's corruption in the Dome and within the Crystal Gage Administration, but what's the bigger picture? Dad wouldn't tell me."

"The less you know, the safer you are." His voice is so low I can barely hear him.

I bristle. "Look, if I'm going to help you in this cause, I at least deserve an honest answer of what I'm fighting against."

Darius crouches to an alert seated position, and I lower myself back onto my cushion couch to hear his words. "Okay, you already know about the satellites, right?"

"I know that's where they send prisoners, and that most people never return."

"No one ever returns."

"But what about short sentences?"

He snorts. "Doesn't matter. Think about it. Have you ever met someone who's returned from a satellite?"

I sit quietly. I can't think of one.

"Exactly."

"So why doesn't anyone come back?"

"Because if someone did, they might tell the ASU's dirty secret."

"Which is?" I hold my breath.

"The state uses prisoners for slave labor to mine the mineral deposits that formed during the Apocalypse. Between the eruptions and earthquakes, there's more than enough raw deposits for slaves to harvest."

"But why?"

"Ah, that's the really ugly part. Why did the Rosh League attack us with EMP warfare in the first place? They weren't content to cripple us. They wanted to conquer us."

"And have they?"

"A long time ago. The first Friend—and every one since—has served as their political puppet. The populace is led to believe they enjoy the privileges of a free society. They're only free because our prisoners' blood pays the tribute we owe."

"In other words, our 'New Jerusalem' is nothing but—a lie?"

Darius snorts. "The only ring of truth about it is the ASU's interest in our so-called foundation stones and the wealth our soil holds. As for our society, you could call it a lie. We've been taught nice words like "equality," but we don't know what they mean. There's nothing fair about how the Dome treats citizens. Our society is built on a false premise, and that's why it's going to crumble."

"What do you and the brothers hope to achieve? Surely our numbers are too small to make a difference."

"Too small? Since when has size kept you from going after what you want?"

I smile in the darkness. He knows me so well.

"We may be small, but our bands are growing. We're fighting to overthrow the Dome and shut down the machine that drinks our people's blood. What's the Rosh League going to do? Bomb us?"

"Rosh League? You mean they're still our enemies?"

He grunts. "They're more like our landlords now and won't dare destroy the resources they want. Besides, rumors indicate they're waging war with other global powers that may take the attention off us for a while. Either way, this soil cries to be free again. That's what we're fighting for."

It sounds so poetic, so impossible.

"What can I do?"

"Our last mole—or insider—accessed the blueprints for the underground headquarters. There's an intel room next to the archives. It's a computer room called the portal."

"I think I know where the room is."

Darius's eyes widen. I hurry to explain, "I've been to the archives once. There was a locked door at the base of the stairway."

He nods. "That's good."

"But how does the portal work?"

"We believe it has the ability to transport communications to the Rosh League and receive their orders. It's the bridge between taskmaster and slave, so to speak."

"That sounds similar to the technology we use in my Simulation class," I say. "It lets us engage with ancient codices and people from past civilizations."

"That's crazy."

"It's crazy lifelike," I agree. "It only makes sense that the same technology would apply to communicate with people in real time."

"Sounds like you're the girl for this job." He grins. "Do you think you can get there?"

I warm with his compliment, but my pulse races at the risk. "I'll try. If I can, what am I supposed to do then?"

"Use this." He presses a small drive the size of my thumb into my palm. "The design shows there's a port for this drive, and that's what activates the computer. This replication is an older model but should still work. It's programmed to plant a virus that will allow us to eavesdrop and even take over systems. With this virus planted, my hackers can do anything from open jail cells in satellite camps, reroute cargo trains full of supplies, and spy inside restricted chat rooms. We can then better plan our offensive and know when to strike hard."

I finger the drive in my hand. "Strike hard? How?"

Darius hesitates. "The less I tell you now, the better. Just in case ..."

"In case I get caught."

"Don't let that happen." His voice is quiet and grave.

"But if I do?"

"I trust you won't betray us."

I straighten my chin. "Never. You have my word."

He reaches to cup my chin in his hands. "I'm proud of you, Portia. My brothers will protect you as best as they can. And whatever happens, I will come for you."

"When?" I whisper.

"The runner will tell you."

"The runner?"

"Fox—I guess you know him as Foxworth. He's the fastest we have and runs our messages through the underground."

Underground. My last glimpse of Dad was disappearing into a tunnel …

"And our other insider?"

Darius stands. "Haven't you already figured that out?"

Maybe I have, but I don't want to believe it.

"Gath is our most valuable mole. I owe him my life, and he owes me his."

I shiver and stand as well. "If you say he's on our side, I'll take your word for it."

"One day, you'll see him the way I do. Trust me. If your world's about to end, you want that man by your side."

I wrap my arms around him, and he squeezes me hard. I feel safe.

But just for a moment. He kisses my hair, releases me, and slips away into the darkness. *Fraternitas Veritas.* His whisper is all that remains.

I grasp the air, wishing I could make him magically reappear.

Falling back onto the cushion, I clutch the blanket and wrap it tightly around me. Then, I lie face down onto my couch so no one can hear my sobs.

Two loud knocks jar me from my fitful sleep. Soft, early morning light trickles through the hall's windows and gives the loft a gentle glow.

My first thought is that I'm late. My second is to wonder if I dreamed into existence my nightly visitor, or if Darius were really here.

But I felt him. I smelled him. He was flesh and bone. I cling to the night's memory and clutch the drive in my hand.

Abandoning my secret loft, I slip through the hallway and to the small bathroom. The other three girls huddle inside, washing away what they can of last night's horrors. I stay no longer than necessary, having no desire to remind them that they had been warned.

Randolph offers steaming plates of sausage and toast. I join the boys and help myself to a hearty portion. Gath calls a five-minute departure warning as the girls appear. They greedily devour what they can.

There's no trace of Red, his cloaked companion, the Trader, or even Lucius when we call our thanks and farewells to Randolph.

He waves, then turns to busy himself with other customers.

We hike to the train station, all of us hoping that today, we won't have to walk as far to get back to Crystal.

I fall in step beside Gath and try to picture him as an ally, but this morning, he just looks like an enforcer. "Where's Lucius?"

"He left—early this morning."

"He couldn't wait for us?".

Gath shakes his head and proves stubbornly tight-lipped.

Once we reach the station, we don't have to wait long for the train. We've no sooner climbed into an empty cargo car than the wheels begin to turn. Gath pulls the door shut, and I choose a lonely corner to curl up and sleep.

It's afternoon when I collapse into my bed back in my dorm. Lydia gives me an "I-told-you-so" look but doesn't press me for stories.

I don't have much to say anyway. Dozens of times, I replay Darius's conversation and come away with more questions than answers.

My concerns only grow when Monday arrives.

After a fairly calm morning, I arrive early to my Simulation class. My desk provides a perfect window to a muffled conversation taking place among Professor Mortimer, Felix, and Gage Eliab. Why are those three in a pre-class conference?

In front of me, Jael fidgets with a napkin on her desk. She brought another container of cupcakes.

I've no sooner taken my seat than Eliab disappears out a side door.

"What's going on?"

Jael hands me a cupcake with one hand and wipes crumbs off her desk with the other. "I don't know. I guess Felix had a question for Mortimer, and then the Gage joined them. I'm glad it doesn't involve me. Gages make me nervous."

"Yeah, me too." I unwrap the cupcake.

Once he finishes talking with Mortimer, Felix stops at my desk. I ignore him and flatter Jael about her delicious cupcakes.

"Hey, you," Felix says at last.

"Oh, hey." I continue chewing.

He leans on my desk. "You're looking—more like yourself."

Warning flags go off in my head. It's only been a week since my compatibility test. Surely, the results aren't in the system yet. Felix can't know that my fresh flesh is hitting the market, and if he does, why should he care? He doesn't need me anymore.

"Jael, these cupcakes are really amazing," I say. "May I have a second?"

She blushes in pleasure and hands it to me.

Felix clears his throat. "I say, you're looking good, Portia."

"Cupcake, Felix?" I turn and push it toward his face. He instantly leans back and away from my desk.

He checks his shirt. I may have grazed it with icing. "No, thanks," he mutters, walking toward his seat. "Guess you're dimmer than they thought."

Luther's warning rings in my ears. *Everyone is going to notice that you're not a mindless zombie anymore.*

Mortimer calls the class to session. I determine to stay alert and not give my enemies an opportunity to find fault with me. I can't let anything get in the way of my helping Darius, whenever he decides that he needs me.

"Last week, we finished your group projects," Mortimer says, peering at us over his spectacles. "Now, in addition to your daily reading, you will be individually responsible for your second project, a biographical research Simulation on a presidential figure of the past civilization. You must uncover their worldviews and then defend or debunk them based on their congruity with our Codex. Some presidents will be easier than others. Earlier presidents tend to be more difficult, as they were much more prone to believe in individual rights instead of sociological ideals. Later presidents, with a few exceptions, were more likely to agree with the basic framework of our Codex's early platforms.

"Once again, we will start alphabetically with assignments."

So, that's it. I'll be assigned the first president, who is doubtless an individual whose ideals the Codex would consider subversive.

I stare straight ahead and sit up straighter.

That's okay. Two can play this game.

Mortimer clears his throat. "George Washington—Abernathy."

The assignment pops on my tablet screen. I select it to review brief biographical information on the man who became the first president of the United States of America, the man from the statue at Tavern Hall.

Mortimer drones on with dozens of other assignments. I don't know why he feels the need to read them out loud when he programs them to appear automatically on our tablets.

I form threads of Washington's character from my preliminary reading. He was a military man, a natural leader. He was chosen Commander in Chief of the Continental Forces in the Revolutionary War and later elected President of a Constitutional Convention and eventually first President of the newly-formed USA. Unanimously. After a second term, he stepped down of his own accord, setting a precedent for future leaders to follow.

I reread the information again. What kind of man would give up power like that? The Codex would consider a leader careless for stepping down. The Friend serves a ten-year term, at which time he or she is succeeded by the man or woman chosen next by the Dome to serve.

"Psst, Portia! You're up."

Jael's intense whisper brings me to the present.

The class is silent. Mortimer's eyes are on me.

He taps impatiently on his podium. "Candidate Abernathy, would you please prepare for your introductory Simulation?"

I slide out of my seat and clutch my tablet. I'm not prepared for this. Perhaps that is what Mortimer wants.

"The rest of you will begin reviewing your biographical source materials," Mortimer continues. "The next four candidates should also prepare themselves for initial Simulation encounters this period. Each of you will have a turn over the next week."

I step onto the platform where a small patch glows blue. The space is sufficient for one person. Me.

Mortimer enters a code. "Ready, Candidate Abernathy? Things are about to get a little cold for you."

There's a sinister glint in his eye.

I brace myself and close my eyes as the green glow envelopes me.

When I open them, I can hardly see. A brutal combination of wind and snow slap me in the face and take my breath away. My tights and black dress are no match for this weather.

Fingers trembling, I fumble for my jacket zipper. It breaks.

I have got to get out of the wind.

A horse whinnies behind me. Maybe its rider can help ...

I press my fingers into my temple. No, I am in a Simulation. Even though I feel frozen, I can't die. But Mortimer is watching my every move and hoping I'll make a mistake. I have to distance myself from the scene.

I run behind threadbare bushes and a cluster of trees as a chestnut-colored horse with a white face[iv] appears in the clearing. Its rider is pale and gaunt but with a striking nobility of demeanor.

He dismounts his horse and falls to his knees, which sink deep into the snow. One hand grasps his hat. The other, he balls into a fist and brings to his chest.

It's George Washington.

And he's praying.

The wind snatches away most of his words, as if to chide me that eavesdropping on a desperate man's prayer is unorthodox.

I strain to catch snippets of his words. He speaks of his men's desperate condition, the absence of proper clothing and food, the sick and the nearly dead. He prays for provision for the new widows and orphans who will never see their husbands and fathers again. He speaks of his country's cause, all the while acknowledging their utter dependence on God's providence.

I'm mesmerized. The man's heart is broken. For his soldiers. For his country. Here is one who loves deeply and bears the heavy responsibility of a fledgling nation's dreams on his shoulders. Here is one brave enough to risk his life and meek enough to know it is not his to own.

This is a man worth following. This is a strong man, a humble man. A man who fights bravely on his feet but finds solace on his knees.

Though chilled to the bone, I feel a new fire in my soul. If men like this lived once, perhaps they can live again.

Perhaps their strength and sacrifice can be reborn in a girl like me.

The snow turns into a green whirlwind. I'm back on the auditorium's platform, and Mortimer's keen eyes level on my face.

He's looking for something and seems dissatisfied not to find it.

"Well, Candidate Abernathy?" He rubs his cane with long, bony hands. "What did you think of Washington and Valley Forge? A picturesque place, was it not?"

"It seemed rather desperate to me," I say flatly.

"Go on."

The cold and the snow. They seem less bitter company than the man standing over me now.

I begin in a monotone voice. "The setting was harsh and cold, and based on the threadbare nature of Washington's attire, had not been kind to the man and his army. I will need to do more research on their circumstances to determine if their plight was the result of poor judgment or an unsmiling Providence."

"Providence." Mortimer pounces on the word. "What is your interpretation of Washington's belief in this Supreme Being?"

"According to our Codex, the man's judgment is faulty," I say. "As we have discussed in class before, the belief in Providence, a Supreme Being—God, if you will—shows a scientifically limiting and superstitious mindset. It is no doubt the result of desperation, a final plea for divine intervention in a dire situation."

Even as I say the words, I burn with shame for criticizing the faith of a man like Washington. And then my throat goes dry, for if his God is real, how much better might my life be for knowing more of him?

Mortimer nods. "Your initial assessments are very good, Candidate Abernathy. You may return to your seat. Jael Bennett, please approach the Simulator for your introduction to John Adams."

As I step down, a man moves in the shadows by the exit.

Eliab.

He has been there all along, watching me, no doubt hoping I would make another incriminating mistake in Simulation.

Jael walks past me, trembling.

"You'll be fine," I whisper. "Observe only. Recite the Codex, and keep your response short."

She smiles weakly back at me before mounting the steps and starting her own Simulation.

Felix tries to catch my eye. I look past him and read on my tablet, with one ear open to Jael's Simulation.

Hers is much less dramatic than mine. All she has to do is observe John Adam's inaugural address and criticize his speech.

In fact, all the following Simulations are low stress, compared to mine.

After the final Simulation, only a few minutes remain in class. Mortimer returns to his podium.

"A week from today, you will sign up for a Simulation time outside of class for the research project on your president. I will be assigning some of you to oversee these Simulations. In the meantime, I advise you to get busy with your research.

"Class dismissed."

No sooner do the words leave his mouth than a notification appears on my tablet screen.

Revisionary Cabinet meeting in D, Level 5 starts in one hour. Present yourself to Professor Mortimer for transportation and briefing.

I look up to find Felix smirking at me.

"What?" I stuff my tablet in my bag and collect my things.

"Did you get the invitation to the Dome meeting too?"

I have a feeling he already knows the answer to his question.

"Yes, I am to report to Mortimer," I say in an automatic tone. The approving look in his eye almost makes me wish I were ghost gray again.

A small group of Revisionary candidates forms at the front of class, and I trail behind Felix to join them.

"Wait for me!" It's Jael's voice.

Felix hurries ahead, but I pause. If I'm to be part of this traveling circus, at least I get to pick my traveling companion. And I choose the red-velvet-cupcake-loving Jael.

Chapter 22

Monday, 11.2.2149
Crystal

We total five candidates. I stick close to Jael and far away from Felix while Mortimer explains our purpose. "You are an honored group, acknowledged for your current achievements in study. I realize this is a last-minute trip for you, but an incident has occasioned a meeting of the Revisionary Counsel in the Dome. They will be examining our Codex to determine whether changes are needed in the area of our coastal defense language.

"I warn you that anything you witness is completely confidential. Any indiscretion on your part will result in your immediate exclusion from your study and extreme correctives."

Mortimer casts a warning look at me. Don't I feel special.

We cram into two small, gray vehicles. Some whisper, but most say nothing during the ride, which takes around fifteen minutes.

It is only the second such ride of my life, the first being the one that took me to Gage headquarters. Why we have roads in Crystal still puzzles me since only Dome officials and Gages drive vehicles. A civilian owning one is absurd. Everyone walks or takes the train.

I jump out behind Jael and stare at the Dome. The colossal structure overwhelms me. From my apartment window, it looks like a beacon in the distance. Up close, it is more severe, the handiwork of giants.

For years, I've planned to earn a seat representing my profession here. Now as I stand in its shadow, it seems to frown sternly at me as if I'm an imposter who doesn't belong.

"Come on, Portia." Jael tugs at my sleeve as the rest of our group mounts the steps. My knees are shaking when we reach the top, not from exhaustion, but from a growing dread.

Mortimer proves remarkably nimble and leads us through two wide double doors, plated with brass and adorned with the symbols of our nation.

Armed Gages stand post at every corner. Real handguns, not Tasers, are mounted on their belts.

A large, circular desk serves as the hub of downstairs traffic. Mortimer approaches the man behind it while we five form a cluster of silence.

Felix is the only one who looks at ease, but then, he probably grew up walking these halls.

Mortimer turns his attention back to us as a two-Gage escort joins our group. "We have fifteen minutes before the cabinet meeting begins, and I have obtained permission for a brief tour of the chamber. A small debate is in session, so at all times, you must remain silent and obey our orders exactly."

We nod and follow our professor into an elevator. The doors open on an upper floor, and we enter the outer hallway of a wide rotunda. The interior wall features wooden doors every twelve feet or so. Our Gage escorts address a sentinel posted at one such entrance.

Silently, the man opens the doors and motions us to follow.

The inside is less ornate but no less intoxicating. Rows of tiered seating levels focus inward to a central platform where a panel and chairman reside. Above the tiered levels shine luminescent signs which designate professions. We have entered by the Tooler section. To our immediate left is Coastal Defense, and beyond that, a group designated Technology.

That profession must be limited to Crystal. Technology majors are unheard of in 'Prase.

The small debate takes place among these three groups. The rest of the auditorium is empty, except for a few representatives who punctuate the remaining space.

A stone-throw away, a lone man addresses the three professions. The lighting of the Tooler sign turns his dark hair a shade lighter and creates hollow shadows in his cheeks.

His voice rises to a shrill cry. "If the CGA does not impose strict command of our defense outposts and seize possession of all tooling factories, we will continue to suffer from subpar operations and risk having more Rogues infiltrate our ranks."

I shudder and stagger into Jael.

Jotham Danforth.

"This is an outrage!" An older woman, his colleague in the Tooler section, stands. Her chopped gray hair falls around her face. "Each square is responsible for its own factory production. You're suggesting we nationalize all factories and impose—what? Crystal

Gage Enforcement? The CGA has neither the manpower nor resources to handle the population's objection to such abuse."

She continues without stopping for breath. "The decreased production levels at the factories *you've already seized* should speak for itself."

Jotham's face blackens into a scowl. "That's because representatives like you keep blocking the motion to employ correctives on protestors."

A wiry woman from Technology joins the debate. "You forget, Madame Alexis, that our correctional technologies are no longer primitive."

Madame Alexis's face turns four shades of scorn. "I've read the papers on your *torture* technologies. Their practice on criminals is already a question for our Ethics professionals, but their employment on the general population is an obscene suggestion."

"There are different levels of correction," the wiry woman counters. "And it is up to our Gages, not Tooler representatives, to define criminal behavior."

"No, that is a matter for our Revisionaries to interpret based on our Codex," Alexis disagrees.

"Some things cannot stew in committee forever." The argument between the women intensifies. "Gages have been employing our corrective technologies in the Crystal Globe for two terms now, with impeccable results."

Alexis spats. "Mind-controlled zombies aren't my definition of impeccable results."

A burly man from Coastal Defense jumps to his feet. "Would you continue to have Rogues undermine our operations? In Chrysoprase alone, our main port cannot account for the loss and damaged equipment we've experienced. Incident reports are growing in number and ambiguity, and we strongly suspect Rogue insiders are to blame."

Jotham roars in rage. "Then interrogate senior members until you get answers!"

"Even if they are innocent?" Madame Alexis demands.

"Would you rather we not fulfill our quarterly quota? Don't you know what that will mean?" Jotham suddenly notices our group and whirls to face the Gage escort.

"What are they doing here? This is a restricted clearance meeting, not a mock session for a field trip. Get them out of here!"

His eyes rest on my face for a split second before the Gages hustle us out of the chamber and into a waiting area.

Minutes later, a tweed-dressed woman bustles toward Mortimer and our Gage escort. "I'm sorry, Professor Mortimer, but there's been an oversight. The Revisionary Counsel meeting contains classified material and is not something candidates may observe. The Friend will be arriving soon, and security demands we clear the chamber of all guests."

"Of course," Mortimer murmurs and motions for us to leave.

Felix steps toward the woman. "Permission requested to remain behind."

"Why, Mr. Caesura, of course." She nods in approval. "I didn't see you in the group."

"These are the other outstanding Revisionary candidates in my class," Felix continues. "I would like to do them the honor of meeting the Friend before they leave."

The woman hesitates. "They would need a security examination first."

I brush my skirt and look down so no one sees the color leave my face. My karambit and Taser will surely be discovered in such an exam.

"I'm afraid we don't have the time for that now," she continues. "But if you would like them to meet the Friend, they may in the Citizen Screen Room." Felix nods in agreement, and the woman pulls out a handheld radio. "Gage Escort for the Friend, please detour to the Screen Room at the request of Felix Caesura. Five minutes."

She returns the handheld radio to her belt holster and motions to our group. "This way, please."

We take an elevator to ground level and enter a long, open room. Dividing it is a floor-to-ceiling transparent glass wall.

"Form a line, please," the woman says. The Gages herd us into place, and I'm sandwiched between Felix and Jael.

A woman wearing a dark purple suit appears through a door on the other side of the glass. Half a dozen Gages trail behind her.

Her posture is queenly. Her fair features appear to be chiseled by gods. Felix clearly takes after her.

Of course, I've seen pictures of her, but she is so much *more* in person.

She acknowledges us with a nod and terse smile. Like dominoes, we bow at the waist, and I hesitate for only a moment before following the example. I can't afford to call attention to myself.

Felix straightens and addresses her through the glass. "This is my esteemed Professor Mortimer and respected classmates."

He pauses and sweeps his hand left toward me. "These are my Simulation partners Portia Abernathy and Jael Bennett."

I straighten to find the Friend's eyes trained on me. I read approval and suspicion in her gaze.

"It is an honor to meet you all," she says without taking her eyes off me.

They are piercing like her son's. I bow again to break their hold on me.

I push open the restroom door and breathe easier as the stall latch clicks behind me. Our meeting with the Friend is over, and I have only to board the vehicle back to the Globe before this afternoon at the Dome fades into memory.

In the stall's privacy, I unsheathe the karambit and Taser holsters from my thighs and bury them deep in my messenger bag. I have to get them off my person, if but to ease my burning conscience.

"Hurry up, Portia, we're leaving!" Jael calls inside the bathroom.

"Coming!" I sling my bag over my shoulder and meet Jael outside. She steps into the cramped vehicle, and I squeeze into a middle seat next to her. Felix sits next to a leggy female in the row ahead of us.

The driver has just shifted gears when two Gages dart in front of the vehicle and hold up their hands. One stands blocking our way, while the second motions for the driver to roll down his window.

"Is Candidate Abernathy in this vehicle?" The Gage enunciates each word for emphasis.

I grip my bag tighter on my lap. "Present."

"Come with me. The rest of you are free to proceed."

Felix glances back, but it is only to smile. I don't know

whether to feel reassured or more frightened.

"Take this," I whisper to Jael and hand her my bag. "Would you drop it off at my apartment? I'm in Commons 7, Room 604. I don't need it here."

She has on her frightened mouse expression but nods that she understands my request.

I slip out the vehicle and follow the Gages up the steps toward the Dome. They lead me to a private security room where a female Gage searches me. Once cleared, I follow the two male Gages deeper inside the building, past required clearance areas, and into an executive meeting room. A polished, oblong table fills most of the room, and the Gages motion for me to be seated at a far end. They stand watch at the door as I take in my dim surroundings. The chair is queenly. At the opposite end of the table is another such chair, behind which is a screen and control panel, much like the one in my Simulation class. I wonder what purpose it has in a conference room.

An hour passes. Maybe more. Maybe less. I'm tired of sitting. A Gage brings me a glass of water without saying a word.

All the while I'm left wondering why I'm here.

At last, a small man appears. He is dressed simply in black and wears spectacles, much like Professor Mortimer.

He doesn't acknowledge me but busies himself at the control panel. The screen hums and turns an opaque blue. The man pecks at the control panel, adding additional parameters and extending the blue from the length of the screen to the entire table.

It is like Simulation, but different. I get the impression that instead of my being transported to a different time dimension, someone is coming to me.

I am not disappointed. Moments later, the Friend herself sits opposite me. The blue fades into the background.

I want to ask questions but bite my tongue and wait for her to begin.

"Portia Abernathy." Her charming smile is just like her son's. "I am she."

"No doubt you're wondering why I summoned you here." A purple gloss coats her lips, which part to reveal even, white teeth.

I hate roundabout games and have never been good at diplomacy, so I do what any good liar does and respond with an equally uncommitted statement. "I'm wondering how we are speaking."

"Oh, this?" The Friend waves her hand. "I thought you would have recognized it."

"The technology is similar to my Simulation class, but it is also different."

She folds her hands. "You are correct. We call it Translation. It allows two or more parties to communicate across the same time spectrum. In a sense, we are translated into the same plane—although I am very much sitting in my office right now. You're seeing what we call a hologram, although a very lifelike one."

Darius's words echo in my memory. This must be the technology rumored to be used in the portal.

But the Friend is staring at me with searching eyes. I clear my throat and recover. "How fascinating."

"You sound critical."

"I am amazed that such technology favors one square while the rest sit in darkness."

"The others are not ready. Perhaps one day. Perhaps never. There is something unspoiled about citizens who enjoy a simple existence without having to bear the burdens of knowledge."

I could not disagree with her more. "What is it you want of me?"

She chuckles. "How mercenary you make me sound! Perhaps I simply want to get to know you better."

"With all respect, you are the governing head of our nation," I say, politely. "You don't have time to enjoy a leisurely conversation with an ordinary candidate."

"My, you are direct. But have it your way." She straightens in her chair. "The truth is that I should like to make out your character. The accounts I hear are contradictory."

"Oh?"

"On the one hand, you are in the top of your class, along with my son, and appear determined to win a seat in the Dome. A worthy goal.

"On the other hand, you have family ties to a traitor and yourself have received an alarming number of correctives."

I grip my hands in my lap where she can't see them. One wrong word, and I will never have the chance to help Darius.

I nod. "Those statements are true."

"Your records indicate you have responded positively to the treatments but with a remarkably resilient personality."

I don't know how to respond, so I lean on my experience with Professor Mortimer. "Personality? If it serves an individual interest, it is an unfortunate flaw, but if it advances our social organism, it can serve the general good."

"Of course." She pauses, then leans forward on the table. "I'm going to square with you, Portia. My Commanding Gage questions the effectiveness of your corrective treatments. As a precaution, he would see you transferred to a satellite and *reformed* there. On the other hand, my son thinks your correctives have taken successfully and sees you as the resource he needs to help find the suspected Rogue insider from Chrysoprase. He is prepared to award you a Dome seat for your support and loyalty. Clearly, these two wishes are not congruent.

"You see, I have a vested interest in you either way. Are you my son's ally, or are you a threat to national security?"

"I'm a simple candidate wanting to make a difference in her world."

She smiles and continues to observe me. I meet her gaze, but its intensity makes me blush.

"I think you are more than that. Your records boast your intelligence and resourcefulness, but perhaps I have mistaken my son's interest in you as purely political. There is another matter I should like to make out."

Breathing. I need to remember to keep doing it so the Friend doesn't detect my anxiety.

"We both know you applied for a compatibility test last week. I can only surmise you did so with someone in mind."

"And you think that someone is your son," I say quietly.

"If it is, I would understand your ambition for such an advantageous match, but I question your motives."

I swallow to keep my throat from going dry. A match with Felix is the last thing I want.

The Friend continues, "That is why your results will not be released until I authorize them—and until I am fully satisfied that you are the right girl for his next match."

His next match. I pinch myself hard on my leg. Yes, that hurts. This is real. Just like Candace's rope.

I take a deep breath to stem a rising panic in my chest and give my mind the chance to think. Of course, Felix has had several girls before me, but is this conversation really about Felix?

The Friend and Felix are cut from the same cloth. The Friend doesn't care about her son's heart. He's simply another pawn on her board. Felix doesn't care about his mother's career. He only wants to ensure the Dome chooses him as her successor.

I focus on the Friend's next words. My life may depend on it.

"And so, I have arranged a sort of test for you. Memorize this code: 070476. Starting tomorrow, this override code will gain you access to any room, restricted or otherwise, in the Crystal Globe for ten days.

"It will gain you access to the archives, to the lower administrative levels of the Globe, even to my son's apartment. If someone questions you, all you have to do is repeat the code, and they will respect your presence as authorized.

"You can choose not to use the code at all. You can choose to provide my son the intel he thinks you're capable of providing. Or, you can choose to betray my confidence and give my Commanding Gage all the evidence he needs to nail your coffin shut."

I stare at her. "You would take such a risk on me?"

"Yes, it is a risk, but I am not afraid—even if you should choose the last alternative." The Friend smiles again. "I said when we began that my goal is to determine your character. By the end of ten days, I hope to be congratulating you—on a future Dome seat and a match well made.

"Do not disappoint me."

When my private escort lets me off at my dorm's entrance, I ignore curious stares from the other residents and hurry up to my room. I kick off my pumps and replace my nice dress with my running outfit. If I don't hurry, I'll miss my daily routine with Luther.

A handful of runners are on the track, but none notice me as I join them.

One lap. Two. Three. Four. Five.

The Friend's words burn in my memory. One code. Ten days to use it. That's a golden window of opportunity to help Darius. She must suspect I am helping him, or she would not have hung such juicy bait before me. But one bite of it, and I'm done. Anywhere I use the code, the Friend and her Commanding Gage will know. It will be the incriminating evidence Eliab needs to destroy me.

Luther is late. Six. Seven. Eight. Nine.

I gasp for breath and slow to a stop outside the track. I brace my arms against my thighs and pant. I'm tired of running. And the next ten days stretch out before me like a marathon.

Another runner is suddenly beside me. It's Foxworth. "Get back on the field. You must never give up. Train, Revisionary. Train."

He slows only long enough to whisper the words before taking off down the track.

I jerk my head. "Hey, wait up!"

He doesn't slow down. I ignore my burning thighs and sprint faster to catch up.

When I finally do, he glances at me with simple approval in his eyes. "Are you ready?"

"Yes?" I pant, not sure I understand the question.

We jog together in silence as we pass another runner. Our movements mirror each other's. I ignore the burning in my lungs and keep up with him. We then pass another runner, then another.

A cramp tears at my side, but I stay with him.

When I can't bear the pain any longer, he relaxes his stride to a speed-walking pace.

"November 11." It's an intense whisper.

"What?"

"That's the date. You have the drive, right?"

I grit my teeth to fight the sting in my thighs. "Yes."

"Once you've planted the virus, you will need to return the drive to me. I'll be watching—and waiting for you. Be ready."

He takes off like the wind. I collapse onto the ground and wish I could die.

I don't know how long I've lain there when I sense someone standing over me.

"Are you all right?" It's Luther's shadow.

I crack open an eye. "Do I look all right?"

"That's a loaded question. You've looked better." He reaches down, offering me a hand, which I accept.

He glances at my arm patch. I'm so used to it that I forget it's still there.

"Whoa! You just ran a 5K?"

"I did?" I laugh with whatever air is left in me.

"If you're trying to impress me, you have." He slaps me on the back. "It's a good thing you didn't wait for me to run, because I came to tell you I won't be able to make our track appointments for a while."

My face must show disappointment, because he hurries on to say, "Clearly, you don't need me anyway!"

I give him a lop-sided smile. "Thanks. Is everything okay?"

"Everything's fine. I just won't have time to spare until after

I complete my Court Scene."

"That's right. When are you scheduled?"

"It could be as soon as next week or as late as next month, whenever the Gages schedule another trial. There's one candidate ahead of me in line, and she's slated for a case on Friday."

"I'm sure you'll do great." The words sound empty to my ears.

"Thanks, I hope so. I have to perform well to keep my top rankings."

I clear my throat. We've already had this conversation, and I'm not up for a replay. He knows how I feel about the subject.

We linger on the field, sauntering toward the bench.

"So how was the trip?" he asks at last.

"Trip? Oh, it was—fine." I wish I could tell him about the statues I saw. I wish I could tell him about Red's appearance, the Trader, and his mysterious official orders. I wish I could tell him about Darius and what he's asked me to do. Most of all, I wish I could tell him about my meeting with the Friend and the choice that lies before me.

But I can't. With his Court Scene so close, he would surely try to talk me out of my plan.

"Well, thanks for stopping by the track tonight to see me."

He looks longingly at me. "I'm glad to see you're not mad at me."

"Mad? Why would I be?"

"I thought a lot about our disagreement on the train."

That feels like ages ago. "Don't worry about it."

"I do worry—about you and what crazy idea you'll cook up next for saving the world." He walks me back to my bag on the stands. "Give me time, and I'll save it for you the lawful way."

Oh, Luther. A hero trapped in a rigged rulebook.

"Luther ..."

He puts a finger to my lips. "I miss you, Cotton. I'm sorry I've been so busy with my studies. Once I get through my first trial, we'll have more time together. It's just that this is important."

His dark eyes brim with hope. I swallow the lump in my throat. "I'm starting another big Simulation project, so we'll both be busy. It's okay."

He reaches for my hand. "Things will be different one day. You'll see. Things will get better. For us. For everyone."

I accept his hand and squeeze. "Yeah, let's hope so."

We walk in silence back to my dorm. He plants a respectful kiss on my head that leaves me wishing our paths weren't taking us down different forks in the road.

I crawl into bed that night, stiff and sore and emotionally spent. How am I going to accomplish the mission for Darius under the Friend's scrutiny? What else is Felix going to ask of me, and what will I say? And how can I do the right thing without breaking Luther's heart?

My head aches. I toss on my bed, long into the night, as Foxworth's words play in my mind. *Train, Revisionary. Train.*

Chapter 23

Tuesday, 11.3.2149
Crystal

I wake in a cold sweat and kick my comforter the rest of the way off the bed. What's left of my sheets are twisted like a serpent. With a moan, I roll over and stuff my head into a pillow.

Even the aroma of Lydia's coffee can't tempt me to get up.

"What are you doing still in bed?" she asks. "You're going to miss breakfast."

I groan and twist my neck to squint at her. "My head is killing me. I must have picked up a cold on the trip to Lapis."

Her cool hand presses against my forehead. "Yikes! You've got a fever. Here, let me brew you some tea before I leave. You shouldn't go anywhere today."

"I have to," I grumble. "I can't miss class."

"At least you only have two this morning, now that you're done with P.E." It's a small consolation, but two classes sound bearable.

I layer myself in clothing and brave my first class. I look terrible and know it.

As I expected, Felix starts for me in class but stops short. "What's wrong with you, Frosty?"

"Woke up with a cold. I feel awful." My voice sounds like fingernails on a chalkboard.

He grimaces. "You don't look much better."

"Thanks." I cough.

He maintains a healthy distance between us. "Let me know when you feel better. I need to talk to you about something."

"Sure." I cough louder, and he slides into a desk several seats behind me.

I barely stay awake in my second class and stumble back into bed, sleeping most of the afternoon. I wake for a meal, plug in my earbuds, try to concentrate on some work, and fall helplessly asleep again.

Day two isn't much better, but by day three, I'm feeling more like myself.

My classwork threatens to drown me, so I retreat to the library. I'm sick of my room anyway. I can't find answers to my larger dilemma within the confines of its walls.

I spend hours in the library, moving about from different corners and study rooms, all the while observing the librarians and the staff who come and go. I finally find a nook that lets me keep tabs on the personnel who enter and exit the archives door.

I had no idea it was such a popular place.

Even Dean Augusta slips through the door on occasion, but she doesn't see me. She's accompanied by a uniformed man.

The temptation to enter nearly overwhelms my better

judgment. What keeps me from taking action is the fear of what will happen the first time I use the Friend's code and if it will simply serve as a mousetrap for me.

I have to find another way inside the archives and the portal without it.

But Wednesday, Thursday, and Friday pass without any new discovery. I'm at an impasse, afraid to make a move but knowing my window of opportunity is shrinking.

My time is not completely wasted. I make a new friend out of an elderly librarian named Thomas who is prepared to adore any candidate who listens to his ramblings.

I also begin to understand the library's traffic flow, to understand its peak activity and slow times. Around noon, the library is mostly empty since all but one or two staff stay behind during the lunch hour.

Lydia tells me that Felix has been looking for me. But with classes done for the week, I manage to avoid him Saturday.

Sunday dawns. If I can't discover a way underground today, I will have to face Felix tomorrow.

After breakfast, I camp out in the library. Most of campus is still asleep on a non-class day. I pass through the double doors and the librarian's desk. Thomas waves me over.

Though I don't have the patience this morning to listen to him for long, I manage a friendly, "Good morning."

"I have something to show you." He taps on a laminated sheet taped to the counter. It's a schedule of some sort, complete with a bright orange border and bold formatting.

The pride and excitement on his face make me smile. "Did you design this?"

He nods. "Yes, it's the schedule for this quarter's

extracurricular modules."

I am still smiling, but the look on my face must show this news holds no importance to me.

Thomas sighs. "I forget. You're a Revisionary candidate and have your own Simulation lab. Classes in some of the other fields use the library's module since the technology is not essential to their curriculum but offers a supplement to it. These modules are intensives, elective labs that give them a new perspective on a particular subject."

I remember Lydia telling me about the library modules for her Court Citizen class. "Can anyone participate in them?"

"As long as the module has room and doesn't require a special clearance, I don't see why not. I've participated in several, and they are fascinating."

I scan the list. There's an astronomy module tomorrow evening at 1900 hours. Before I can ask about it, Thomas says, "Would you want to join me in one tomorrow? Solar modules are some of my favorites."

"Why not? Sure, sign me up. Where does it meet?"

"It's on the other side of the staircase, downstairs past the art gallery."

I know the place. I've walked past the candidate study lab dozens of times, but I didn't realize its double purpose.

Another candidate approaches the desk, and I slip away before Thomas can detain me with a story. I mount the stairs and retreat to my favorite study nook within view of the restricted access door to the archives.

The Friend's code taunts me. I have the knowledge to make the door open but not the nerve.

I close my eyes and try to remember the pattern Felix's fingers ran over the access panel, but his large palms kept most of his fingers covered. I watched him press the keypad four times.

Then, we had descended. At the base of the stairs was a door. According to Darius, that is the portal entrance.

Again, I wonder why the basement access is on the second floor when the portal is at the base of the stairs, at the same level as the library's main floor.

Perhaps there is a second entrance. The thought has crossed my mind several times.

I try to focus on my tablet and coursework, but it's no use.

I descend the stairs and circle around the staircase. On one end, an art display showcases portraits of the successive Friends who have governed us. My eyes stop on the portrait of Juliana Caesura, Felix's mom. It is an amazing likeness of her. Her blonde hair is now speckled with gray, but her features remain clearly defined and arresting.

Those pale gray eyes … What secrets is she keeping from the people, and how much about them does her son know?

On the other side of the wall is the candidate study lab, the location for tomorrow's module. Two dozen stations form the seating area. The accordion dividers that stanchion the space off-limits during guest lectures and modules are pulled back. Slid fast against the wall is a podium with a built-in computer.

A few candidates mill about the area, studying at stations and charging their tablets. I walk past them to the white board up front and immediately recognize a flyer with a bright orange border. It's a duplicate list of the upcoming modules.

A second sheet contains information about registering for them.

I slide into a station and start charging my tablet. It gives me a place to hide while observing my surroundings.

The glow of the module tomorrow begins to wear off. There is nothing here that looks like an entrance to the hidden room, which must be just out of reach inside the stairwell walls.

Then a new thought strikes me. Maybe those who designed the portal didn't want a second entrance apart from the restricted archives. Limited access makes sense for the Globe's central computer hub. Translations, like the one I had with the Friend, aren't bound by location constraints, because they let people in different places communicate face-to-face.

Remembering the Friend's holograph makes me shudder. It was stunningly lifelike yet not real. The concept of a Simulation-like experience across the present time dimension is still a hard idea for me to grasp.

I scan the perimeter of the candidate study lab, defined by the accordion divider tracks and see the opaque, hard floor for what it is: the boundary of a technology module's reach.

A wild thought strikes me. If tomorrow's module is a Translation, can I hijack it to a different location and see inside the portal without really being there?

Knowing the layout and port location could save precious seconds when I'm able to breach its physical walls.

But how does one schedule a location? I don't even know how to program a Simulation.

My tablet buzzes.

And I frown. It's Sunday. The one day my tablet shouldn't be buzzing.

I swipe to unlock the screen and read the notification:

Report to the Simulation Lab at 1400 for training.

On a Sunday? I glance at the time. It's barely 1000 hours. I have plenty of time to worry about this new meeting.

I pull out my research on Washington. It's the only task that might distract me for four hours.

When I reach the lab, there are three chairs lined up on the platform, and two of them are full. I would know the backs of those heads anywhere.

Felix and Jael.

The third chair is empty, and it is next to Felix.

Professor Mortimer stands by the Simulator controls with his back turned to us.

"You're looking better," Felix whispers. His voice holds both a compliment and reproach.

"I'm finally feeling like myself again." I keep my eyes on Mortimer.

"I think you've been avoiding me."

"I've been avoiding life."

"You can't run forever."

I flinch and straighten. If that is a warning, I'm going to pretend I don't know what he's talking about. But I can't hold back my sarcasm. "Well, I didn't know being ill was a crime. I'll be sure to forbid my body from ever being sick again."

Felix snorts. "That's not what I meant."

"What's this meeting about anyway?"

"Don't you know? We've been selected to help oversee individual Simulations this week."

Mortimer turns to face us. "Thank you for taking the time out of your weekend to learn how to operate the Simulator.

"The three of you have been selected, not only because you individually rank in the top of your class, but because your group project showed a phenomenal ability to work together. It warms a professor's heart when candidates learn that together they are more valuable than separate."

There he goes on his social organism theory again.

"I have decided to delegate oversight of individual Simulations to you three. Today, I am going to teach you the rudimentary elements of programming a Simulation. For each candidate, I will supply you with the codes you will need to enter. All you have to do is follow the steps to program them properly. I advise you to take notes, because I will not be repeating these steps."

I pull out my tablet and create a blank document, my fingers itching to type and learn.

"First, you need the Simulation access code. Ours is 003. Next is my authorization code: MOR. After that, you must add the eight-digit date code followed by the four-digit time. These are critically important to enter correctly, because a minute or second too late, and the candidate will miss the most important element of the Simulation.

"Following the date and time is the candidate's individual code. This is a four-digit code registered with the tablet and can be found under the settings tab.

"Finally, enter the duration code. This can be no longer than six digits as Simulations may not last over 24 hours. Two digits are for hours, two for minutes, and two for seconds. You will not need to figure this out for the candidates as I will have a predefined list for you before class on Monday."

He pauses. "Really, all you have to do is follow the directions and specifications I leave you, and nothing can go wrong."

None of us says a word.

"Today, we're going to do an example. Candidates Caesura

and Bennett, would you please step forward?"

Mortimer instructs Felix to stand on the platform and become the subject of the Simulation, while he shows Jael how to enter the codes on the control panel.

"Now, Miss Bennett, first enter the Sim code and my access code."

"003MOR," I mutter under my breath, and hope Jael can remember.

"Very good," Mortimer says. "For today's short example, Candidate Caesura will travel back to the date and place of Jefferson's birth. The eight-digit date code is 04131743."

Jael pecks at the board, hands shaking.

"Once you enter the date, a selection screen will appear. As advanced as the Simulator is, we have only been able to program the events that our archives have revealed to have occurred. The database is extensive, but the date narrows down the matches considerably."

"Ah, there you see." Mortimer taps on the screen with a long fingernail. "You have five matches. Select the one that reads: Thomas Jefferson birth."

Jael makes her selection, and Mortimer continues. "Then, add the duration, which in this case, is 000200 or two minutes."

The Simulator comes to life, enveloping Felix in a blue mist. While his body remains transfixed on the platform, the screen shares his historical encounter with us.

Jael cringes, and I glance away from the screen.

When Felix returns, he looks paler. He takes his seat next to me and mutters, "Births are a beastly business."

"They make you grateful to your mother, for sure."

He raises an eyebrow. "Is that supposed to mean something?"

"Just that our mothers must have really loved us." And a fuzzy fragment of a memory is all I have left.

But Felix doesn't share my sentimentality. "Ha! You don't know my mother."

"But we have met."

He grins at me with a glint in his gray eyes. "I know. We'll talk later."

Mortimer then demonstrates the prompts to follow for turning off the Simulator.

He leans against the podium. "Since I have access to your calendars, I have taken the liberty of blocking out some of your available, non-class time for administering Simulations. I've printed a sign-up sheet I will share with the rest of the class on Monday. However, since you three have kindly *volunteered* your time today, I'm giving you the opportunity to choose your times first."

I am strongly growing to dislike the word *volunteer*.

Mortimer continues, "Keep in mind that you will need to administer each other's Simulations as well."

He hands me a clipboard. The dates begin on Tuesday, and both Felix and I are scheduled to administer the Simulations for that day.

Jael has openings for early afternoon on Wednesday, right before some of the other slots I'll be supervising.

I write my name next to her 1400 hours' slot. I'd much prefer to have a friend behind the controls.

"Any questions?" Mortimer asks.

No one moves.

"You are dismissed."

I thrust the clipboard into Felix's hands and stand, hoping to put off our conversation a little bit longer.

No such luck. "What? You don't want me overseeing your Sim?"

I stiffen. "Wednesday works better for me."

"Then Wednesday works for me too." He crosses out Jael's name and writes his own above it. "In fact, Frosty, you're in luck. I'm free from noon onward that day. Meet me for lunch in the cafeteria before your Simulation, and I'll treat you to a *special date*. That gives you plenty of time to have an update ready for me."

"Update? I don't know what you mean."

Jael watches us with a confused frown, then scurries off without another word.

"There's no need to pretend." He guides me toward the door and lowers his voice. "I still need to know who the insider is, and you're my key to finding out."

I cross my arms. "From what I hear, you're doing fine on your own."

He leans against the door frame and smirks. "What? You don't think I plan to keep my end of our deal?"

I want to tell him there is no deal, but the Friend expects me to be Felix's ally. If I snub him now, she'll know Eliab is right about me.

I uncross my arms and shrug. "I know less now than I did a few weeks ago. Lydia's been disqualified from her Dome seat due to her Court Scene ruling, so I don't see her as any possible threat. Luther, on the other hand, is determined to reach the Dome and will do whatever it takes to prove himself loyal. I'm sure he'll judge harshly whatever offender stands trial."

"And what about the other 'Prase candidate?" Felix stands

inside the exit.

There's no way to escape the question. "I don't know much about him."

"Come, come, Frosty, what have you been doing the last several weeks?"

I want to say *regaining my personality*, but that won't do. "I'll find him, and let you know."

"That's more like it." He straightens and tips my chin. "Until Wednesday."

"Yes, Wednesday."

He moves his hand to my lips. His familiarity makes me wince. "This is your virgin mission, you know, but I believe you're going to give me what I want. I always get what I want."

"Then I would be unwise to disappoint you."

He jerks back his head and laughs. "Oh, Frosty, you are a quick study. I have no doubt you'll pass my mother's test."

"Oh?"

"We've talked about you—The Friend, Gage Eliab, and I. After your little outburst in class, I thought Eliab might be right, but I'm a firm believer in our correctives. And you, my pet, are living proof that beauty and fidelity can be made to serve a greater cause."

"And the Commanding Gage? Does he agree with you?" I hold my breath.

Felix grins and slides an arm around my waist. "I don't have him convinced yet, but you've managed to avoid the worst of his wrath."

The Trader. Who else but Eliab's henchman could he be?

"But don't worry about Eliab. You place yourself as clay in my hands, and I'll have no trouble proving he was wrong about you."

"I'll have something to report by Wednesday," I whisper to hide the revulsion I feel.

He pinches my waist. "Good. Just keep thinking about what you want the most."

I nod tersely, resist the urge to slap his face, and hurry out the auditorium.

Chapter 24

Monday, 11.9.2149
Crystal

Monday dawns. I keep my distance from Felix as one would a pet with rabies. When I enter the library that evening for the module, Thomas is already waiting in the candidate study lab, and I choose a station next to him.

He scoots his chair back to talk to me since he's short too, and neither of us can see over the dividers separating each study station from the next.

"I'm glad you came." He shoves his glasses up his nose. "That's Professor Wiggins up front. He sponsors the Astronomy Club and teaches several classes too.

"Here, let me help you log in." Thomas stands so he can look over my shoulder. "Take out your tablet, and go to the library page. See that icon at the top, right? That's for clubs. Click on it, and select Astronomy Club."

Professor Wiggins begins addressing the group. "I'm delighted to have all of you joining me for tonight's module. If you have not done so already, please sign in on the library page of your tablet."

"It's asking for a username and password," I whisper to Thomas.

"Oh that," Thomas mutters. "I forgot. Use mine for now. It won't matter that we're both logged in at the same time."

He falls back into his chair. "Here, give me your tablet." I'm more than willing to do so. If I'm not signed in, the Friend can't track my movements.

My only fear is that I might cause trouble for this librarian who's taken a liking to me.

"There, you're all set." Thomas hands it back to me. "Now, listen to Professor Wiggins. He'll tell us the rest of the information we need to access the module."

Professor Wiggins flips on a small black switch built into the wall, activating the computer. One of the candidates closes the dividers, while another dims the overhead lights as a low humming fills the space.

"Tonight, we're going to travel toward the Pleiades star cluster in the Taurus constellation," Wiggins resumes his introduction. "We're going to examine this star cluster, also called the Seven Sisters, and learn about the mythology surrounding it."

He sounds as excited as a child on an adventure. "Now, please follow these directions on your tablet."

My hands begin to sweat. The fields on the screen are somewhat different than the ones Mortimer showed us for Simulation.

"Your access code is 012WIG," he begins.

The next screen has a field that reads "Time Zone." I don't know what that means, and my eyes rapidly scan all twenty-four of them.

"Select the one that reads EST," Wiggins says. "You're already logged in, and the next screen should be pre-populated with your personal code."

Thomas's digits flash on the screen, and again, I feel guilty.

"The next screen is preset for both location and duration, so you do not need to change anything. This module will last half an hour."

I tap on location, wondering if I'm even allowed to change it.

And in that moment, I realize Darius is right, and my bubble is very small. The screen selection expands to multiple pages of locations, organized under a variety of headers. Much of the terminology is foreign to me.

There are seven *continents. North America* is preselected, and I don't change it.

Then, I must choose among the Black Tundra, a myriad of satellites, New Mexico, and the ASU.

I select the ASU.

I select the Crystal Square, then the Crystal Globe, then the Globe Library.

The next screen loads. There are dozens of locations below ground I can choose for Translation. Most are probably university operation centers like the dean's office.

Places I want to avoid.

I scroll alphabetically and hover over P and the word portal.

There's no going back now.

I hold my breath, and make my selection. For a second, I feel queasy as the overhead projector up front flashes along with the other candidates' tablets. They begin their Translation in the night sky.

I begin mine at ground level.

I squint my eyes hard in the dim interior.

I'm in.

The portal is a small rotunda. Half its semi-circle is a screen with a computer operating station. The other half is plush seating, as if for a private screening of an Entertainer's play.

The room provides a luxury Translation experience for the Dome's representatives, no doubt.

I find the black switch to turn on the computer and feel the port where I can insert the drive.

My hands tremble with excitement and dread as I pull the drive from my messenger bag. Half an inch separates the drive from the port. I forget for a split second that I am in a Translation and shove my drive into the port.

Nothing happens.

But of course, nothing can.

Mortimer's words from my first Simulation class echo in my memory. *We're reopening history's pages, not changing it. The only change we hope to accomplish is in ourselves.*

Simulation or Translation makes no difference. While in its confines, I have no power to change anything but myself.

And perhaps my future.

The thought hits me with force. Yes, I'm a *Rogue*. I am a sister of the Brotherhood. I'm a traitor to the Crystal Globe, the Dome, and all my plans of becoming a Doctor Revisionary.

I jam the drive into my pocket and survey the portal exits. There are two doors. One has a plush red rug just inside it and can only lead inside the underground levels of headquarters to places with sterile white walls and heavily guarded entrances.

The other door has a black wire mat in front of it, surrounded by dust. It must be the door to the archives.

In the remaining time, I examine the room and train myself how to find the switch and port with my eyes closed and in the dark.

When I do this mission for real, I'll make the most of every precious second.

The Translation ends. It's a good thing I'm still seated at the station where I started, because I'm exhausted from my mental efforts and drenched in sweat.

I close out the screen on my tablet and hope no one noticed I was missing in outer space.

"Are you okay?" It's Thomas's voice. "I didn't see you in the group."

"I think I got sick."

He glances at my damp forehead and shakes his head. "Sorry to hear that. You missed out on an amazing galactic show."

"Yeah, I'm sorry too. Maybe next time will go better." I gather my things together, excuse myself, and slip outside the dividers.

And then I see him.

Felix leans against the wall next to his mother's portrait. "Hey, Frosty."

"Oh, hey!" I clutch my tablet under my arm. "I didn't expect to see you here."

He smiles, but it feels forced. "How's the research coming?"

"Which one? My project on Washington isn't going anywhere fast. I could really use access to the archives again, but Mortimer hasn't authorized that yet."

"I might be able to help—once you're done with the research

for my project. Or maybe you're done already?"

I clear my throat. "Like I said, I'll have something for you by Wednesday."

He doesn't look impressed. "Why are you wasting your time in a library module?"

"I was clearing my head. I needed a distraction, so I joined an astronomy module for fun."

"Frosty, if you need a distraction, you know my apartment number."

Play along, Portia.

I laugh lightly. "Ha, I don't plan to bother you until I've got what you want."

"That gives me another reason to look forward to Wednesday." His words hold both promise and poison. "I'll meet you in the lunch room at noon. I've arranged a surprise for you."

I offer a weak but encouraging smile. "Until then."

Back in my dorm, I douse my fears in a cold shower and crawl into bed.

I have three more days before the code expires and one more day from Foxworth's deadline. Either I risk using the code and hope for a chance to activate the virus before I'm captured, or I get Foxworth to help me fool Felix into believing I'm on his side for a little longer.

But how can I without putting Foxworth in harm's way? I rack my brain for options, but the more I think about them, the more I like none of them.

They all feel like different ends of the same knife.

I drift through Tuesday morning, going through the motions of my classes, but my heart is not in these routines.

As soon as classes end, I hurry to my room, change, and slip into my running shoes. I can only hope Foxworth will be on the track today.

He is, and this time, he doesn't wait for me to catch him. "Everything is in place for tomorrow. Are you ready?"

I steady my voice. "I think I can get in. Insert the drive into the port. Then what?"

"You think? Or you can?"

I grit my teeth. "I can."

Foxworth seems satisfied. "When the drive flashes blue, remove it, and get out of there. Meet me here at the track. I'll be watching for you."

He starts to run away, but I touch his arm. "I do have a problem, though, and I'm hoping you can help."

He falls into a jog beside me. "What's wrong?"

In as few breaths as possible, I tell him about Felix and the Friend. "I don't know what to tell him. He suspects you're the *third musketeer* and wants me to report on your movements, but the last thing I want to do is jeopardize your safety."

"There's nothing safe about any of this," he says. "If I can be the red herring to draw attention away from you, that's good with me."

"What do I tell him?"

"Don't tell him anything. Show him." With that, Foxworth takes off running for the woods. I follow him down the deer trail that leads to the old graveyard.

He is fast. No wonder Dad calls him *the runner*.

I reach the first patch of headstones and scan the overgrown field. My eyes rest on the towering winged woman. Foxworth waits at its base.

Hurrying to his side, I hope for an explanation. "Where are we?"

"A graveyard, of course." His lips hint at a smile.

"Why are we here?"

"You need something to excite your Mr. Felix, right?"

"He is not *my* Mr. Felix," I mutter.

"But we can't let him know that." Foxworth turns and presses his lean but powerful build against a boulder behind the statue. It moves just far enough left to reveal a narrow crevice.

"A tunnel?" I whisper.

"It's how I run among the squares." He wipes cobwebs out of the way. "Thanks to your father, we have a whole underground network."

Dad with his knobby fingers and dirty nails. All these years, he's been keeping this secret.

"Where are we going?"

Foxworth reaches into a nook and pulls out a lantern. He strikes a match and lights it. "You'll see."

The space gives way to a slightly wider tunnel with enough room for two small people to move comfortably, single file. Height is on my side today.

We reach a modest-sized room, and Foxworth pulls a leather pouch from a crack in the wall.

"What's that?"

"Coins—original currency from the past civilization. Really old." He hands a piece to me, and I wipe my finger over the marred face. Despite the years, it shimmers in the lamplight.

"It's pretty."

"It's gold."

"Gold?"

Foxworth smiles at my surprise. "Yes, it was the original tender of the USA and later backed the paper currency. But the government overspent and fell into gross debt, so leaders ordered the paper currency be printed on demand, even though there wasn't enough gold to back it all."

"Then the currency value decreased?"

"Exactly. The currency inflation devalued our money in the world market's eyes and served as one of many reasons the economy collapsed."

I reach to give the coin back to Foxworth, but he shakes his head. "Keep it."

"But isn't private possession of gold illegal?"

"Of course, it is. That's why you're going to give it to Felix."

"Felix!" I grip the coin. "But ..."

"You said he wants you to find evidence to prove me either innocent or guilty. He probably won't be satisfied if you say I'm innocent—so give him something to make him trust you."

"But what about you?"

He grins. "I'm a runner. Once I get you out tomorrow, I'll disappear myself."

"You're going to help me escape through here?"

"That's the plan. I have another errand to run tonight, so you'll need to head back on your own."

"But what about the boulder? I don't think I can move it."

"Don't worry about it. I'll replace it later when I come back."

"Okay, thanks." I slip the coin into my bag and clutch it tightly.

"Until tomorrow."

Foxworth disappears down another corridor, and I look after him. He's close enough to my age to be a second brother or a "match," as Dad once said.

Maybe—if I didn't know Luther.

I crawl back into daylight. The empty graveyard gives me chills, and I hurry towards the deer trail. I have just passed under the cross's shadow when something moves on the far end of the clearing. It's probably a rabbit.

I'm out of breath again when I emerge onto the track but try to look casual by running another lap. At least exercise helps exhaust my nervous energy about tomorrow.

When I reach the bleachers, a familiar figure steps toward me. Although I'm coated in sweat, Luther's eyes light up when he sees me.

"I've missed my running buddy. Lydia says that you've been sick. Are you feeling better?"

"Yeah, much better than last week." It's a half truth. I'm over my cold, but the longing to tell him my secret makes me more miserable. "But hey, I thought you didn't have time for the track."

"I missed you too much."

"Well, I've missed you, too." I sit and pat the bench beside me for him to join. "How's your Court Scene preparation?"

He falls next to me and rubs his temples. "I want it to be over. I've done as much prep as I can do. What will be will be."

"Do you have a date scheduled?"

"That's just it. There aren't any trials. I guess everyone's decided to be good."

I laugh nervously but feel sick inside.

He studies me. "Is something bothering you?"

"You have no idea." I sigh. "Luther, there's so much I wish I could tell you."

He gives me a searching look. "Then, tell me."

"If I do, you might try to stop me."

His brow creases. "What do you mean?"

I shake my head. "I don't want to say anything that might compromise your position. You believe you can reform our government from inside. I no longer think that's possible."

Luther groans. "Not this again."

"Hear me out." I jump to my feet. "You've been the friend I never thought I'd have. You believed in me. You trained me. I can never thank you enough."

He pushes himself off the bench and faces me. "Cotton, what are you saying …"

"But our visions for the future are different," I press on. "No matter what happens, I know you'll do what you think is right. And I'll trust you for that."

I close my eyes. I never imagined that doing the right thing would hurt so badly.

He presses a hand on my shoulder. "Portia, what are you talking about? What's wrong?"

"Our world is gasping for freedom, and I'm going to do the only thing I know to give it a chance to breathe again."

Impulsively, I kiss his cheek. "Goodbye, Luther. And good luck."

Then I run. Run away. Run as Luther's voice calling out my name fades into the night.

Chapter 25

Wednesday, 11.11.2149
Crystal

Hands trembling, I reapply my lipstick, study myself in the mirror, and check the time on my tablet. Five minutes to noon.

When I woke this morning, the thought struck me that today marks the anniversary of the signing of the Mayflower Compact. The Separatists risked everything for the chance at a better life.

Over 500 years later, I'm risking everything too.

I slip the lipstick into my messenger bag, my hand checking for the coin and brushing against my hidden Taser. I unbutton the top of my sweater and then adjust the holster under my skirt where Dad's black blade has resumed its reign in my thigh holster.

It's show time.

I step out of the girls' bathroom in the dining commons and spot Felix talking with a waiter who guards the entrance to the reserved seating area. I've never eaten there before but have caught glimpses of balcony seating and finely decorated tables.

Felix sees me and waves me over to him. He pecks my cheek and pinches me. "I hope you like my surprise."

I flash a smile. "And I hope you like mine."

The waiter escorts us through the dining room to a small balcony where a table for two waits. Steaming bowls of soup and savory bread rouse my appetite, but it all seems too much like a last meal to enjoy it.

I unfold the fabric napkin on my lap and determine to try anyway.

"Isn't this delightful?" Felix pours himself a glass of wine. "This is one of my favorite places. It's quiet, unhurried, and private."

"It's very nice," I agree.

"Have some wine." He starts to fill a crystal glass for me.

"No thanks," I say. "I can't get too relaxed. Remember I have my Simulation in two hours."

He pours it anyway. "You have to live a little, Frosty. Life's too short not to enjoy it."

"That's easy for you to say, but I don't feel at all prepared for my next Simulation."

Felix clucks his tongue. "Oh, Frosty, relax for once, and enjoy yourself. You need to learn to govern yourself less with your head and more with your heart."

"And how would you see me governed by my heart?" The waiter appears with steaming plates of chicken tenderloin. The fragrance disarms the knots in my stomach.

Felix cuts into a delicate piece. "Start listening to your feelings, and follow them." He takes a bite. "For instance, what do you feel right now?"

I stare at the culinary masterpiece before me. "Hungry."

"Then eat."

He doesn't have to tell me twice. I savor my first bites, yet the smirk on his face makes them hard to swallow. "Do you always govern yourself by your appetites?"

"Always," he says. "If you're hungry, you eat, right? Appetite is a powerful motivator for achieving what we want most. I know what I want. The question is, do you know what you want?"

I wash the meat down with water. "That depends on what you mean."

Felix laughs, but the glint in his eye is serious. "Oh, Frosty, do you only answer in riddles?"

I sip a glass of water instead of answering, but the expectant look in his eye tells me his banter is a cover for the real reason of our lunch date.

I set the glass down and square my shoulders. "You'll be pleased to hear I have something for you."

He breaks a piece of bread in half. "I was hoping you'd say that."

I reach into my bag and feel for the coin. My fingers brush the drive. I have only a few hours to complete my mission. I can't blow my one chance.

Pinching the coin, I pull it out and slide it across the table to Felix. His eyes grow wide, and I scoop a spoonful of soup to hide my growing anxiety.

"Where did you get this?" His voice is low, deadly.

I level my chin and hope my voice won't betray me. "You asked me to find out more on Foxworth, so I followed him on the track. I used to be in the same P.E. class with both of you. He dropped this when he was running, and I thought you might be able to tell me what it is."

Felix clutches it in his fist. "Know what it is? Of course, I do. This is illegal gold, a relic of the USA."

"But where would he find such a thing?" I lower my eyes, hoping I haven't signed Foxworth's death warrant.

"Rogues," Felix mutters. "They're trying to undermine the dolari. This is the evidence I need to bring him in for questioning."

I suddenly feel sick and set my spoon down. How can I feast when I've put Foxworth in such danger?

I remind myself this was his idea, to help me buy the time I need, but I feel like a traitor.

Felix slips the coin into his vest pocket. "Good work, Portia. I knew I could count on you."

But the lilt to his voice warns that he doesn't trust me.

Felix finishes every morsel on his plate while I rearrange the food on mine ten times. I have to get him to take me to the archives. He mentioned it yesterday, but I can't risk losing my one opportunity.

He finally breaks the silence. "You're not eating very much."

"I'm nervous."

He laughs. "Do I make you nervous?"

"Not like Mortimer does."

"You're still worried about your Simulation. Is that it?"

I nod. "I'd feel a lot better if I knew more about this Washington character."

Felix studies me a moment as if deciding something. "Then perhaps we should pay the archives a quick visit before your Simulation today."

"If it wouldn't be too much trouble …" I smile demurely.

He dips the last of his bread in the soup. "It will be no trouble, my pet, although I don't know how much help those books will be. As far as I'm concerned, the archives contain nothing but dust and the breath of death."

"All the dust is rather unpleasant, but I think I can find the American section again without wasting too much time."

Felix wipes his mouth with a white cloth napkin. "Very well." As he does, another man appears. He's dressed similarly to the other waiter, but there's something different about him. He glances at me and whispers to Felix. His face remains impassive but grows harder. Felix glances at his watch, replies, and waves the man off without another word.

"Is everything all right?" I fidget with the napkin on my lap.

"Yes, quite." He studies me for a moment, and I feel exposed as if somehow, he knows my secrets.

Felix pushes his chair back and motions for me to rise. "We'd best begin, then. We have only an hour before your Simulation, and we can't have you missing that." His tone is civil but twenty degrees colder than it was moments ago.

When we reach the library and the second-floor door to the archives, Felix pauses. He doesn't say anything but turns and looks at me.

"What is it?" I ask.

"Oh, it's just that—It's nothing." I watch closely as he enters his own four-digit code, and the door opens.

We continue in silence as the library door closes behind us and begin our descent down the stairwell.

My hand brushes the portal door at the base of the stairs, but still, I follow Felix into the archives. I will come back and get in.

"Washington, right?" Felix flicks a switch on the wall, bringing to life the dull lights overhead. They pulse and flicker, casting their half-life glow into the gaping space.

Felix leads me past narrow aisles stacked tall with books. The last time we were here, he said he didn't know where anything was. Now, he draws me further into the cavern-like depths.

But I have a good memory too. We passed the aisle with the books about America five rows back.

A small sound echoes from the space beyond, and I slow my steps. Perhaps I am not the only one with a motive for coming here today.

"Wait, I think I've found something." I step inside an aisle. From the angle, I can see him, but he doesn't see me.

He spins around, frowning, then jerks back to face the far end of the archives. He flashes two fingers and turns again to find me.

A signal. Who else could be in the archives? What had the waiter whispered to Felix?

Two can play this game.

I pretend to engross myself in a book.

Felix finds me, annoyance written on his face. "Come on, Frosty. It's this way."

"Funny, I thought it was back the other way." I snap the book shut and study him. "What's wrong, Felix?"

Sparks fly in his eyes. He slaps it out of my hands and grabs my wrist. "What's wrong? Maybe you can tell me."

"You're hurting me." I try to yank away, but he doesn't let go.

"If you've been lying to me ..." There's poison in his words.

"Lying? What on earth gave you that crazy idea?" I demand.

"Eliab's birddog saw ..." But he doesn't finish. A man emerges from the shadows behind him, towering over us both.

He leans heavily on one leg. The dim lighting offers an imperfect look at the Trader's dark face, offset by sharp eyes.

I gasp and twist away from Felix, but he pins me against the bookcase. Hunger, anger, and control fight for dominance on his face.

He snarls, "He saw you—saw you follow Foxworth into the woods. He didn't drop that coin, did he? He gave it to you so you could deceive me."

I fight to calm my fear. I have to focus if I'm going to get out of this alive. "He's lying." I stare defiantly back at Felix. "It's another lie Eliab is feeding you about me."

A rumble sounds deep in the Trader's throat. It grows louder until it breaks into a demonic laugh.

Even Felix looks unhinged as if he's trying to decide which of us to believe.

The Trader's hand digs deep into his pocket and hurls a fistful of coins onto the ground. They clank and clash on the hard flooring, echoing like a crowd of condemning witnesses.

"Fool girl." His voice penetrates the archive air like a knife. "I followed you down the trail. I saw you leave the tunnel and found these there. Your ruse is discovered. In a matter of hours, my men will ferret your Rogue friends from those tunnels. It was a genius plan, really. It explains how Rogues have slipped out of our fingers many times before. But not this time. We'll trace those tunnels back to your leaders, and there will be no one to warn them we're coming."

He pulls a long blade from a sheath, making the air hiss. "Thanks to you, it will all be quite simple, and I'll still collect the payment for my services." The black presence steps closer.

"Rogue!" Felix swears. "You're the insider from 'Prase I was looking for, and now, you'll serve as proof to Eliab of my unquestioned loyalty to the CGA."

He brushes his lips on my ear. "It's a shame to waste you, my pet, but there are plenty of other pretty faces."

For that one moment, Felix relaxes his grip. It's all the chance I need. I shove Felix back and whip out my Taser. It won't keep the Trader down long—but I only need to buy a little time.

He curses the moment it contacts his skin. His hooded form staggers to his knees.

Felix rebounds back into me, knocking the Taser from my hand. We tumble to the ground together, kicking and scratching at each other.

His soft hands are at my throat. I won't have the breath to fight him for long.

I claw at his face with my right hand and, with my left, feel for my skirt and sheath.

The black blade is sharp and doesn't require me to slice hard.

Felix falls back, screaming. A red streak seeps out along his gut.

I release the karambit and gasp for breath. Crawl to my feet. And run.

At the base of the stairs, I reach the padlocked door. Bloody fingers press the code 2150. It's next year, the year the Dome will choose the new Friend, and the code I watched Felix enter at the archive entrance.

The door opens. I kill the lights behind me and enter the portal.

The interior is black, all but for an emergency light at the top of the doors. The light is all I need. I use a clean part of my sweater to flip on the black switch and find the port.

I slide the drive in place and step back, watching as the Translator purrs to life and starts reading the drive data.

Seconds feel like an eternity before the drive turns blue and I can remove it.

The Translator goes black, and I don't even wait to flip the switch again. What's the use of caution when the Friend's son knows you're a Rogue, and a Trader is hunting you?

I make a crazed run up the stairs but have enough discretion to remove my sweater to hide the blood stains on it before exiting the library door.

With all the caution I can muster, I slip past other candidates, out the library, and start for the track. The sidewalks are full of candidates, hurrying about their days. Few notice me—the girl with the disheveled hair, clutching a sweater to her chest.

The track is empty. Most candidates are still on their lunch hour.

I ditch the sweater in a dumpster and wash the blood off my hands in the girl's locker room, keeping my eyes alert and hoping Foxworth will be outside when I emerge.

He isn't. Another man is. His square, black shoulders crouch by the bleachers, waiting for me.

"Gath!" I gasp. "The tunnel—It's been jeopardized. We have to warn Foxworth."

He pulls me down to a kneeling position so I can hear his whisper. "He already knows."

"The Gages are going to get into the tunnels, and then all our brothers will be in danger."

His face is grave. "I'm in charge of the unit leading the Gages there."

"Then what are you going to do?"

"Leave that to me." He glances around us and stands. "Do you have the drive?"

His eyes lock onto mine. I meet them and press the blood-stained drive into his hand. "Yes, the virus has been planted."

He takes the drive and squeezes my hand. "Well done, sister."

The strain hits me, and I fall to the dirt by the bleacher. He squats to his knees and places a firm hand on my back. "Are you okay? Did anyone see you?"

I bite my lip and nod. "Yes, I'm fine, but I had to fight my way out. The Trader was there—I tasered him again, but that won't keep him down for long. I sliced Felix up too. It's only a matter of time before Eliab has his hounds looking for me.

"But there's no way out now, is there?" My voice sounds hopeless to my own ears.

He shakes his head. "We'll find another way, but first, I have to protect our brothers and stop Eliab. Then, I'll come for you."

"But where will you find me? What can you do to keep me out of their hands? Gath, I can't …"

He holds up a finger. "Never say can't. Go to your class, and I'll find you there." Even in the bleakness, there's a twinkle in his eye. "If all goes well, I'll be the one to arrest you."

Gath pulls me to my feet and without another word, disappears. With him goes my only hope.

Inside my messenger bag, my tablet buzzes the fifteen-minute warning for my Simulation. I wonder what will happen since Felix won't be there to administer it.

Trembling, I smooth my hair into place and start for class, all the while training my mind on the most important game of *Forget and Remember* I've ever played.

My footsteps echo in the nearly empty Simulation auditorium. I take a deep breath and stroll toward the front. Jael has just finished administering her last Simulation. The classmate thanks her and disappears.

She glances up when she sees me, and I hurry over to her. "Hey, Jael, would you mind administering my Simulation before you go?"

"I thought Felix was going to do that?" Her words hold a reproach.

I smile disarmingly. "I'd much rather you take the wheel for my turn."

Jael sighs. "If you want to, but let's make this quick. I'm really hungry."

"Quick works for me."

Jael resumes command of the controls and nods for me to step onto the platform, but her movements are awkward and jittery.

Then I understand why. On the far side of the auditorium by the exit, someone is watching. It's Professor Mortimer.

Why is he here?

Jael pulls something out from the podium and steps toward me, forcing me to focus on the present. She holds out a jacket. "Here, you might need this. The winter of 1776 might be—cold."

There's a warning in her eyes.

"Ready?" she asks. My fearful little Jael has never looked braver.

"Ready." I clutch the jacket.

If she can be brave, so can I.

Chapter 26

Wednesday, 11.11.2149
Crystal

The blue lights of the Simulator blur the auditorium. I look down at my black boots and leggings and watch them fade in the swirling snow.

The brutal wind bites through my clothes. I march along a haggard line of soldiers in the dead of night. The only sound is the crunching of snow and the hacking coughs of some soldiers.

The man beside me is barefoot, and his clothes, nothing more than rags. His raw hands seem frozen to the musket and flag he's holding. I cringe and look away.

A blast of wind whips my face until tears freeze on my cheeks. The man beside me glances strangely at me, and I pull on Jael's long jacket to help hide my face and dress. Perhaps with my cropped hair and height, I can pass for a boy.

A faint roar grows steadily louder.

"That sounds like the Delaware," the man next to me mutters.

"Yeah, and this weather is getting worse," another adds. "Merry Christmas to us."

"It's Christmas?" I ask before I can stop myself.

"Yeah, ain't you been counting?"

I shake my head. This is the last place I want to be on any day. I can no longer see my feet in the darkness, only feel my way through the snow.

A horse appears through the blinding streams of snow and sleet. A wavering torch illuminates the rider's face.

It's Washington.

"We cross ahead," he shouts into the wind. "The Marblehead Militia[v] is ferrying us across. Step lively. We need to hurry."

"Where are we going?" Once again, I can't help myself.

"Only God and Washington know." The man beside me clutches the flag pole tighter. "Just follow orders."

Washington pauses on the river bank and calls a command to one of his generals. The man nods and pulls a pamphlet from his coat. The soldiers huddle close, and I squeeze between them to hear what's being said.

These are the times that try men's souls. The summer soldier and the sunshine patriot will, in this crisis, shrink from the service of their country; but he that stands by it now, deserves the love and thanks of man and woman. Tyranny, like hell, is not easily conquered; yet we have this consolation with us, that the harder the conflict, the more glorious the triumph.[vi]

The general stops reading. My body is numb, but my mind is on fire.

"Who wrote that?" I whisper to no one in particular.

A scrappy man next to me replies, "Thomas Paine." There's a

note of awe in his voice. "He published it a few days back—that's what I've heard anyways. Makes a man feel brave enough to keep living, it does."

He looks up as Washington issues the command to begin boarding ferry-like boats.

Following closely behind the man in front of me, I shuffle onto a ferry to cross the Delaware River.

I stay close to the flagman on the crowded ferry, relieved that no one hands me an oar. I close my eyes as we heave into the churning waters. Chunks of ice crash into us, cling to us. The men pound with their feet to help break them off. Some jump up and down. I join them to stay warm.

A green flag flies in the torchlight, and its pattern offers a distraction from the cold. In the center of the flag is a red box that pictures a soldier fighting a wild cat. Below that, a Latin banner reads, "*Dominari Nolo.*"[vii]

I want to ask what it means but hold my tongue. Another ice chunk drives us downstream into the seething current. I tell myself no one can die in a Simulation.

We ram into the other shore, and I jump off behind the flagman, following him up the bank where Washington waits.

He's pale as a ghost. He watches the ferries' slow progress with agony in his eyes as his generals organize the men who have already crossed.

Hours pass, and I wonder if the Simulation will ever end. I'm nearly frozen in place. The flagman beside me looks paralyzed with cold. His bloody feet invite infection and amputation.

Do not intervene.

The last ferry arrives.

Washington stares ahead with grim determination. He finally

gives the orders to his generals. The command is to march ten miles south to a place called Trenton and surprise Britain's hired Hessian mercenaries.[viii]

According to the mumblings of the man beside me, a victory will be a much-needed shot in the arm to keep the Revolutionary army alive.

Ten miles. I hope the Simulation might end upon the announcement, but instead, I trudge behind the shoeless soldier in a blizzard.

What feels like a lifetime passes in silence.

Finally, sometime in the early morning hours, the town of Trenton appears over a ridge. All is quiet, and no Hessian defense waits for us.

"They're probably stone drunk," a soldier mutters.

"Hmm?" I ask.

"Why, after a long night of merry-making, naturally."

Yesterday was Christmas, after all.

Washington's men fall into position for the ambush attack, and I sink lower in a patch of snow, overlooking the town's entrance.

On no account am I participating in the battle. *Observe. Observe. Observe.*

Then I see it. Blood in the snow. Footprints of blood.

The soldier I've followed most of the journey staggers beside me. He can't keep up with the other men.

His flag falls to the snow. He gasps in anguish and falls to catch it, dropping his musket. Though half buried in the snow bank, he holds the flag above his head.

He's trying to pass it on.

His bloodshot eyes search my face.

"Take up the flag," his hoarse voice pleas.

The man is freezing to death. I close my eyes and shudder, unable to get him out of my mind, unwilling for his memory to haunt me forever.

"Take up the flag." The voice is weaker.

I flash open my eyes and jump to my feet to stand over him. "The flag," I shout above the storm. "What does it mean?"

"Dominari Nolo," he wheezes, imploring me to take it. "I will not be dominated."

His eyes freeze in place as his body stiffens. Still, his outstretched arm beckons me to take up his fight.

Dominari Nolo. It's a benediction to this nameless soldier, frozen to death in the snow. Even death has not defeated his cause or quenched the fire of his spirit.

I grasp the flagpole from his lifeless fingers as a volley fires in the distance. "Dominari Nolo!" I scream into the wind.

And for a moment, forget that I belong to another world.

No sooner do I grasp the flag than the green mist surrounds me.

The flag. It was a trap. And I fell for it.

The Simulation platform becomes a busy place. Eliab and Mortimer march over to where I'm lying on the floor. Jael stands frozen behind the podium, her face pale and terror-stricken.

I scan the auditorium for Gath, but he is not there.

"Portia Abernathy, you're under arrest for sympathizing with subversive ideologies." Eliab grabs my arm and yanks me to my feet.

"Subversive ideologies? I'm thrown into an emotionally-charged Simulation and blamed for responding to a dying soldier's plea? You walk ten miles in snow and see how fatigue can wear on your sense of logic."

"But every Simulation is a test of your logic," Mortimer hisses at me. "And you failed."

"You set me up," I retort.

"We'll let your peers decide." Eliab sneers, pulling me toward the exit.

"Peers?"

"Yes, peers. You haven't responded to correctives. You've proven time and time again that you don't uphold the values of the ASU. And I've received word from one of my men that he has hard evidence to link you with Rogues. The only thing left to do is let a courtroom decide your fate, and that seems almost too generous to me."

Eliab leads me down the narrow hallway to the exit where his vehicle is parked. We reach it as an earsplitting boom rocks the ground. I stagger into the door, and Eliab shoves me inside while barking orders to the Gage beside him.

Gath. The noise reverberates in my ears. What happened at the tunnel? I can't squish the cowardly thought that follows: What will become of me if he doesn't come back?

For now, the explosion distracts Eliab from my case. He assigns me to a subordinate Gage who delivers me to a white-washed cell with nothing but a cot and basic stall. The hours drag before a guard reports that I'm slated for a trial on Friday at noon.

I'm too stunned to think. Ten years later, I'm now in Darius's shoes. And I don't feel big enough to fill them.

I sink onto the thin cot and cover my face with my hands. *"Dominari Nolo,"* I tell myself, over and over. *I will not be dominated.*

The frozen soldier's face haunts my memory. Perhaps I can be like him. He died nobly. He died true to himself.

Only, I don't want to die.

Hours pass. The loneliness serves to mount my fears.

"Portia, is that you?" Lydia's voice calls down the hall.

I jump to my feet and rush to the bars. "Lydia!"

"Two minutes," a guard mutters from the hallway. Lydia runs to the bars, grasping my hand through it.

"Oh, Portia!" Her voice cracks. "Are you all right?"

I nod, dumbly. "Any news?"

"Your trial is Friday. I can't believe it's that soon. Someone must really want you …" She lowers her eyes.

"Gone," I finish for her. "I don't stand a chance."

"Yes, you do." Her brown eyes flicker with hope. "Luther is acting Court Citizen."

My fear has become a reality.

"If anyone can ensure a fair trial, he will," she assures me.

Oh, Luther.

My heart dies within me. "Does he know?"

"I'm sure he does," she says. "Despite the efforts to keep your trial hushed, word has slipped out, partly because you're not the only one standing trial Friday."

"There's someone else?"

Lydia nods. "And he's fairly high-ranking, from what I understand. Rumors say he's someone connected to that explosion from earlier today. That was really something, wasn't it?"

A new fear grips my chest. "Do you know his name?"

She shakes her head. "No, but all I care about right now is you. I want you to take hope. Luther will help you. I'm sure he will."

"But it's not just up to him," I protest. "There are two peers from my class, and lately, I'm not very popular."

"Keep your chin up. Luther won't let you die."

A small comfort. There are worse things in life than death.

"Time's up!" the guard bellows behind Lydia.

She presses her face against the bars. "Don't give up hope, Portia."

The guard loudly clears his throat, and she releases her grip, disappearing down the hall.

The evening passes. And then the next.

I pick at my tasteless meals while the thin-lipped counsel assigned to me maps out a weak plan for my defense.

I hardly sleep. My dreams are haunted by Darius. Tomorrow, I'll relive his nightmare.

I'm living my own already. Even if I'm found not guilty by some miracle, there will be nothing left for me at Crystal. My chances at a Dome seat are gone, and my chance at a future, dim at best.

The next morning, I'm permitted to shower and change into the drab clothing of an accused prisoner.

An hour to noon, I'm read my "rights" and then left in a conference room. I sit at the table, head down.

Another guard appears and ushers me to a packed courthouse. I spy Lydia in a row with her Court Scene classmates. My Simulation class takes up another two rows. Candidates I don't even recognize squeeze onto benches.

The other half of the room swarms with Gages, some on duty, some not.

My weasel of a defense counsel waits for me at a front row. "We're scheduled second on the slate today. We wait here until the first case has been heard."

I drop into my seat, dreading the delay. I would rather it all be over.

A murmur fills the room as the counsel for the first defense enters, followed by the charged official.

I fight a surge of nausea rising in my throat.

It's Gath.

He catches my eye as he walks to the table in front of me. His hands are bound, but his posture is tight, erect, and defiant.

The tunnel. The words are on my lips, though no sound passes through them.

He seems to understand. He gives me a terse smile and then glances away.

His smile, though grim, gives me hope that although we are lost, our brothers might be safe.

The courtroom crier interrupts my thoughts. "All rise for the Honorable Court Citizen Danforth."

Luther enters and walks to the judgment seat. No flicker of recognition passes on his face as he looks from Gath to me.

He takes his stand. "Ladies and Gentlemen of the Court, you are witness to two cases today. The first is the case of Gage Gath versus the Gages of the Crystal Globe. Gage Gath is accused of subversion, aiding and abetting the Rogues responsible for the recent attacks on our electrical grid. Moreover, he is accused of conspiring with Rogues while under the guise of supervising Greek outings and undermining the objectives of Crystal agents in the process. Lastly, he is believed responsible for the explosion that allowed the escape of Rogue conspirators within our very borders.

"The Court's intent today is to examine the evidence against him and determine the extent of the Gage's treason and what consequences are appropriate for his crimes.

"Acting as peers are two members of the defendant's graduating class: a fellow Gage who will remain anonymous and a staff member who co-chaperoned Greek outings with the accused, Lucius Kline."

I gasp and turn to see Lucius's buzzed black head. Gath's fellow alumni and coworker now sits in condemnation, his eyes smoldering behind his red-framed glasses.

My heart sinks. Lucius is another Jotham, another friend turned betrayer.

Luther pounds his gavel to silence the murmuring in the room. "We will hear the defendant's counsel first."

If my counsel looks like a weasel, Gath's looks like a vulture. He doesn't inspire much confidence.

"Ladies and Gentlemen of the Court, I present the defense of Gage Gath, a veteran Gage of the Crystal Globe and long-standing defendant of its citizens. He has risen to the occasion during satellite conflicts, including the infamous Baytown crisis, even at the jeopardy of his own life."

Baytown crisis. Did that involve Darius? I suddenly wonder how Darius and Gath began their unlikely friendship.

The counsel's rasping voice proceeds to list a long record of Gath's feats and services, arguing that the current accusations do not coincide with the defendant's proven character.

"The defendant therefore pleads not guilty. The charges levied against him are nothing more than happenstance rumors of peers, jealous of the defendant's flawless record and position in the

Globe."

The defense counsel takes his seat as Luther speaks from the bench. "Will the prosecution rise?"

I recognize the man. He is the same one who served as prosecution during the last trial I witnessed.

"Ladies and Gentlemen of the Court," he begins with the same efficient charm, "the defendant failed to address the specific accusations brought against a man entrusted with the heaviest of responsibilities. The position of a Gage demands utmost fidelity to the ASU, and here we have a man whose actions stand in sharp contrast to the ideals he's promised to uphold.

"I would like to bring Mr. Lucius Kline to the bench for questioning. He is an eye witness to the events that call into question the loyalty of the defendant to his station."

Luther pounds his mallet on the base. "Request denied. As you well know, Mr. Prosecutor, Mr. Kline has been assigned the role of peer. To testify against the accused presents a conflict of interest. Mr. Kline may either serve as a witness or a peer. He may not serve as both."

Another wave of murmuring flows through the courtroom as the audience realizes the prosecution's attempt to compromise the jury of peers.

The prosecutor flushes. "Request adjournment of the case until this oversight is resolved."

The defense springs to his feet. "The defense protests adjournment."

Luther calls for order. "Adjournment granted. However, the defense may present a condition."

The defense nods in approval. "The defense will determine the selection of a peer replacement for Mr. Kline."

A guaranteed not-guilty vote. It will keep Gath alive anyway, though how long he'll survive on a satellite is anyone's guess.

"Granted." Luther bangs the gavel again. "Case adjourned until tomorrow at noon. May the parties for the second case prepare themselves? We will convene in half an hour." Luther exits a back door for a brief recess. The courtroom buzzes with gossip at the turn of events.

My eyes linger on the door where Luther disappeared, and my chest surges with pride. He didn't let a seasoned prosecutor trick or bully him into breaking the rules. He judged wisely. I can only hope he will do the same with my case.

Chapter 27

Friday, 11.13.2149
Crystal

Once the first counsel leaves, my defense and the prosecution move to the front tables. The hard seat grows more uncomfortable. I would rather know my fate than endure this merciless wait.

But when Luther returns to the bench, my legs tremble.

The courtroom crier drones. "All rise for the Honorable Court Citizen Danforth."

With stoic expression, Luther begins again. "Ladies and Gentlemen of the Court, you are witness to a second case today, the case of Revisionary candidate Portia Abernathy versus Professor Mortimer, the Gages of the Crystal Globe, and Felix Caesura."

My throat goes dry. Luther spoke my name with all the detachment of a stranger. I would give anything to hear him call me Cotton again.

"Candidate Abernathy is first accused of infidelity to the ASU Codex," Luther continues. "Through Simulation exposures to the codices of the past, she is accused of sympathizing with said failed codices instead of applying the proper principles and procedures of a Revisionary candidate. Moreover, the Gages of the Crystal Globe accuse her of subversion, infiltration, and sabotage of classified technology. Finally, Felix Caesura accuses her of personal battery while attempting to escape arrest.

"The Court's intent today is to examine the evidence against the accused, gauge its authenticity, and determine what consequences are appropriate for the candidate. Acting as peers are two members of the defendant's Simulation class: Benedict Whitmore and Jael Bennett."

I close my eyes in relief. Jael is on the jury of peers. Surely between her and Luther, I can escape a death or satellite sentence.

"We will hear the defendant's counsel first."

My defense takes the stand, his posture crooked, and his face, twisted. I do not like him. How will the jury like him?

But his words are stronger than his stance. "Ladies and Gentlemen of the Court, I present the defense of Portia Abernathy. Miss Abernathy is one of the brightest and best candidates in her class. Her marks are the highest, and her fidelity to the ASU, unmatched. The prosecution will have you to believe she is disloyal to our Codex and her training. Nothing could be further from the truth. This candidate is passionate. Her passion is so extreme that the prosecution would have you mistake it for subversion.

"The first accusation against the defendant is that she is disloyal, even sympathetic, to previous codices. Through her Simulation class, she encounters these codices as part of her training. Her job is to observe, criticize, and learn from them.

"But the accused took her learning experience to a new level. She dared to *engage* history. And because this has not been done in the past, her professor automatically assumes she is sympathizing with past civilizations and codices.

"In fact, she is *empathetically* learning. To understand failed civilizations, she made herself vulnerable. This vulnerability is the sign of bravery, not treason. To fully learn from a civilization's mistakes, she exposed herself to the civilization's heart, open to both its beauty and its shortcomings.

"That is not treason. That is the mark of self-sacrifice, in order to completely grow from past failures and ensure the present success of our own Codex."

The defense pauses for effect. I sit, spellbound by the story. He's made me out to be a hero, not a turncoat. Some members of the audience break into applause.

Luther pounds his gavel. "Order!"

"Moreover," my defense continues, "the prosecution would have you believe the accused is guilty of subversion, aiding and abetting Rogues to bring down our technological infrastructure. But I say to you that they have no evidence to that effect. They are looking for a scapegoat, someone to blame for their own poor mismanagement of technology. If Gages find a young woman of unmatched intelligence a threat, they are to be pitied. The accused's intelligence is not a liability but an invaluable asset to the Crystal Globe.

"Finally, if you believe the story that a petite young woman of Miss Abernathy's stature is capable of battery against a man like Felix Caesura, you are poorly mistaken. Perhaps this is the question we should be asking: what were Mr. Caesura's intentions toward Miss Abernathy that provoked her to do him bodily harm? I hope the court will search out this matter in all honesty.

"Therefore, I set before you a plea of not guilty to any of the charges brought against the accused."

The defense finishes with flair, pounding his words into the air with his fist, and returns to his seat.

Luther turns his attention to the other side of the courtroom. "Would the prosecution please rise?"

A man with polished posture stands and addresses the courtroom. "Ladies and Gentlemen of the Court, do not be deceived by the portrait the defense has painted of the accused. Of her intelligence, there is no question. Of her loyalty, there is strong doubt.

"First, I would like to examine the evidence of her subversive sympathies. I bring her Simulation professor, Doctor Mortimer, to the stand for questioning."

I play games in my mind to help drown out his words. For the first time, I'm thankful my professor is unlikable. Nothing he says outmatches the elegant defense my counsel outlined.

The prosecution frowns when Mortimer leaves the stand, but he quickly collects himself and calls his second witness.

Felix Caesura.

The audience collectively gasps as a Gage wheels the Friend's son into the courtroom. His waist is heavily bandaged. Even my defense sinks lower in his seat.

The prosecution smirks. *Trump card.*

"Mr. Caesura, please tell the Court what relationship you have with the accused."

"With pleasure," Felix begins. "Abernathy and I share the same area of study and at a superficial level, the same objective:

We both covet the honor of representing in the Dome one day.

"But her motives and mine are distant worlds. I witnessed this firsthand in our Simulation class, which I share with her and my many other outstanding classmates."

Murmurs of appreciation fill the room. The crowd sways to Felix's side.

"What have you witnessed that speaks to the accused's disloyalty?" the prosecution asks.

"When I first met Abernathy, I was immediately impressed with her beauty, brilliance, and charm. It's hard not to like a girl like that." He laughs, building crowd identification.

"But then, I watched her in class. At first, she asked seemingly innocent questions. Then, when she started participating in Simulations, her motives became more transparent: she was not here merely to learn from past civilizations. She wanted us to learn from them."

Mumblings of protest echo behind me.

"Order!" Luther's face tightens, and he refuses to look at me.

Felix continues. "The defense suggested that to engage with past civilizations through Simulation was a mark of bravery, but you have to understand. Simulations are not designed for engagement. They are designed for observation only. The reason is that in a Simulation, we can't change history. But unfortunately, it can have the power to change us.

"That's why our professor laid down the rules early on. Observe only. Ask questions after. Those of us new to the technology of Simulation can be easily deceived by its charms. We need the guidance of our professor to help us learn and grow.

"Abernathy went rogue in her Simulations. She engaged with its characters, wanting to get inside their heads. Engagement brings in the element of emotion and ultimately empathy.

"I don't present the idea that Abernathy intended to become disloyal to our Codex, but that's what happened because she refused to follow the rules. And candidates who don't follow the rules can never be trusted to make them."

He curls his lip. "I confess to being a fool, though. Her passion, misplaced though it was, drew me to her. She coaxed me to introduce her to our archives, so I did. But when she asked to see them again, I became suspicious. When I confronted her about her behavior, she attacked me."

Liar! I want to scream but bite my tongue. An outburst will accomplish nothing, and as much as I despise Felix, he is no more a liar than I am.

He draws in a deep breath. "When a beautiful woman, you wanted to trust, cuts open your gut and leaves you to die—" His words hang suspended.

The crowd roars, some cursing my name. Luther wears out the gavel to restore order.

"Thank you, Mr. Caesura."

I search Luther's face for forgiveness but find none. What he must be thinking makes me want to die. He must think I'm a player, a seductress, a cold-hearted killer.

The prosecution continues its relentless barrage. "Now I would like to call to the stand Gage Eliab."

The grizzled Gage steps into the witness stand with a manner of ease. He has stood there many times before.

"Gage Eliab, please explain your involvement with the defendant."

"With pleasure. I first met Abernathy at her brother's trial ten years ago. She was a rebellious child then, but I had hoped she might learn from her brother's mistakes.

"Instead, she's followed in his footsteps. The night of Greek Rush and the Rogue attack on our power grid, she was the last candidate to report to her dorm. Her story was sketchy, so we brought her in for questioning. She could not provide a satisfying answer for being out after curfew, but I wrote her off as a freshman who probably had one too many at Greek night."

He pauses to chuckle. "It was a decent guise, but I underestimated her.

"I confronted her again after an uprising in her class. She defied Professor Mortimer after a Simulation. As is procedural, we brought her in for correctives, and, I might add, it wasn't her first time. Her own adviser had to apply correctives the first day she was on campus.

"But the correctives didn't take. Only, we didn't learn that until it was too late. She participated in Greek field trips. With the help of one of our own, she began communicating with Rogues— or perhaps she has been communicating with them all along. We sent a tracer to trail her, and she avoided him. But he discovered her dealings with Rogues.

"Still, as of yet, she had committed no actual crime against the ASU, just against our ideals. That in itself was worthy of punishment, but this morning, we found evidence to link her to an attack on our technology."

Eliab stares hard at the courtroom. "We found her fingerprints and traces of blood on a padlocked door leading to one of our operations rooms. The computer had been tampered with and a virus planted. Our experts are trying to undo the damage, but much has already been done.

"The fingerprints match those of Portia Abernathy. The blood belongs to Felix Caesura."

Eliab pauses for effect as the room again stirs. "Abernathy is a traitor, like her brother was before her."

"Objection," my defense stands. "The witness was not called upon to pass a verdict, only to answer questions."

"Order!" Luther's voice is angry and loud. The room hushes, and he repeats with a steadier voice. "This Court will have order."

My counsel casts a nervous glance at me as the prosecution clears his throat. "Thank you, Gage Eliab." He turns to Luther as Eliab exits the witness stand. "The prosecution requests permission to question the defendant.

"Objection!" My counsel jumps to his feet.

"Objection denied." Luther's voice is low and grave. "The prosecution may now call the defendant to the witness stand."

Luther wants to know the truth, but can he ever understand it? The prosecution smirks as I stand and take my place.

"Miss Abernathy, did you arrange to meet with Felix Caesura two days ago?"

"Yes."

"And did you ask him to take you to the archives?"

"Yes."

"And did you stab him?"

"In self-defense, yes."

A new murmur fills the courtroom as the prosecution narrows his eyes. "Simply answer my questions, yes or no."

I look him squarely in the face. "Your questions are not seeking to discern the whole truth."

That does it. Now the crowd demands to hear my story.

"Order!" Luther grows impatient in his attempts to stem the quelling tide of emotions flaring up inside the room. His handsome face tenses with strain.

The prosecution does not wait for the room to quiet. He raises his voice and continues. "Gages found your fingerprints on the keypad outside a door that requires a special clearance. Do you deny that those were your fingerprints?"

"No."

He sneers in triumph and turns to Luther. "Thank you, Your Honor."

My defense does not wait for him to take a seat before approaching the bench. "I request permission to question the defendant."

Luther nods. "Request granted."

My counsel steps toward me, his demeanor marked with new confidence. He gives me a knowing look.

He guesses I'm guilty. But he is a weasel nonetheless, and he wants to one up the prosecution. Now is his chance to shine and my moment to weave the most convincing lie of my life.

"Miss Abernathy, you said you stabbed Felix Caesura in self-defense. Is that correct?"

"Yes."

"Why would you do that?"

I take a deep breath. "I asked Felix to show me the archives so I could do research for my Simulation project."

"Had you been in the archives before?"

"Yes, once."

"And Felix had taken you then as well?"

"Yes."

"So, you trusted him."

"Yes."

He smiles, calculatingly. "You were—lovers then?"

I recoil in my seat. This is not what I had expected from my own defense, but I recover quickly, knowing what he has in mind.

"Lovers, no."

He frowns. "But more than friends."

I struggle to answer the question. "Perhaps."

I don't dare look at Luther. I wish I could explain how things really were.

"What action on Mr. Caesura's part provoked you to defend yourself?"

Now it's my turn to tell a half-truth. "He led me into a trap. He tried to turn me over to a Trader. You see, I asked too many questions, wanted too many answers about past civilizations and how we could learn from them. Ignorance is a powerful population control. When the Dome doesn't like the questions you ask, it resorts to cruel correctives—or more permanent ways to silence you. It will even use people who you thought were your friends to betray you."

A hush falls on the room.

"When the Trader appeared, I retaliated against him. Felix tried to stop me. I had no option but to defend myself and flee."

My defense presses a final question, the answer to which I have already rehearsed. "How did your fingerprints get on that door?"

"I tried any and all doors I could to escape. I must have grabbed that one in the process."

"Thank you, Miss Abernathy." He turns to Luther. "Thank you, Your Honor."

The sparring match is not over. The prosecution pounces again immediately. He places something wrapped in small, black fabric on the table beside him and turns to me. "Miss Abernathy, how did you know the man who met you in the archives was a Trader?"

The truth is sometimes the best defense. "I met and escaped from him on a Greek outing."

"Our evidence suggests you did more than cross a Trader in those outings. You consulted and schemed with Rogues to plan an attack on our technology. Of the two, a Trader is a lesser evil than those bent on wronging our own people. Do you deny meeting with these Rogues?"

I set my jaw. "I deny meeting with anyone who intended to harm our nation."

He raises his voice. "Answer the question. Did you meet and consort with Rogues?"

"No." Unflinchingly.

He leans over the table and reaches for the black object. "Then how do you explain your possession of this?" He unwraps the small, black karambit Dad had given to me—still stained with Felix's blood.

I had forgotten all about it in my haste to escape.

The prosecution holds the karambit up for all to see. "This is the weapon you used against Felix Caesura. Inscribed on it are the words *Fraternitas Veritas*, the slogan of the Rogues responsible for unlawful and destructive behavior against our society.

"Your fingerprints are all over it. Do you deny it?"

"No."

"Yet you denied meeting and consorting with Rogues."

"Yes." I know I am trapped, but I am not finished. "I did not consort with Rogues. I met only with those who love freedom and solidarity and truth, virtues long dead to many in our current civilization. There are those who believe they are not lost forever."

"Then with your own mouth you condemn yourself." The

prosecution sneers. "That is all, Your Honor."

The questioning is closed. The evidence is laid bare. But the courtroom is far from content.

Luther brings down the gavel again, but he looks tired. There's a heavy weight in the air. "The jury will now adjourn for half an hour."

Jael and the second peer follow him into a back room. I can only imagine what they will say. Poor Jael looks ready to cry.

My defense doesn't say anything as the guards usher me out of the courtroom. Stares, glares, curses, and cheers break through the crowd. The room starts to swell with emotion, much like the way it did ten years ago, at Darius's trial. Two Gages lock us inside a small room. The door has no sooner shut than I hear shouting and screaming. Stomping of feet.

The guards don't budge from their post. My defense returns to a lesser form. His eyes show fear, which leads to self-preservation. He will not risk compromising his reputation to defend me any further.

Nearly an hour later, the Gages lead us back into the courtroom, now silent and empty.

It is not too difficult to guess what happened. A commotion must have broken out, and Gages forced everyone to leave and arrested the protestors.

No one will witness my sentence but the prosecution, defense, jury, Luther, and me.

Then I see him. Eliab sits next to the prosecution, no doubt ready to ensure that my sentencing is swiftly carried out.

A weary Luther calls the Court back into session. "The jury will now present the verdict."

Jael's whole body shakes. "Not guilty." It's a mouse's squeak, but it's a brave stand.

I am moved.

The second peer named Benedict stands. "Guilty." His vote does not surprise me. Why should he risk his reputation for a candidate he doesn't even know?

Luther rises from his seat and gazes straight ahead. I hold my breath. I trust him with my life.

"The Court finds the accused guilty."

His words knock the wind out of me. I lower my eyes to my feet. The feet he trained to run. The feet he now condemns to shackles.

I squint back the tears threatening to fall.

"The Court hereby sentences Portia Abernathy to twenty years at the Baytown Satellite."

The same satellite where Darius went.

Eliab leans over and whispers to the prosecution who jumps to his feet. "Objection!"

"Acknowledged," Luther says.

"Two guilty judgments should equal an automatic life sentence," the prosecution demands.

"Under normal circumstances, yes," Luther says. "The evidence presented reveals the prisoner is guilty of subversive beliefs, behavior, and consorting with Rogues. However, it does not present undeniable evidence that she is responsible for the technology breach. Neither defense nor prosecution presented the alternative that another insider is to blame. I would strongly recommend that our Gages pursue this further. Even if the accused abetted the operation, suggesting she worked alone is highly questionable.

"Therefore, the reasonable and fair verdict is to sentence her to pay for her crimes while withholding unusual punishment."

The prosecution nods and takes his seat.

While part of me wants to recognize Luther's gesture of mercy, the other part reminds me that he knows as well as anyone that no one ever returns from a satellite.

"The prisoner will hereby be transported to the Baytown Satellite on Sunday's cargo train." Luther reads the sentence with all the aloofness of a stranger. "In the meantime, due to the disturbances experienced today, she will be kept under apartment arrest until Sunday."

"Objection!" Eliab shouts, forgetting his place.

"Objection denied. In light of the high visibility surrounding this case, it is better that no one knows the outcome of the trial until after the Sunday train leaves at dawn. Apartment arrest will imply that her case has been adjourned. I have submitted the request for two female Gages to remain with the prisoner until Sunday's train. Her current roommate will be moved to a different apartment. No visitors will be allowed without written consent from this Court."

Luther pounds the gavel one last time. "Case dismissed."

The Gages guarding me move to my side. One dangles a pair of cuffs. I rise and fold my hands for him.

I sense Luther's eyes on me, but I keep my eyes focused on the marble floor. At least it is constant in its character. I expect nothing from it but to be hard and cold.

The turmoil outside the courtroom, the rush to an armed vehicle, the armed Gages stationed in the apartment I once called mine—none of it matters. My fate is decided.

I slouch on the edge of my bed and stare out the window. Hours pass. The golden Dome turns ash gray as dusk falls.

I close my eyes and try to sleep, hoping the new day will hold some visitor, some relief. It brings mounting disappointment. Lydia does not come. Luther does not come.

No one comes. I feel alone and am tempted to cry. The Gages are silent and forbidding as stone. They never let me out of their sight, not even to shower. They must fear I will kill myself.

I change into my drab prisoner uniform: a heavy gray pair of pants, a long black shirt, and simple jacket that offers no promise of warmth. I close my eyes and try to sleep the last comfortable sleep of my life. My train leaves in the morning.

I wonder about Gath and what has become of him. I wonder what happened at the tunnel, if Foxworth escaped, and if Dad is safe. I wonder if Darius knows what happened to me. I wonder if Luther can live with himself.

Hot tears. I should never have trusted a Danforth.

At some point, I fall asleep, because I wake to a Gage roughly shaking me. "Get up." She shoves a cold bowl in front of me. "Eat this. We leave in ten minutes."

But I can't eat. I'll regret it later, but right now, I don't care.

The frozen darkness slaps my face as we exit the dormitory in the dead hours before dawn. An armed vehicle waits, and I climb inside. A female Gage takes one step into the vehicle when it suddenly accelerates, and she's thrown out.

I grab the seat as the door flaps open.

For a split second, I hope for a rescue, but then Eliab turns from the front seat and trains a handgun on me.

I glance at the door, still ajar.

"Make one move, and you're dead."

I dig my nails deeper into the seat. "What's going on?"

"Shut up. You're a prisoner. You don't get to ask questions."

With the gun still pointed at me, he barks an order at the driver who hangs a sharp left.

When we finally park, we're at a large covered structure. Hissing and smoke vent from the open ceilings like a dragon slumbering.

I've never been to this station before. It's surrounded by nine-foot barbed wire fences.

The driver and Eliab shove me toward a metal door, leading underground. The train station above grows more muted as we descend. We reach a solid white door. Eliab punches a code, and it springs open.

Inside is a white-walled room with a large translucent chair opposite a simple metal one. Strapped to the fantastical chair is Gath. His head hangs to his chest, eyes closed. His skin looks burnt.

I gasp in terror. At the noise, he cracks open an eye and struggles to focus his gaze on me.

"What have you done to him?" I demand. The driver restrains me from rushing over to him.

Eliab walks to the chair and unfastens a singed strap holding down one of his arms. He nods to a third Gage in the room to finish unhinging the rest. "He has brought this upon himself. He refuses to cooperate with us."

With the restraints undone, Gath collapses onto the floor. The third Gage drags him to the opposite metal chair. His back arches unnaturally against it.

"And so," Eliab continues, "we thought we'd try a different tactic. You see, the Court Citizen was right when he suggested you could not have breached our computer technology alone. You had help. Gath helped, but there was someone else, too. And we have reason to believe he has escaped with sensitive information. Unless he is detected and caught, we cannot prevent him from interfering again. But Gath won't talk."

The Gage holding me pulls me toward the chair, now unoccupied by Gath. I resist only to buy time and to hope Gath will emerge from his stupor to help me.

"I don't know anything." I try to squirm out of his grasp.

"We know there was a third man," Eliab glowers. "Who is he?"

"I don't know." And wonder when I will ever be able to stop telling lies.

The Gage locks the restraints over my arms as Eliab moves toward a small control panel. "You've experienced our technology before. You would dare tempt it again?"

I struggle frantically against the manacles as Eliab begins entering a code.

"Stop!" It's Gath's voice, tired but strong. "She doesn't know anything."

A smile plays across Eliab's lips. "Perhaps you are right. Then, tell us what you know."

Silence.

Eliab laughs. "Very well. I hope you enjoy the show."

My skin crawls as the chair comes to life. Subtle pins and needles grow forcefully stronger. I clench my eyes. There is no anesthetic to numb the pain this time.

Moments grow to seconds and stretch to minutes while the chair claws at the fiber of my being. It feels like fangs and burns like fire.

My first scream echoes off the walls, sounding less than human to my own ears.

"No!" It's a roar of rage. Metal hits bone. I convulse in the chair and squint through the pain. Gath wields his chair like a lethal weapon. Eliab lies motionless on the floor, while the other two Gages pounce.

My vision blurs as the door bursts open. Someone's shouting.

The pain subsides, but there's a lingering bite even as the chair falls into slumber. Boots hit the hard floor. Come and go. I'm dizzy and unable to make out anyone's form.

Someone releases my restraints, and I fall into his arms. He's cradling me, kissing my face.

"Portia, Portia." It almost sounds like a sob.

The fuzzy face comes into focus.

"Luther?" I whisper.

"I tried to protect you and get you on that train—found out about the prisoner hijacking just in time and came as soon as I could.

"Your train leaves in five minutes. We have to get you and Gath on board before Eliab regains consciousness and challenges the Court's verdict. He wants you here to interrogate. I can't prevent him from doing that if you remain in Crystal, but I do have the power to carry out the current sentencing without cause for suspicion."

"You want me to die on a satellite?" It's a slurred whisper.

"I never said that." He lifts me in his arms. Gath is by his side, allowing a Gage to cuff him again. Luther hands the Gage a folder and steels his voice. "Give these documents to the Gage in charge of the transport." The man nods and heads for the front train car.

Why Luther is still carrying me, I do not know. Ahead of us, another Gage marches Gath toward a train car as steam fills the depot.

"I can't survive twenty years."

"I'm not asking you to."

His face finally takes clear focus. His eyes are dilated and full of warmth. But with each step he takes, we draw closer to the train car that will dump me off in a satellite graveyard.

"You condemned me as guilty."

"I condemned you to save your life." He presses a kiss into my hair when the Gage isn't looking. "If you had remained behind in Crystal, you would have been food for Eliab. I had to get you out and Gath, too. Maybe out there, you'll find a new life."

"In a satellite? You're crazy."

"We knew our paths had to part."

"Not like this."

Gath disappears inside the train car while a Gage stands watch on the platform. Luther utters a few words to him and disappears inside the car with me.

He lays me down on a mound of hay and brushes his lips against my ear. "You're a runner again, Cotton. Don't ever stop. I promise one day, I'll catch up."

With that, he is gone. I roll to my knees and grip a fistful of hay as more steam floods the car and burns my eyes.

The Gage outside gives the cargo door a hard yank. It groans and begins to close. This is Gath's last chance to break away, to save himself. His satellite sentence can't be any lighter than mine. What hope does he have once he gets there?

Yet he stands motionless, resolute. I crawl toward him. He reaches down for my hand and pulls me to my feet as the train wheels turn.

The platform and the shadows of the men standing there fade into phantoms as dawn streaks through the haze. We watch in silence as our old lives die with the coming of day. Our new lives promise nothing but toil and hardship.

The door thuds in place and locks. A small slit of light seeps through a crack by the latch.

Gath looks at me, a faithful glint in his eyes. The giant is burned but not broken.

"*Fraternitas Veritas.*" It's the sound of freedom on his lips.

And it echoes in my soul.

Notes

ⁱ The Mayflower Compact

ⁱⁱ Proverbs 1:7

ⁱⁱⁱ "Declaration House." NPS.gov.

^{iv} "Nelson (Horse)." MountVernon.org.

^v "Washington Crossing State Park." NPS.gov.

^{vi} "Washington leads troops on raid at Trenton, New Jersey." History.com.

^{vii} "Historical Flags of Our Ancestors – American Revolutionary War Unit Flags." Loeser.us

^{viii} "Washington Crossing State Park." NPS.gov.

We hope you enjoyed reading
THE REVISIONARY. If you did, please consider returning to the Amazon page and leaving a review for the author. And watch for Book 2 of The Rogues Series,
THE REVOLUTIONARY

Acknowledgments

Hemmingway said, "There is nothing to writing. All you do is sit down at a typewriter and bleed." His exaggeration reveals the truth: writing is hard, often painful work. Writers might "bleed to death" were it not for those who come alongside them and strengthen their hands. I want to thank those who have strengthened mine and made this book possible.

I would not be writing today were it not for my family's faith and patience with my endless scribblings. I also want to thank Amberlyn Dwinnell whose friendship and editing expertise are a treasure. I am indebted to my editors, Marji Laine and Karen Harrison, for believing in this story and for their thoroughness; and to Fay Lamb, for generously mentoring writers and introducing me to the incredible team at Write Integrity Press.

Like it or not, we all judge a book by its cover, and graphic guru Kelli Sorg (Make It Snappy) eloquently captured my vision. I'm truly grateful for her design expertise and beyond that, friendship.

I want to say a special thanks to my Page 5 Word Weavers and especially to Ashley Jones for being my friend, cheerleader, and sounding board.

There's a reason I dedicated this book to Devon and Timothy Curtis, my friends going on too many years to count. They both smiled kindly and said nice things when I slid the first chapters their way. Their encouragement was what I needed to pursue this project.

Many others have prayed for me and endured my ramblings as I hashed out this book. To all these, I give my heartfelt thanks.

About the Author

Kristen Hogrefe is an author and teacher who challenges young adults to think truthfully and live daringly.

Her publishing journey began in 2010 with the first book in her young adult suspense trilogy Wings of the Dawn. She completed the trilogy in the fall of 2014 and has contracted with Write Integrity Press for a new young adult trilogy: Rogues.

Kristen also has the heart of an educator and mentor. She teaches secondary language arts for Alpha Omega Academy and serves as the middle school girls' director at her church's youth group. She is a motivational speaker for graduations and a workshop presenter at writers' conferences. She also serves as a Word Weavers mentor and leads an online writing group.

Kristen enjoys meeting her readers, and you can connect with her through her website and blog at KristenHogrefe.com. She is active on Facebook, Twitter, and Instagram as well.

Discussion Questions

1. Even the best-laid plans can miss the mark. When the Pilgrims landed in Cape Cod, Massachusetts, they were miles off course from their planned destination. Before they disembarked, they penned the Mayflower Compact to hold themselves responsible to each other and their purpose.

Portia reviews this document in her Simulation class. What does it reveal about the character of these voyagers?

2. A *logical fallacy* is an error in reasoning that often appeals to emotion, overlooks possibilities, and ignores all the facts. It can take many forms, including:

- *Argumentum ad hominem*: an appeal that questions a person's character (often with slanderous implications) rather than examines the actual issue.
- *Either-or*: an appeal that implies there are only two possible options from which to choose (when there are, in reality, several).

What faulty logic does Professor Mortimer use in his class discussions of the Mayflower and Declaration? Why would someone intentionally use a logical fallacy?

3. Portia meets Samuel Fuller, a historical character, in the Mayflower Simulation. In this fictional encounter, he paraphrases an old proverb (Proverbs 1:7). Find a Bible, or use a Bible search

engine like BibleGateway.com to read the full proverb. What does this proverb mean?

For more discussion on this question, visit KristenHogrefe.com and search for the post "Fools in Fiction."

4. The coin Foxworth drops makes Portia consider the value of currency.

Who decides what a piece of paper is worth? Is it worth anything if not backed by something?

In 1933, the U.S. abandoned the "gold standard" for backing currency. Now, America's currency is considered "fiat money," which means it's backed by nothing but debt. How does this debt-based standard make you feel about the value of the bills in your wallet?

5. George Washington had a favorite horse named Nelson, and Portia spies him riding this "chestnut-colored horse with a white face" at Valley Forge.

Does Washington seem less like a name in a history book and more like a relatable person to know he named his horse like many do today? What do you learn about Washington in the story that might make you curious to find out more about him?

6. When Portia follows Foxworth to the graveyard, there's a weatherworn statue shaped like a cross in the center among the headstones. She questions why the cross, a barbaric means of

execution (made infamous by the Romans), would be chosen as a centerpiece for the dead.

Little does she know that the cross symbolizes eternal life for those who trust in Jesus, the Son of God. According to John 3:16, why did God send his Son to die on a cross? (You will need a Bible or online Bible search engine to look up this reference.)

For more discussion on this question, visit KristenHogrefe.com and search for the post "The Paradox of the Cross."

Runners Up for the ASU Flag Design

We appreciate the talented students of
Alpha Omega Academy and their beautiful designs!

Kyrah Walker

Emily Faria

Nikole Jaskula

Enoch Chow

Gabe Harrington

Kyrah Walker

Hannah Marella

Brianna Ford

Kyrah Walker

Other Young Adult Books

For her mom's birthday, Wendy finds an old jewelry box at a flea market—the perfect gift for someone who loves salvaged junk. But inside the box is a cryptic note that appears to have been written recently. Wendy's curiosity leads her on a search with boyfriend David at her side, eager to help.

But when Wendy's stepfather loses his job, she needs more personal and urgent help—the financial kind. The family's plan to visit Alaska on vacation is headed down the sewer like a hard Louisiana rain. How will Wendy ever see Mrs. V or Sam again?

An opportunity arrives in the form of tutoring Melissa, one of the Sticks, and Wendy's money problems appear to be solved. Until the arrangement takes a turn that gets Wendy into trouble like never before.

Sometimes you flee from your enemy ...
sometimes you stand and fignt.

Haven Ellingsen enrolled in Life Ventures Therapy Camp in the Cascade Mountains to help her heal from horrible memories of her mother's violent death at the hands of an armed robber. But now, a greater fear dogs her steps. The rustle of leaves or the snap of a twig could be nothing. Or it might signal the presence of the stalker who won't stop following her. It seems like a cruel trick from God to throw Haven into another dangerous situation only a year after her mom's murder.

Can one month of survival training exuqip a girl to face all that the rugged wilderness and a madman can dish out?

Both are available at Amazon.

**Thank you
for reading our books!**

**Look for other books
published by**

Write Integrity Press
www.WriteIntegrity.com

Made in the USA
Lexington, KY
22 June 2017